CLOUDGAZER

To Sue,
hope you like!

CLOUDGAZER

Azimuth Skies Book 1

Cover art & design by Alexander Webb.

ISBN: 9781798765340

www.novodantis.com

Contents

~ For Lucy ~

1 - Prologue

Laronor, Brazak West
July 22nd 9329

He looked down at the sky.

It spread out below like a boundless ocean, a vast blue universe filled with rolling cotton clouds. Up ahead, misty tendrils curled and snaked around the foundations of the floating city. Sprawling structures populated a dozen islands hanging in midair.

Moving closer, he could hear the hum of spindle-like cloud farms, their arms stretching out to grasp and absorb moisture from the air. The clink-clank of the carbon refinery pattered across the morning sky, and factory smoke rose serenely from tapered stacks. The air smelled of things being made.

Forming the base of each of these isles was a gigantic mass of floatrock, the material that kept them suspended in the sky, as though they were too big to respond to gravity's will. And around each of the islands was a shifting mass of autocabs, their metal frames like glittering ants, shuffling back and forth. Long walkways weaved through towers of masonry and steel, with great arching bridges leaping from one isle to another.

In short, the islands formed a city in the sky, much like any other.

Well—not quite like any other. For all the years that had passed since providence had brought him this way, for all the city's decline, poverty and lowlifes, this was *his* city.

This was Laronor.

Kiy Tanthar had visited just about every corner of Azimuth, despite still being only in his early twenties. But it was always Laronor that kept him coming back. Perhaps because he was born here; perhaps because it was the place his parents had called home. Or maybe it was Laronor's churning underworld of thieves and scoundrels that made it an appealing target for his sort of work.

Wearing an old brown duster and knee-high boots, Kiy looked the part of a drifter. His hair was unkempt and his lean face unshaven and ill-nourished, though strong of bone. A worn-out satchel lay at his feet. Around him, the deck of the small passenger ferry *Pinta* was empty apart from an old man a few strides down along the railing.

'Quite the sight, eh?' the old man said.

Kiy looked over at the man, then back at the city. 'Yeah. I've been here before.' He was reluctant to engage in chat at this point of the job. Wouldn't be wise to draw attention to himself.

'Ha! A flakking dump, in't it?' the old man mumbled.

Kiy vaguely recognised him as the ship's captain— Garinov, if he remembered correctly. Clad in a scruffy green jacket and flat cap, the old man seemed to be staring at Laronor with a mix of awe and revulsion. Kiy imagined that was how most people perceived it.

Kiy nodded. 'I was born here.'

'Heh. Hard luck.' The captain laughed again, which became several hacking coughs. Recovering, he took the opportunity to light a cigarette from a box in his chest pocket. 'So what made you come back?' he asked, shaking his match to extinguish it.

Kiy smiled to himself. 'Just a little business to see to. I won't be staying long.'

Garinov nodded politely, his attention distant. Some way off, towards the port side, a collection of warships had gathered in a cluster, sleek profiles set against a backdrop of gnarled grey clouds moving north.

The *Pinta* slowed as it approached Southport Harbour. Large skeletal pillars loomed up ahead like giant statues; the metal supports of the city's cabletram system. Each great column rose from a sturdy anchor of floatrock and suspended three cables on either side. As the ship made to pass beneath the tram line, two carriages were moving to cross each other just ahead.

Kiy's attention was drawn to a sudden commotion down the deck. A round, red-faced man had emerged from the cabins in a fit of rage, yelling something at the wind, then at a man in a grey uniform who had stepped out behind him. The two launched into a heated conversation, though it was too far away for Kiy to make out the words.

That's my cue, thought Kiy, stooping to his satchel and extracting a long metal device. It was a slender, mildly tapered block that, with the press of a button, extended to near twice its length. At the narrower end was a small square nozzle; at the other was an opening.

Kiy slipped his hand into the opening, in much the same casual manner as one might don a glove. The device encased his forearm like a bulky gauntlet, running up to his elbow.

The cigarette in Garinov's bony fingers went limp. 'Well I'll be damned. You're a cloudgazer?'

'Nah, I'm the king of Serulia.' Kiy grinned at him with an air of self-assurance.

Hurried steps rapped across the wooden deck towards them, accompanied by an angry yell:

'Tanthar!'

Kiy vaulted over the railing into open sky.

'Gah, stop!'

Detective Inspector Kerutz huffed as he collided clumsily with the railing, stopping him from going over the side too. The cloudgazer fell from view, becoming lost in cloud. Then a black line shot up and connected with the cabletram that the ship had just passed. A moment later, the cloudgazer re-emerged, being pulled along the line by the device on his wrist. Soon he was just a swinging speck quickly retreating into the mist.

'You let him get away.' Kerutz straightened his grey uniform as he turned to the docile figure of Garinov, who was pulling on his cigarette.

The old captain held up his wrist illustratively. 'Left mine at home, Detective.'

'Very funny.' Kerutz glared at a passing cumulus as though it were somehow responsible. 'I told you Kiy Tanthar was on your ship.'

'Din't ask the lad his name.'

Kerutz sighed wearily, his shoulders drooping with resignation. 'Damned kid could be anywhere by now...'

2 - The Lykomin

Three kilometres north of the Junders Neutral Zone,
Nezzu Strait
August 2nd

Lieutenant Feodora Litvyak stepped out onto the deck of the *Lykomin* and took a deep breath of the cool night air. There were no moons visible, but the sky was clear, above them at least.

She ran her fingers along the cold metal handrail, allowing herself a moment's contemplation. She was due on the bridge in just a few minutes, but between her quarters and her station she could steal a quiet walk in the night. She ascended to C deck and headed towards the centre of the ship.

Pausing, she indulged a simple whim: watching the huge, wheeling tri-blades of the starboard megaprop engine. She found its repetitive, monotone 'whump'—and the vibration of the great turbines through the ship beneath her feet—soothed her. She felt these vibrations when she slept, when she woke, when she ate. They'd been in flight for just over eight weeks, but in that time, Feo had never once missed the eerie, odd silence of floatrock, the stimulus that most people seemed to prefer. To her, the sound of an engine meant all was well.

She reached the foot of the observation mast and decided to take a look for herself. She climbed up the mast rungs with steady, deliberate steps. The small, two-person nest was occupied, but the man on duty was asleep. Just as she'd expected, in truth.

'Ryke! Wake up,' she said sharply in his ear.

Ryke woke and half fell off his seat. He looked up at her, startled, then realised who it was and sighed lazily.

'Your shift is over in forty minutes,' she said in wry amusement. 'Try to stay awake, if it's not too much trouble.'

'Ah, can't wait.' He grinned. 'Hard to sleep with that cold breeze, you know.'

'You might wanna try sleeping *between* watches,' she said, tilting her head disapprovingly like a mother.

'Oh come on, Feodora, stop being a tail-dragger. I don't have to do anything; why can't I catch some kip up here?'

She folded her arms. 'Just because it's quiet, doesn't mean you can muck about. What if something came up, hm? What good are you asleep?' The ship did have radar, but that was only enough to know there was something there. It took a good pair of eyes to know what it was. And some days the electromagnetic noise was so bad, radar was next to useless. Today was such a day.

Ryke rolled his eyes. 'Are you kidding me? Have you noticed what boat you're on, honey?'

'Yeah, Border Control,' Feo reminded him.

'Hmph. *Boredom* Control, more like.' He shrugged her off. ''S'alright for you, it's all nice and warm on the bridge.'

'That's not the point, Ryke.' She ran her hands through her long hair, and her eyes, habitually scanning the horizon, spotted something. She froze.

'What?' Ryke frowned.

'Is that a ship?'

'Shyut, that's not funny.'

'I'm serious! Look! Over there.'

Ryke's face crumpled irritably. 'That's the Junders Zone, there's not gonna be anything that way.'

'No, *look!*'

He followed her gaze out across the thin clouds of the Junders Neutral Zone. Then, as is often the way when searching for an object in the sky, it was suddenly as though it had been there all along. An unmistakable dark shard, a dozen or so kilometres off, set against the poor weather to the south. It seemed to be headed north-east steadily.

'Flak. This m-must be a mistake,' Ryke said, face wrought with regret. 'Feo, I never meant to miss it, I just—'

'Stay calm. It'll be fine.'

'What do we do? Sky and Moons, what in hadnar do

we—'

'I'll inform the bridge; just keep your eyes on it,' Feo instructed, picking up the handset for the ship's phone and waiting for the confirmation click from the switchboard. 'This is Litvyak; status red. We have a possible infringement. I'll be there in two.'

Slamming the device back onto its hook, she made for the ladder.

'Feo, what does this mean?' Ryke asked, glancing about. 'I've not... I mean, we've never spotted anything before.'

Feo found a smile. 'It's probably nothing. Just keep watching. And don't fall asleep!'

She figured the adrenalin in him would ensure that, if he was feeling anything like she was now. Nervousness and anxiety mingled as she skipped the last rungs of the ladder and broke into a hurried jog. The warning klaxon began to wail across the ship, a deep throb that rose and fell. In a matter of moments, the day's tranquillity evaporated in a roar of activity, as crew scrambled from mess rooms and cabins to take up their stations. Feodora jinked between two midshipmen and took the stairs of the port-side deck two at a time. When she got to the upper level, she rounded the corner and burst onto the bridge.

Captain Deen was stooped over a bank of readout dials with grave concern. He was a stout man, bald and heavily stubbled, in his forties or fifties. He'd been captain of the *Lykomin* ever since she saw action back in the Liberation War, making him one of the few officers in the Brazak fleet with much combat experience these days.

'Captain,' Feo said, announcing her presence.

'What's going on, Lieutenant?' He didn't look up.

'Sighting in demilitarised airspace, sir.' She spread out her instruments on the navigator's desk, making hurried calculations in her head as she began making markings on the map. 'Bearing: one-zero-zero. Fifteen kilometres from the border, heading maybe three-four-oh.'

'From the south?' Deen's brow furrowed. They both knew what that meant: the ship was almost certainly from Ganzabar. 'What the flak are they trying to do? Start another war?'

'It would, ah, appear that way, sir.' Feo found it odd that the notion didn't frighten her. She knew it should, but it sounded so preposterous. Perhaps because it was madness, and she'd like to think madness was not apt behaviour for the most powerful nation in the world.

'We have confirmation,' called one of the bridge crew, the comms officer Nyjel Roslyn. 'Verified as Ganzabi, Poltiax class.'

'A civilian freighter?' Deen sounded doubtful.

Feodora shook her head in confusion. What was a lone Ganzabi cargo vessel doing trespassing in the demilitarised zone?

'How did it get so close without us spotting it?' Deen demanded.

'Uh... visibility to the south is poor,' Feo offered. She doubted that would get Ryke entirely off the hook, but he only had himself to blame.

Captain Deen sank into thought for several moments, chin leant on interlocked hands. 'It must have made some navigation error.' He stared across the horizon. 'Hit up a shortwave with them. They can't just wander around here, lost or not.'

There was a pause as Roslyn fiddled, then transmitted a call to respond, his voice tense but professional. After half a minute or so of vain attempts, he turned to the captain. 'No response on the shortwave, sir. No transponder broadcast either.'

'Hmm. If their radio is out, that might explain the poor navigation. Litvyak, how long before they cross the threshold to Brazak airspace?'

Feo was hurrying through the calculation in her head, thumbing the map, re-checking distances. 'About three minutes at current speed, sir.' She took a counter from her navigational tools, a simple mechanical device known as an apochrometer. She clacked a button on top a few times until the digits flipped to fifteen thousand, then set the dial to the speed estimate. She hit a switch on the side, which set the digits whittling away at an alarming rate.

Captain Deen rubbed his jaw and exhaled—a long, drawn-out grunt. 'Very well, then. Go to full alert. All hands assume battle stations.'

'Sir...' Feodora looked up from her work. She felt a lump in her throat. She'd had nightmares about this—but it was all a worst-case scenario, something she'd taught herself not to worry about. *Nobody wants another war.* That's what they always said. But these Ganzabi didn't seem to think so.

'We follow the drill, Lieutenant,' said Deen. 'I don't want a war any more than the next sane man. But we have to get their attention and make it clear they must turn back. A warning shot is necessary.'

Feo nodded, assured that Deen knew what he was doing.

The captain strode up onto the small raised platform at the rear of the bridge and gripped the rail that ran along the front of it. The position of a captain on a ship at war. 'What's the status of the *Opekun* and the *Zaputsk*?'

'They are confirming the sighting and going to battle alert, ready on your command, Captain,' Roslyn replied.

The captain exhaled audibly. The *Lykomin* was a respectable destroyer, but the two ships with it were just light escorts, little more than barges with a single five-point-six calibre. The patrol was not really meant to do any serious fighting. The Ganzabi ship appeared to be unarmed and alone... but if more ships turned up, they could be in trouble. It would be wise to inform the Admiralty of the situation.

'Roslyn, do we have a channel to a transpulse beacon?'

The comms officer persisted a moment with several switches before shaking his head in frustration. 'I can't seem to locate it, sir. The beacon may be having technical issues.'

Deen narrowed his eyes. Feodora could see he wasn't ready to consider such an occurrence as harmless coincidence. She looked at her distance timer. 'Ganzabi ship five thousand from threshold.'

The captain rapped fingertips on the rail as he considered the situation. Around them, the *Lykomin* had awakened fully to life. There were shouts and knocks and the furious stamping of boots along metal walkways. The ship's vapour drive, some decks below, had risen slightly in tone as the vessel's power plant shifted to combat readiness. The lighting in the bridge had transformed to a dull red, and the battle klaxon droned intermittently with its deep, warbled wail.

'Four thousand metres,' Feodora updated. *The Ganzies are cutting this pretty close.*

The crew hushed as they finished preparations, looking out of the windows at the distant shape growing closer. The moments ticked by slowly, an uneasy quiet punctuated only by Feodora's distance updates.

'Three thousand...' She bit her lip.

The ship's bridge had gone so quiet, Feodora could hear Deen's fingernails tap the rail. He seemed about to speak, then closed his mouth again.

'Two thousand.' *They're turning back,* Feodora thought. *Any second now.* She looked at Deen hopefully. He was focused intently on the ship now clearly visible from the bridge's windows.

'One thousand five hundred.' Her voice faltered slightly. Surely now? But the speed of the traces remained constant.

The captain finally stirred. 'Prepare to fire a warning shot abeam their position one-fifty.'

'One-fifty abeam, standing by to fire,' the gunnery chief replied precisely, almost as soon as the order was spoken.

Deen waited as long as he could. Then he said, 'Fire.'

There was a thud and rumble from belowdecks, and two bright stars flew out across the dawn sky towards the trespassing ship. They sailed past her starboard side, exploding in a pocket of smoke that left a lingering mark on the sky. The message would be clear to even the most dim-witted captain: the *Lykomin* meant business.

'Any change, Roslyn?' the captain asked after half a minute or so.

Roslyn looked deeply troubled by the response from the lookout. 'That's a negative. Course and speed remain unchanged, sir.'

'Five hundred...' Feodora said, monitoring her countdown timer. The digits whittled away.

'It may be a fire-ship,' Deen said with renewed concern. 'It would be unlike Ganzabar to use a suicide weapon, but any sane captain would either have turned around or opened fire by now.'

Feodora felt her stomach tighten, and her mouth was dry. Something about this whole thing felt terribly wrong.

Her digits froze on zero. She regarded them with disbelief. 'Ganzabar, ah... has crossed the Brazak border, sir.'

'No. This is all wrong.' Deen shook his head. 'They must be having a serious technical problem.'

'Sir, what do we do?' Roslyn's inexperience came through in his voice.

'Put us on intercept course. We'll block their way, and if they still refuse to move we'll have to—'

There was a sudden boom, and a judder rattled through the bridge around them.

Roslyn put an ear to one of the beeping speakers, listening to the encoded transpulse message. '*Opekun* reports it is taking fire from the Ganzabi ship!'

Alarm was written on every face on the bridge—every face but Deen's, whose anger flared and frown entrenched. 'What?'

'Sir, the ship appears to have a twenty-five-pounder main gun!'

'Of all the gall, an armed freighter...' Deen muttered angrily. They were hardly unheard of. But to use one in a surprise attack? It had him at a loss for words. Still, armed they may be, but they were totally outmatched. Enough was enough—they would burn for this. 'All gun crews, aim on target and fire at will. I repeat, fire on Ganzabi ship!'

Seconds later the floor shuddered as the forward and rear cannons launched their shells. Feodora tensed. She'd witnessed the *Lykomin* fire shells many times, but never in anger. And it was all happening so quickly. Ten minutes ago, she had been on just another peace-keeper ship tasked with the most mundane patrol duty; now she was at the bridge of a warship in a battle zone.

The ship shuddered again, but this time it wasn't the smooth throb of a shell being launched; it was the savage jerk of something hitting them.

'Close-hits, taken minor damage!' one of the bridge officers called out.

'Dive one hundred, come to heading one-eight-zero,' the captain barked.

The ship heaved, and the sound of explosions all around them grew louder and more frequent. Feodora saw a ship outside, one of the two escort frigates that accompanied them, swing around to fire a volley at the enemy. A moment later, an angry backlash scorched past it, one shot smashing the frigate's centre.

'Sir! The *Opekun* has suffered a critical hit!'

'It's caught fire!' one of the officers observed from the window.

Feodora felt sick as the small patrol ship was engulfed in smoke and began to dive.

'*Opekun* has sunk!' Roslyn reported.

Captain Deen managed to hide his fury. 'What in Sky's name are they firing?'

'*Zaputsk* has taken hits. It's taking evasive action.'

The ship lurched again. There was a creaking sound and a horrible crunching as enemy shells punched into the lower decks.

'Damage status!' The captain regained his composure. 'What's the fleet situation?'

'We've taken hits near the stern, sir. We've got a damaged dihed, and two broadside crews report casualties.'

'*Opekun* down, *Zaputsk* has taken some damage but is engaging the enemy.'

The captain nodded. 'Come around to zero-nine-five. Fire starboard broadsides on my mark. Use our manoeuvrability to keep one step ahead of them. *Zaputsk* is to keep on the evasive.'

'Coming around!'

'Starboard cannons ready, sir!'

Feodora glanced up at the enemy that swung into the starboard view. It was an angular thing, but no warship: little more than a huge block of metal, long and fairly tall with a tower at either end. She could just make out the main cannon, affixed to the forward top deck where a crane would normally be.

'Starboard broadsides, fire!' The captain's voice was like a thunderbolt.

The *Lykomin* made a defiant roar as its broadside pounded the flank of the Ganzabi ship. A ripple of explosions appeared across the ship's surface, and Feodora felt a surge of vindication. She clenched her fists, wanting nothing more than to see this supposedly civilian merchant ship explode in a ball of flame, but it held together despite a number of gouges in its hull.

The *Lykomin* and its opponent swung around. As the vessels passed each other again, the Ganzabi ship finally began to list to one side, smoke gushing into the pale pink sky.

'Ganzie ship has taken heavy damage to its starboard side,' Roslyn relayed, sounding relieved. 'It is withdrawing south of the border into the neutral zone.'

Deen narrowed his eyes. 'We can't let them escape, not after what they did to the *Opekun*. Come about, port-wards, speed three quarters. Ready the port cannons to use armour-piercing, aim for the engines. We're going to get to the bottom of this.'

'Aye, Captain!'

The *Lykomin* turned and took chase, gradually closing on the wounded Ganzabi ship. As it caught up, it turned to rake the bulkier opponent. The Ganzabi craft splintered and tore with the impacts, black plumes of dirty fire oozing from its wounds.

Then, with a blinding flash that shook the *Lykomin*, the Ganzabi vessel broke in two. Its shattered remains slowly sank, leaving a billowing black column to mark its grave.

'Sir,' reported Roslyn. 'Ganzie ship has been destroyed!'

Captain Deen gave a resigned sigh. 'Likely cause?'

'Unclear, sir. It appears their rear Antimass tanks simultaneously exploded, sir.'

The captain looked suspicious. 'The Poltiax class is more durable than that.' He spoke more to himself than his bridge crew. He looked around to the craftsman—the man who operated the ship's steering and altitude levers. 'Well, in any case, there was nothing else to be done. Bring our heading to two-five-zero and ascend to—'

The *Lykomin* juddered again, but much more violently this time. The bridge tipped to one side and then the other, knocking several of the crew off their feet. Captain Deen held the rail of his station tightly. An explosion plumed up on the deck in front of them.

'Sir, the *Zaputsk* is hit! It's going down!'

Feodora just caught the patrol craft drifting down into the clouds, bleeding its own small column of smoke.

'Damn, what in the name of the Moons was that?' Deen demanded.

Roslyn pressed a finger to his headset. 'We're taking fire, but the source is unknown!'

The captain looked at the comms officer sternly. 'What do you mean, *unknown*?'

'We can't detect any vessel towards aft starboard, but we are definitely taking hits from that direction.'

'Delayed warheads of some kind, to hit our flank?' the craftsman suggested.

'Unlikely, sir,' Roslyn said. 'We would have detected that.'

Captain Deen's expression went blank, and Feo felt a horrible dread. The feeling that something wasn't right returned more vividly than before.

'Sir!' cried Roslyn. 'Two Ganzabi Patriot-class ships emerging from cloud at our ten o'clock, distance forty-five hundred.'

'To port?' Deen's brow rose. 'Shyut. What's firing at us from the other side?'

Feodora bit her lip. She'd never heard Captain Deen swear, and it unsettled her to think of him struggling with anything. If he was struggling, what hope did the rest of them have? 'Perhaps the other ship is invisible?' she offered.

The captain shot her a look. '*Helpful* suggestions please, Ms Litvyak.'

She fell silent.

'We cannot allow them to distract us with something we can't fire on,' said the captain. 'Focus on the ones we can. All guns, fire on the lead Ganzabi ship to port.'

The *Lykomin* advanced boldly, guns roaring at the Patriot-class destroyer. Then a flurry of white flashes erupted across empty sky to its starboard side, sending shells screaming into the *Lykomin*'s side.

The bridge dipped towards port, and Feodora had to grip her station to keep balance while her map and pencils were thrown across the deck with a clatter. There was a glow of fire on the starboard side as hits exploded across the ship.

'Damage status!' the captain shouted, getting back to his feet.

'Starboard Antimass tanks hit!' came a yell. 'We have a leak in tank three.'

Roslyn slammed down the ship's intercom. 'We've taken serious casualties to the broadside teams, and both the dorsal cannons are inoperable.'

'Unbelievable. So much power.' Captain Deen's words came in fits between spasms of pain, his hand clutching his ribs.

'Whatever they're firing, they're punching through our armour like paper. We're not going to take another volley,' Roslyn said desperately.

The captain gave a curt nod. 'What's left?'

'Engines. Half power. Three diheds. Flak-all else!'

Deen looked out at the dark sky and reflected on the moment. This was it. Fight or flight, live or die. He took a deep breath, then said distantly, 'There is no honour in suicide.'

'Sir?' Feodora looked at him fearfully.

'We're surrounded, Litvyak. We have lost three quarters of our guns and nearly all our mobility.' Another impact rumbled, and he paused, clearly not liking where he was going with this. 'We have no choice. Roslyn, strike our colours.'

Feodora's heart sank, but at the same time she felt a strange kind of relief. The battle was over. *While we're still alive, there is always another day.*

Roslyn began to transmit the message. Everything went quiet, until all she could hear was the tap-tip-tap of the transpulse. She'd never learned Pulse Code, but the signal of a ship surrendering was something she'd been taught to recognise. It was like the cry of a tormented creature, begging for release, repeated over and over.

The signal continued, looping around and around, as Feo and the rest of the *Lykomin* waited for their answer. She felt like they had been stripped naked for a thousand foreign eyes to weigh them up and decide what they wanted to do with them.

She tried to turn her thoughts to something comforting. This was all a mistake, of course. Nobody wants a war. The mess would be cleared up, and Ganzabar would be made to return them to their home country. It wouldn't bring back the *Opekun* and *Zaputsk*, or the countless casualties on her own ship. But it would at least be over.

'Captain,' Roslyn said. 'They're attempting to open a shortwave channel.'

'Patch it through.' He took the intercom receiver from its hook. After a moment's pause, he spoke.

'This is Captain Deen of the Brazak West destroyer *Lykomin*. I...' He hesitated, struggling to form the words. 'I hereby surrender this vessel and declare all crew will stand down.' He grimaced, his outrage barely contained. It seemed to Feo as though he were being made to apologise somehow, as though this wasn't the fault of those murderous lying Ganzabi.

His face betrayed surprise when he heard the voice that replied. It was young and female with a strong Ganzabi accent, soft yet voluptuous.

'See? That wasn't so hard now, was it?' the voice said. 'I am pleased to hear your recognition of our superiority. I'm so sorry for the loss of your ship.'

'Two ships, you mean,' Deen said bitterly. 'They were the *Opekun* and the *Zaputsk*.'

'Oh, were they yours too?' the voice said sweetly.

Deen froze, and his eyes went wide. As realisation hit Feodora, the deck upended and a noise like the world ending blasted every other sound to oblivion. Explosions thundered around them. Everything spun, falling and twisting. Fissures opened up in the deck, and pieces of the wall split away, fire filling everything beyond.

Feodora closed her eyes as the air around her screamed with shattering glass and shrieking metal. And before the radio systems exploded, she thought she heard the terrible sound of laughter.

3 - Dinner With The Litvyaks

Brudor, Brazak West
July 31ˢᵗ, two days earlier

The balcony was lined with flowers, herbs and flora of just about every shade. A gentle breeze pushed past the red and purple blossoms like a browsing ghost, sifting through the tall stalks and rustling leaves.

The wind was followed by a clanking sound. Two hands appeared on the railing, and with one easy motion Kiy Tanthar pulled himself up and over.

At the other end of the balcony was a teenage girl, stopping at the last few flowers in the line to water them. She gave him a look of mock annoyance. 'Don't you ever use the door?'

Kiy straightened, then smiled boyishly. 'Where's the fun in that?'

She allowed herself a grin as she turned back to the plants. 'I see you're still alive and well, Kiy.'

The cloudgazer scratched at his hair. 'You seem surprised.'

'Don't take it personally.' She was a short, slender girl with a petite nose. Her bold face was framed by long auburn hair twirled at the ends. Her red-white patterned pinafore was old, the frilled cuffs re-sewn several times, but she wasn't ragged-looking. She had a simplistic, working-girl's prettiness about her.

'Garden seems to be coming along nicely.' Kiy motioned to the rows of vegetables and herbs arranged neatly around her.

She nodded, regarding the plants warmly. 'Ma's downstairs.'

'She got anything new for me?'

'Guess that depends how you did, don't it?' She put down the watering can and turned expectantly. Her expression seemed to challenge him, if only in jest.

Kiy took a coin from his bag. It was a brilliant silver and hexagonal, with rounded corners.

'Oh, you know... only two hundred floril...' he said casually.

She leapt at him to try and grab it, but he held it above her reach playfully. 'Aw, c'mon!' she said with a hint of laughter.

'Goes to Mum'ma first, Hennie.'

She stopped reaching and pouted. 'Just one! She wouldn't miss it.'

Kiy laughed. 'Oh, I'm sure: "Hey Mrs Litvyak, here's the payoff: a hundred and ninety-nine floril..."'

Hennie chuckled. She was sixteen and still had the laugh of a child. It lit up her face, usually so sombre.

'Tell you what,' he said, 'you can have one from my share if you let me try one of those delicious-looking tomatoes there.'

She grabbed one and held it up to him—then pulled it out of reach just as he had done. 'What, these? Wouldn't dream of chargin' you, Kiy, but ya gonna have to fight for it!'

Kiy began to play-fight for the vegetable, giving her more of a chance by holding his sling arm behind his back. She wrestled at the other arm ferociously.

'Hey!' she said. 'Don't go putting one arm behind yer back! I can beat you any day, Tanthar!'

He grinned, and there was a pop and a whir as he fired the sling from behind his back. The grapple clamped on to a second juicy tomato, and a heartbeat later it reeled it back in.

Hennie put her hands on her hips. 'You big cheat!'

Kiy brought the sling back in front of him smoothly and took a bite. 'Never give your opponent the opportunity for an easy victory.'

'Trust you to have a moral there somewhere.' She looked at him with heavy-lidded eyes.

'Hennie!' came her mother's call. 'Hennie, dinner's ready, honey.'

'Coming, Ma.'

She stepped into the apartment, with Kiy following behind. They passed through the large room shared by Hennie and her sisters. Paper patterns, finger paintings, badges, wind chimes, pottery and embroidered patches were scattered along the walls and all over the floor.

They headed down the stairs to find the rest of the family gathered around the table in the small kitchen. Mrs Litvyak was a woman in her mid forties with worker's hands, a worldly face and faded umber hair tied back in a bun. She was dishing out soup to her children: sisters Almay, Naki, Ainu, Olya, and Olya's twin brother, Leo. Hennie took a seat, and her mother placed a bowl in front of her before turning to Kiy.

'Ah, you're back,' she said with a smile. 'And how're you today, Kiy-me-luv?'

'Just fine, Mrs L.' Kiy removed his sling and placed it in his pack. He took a look around the table. 'How's the family today?'

'I saw a Gawker today!' said Olya.

'It was a Sengull, idyat!' Leo mocked.

'Was not, mughead!'

'I think they're just happy to see you back,' Almay said over the twins' continued argument.

Mrs Litvyak set the pan down and removed her oven glove. 'How'd it go then?'

Kiy produced the bag of coins. 'Two hundred floril and no problems. Just another irate detective-inspector to add to my stalker list—'

'Wowww, two hundred?' Naki exclaimed with wide eyes. 'That's a *lot*!'

'Never mind that and eat your soup,' Mrs Litvyak said. She took the bag from Kiy appreciatively. 'Ta, luv, you're a star. You eaten yet?'

'Yesterday,' Kiy replied with an evasive look.

'Gracious.' Mrs Litvyak rolled her eyes. 'It's a wonder your body still moves. You could do with colour in them cheeks, my lad.'

Hennie slurped her soup. 'He ate one of my tomatoes.'

Kiy smirked. 'Dobber.'

'Well, if you're hungry, there's a little left in the pan,' Mrs Litvyak said.

'Wouldn't want to impose...' Kiy held up his hands.

'Not at all. You're puttin' most of the food on this table, luv. Help yourself.'

'Well—gotta admit, it does smell good.'

Hennie shifted her chair aside. 'Come on, Kiy. Sit down and eat!' She offered the stool.

'Oooh, sit next to me, Kiy!' Almay said, smirking at Hennie.

Hennie narrowed her eyes. 'Shut up, peewee!'

Kiy took a bowl tentatively and sat down to the table. On the low footstool, he appeared barely the height of five-year-old Ainu. The children giggled and Kiy went along with it, pretending to be even shorter and sipping at his soup with theatrical foolery.

'So, Kiy!' Leo said. 'What did you get up to that pissed off a detective inspector? Kill anybody, huh?'

'Leo...' his mother scolded.

'Nah,' Kiy said disinterestedly. 'Nothin' like that.'

'Man, I thought you're supposed to be a mercenary or something,' the boy replied. He was barely thirteen, but seemed ready to go out and set the world to rights.

'I try not to kill people. I hear it's really bad for you,' Kiy said.

'Ha.' Leo was obviously unimpressed.

'He's just more mature than you are, see,' Almay told her brother.

Leo sneered. 'Nobody asked you.'

His mother slapped the back of his head lightly, flicking up a tuft of hair. 'Almay, stop winding him up.'

'Wha'd you hit me for?' Leo exclaimed.

'You're brewing it. You'd better start behaving or you'll be going straight to bed.'

The pair returned to their bowls in silence. Kiy wolfed down the rest of his soup as Mrs Litvyak went about the kitchen, clearing up pots and pans and humming some made-up song.

As soon as Leo finished his meal, he was talking again. 'I heard Ganzabar's gonna take over the neutral zone,' he said, almost to himself.

Kiy looked at him sharply; the boy caught the gesture and smiled.

'Leo Litvyak, I won't have any son of mine spreading market rumours,' Mrs Litvyak said sternly. 'I'll hear no more of it.'

'It's okay, Ma,' Hennie said, shooting Leo a cold-blooded look of disdain. 'Feo will be fine.'

'The *Lykomin* is probably the biggest ship out that way,' Kiy said.

'So what?' Leo sneered. 'It's just one ship—'

'Leo!' his mother said, sharper this time.

There was a moment of tense silence, but Kiy defused it quickly. 'Look, it's just talk, short-top. Nobody wants a war.'

Leo used to moan when Kiy called him 'short-top', but now he just got mildly irritable. 'Oh yeah? How can you be so sure?' He scraped his bowl with a metallic grind.

Kiy stood to clean his own bowl, but Mrs Litvyak whisked it out from under his nose and put it in the sink. He looked over at Leo, realising the boy was still awaiting an answer. 'Well... it's all in the history.'

'History is boring.' Leo rubbed his nose.

'*I* don't think so,' Hennie said, now perched on the windowsill.

Leo grunted disdainfully and left the table.

'Well you see,' Kiy began, 'at the turn of the century, Ganzabar was in an all-out war against us. It was complete chaos and destruction.'

Leo lingered at the foot of the stairs, doing his best not to seem interested.

'We were getting beat. Then in ninety-three-oh-two...' He paused for effect, then snapped, '*Bam!*'

Almay jumped.

'Out of nowhere, comes this airship captain. She's just a junior lieutenant, but she traps and sinks a Ganzie fleet twice her own and goes on to smash them in their trails.'

Mrs Litvyak smiled knowingly as she went about her cleaning, no doubt glad to see her children learning something, even if it was almost fairytale by the telling.

'She even manages to trick a whole Ganzabi invasion force into flying below the Understorm! Ganzabar's plans for the war were bunked.'

'Ataryk?' Leo ventured.

'I thought you were leaving.' Kiy smiled, then continued. 'Yeah, Natalya Ataryk, the captain, the revolutionary... and so on. Thanks to her, Ganzabar's invasion stalled.'

Ainu started to bang her little wooden spoon about, oblivious to the narrative, until her mother came over and settled her down.

'So, wait—I thought Ganzabar won the Great Nezzu War,' Hennie said.

'Well, it was looking better. Then Ganzabar sued for peace. They did what they do best: bribery. They forced a surrender, on pretty bad terms.'

'Flakkers,' Hennie muttered.

Her mother cleared her throat.

'Sorry, Ma.'

'I still don't see how that's supposed to stop another war,' Leo protested.

'Well obviously, that wasn't the end of the story,' Kiy said with a wry look.

'So then what?' Hennie cradled a knee on interlocked fingers and swung her leg absently. 'I'll bet it was the USK. It was the USK, right?'

'Well, after the war, we were occupied by Ganzabar. Until ninety-three-fourteen; then the Liberation War changed everything.' Kiy leant forward on the table. 'A small group of independents rebelled against Ganzabar. Embarrassed them on more than one occasion. But the rebels were low on manpower and ships. That's when the United Sky Kingdoms stepped in.'

'Yeah, late as usual,' Leo snorted.

'And that's how we got independent again. With a little help from the USK, we kicked Ganzabar out for good. And so long as the USK are our friends, Ganzabar will think twice before messing with us...'

Kiy stared at the table, his memories washing over him. It had been years, but it seemed perverse talking about his childhood nightmares like a history lesson.

'Yeah, well, I still think we should totally go over there and occupy them, see how they like it,' Leo grumbled.

'I think it's time you went to occupy your bed, young man,' his mother said. 'Come on—story time's over, kids.'

Leo gave a sigh and went upstairs, followed by the other Litvyaks, save for Hennie and her mother. Once the younger children were gone, the three busied themselves quietly, until Mrs Litvyak said, 'You think it's true?'

'What?' Kiy had set down his sling on the kitchen table and was cleaning it with an old cloth.

'All that fine yarn-spinnin' about the USK keeping Ganzabar away. I mean, nobody's seen or heard from Ataryk in over ten years.'

Kiy looked at Hennie, who was watching expectantly, then back to his sling. 'S'worked so far,' he mused.

Hennie nodded and gazed out of the window. 'I hope Feo's okay.'

Her mother turned back to the sink. 'So do I. For all our sakes.'

4 - An Incident

Brudor
August 2nd

Skyswept Creek trickled down the rocky outcrop, darting between the clumps of grass as it made its way to the pool at the clearing. Wistful trees gave shade to a stony path winding through the grass near the precipice where rock and earth abruptly gave way to open sky. A steel rail followed the edge roughly, marking the boundary of Brudor Common.

Located in the middle of the sleepy town of Brudor, the Common was a daily scene to Hennie. After a long day working at the hat-maker's, she would head home along the snaking path, her mind wandering.

Hennie loved losing herself in her imagination as she walked. She pictured the little creek and pool as a mighty canal and grand reservoir. She saw the tiny hill and thought of what it might be like if it were part of a great rolling downs, stretching on as far as the eye could see, a land so big you could not see the edge. Now that was a wondrous thought! It made her think of the parks and commons she'd heard about in the big cities, like Risley and Valyagrad.

She sat down near the edge of the Common and looked out across the sea of sky. The breeze shifted the clumpy white clouds lazily across her view, as though they were on their way home, too. Far below, a carpet of ruffled white seemed to form the bottom of the world. The wind stirred about her, carrying a gentle warmth. She closed her eyes and let it wash over her.

This place was full of memories. Long summers spent playing with her big sister Feo, her little sisters and brother running around chasing insects, since before Ainu was born, even. The excitement of the Harvest Festivals, when the farm ships would arrive from the south with their incredible bounties of fruit and vegetables.

There had never been much to worry about back then. But times changed. On her fourteenth year she'd taken work at the hat-maker's. Hennie hated hats. She didn't like wearing them and she didn't like making them. She wanted nothing more than to go back to playing on the Common. But such was adult life, her mother would always say. Hennie didn't really feel like an adult, but then again, she supposed that sort of feeling didn't arise overnight. You had to gradually get used to the idea.

Reaching into her small leather bag, she pulled out her battered old radio. It was the size of a large book, blue plastic with graceful bronze lines and elegant details. It was older than she was, dating back to Great Brazak, before the days of the Occupation and the Liberation War. It had been given to her by her father, one of the few possessions she had to anchor her memory of him.

She placed it beside herself on the grass with reverence, then clicked the power on. There was a crackle, then the sound of a clarinet floated from the little speaker. The sound of the radio always took her away, far away into the skies.

She flung herself backwards onto the soft grass and stared up at the thin, stringy clouds high above. They were so far away as to seem motionless, like a permanent fixture of the vibrant blue heavens. She imagined being out there in the blue, her arms transformed to wings, the clouds rushing beneath her as she flew. In her daydream, she imagined she could leap from the edge of the Common, over the abyss into the sky. But she felt no fear, for her arms carried her and she soared upwards into the brilliant azure vastness. The whole sky was hers; she could go anywhere she wished.

She savoured that sensation—a sense of complete freedom she could glimpse only in her imagination.

The sound from the radio abruptly ceased, replaced with a whoosh of static. Hennie was pulled out of her daydream with a frown. A moment later the sound returned, although with less clarity and a constant background fuzz. Poor old thing, she thought. It was probably going funny.

She sighed. Dinner would be ready soon. She didn't much care for it right now, but it was easier to just be back home on time and make Ma happy.

Rolling to one side, she propped her chin on one hand and ran outstretched fingers through a patch of Arlands. The tall, graceful stalks parted with the lightest of resistance, their calm aqua blue flowers swaying gently and releasing a crisp fragrance like a breeze after the rain. Her gaze shifted past them to a figure moving hurriedly across the Common, along the path the way she'd come.

She sat up, regarding the figure curiously. It was a boy, about her age, carrying a grey satchel under one arm. He had thick blond hair and a narrow face. And when he looked up, she recognised who he was. It was Martle, the postboy. She'd seen him from time to time on her trips to work in the morning, though she'd spoken to him only once or twice.

The first time she saw him, she'd felt a deep longing for that face. She wondered if it was love, but that just sounded stupid. Anyway, her mother always said she would know when she was in love. And the idea of loving Martle was absurd! You can't love someone you don't even know. Still, he had a handsome face, and she liked it.

She turned away, fixing her gaze on the sky beyond the wooden fence, then flicked off the radio. Only the wind and occasional birdsong remained. The sound of footsteps approached. She tried to look as though she were blissfully unaware.

'Hey.'

She swallowed. What was he doing talking to her? She said nothing.

'Um... Hennie, right?'

She turned to see him staring at her, short of breath. 'Oh, hi!' she said. 'I was just, um... looking at the sky.' She mentally kicked herself. *Looking at the sky? Way to go, Hennie, he's not gonna think you're crazy.*

If it did make her seem crazy, he ignored it. 'Have... have you heard?'

'Heard what?'

'There was an incident. Ganzabar...'

She frowned. 'What about Ganzabar?' She felt sick suddenly.

'They say they're goin' to war.'

Hennie could see the fear in his eyes, but she couldn't believe it. 'Ganzabar's going to war? With who?'

'No... you don't understand. Somethin' happened in the NDZ.' He swallowed.

Hennie shook her head silently. *No.*

'It's true,' he said with great insistence. 'I swear. Ganzabar attacked! The *Lykomin*'s missing! Everybody's getting ready to leave. Here, take this.'

In his hand, he held an officious envelope bearing the government's stamp.

Hennie took it numbly. She stared at it a few moments, and then it was as if everything fell into place. Her mind went to Feo: she saw her standing on the deck of the great ship, a flurry of explosions erupting behind her, rippling up the structure, getting ever closer. Feo's expression was placid, content—a sad, wistful smile. The glow of flame lit the sides of Feo's face as it was engulfed in fire.

'No!' Hennie recoiled, throwing the envelope aside. 'It's not true!'

The boy looked hurt. 'I swear it is! That's an evac order—everyone has one!'

'Shut up! Liar!' Hennie snapped back. She snatched up her radio and ran from the Common before her tears could form.

5 - The Proctor

Nubylon, Azrune
August 3rd

At the centre of the magnificent city of Nubylon stood the ancient Circular Palace, a spire reaching up to the stars. It was like a mountain, building up slowly at first, then with a sharpening curve it transformed into a huge cylindrical tower, shining in white and gold, with a slanted, smooth top. It was elegant and minimal, with such disregard for the rules of material and architecture as to appear made by magic.

Around the circumference of the palace floated a giant ring, just a metre thick and ornately adorned with lavish fractal patterns. Several narrower rings, at offset planes of rotation to the main one, protruded farther from the orbit like some brass model of the heavens. And around the upper portion of the tower, a thicker, habitable ring of metal and white stone encircled the structure, though it did not appear to be attached to the main building at any point. Neither did it seem concerned by the impossibility of its existence, hanging there unsupported.

On one side of the tower's crown, a panoramic balcony protruded from a room with huge, slightly curved windows. Within the spacious room, a fire crackled on an ornamental marble hearth. The glossy stone flooring encased blue carpet squares in repeating geometric patterns. Dim wall lights, shaped like newly birthed crescents, threw milky shadows across the floor.

In the middle of the chamber, looking out at the quiet night, was a tall chair. On it sat a small boy.

His face was finely proportioned, as though it had been sculpted on expert commission. His flawless black hair, finer than silk, was in a loose, natural bob. His clothes were simplistic yet spotless: a tall-collared tunic with epaulettes, cotton trousers and knee-high boots, all in white, trimmed with gold and sky blue. He wore a thin fabric cloak of the same colours—a purely stylish garment, as it was pleasantly warm in the room.

The chair, on which he sat completely motionless, might have been described as a minimalist throne. It was tall-backed, passing his head twice over, with no embellishments but the straight gold trim. It was grand in a way that was both clean and austere.

And it made him look even smaller than he was.

Yet he was easily the most powerful and important 'boy' in the world. He was the sovereign head of state of Azrune, and he had been for hundreds of years. The term 'monarch' would not be apt, nor was he exactly 'emperor', although the word was often used to describe him. No, he was merely an extension of the people's well-being, the common sense of humanity given form. So it had been for countless generations.

Other kings of the world might claim divine birth, but such claims were mere political machinations—they were simply men. They would grow old and die; nothing made them special or gifted them naturally for government. Unlike him. He never grew old. He had always been this way, as long as he could remember. And he had a very good memory.

He was known simply as the Proctor.

The people of Azrune had been his wards for untold generations, along with many other nations that had since declared themselves separate entities: Ganzabar, the United Sky Kingdoms, Lystrata. The Proctor was often curious how much their political independence had changed their lives, but they seemed to delight in screwing things up themselves instead of having things screwed up for them.

'Proctor.'

At the sound of the woman's voice, the boy raised a hand in a beckoning gesture.

The tall woman wore white and blue also, but her outfit was a gown-like tunic. She was about fifty, her terracotta skin weathered and her face possessing a mature charisma. She walked with a haughty stature, tall heels clacking on the polished floor.

'Prime Minister Tendrassi,' the Proctor said.

'There has been an incident,' she said as she reached him.

'So I hear.' The Proctor's voice was light, gender-neutral almost, and far older than he looked.

'A Brazakker warship was sunk in the Junders Demilitarised Zone, after supposedly attacking and sinking a Ganzabi merchant ship,' Tendrassi said with motherly disapproval. 'Both sides blame the other. Tensions continue to escalate. War appears inevitable.'

The Proctor nodded to himself, mulling it over. 'That always seems to be how these things happen.'

'There is something else.'

The Proctor registered his interest with a curious look.

'The Brazakkers managed to recover the wreck of one of the two escort craft involved—they dredged it from the Understorm. It was taken out with a single hit, and the penetration marks were like nothing they'd ever seen. They feared some new Ganzabi weapon, so they petitioned the Ministry of Science for analysis.'

The Proctor perked up as though an answer had been whispered in his ear. 'The Erehwon class.'

Tendrassi concealed her surprise. 'Indeed. Puncture marks match the prototype's munitions. Of course, we declared our analysis inconclusive.'

The Proctor nodded. 'So, whoever has the Erehwon prototype is trying to ignite a war between Ganzabar and Brazak West? And evidently has already succeeded.'

'It seems that way,' Tendrassi agreed. 'Ganzabar's embassy in Risley was abandoned this morning.'

'Well then. Queen moves to counter knight.'

'Sir?'

He looked at her sincerely. 'We should send the *Akron*. The prototype, she... she *must* be recovered.'

'Intervene?' Tendrassi said, then shook off the disagreement as though it were a momentary indulgence. She bowed slightly. 'Of course. Very well, sir.'

The Proctor seemed merely distracted by these official matters. 'You know, I am struggling to find the meaning of independence.'

'Sir? How so?'

'The fates of nations.' The Proctor made a dismissive gesture and went quiet a moment. 'The moons are pretty tonight.'

'Indeed, sir.'

'Reminds me of a Tuesday. Is it Tuesday?'

Tendrassi nodded. She remained attentive, but not patronising.

The Proctor drew in a deep breath and exhaled slowly. He got to his feet, walked deliberately to the window, and looked out at the balcony and the night sky. The city of Nubylon, an artificial star-scape of yellowish lights and glowing spires, glittered from one end of the horizon to the other. The Proctor locked hands behind his back, looking like a precocious child.

Tendrassi followed precisely, remaining several metres behind him. He turned to look at her.

'What do you think of direct intervention?'

She frowned. 'Frankly... distasteful, Proctor.'

'Quite.'

There was a pause, then he added sadly, 'And yet look at where we are.'

'I suppose we have no choice. You said so yourself, Proctor: above all, it must be returned, as the consequences otherwise could be catastrophic.' She pondered a moment, then spoke more earnestly. 'I suppose a little lesson into the bargain wouldn't do a great deal of harm, either.'

'That's how it all starts.' The Proctor returned his gaze to the night. 'The sum of all well-intentioned actions could destroy the civilised world.'

Tendrassi made a troubled face. 'I'm not sure I understand where you're going with this.'

'I apologise, Madam Prime Minister.' The Proctor looked to his feet. 'I am self-indulging. It happens with age. You may go.'

'As you say.' The Prime Minister gave a small bow and left the room.

The Proctor continued to watch the lights of Nubylon, glowing as they had done for centuries.

6 - Evacuate

Kiy watched helplessly as the Litvyaks prepared to evacuate. He had an unreal sense of urgency in slow motion, an impending doom over the horizon that edged closer every day. Somewhere out there, across the sky, a terrible danger was marching slowly towards them.

The *Lykomin*'s status was still being withheld by the military. All that was known was that it had encountered a Ganzabi ship intruding on Brazak airspace—a Ganzabi ship that had sunk a Brazak escort. The *Lykomin* had pursued it to capture, and then contact had been lost. The Litvyaks had been in a state of endless, nerve-shredding anxiety. About the only thing that seemed certain now was that things were going to get worse.

Ganzabar, meanwhile, had claimed that a Brazak warship had chased a Ganzabi merchant freighter through Ganzabi airspace, so they had sunk it in revenge. The reality of the situation was finally confirmed by the politics correspondent for Brudor News Radio.

'I regret to inform you that the Ganzabi ambassador left Risley yesterday morning, and, as of noon today... our nation is at war... with the Federation of Ganzabar.'

The words were haunting, ominous, promising misery and bloodshed that just about every Brazakker had thought they'd left behind. But for Kiy they stung with shame, too. He wondered if the Litvyak children would ever listen to a word he said now.

There'd been no word on the USK's stance with regard to the Brazakkers' cause. The more cynical had noted that the Sterling dollar's strength and the USK's economic situation meant that, unlike during the last war, this was a bad time to get involved, fiscally speaking. Kiy wouldn't be surprised if it came down to the money. In any case, it was too soon to know for sure.

Kiy slumped in his makeshift hammock on the apartment's balcony. It was his usual sleeping arrangement with the Litvyaks, although he normally only spent a night or two there at any given time. The wind could get cold in the open, but he never complained; it was nothing like the winds back home, and it certainly beat sleeping on walkways and in cabletram shelters.

Kiy watched the hurried mass of people around them packing away their lives and trying to find someone who would take them out of town. Brudor wasn't far from the southern border, and a sense of danger hung in the air. The government were trying to move children and families out, but there simply wasn't enough time or enough manpower, and there was not nearly enough transportation.

The chattering along the walkways was angry, impatient, afraid. The incident had riled up the Brazakkers no end. They didn't take kindly to being pushed around at the best of times, but when it came to Ganzabar there was rarely a sympathetic voice. Kiy overheard curses, racial slurs, and defiant declarations.

Unlike the people here, Kiy had few preparations to make. He had few belongings: just the clothes he wore, his satchel—containing his sling, dried biscuits and a flask of water—and his revolver in a holster on his thigh, a relic passed to him from his late mother. He almost never fired it. His only ammunition was what was already loaded on the wheel feed. In a sense, he was always packed. But all things considered, he wasn't even sure if he was leaving.

The Litvyaks had given a lot to him, certainly. Mrs Litvyak treated him like her own son. For almost a year now, she had gotten him jobs, and he'd worked them. They were generally an honest sort, too. Besides, he'd never been good at the business side of freelancing. He'd always found the actual looking for work tedious, while Mrs Litvyak seemed to know a guy who knew a guy for just about everything. Kiy gave her half of the sum for every job, which was generous by the going rate, so she was ever grateful. He didn't mind; her family seemed to have more need for it than he did.

The arrangement was as stable a one as a cloudgazer could ever hope for. Still, he was beginning to think it might be time to go his own way. If Ganzabar really was committed to a war, he'd be naïve to not be near it—where his kind should be, and Hennie and the others definitely shouldn't. He'd only be a liability to them, another mouth to feed in a household on the run.

'You look so strong.'

Kiy turned to see Hennie looking up at the Brazak Flagship *Municipal*, docked in the harbour. It had arrived that evening with much of the Home Fleet, heading south to intercept Ganzabi invaders. The ship hung at the side of the harbour building there like a huge bird of bronze and blue, nestled amongst the lattice of gantries and docking beams. The flocks of smaller ships that surrounded it dwarfed Brudor's little harbour.

Kiy nodded, appraising it too. 'She certainly does.'

'She will kill the Ganzies.' Hennie quivered. 'She'll get them back.'

He looked back at her expression: eyes ablaze, lip curled. At first, the question of what had happened to Feo had left her in a state of desperate hope. But that hope had quickly turned to rage as the truth looked ever more dire, and now she searched for someone to blame. As the second oldest Litvyak, Hennie was perhaps closest of all to her big sister. Kiy knew she felt as though a part of her had been ripped away, though she still fiercely denied Feo could be gone.

It was almost like losing their father all over again.

Mrs Litvyak was remarkably unchanged, but Kiy knew she was putting on a brave face for her son and daughters, trying to keep their spirits up as they patiently awaited passage out of Brudor, unsure of when they might come back, or if their home would even still be here when they did.

So much loss. A daughter, a sister, their security. And now… now they had to leave their home behind and take refuge in the north.

Kiy's gaze fell. How could he leave them at a time like this?

No, stop, he berated himself. He liked the Litvyaks—that was certainly true. But he wasn't their father. He didn't want to get involved in the complications of a family. His relationship with them had to be professional; Mrs Litvyak was his client. He'd be compromising his way of living if he let it be otherwise.

'Ma's managed to book us passage on a liner,' Hennie said. 'It leaves tomorrow evening. She only got seven tickets, but I guess you'll just be slipping aboard in your own way?'

Kiy looked away. 'Hennie...'

She didn't seem to hear him. 'I just can't believe it, you know. A week ago everything was great. And now...' She let out a frustrated sigh.

'Hennie, I won't be leaving with you.'

She suddenly stared at him as though he'd declared himself the Sultan of all Lystrata. 'What? Why not?'

He shook his head. 'I *can't* go with you.' He motioned towards the harbour, where the fleet sat dormant, its guns bristling. 'The opportunities will be here now.'

'*Opportunities?*' she said bitterly. 'To make money, you mean?'

Kiy sighed. 'It's not that simple. I'm a cloudgazer, Hennie. I belong here, where the problems are. I can't explain it very well. That's just the way things are.'

'I don't get it! What about Ma? What about Leo, the girls? They need you, Kiy.'

Kiy noted she omitted herself, but he suspected that was only because she didn't like to admit needing anything. 'You can have the rest of my share if you want. I'm sure it'll see you through for now—'

She kicked a heel into the floor plates angrily. He looked at her, but she wouldn't meet his gaze.

Finally, she spoke. 'I don't mean money. We just... we need you to be there, y'know? For a little while. Please?' She looked up. 'Ma, she's fighting a battle too, y'know. Never mind them!' She motioned to the *Municipal*.

Kiy exhaled slowly, then stood. 'I think I've overstepped my place here. I am grateful for what you've given me, you and your mother—all of you. But I don't belong here. I never have.' He shook his head irritably, as though annoyed by his own words. He placed his sling on his right arm; the device rippled with a sequence of glowing edges and lines as it came to life.

'Wait...' she began, then seemed at a loss for words.

He tossed a small bag on the hammock; it jingled as it landed. Then he raised his arm.

'Take care, Hennie.'

The clamp fired, attached, and a few moments later Kiy was whisked off the balcony and into the skyline.

Hennie watched him go with resigned disappointment. She watched him until he vanished beyond a spire of the Old Refectory. Then, sensing someone was behind her, she turned. Her mother stood in the doorway.

'Ma!' she said with surprise. 'Did you...?' Her voice dwindled.

'Yes.' Her mother nodded. 'I was pretty sure he wouldn't come with us, darling.'

'But why?' Hennie lamented. 'Feo's gone away, Kiy's gone away... oh, things just can't get any worse!'

Her mother stepped up and put an arm around her. 'Now, dear,' she said evenly, ruffling her daughter's long hair and kissing her head, 'let's not invite trouble's custom, shall we?'

7 - Bombs

Brudor
Early hours of August 5th

The siren woke them. It was a ghastly sound, a rising wail that screamed across the dark sky. And in the distance was the sound of engines—bombers and skyfighters, humming in unison.

Hennie hurried down the stairs with Naki and Ainu on either side, as her mother and Almay gathered a few more things into a large bag.

'Come on,' Mrs Litvyak urged, trying to get her kids together. 'We've got to go!'

'I want to take Sibby!' Naki said.

Her mother took the large doll from Naki's hands. 'Leave Sybil here, darling. Almay, you don't need all your books! Come on, come on! Olya, where's your brother?'

'Don't know.' Olya shrugged, her voice stubbornly indifferent.

'He said he gone to the war,' Naki offered.

'Naki!' Olya said to her little sister. 'You little dobber!'

'*What?*' Their mother gasped, her pupils shrunken to pinpricks. She turned to Naki. 'Where did he go?'

Faced with her mother's anger, Naki began to cry.

'Naki, honey, I need you to tell me,' Mrs Litvyak said, fighting impatience.

Olya stammered, 'He-he-he's gone t-to join the fleet. He's gonna fight Ganzabar for Feo. We promised not to tell —'

Their mother shook Olya by the shoulders with frustration. 'Oh, Sky be damned! What do I do now?'

She looked at Hennie, her eyes betraying desperation.

'I'll go look for him—' Hennie began.

'No!' Her mother closed her eyes, inhaling deeply. 'No, dear, not now.' She hurried them all out the door. 'Hurry, we've got to get to shelter! Come on!'

They ran alongside her as the droning got louder, an angry, insect-like buzz over the siren's awful cry. The walkways and gantries were relatively deserted—most had evidently already got out or were sheltering in cellars dug into floatrock. Below them, between the walkways, the sky was a vast and endless void of dark purple, almost black.

The gantry beneath their feet rattled as the first bombs impacted. Children screamed and parents cried out for them. Hennie tried to comfort her younger sisters as they ran. She stuck to the back of the group, helping her mother keep everyone together.

At Independence Square, a crowd surged around the central cabletram station. The station was a wide, thick-walled building, mostly sunken into the floatrock of the town's central island. As the Litvyaks arrived, the crowd was exchanging heated words with a soldier blocking the entrance.

'What the hadnar are you doing? Let us in!' a man yelled.

'You need to head for the airfield!' the soldier replied, his voice weary from repetition. Behind him, another soldier was evacuating those already inside back out again, to join the masses headed down Ashgrove Prospekt.

'Get going,' the first soldier added. 'The station's not safe. The whole Ganzie fleet is coming down on us.'

'You can't airlift the whole town!' shouted one man.

'Crazy talk!' said another.

'Get outta the way!' a woman cried, her hands on the shoulders of her son.

'For Sky's sake, love, you need to go, now!' the soldier protested. He and his colleague stood braced in the entrance, their rifles held across their chests. There was no getting past them.

Hennie turned to her mother. 'Ma, the airfield! Let's go!' she said, heading to join the groups that were heading for the airstrip. Her mother assented, and they pressed on, dragged along by a human tide of panic.

All around them, fires had sprung up, and the pre-dawn horizon was tinged with a hellish red. Bombs beat percussion on their heels, shaking the floatrock with each detonation. As Hennie strained to look back, trying to make out the silhouettes of the bombers on the night sky, her foot caught on something and she tumbled. She yelped, cradling her scuffed knees.

She'd barely begun to stand when she was thrown to the side by an immense blast and a wave of heat. It was so loud, she wondered if a bomb had landed right beside her.

She stumbled in sudden silence. What was going on? Blurs went past. Her vision was filled with flaming wreckage. She wasn't sure what she was doing here. She couldn't be dead, because she was still alive. That was generally a pretty good sign, she thought.

Then, gradually, she heard voices again. The siren and the bombs returned again too. She turned behind her. A fire raged in the ruins of what had once been the Square, with tiny pieces of rubble and flaming wreckage spreading into the sky. She thought she heard distant screams.

Glancing around, she felt her heart skip a beat. Where was Ma? Her sisters?

'Hennie!'

She looked around, then saw them: her mother and the rest of her siblings were on the far side of a fallen tangle of power lines and girders.

'I'm okay Ma!' Hennie managed.

'We can't get to you, Hennie!' Almay yelled, panic-stricken.

Hennie got to her feet. 'It's okay... I'll catch up! Keep going!'

Her mother seemed to doubt a moment, then nodded. 'Come on, kids.' She scooped up Ainu and ran. The others followed her out of sight, and Hennie ran into an alley between two buildings to try and find a way around the wreckage.

As she rounded a corner, she tripped again, though this time she kept her feet. She spun and hit the wall—then put her hand to her mouth when she saw what it was that she had tripped on: a dead body. With sickening nausea, she realised she recognised the face that stared upwards with lifeless eyes.

'Martle...' she whispered.

He had done nothing to deserve this. And the last time she saw him, she'd shouted at him and called him a liar. Her unjust rage came back to her now, only it was the dead face of Martle yelling at her...

She turned away from the body and ran.

She quickly became lost. Every side alley was a false promise. She wished she'd spent more time learning her way around the west side of town. Gradually her gait faltered and she came to a stop, suddenly noticing how alone she was. Nothing around her moved; the sound of the bombs and the screams was far off now. Brudor was dead. Only the drone of the bombers remained.

Fighting rising panic, she hurried down a flight of steps to a lower platform, hoping it would lead back up to the far side of the Square. But when she came around a corner, she let out a frustrated groan. The gantry came to an abrupt end. A large gap separated it from another, higher-level walkway.

She eyed the gantry she stood on, then the one up ahead. Could she cross the gap? Gathering courage, she carefully clambered onto the railing and began to reach up to the next level. An explosion some way off caused the walkway to shudder, and she clutched a loose cable to keep balance, trying desperately not to look down into the sky.

She reached out again for the upper platform with her free hand, but it was still just too far away. *Come on!* All she wanted was to be back up there so she catch up with mother and the others. Every second they got farther away. Every second death marched closer. Her panic escalated. *Just... jump for it!*

She leapt.

She stretched for the upper platform, but her hands couldn't find purchase. They slipped from the smooth metal and she began to tumble. She let out a scream, falling through the gap towards the sky, spinning, tumbling towards the void of the night.

Then, abruptly, she stopped.

It was as if the world had paused for her. Was this what happened when you fell to your death? You were given a moment to reflect?

Then she realised something was gripping her wrist, and she looked up. Her eyes went wide as relief swept over her.

'Kiy!'

Kiy hung from his sling cable, with his other hand firmly around her wrist. 'Flak, girl! You scared the crap out of me for a moment there.'

'How did you find me?'

'Bumped into your mother.' He pulled her up to the higher gantry, and Kiy caught his breath. 'What the hadnar is going on?'

'I don't know! The Square just exploded! We've gotta get out of Brudor. They're destroying everything.'

'Shyut. Thought I heard bunker shells.'

Hennie tried to calm her nerves after her brush with death. 'Ma's gone to the airfield; they're flying people out.'

Kiy looked troubled. 'So she said. I don't see how that's possible, though.'

'Well, that's what the soldier said.'

He mulled on it. 'Well, shyut, I don't have any better ideas. Come on.'

They ran together, Hennie fighting to keep pace with Kiy's long strides. As they cleared the crest of Rosebury Rise, a group of four Brazakker fighters flew low overhead, their twin turboprop engines making a deafening whump and a roar.

Hennie gave a vindictive cheer as they screamed past, heading for the sound of the bombs. Like any Brazakker, Hennie recognised the Foxtail duplane, distinctive skyfighter of Brazak West. A common postwar slogan claimed three things won the Liberation War: 'Foxtails, Foxtails and Foxtails'. Of course, the money to build them came from the USK, but patriotism rarely courts sensibility.

'They're gonna show the Ganzies a thing or two,' Hennie said, fists balled.

'Then we need to hurry up get out of their way,' Kiy reminded her. They broke into a run again.

As they neared the airstrip, a small high-wing passenger craft was coming down one runway, while on the adjacent one a large cargo plane was accelerating away.

'Looks like an airlift was already underway,' Kiy said. 'Bet they weren't counting on coming into a combat zone, though.'

He pointed his sling at the airfield. A small telescopic lens flicked out of the sling, and he surveyed the scene with its aid.

'There,' he said, withdrawing from the scope. 'I see them. They're near the front of the crowd.'

'We gotta get to them! Let's go!' Hennie ran forward. Kiy bolted after her.

At the taxiway, a crowd of people were all trying to be first onto the aircraft, swarming the queue. Kiy and Hennie fought their way forward, trying to see over the tops of people. Then Hennie caught sight of her family just as they boarded a plane. As Mrs Litvyak stepped aboard, she turned back for a longing look at Brudor. Their eyes met, and her mother immediately began to shout something, but Hennie was too far away to make it out.

'Ma!' she yelled back helplessly.

Mrs Litvyak tried to leave the plane, but soldiers pushed her back into the cabin and sealed the doorway. Hennie saw her mother's face appear in one of the plane's windows as the engines fired up.

'Kiy, you gotta do something!' Hennie said. 'Use your sling!'

He shook his head. 'I'd end up crashing it. If that plane could carry any more, they'd be on there already.'

Hennie watched, powerless, as the craft trundled to the start of the runway and began to accelerate down the strip. It reached the end and dipped a little off the edge before climbing up into the air. As it shrank away into the vast expanse of sky to the north, a curious sense of calm washed over her. Her family were out of danger now; she only had to worry about herself. Well, her and Leo.

Leo...

'Leo wasn't with them, was he?'

'I didn't see him, but he must have been. Why wouldn't he be?' Kiy said.

She looked away. 'I guess he really did it.'

'Did what? Where is he?'

'Sky knows! He went off to fight the Ganzies. After he found out you'd abandoned us.' Her gaze fell. 'Yesterday, he told me... he thought you might avenge Feo for us. I think he decided he wants to do it himself.'

'Oh, he's going to get himself killed—' Kiy cut himself short. 'Hennie, I'm sorry—'

'It's okay,' Hennie said, but her voice sounded empty. 'I don't blame you for this. I don't know why you have to be out there in all this, but I guess that's what you've gotta do.' She looked up at him, her mouth a thin angled line. 'He must have got on that ship that was docked here last night.'

'The *Municipal*? It's head of the Home Fleet. They haven't gone far; holding at Mosleyhead, if I recall.'

Hennie didn't think to ask him how he knew these things. He always seemed to know so much about the goings-on in the world. But then, he was almost literally a fly on the wall at times.

'Kiy...' She fixed her eyes on him with a stern look. 'I want to give you a mission, if I may.' She paused, constructing her proposal carefully. 'I want you to bring back my little brother. Wherever he's gone, it can't be good. Please?' She put a hand on his arm 'Even if Ma won't pay you to do it, I will.'

Kiy paused as though in thought, then looked at her with a smile. 'I wouldn't dream of charging ya, Hennie.'

Her face was awash with relief and gratitude.

'Of course I'll look for him. You know I would anyway.' He motioned towards the diminishing crowd clambering onto planes. 'As for you, you need to get on one of those.'

'To where?' she said in a small voice. 'I don't know where Ma's gone to.'

He took out a handful of floril and gave it to her. 'Head for the city of Laronor. When you get there, look up a man named Miles Rathbone. He was a friend of my parents. Tell him I sent you. He'll look after you till I get there.' As he explained, he scrawled out a note on a scrap of paper from his pocket. 'I'd see you there myself, but Leo's gonna wind up in trouble sooner than later, I feel.'

Hennie made a face as though he was talking nonsense. 'Don't worry about me, you softy. I'll be fine.' She took the paper. It had several lines of names and some numbers, though the writing was barely legible. She stowed it in her shoulder-bag, noting grimly that the bag's contents were now all she had.

As Kiy backed away, she realised she'd be alone again. But this time, she was invigorated with a new sense of hope. If anyone could get Leo back, it was Kiy. And she would be safe for now in Laronor, far away to the north.

'Good luck.' She sprang forward and gave him a kiss on the cheek. 'And thanks.'

She ran for the planes and didn't look back.

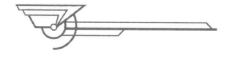

8 - Sky Hop

Brudor

The once peaceful town of Brudor was in smoking ruin. Most of the structures were crumbling or ablaze. Chunks of rock and concrete hung by pipes and cables; some broke off and tumbled into the infinite expanse below.

Kiy vaulted onto the side of a tall tower that had taken the brunt of a bunker-piercing torpedo. He toed along a line of shattered masonry and then, with a fluid flick of his sling, pulled himself up to the crest of the tower's remains.

Across a massive gap of empty sky, the form of an airship drifted slowly along; a Ganzabi warship, its searchlights scanning in the dim light of the foggy morning. They were all over Brudor now, seeking out any remaining pockets of Brazakker resistance.

Kiy wasn't too worried about being spotted, though. They wouldn't be looking for him, so they weren't likely to see him. He had evaded the search teams with ease so far, keeping to the underside of the islands as he'd made his way back to the harbour.

All he needed now was a ship going to the battle zone; the Brazak Home Fleet was reportedly massing to the north, and the *Municipal* would likely be at the head of them. A ticket with the Ganzabi military would do.

Of course, he wasn't Ganzabi military personnel.

He was, however, a cloudgazer.

Leaping to another spire, he swung up onto a steel girder and steadied himself. With his free hand, he took out a small shortwave radio receiver and flipped it on. It crackled and hissed as he adjusted it, scanning for transmissions in the immediate area. Snippets of words fought with whooshing static and harsh electrical pops and clicks.

Kiy casually leapt forward and fell several stories, firing out the sling's clamp as he did so. The clamp found purchase at the tail of a Ganzabi ship, and he reeled himself in, keeping out of view. As he steadied himself below the belly of the ship, he saw that the craft was moving into a clearing of improved visibility. And as it did, his radio hit on a clear transmission.

'—this is the *Pious Son*, ready for orders.'

'Copy, *Pious Son*. Rejoin invasion group, task-force Dagger, vector zero-zero-five.'

Kiy smiled to himself. *Headed north. Perfect*.

'*Pious Son*, copy. Rejoining task-force Dagger.'

A small airship began to move, its central megaprop engine gradually spinning up. It was no more than fifty metres long, but looked tough enough to be joining the battle to the north.

Kiy slipped the radio into his pocket and took hold of a metal pipe protruding from the ship's hull. With his sling-arm freed, he aimed down the telescopic viewfinder. On the wedge-like prow of the distant airship were tall white letters spelling out its name.

'There you are, *Pious Son*,' Kiy muttered. 'Wouldn't mind a lift if you're offering...'

The craft in his sights was probably almost two kilometres away, near the limit of his range. The sling was able to store a cable two and a half thousand meters in length—a cable strong enough to support the weight of more than two people—and yet it all fit in a space the size of a shoebox. He couldn't say how it worked; such were the long-lost wonders of Gold Age technology.

He fired the clamp, and it whirred furiously across the gap for several seconds, accelerating as it went. The line tensed when the clamp found its mark.

Kiy let go of the ship from which he hung, and as he fell, he reeled in the sling. Acceleration took his stomach away, and then he was flying across the grey void like a bullet, the wind buffeting his coat, the wet mist of cloud soaking his hair. He grinned. There was nothing in the world that came close to the thrill of a sky hop.

The *Pious Son* closed fast. When he began to swing into its shadow, he steadied the reeling. His swing slowed, then stopped, and he swung underneath the airship. As he swung back again, he clicked the sling vigorously into life again. It pulled him up sharply, catapulting him up above the deck line. Kiy inverted and landed smoothly.

The deck was deserted—a fact that momentarily disappointed Kiy, as he considered that to be one of his very finest inverted landings. He removed the sling, stowed it in his satchel, and made his way to an access hatch. Finding it unlocked, he stepped through onto stairs leading down.

The interior hummed to the tune of the engine. Kiy crept along, peering into a few of the nearest rooms, but they were deserted.

He wandered deeper inside. The sounds of engine parts clanking and shunting grew around him, getting louder as he descended into the Drive Room. But still, there was not a soul in sight.

Who's running this ship, anyway?

An empty deck was one thing, but there should be someone around the engines at all times, even on a small ship like this. This was definitely the *Pious Son*, which he'd heard transmit, so there had to be somebody—

He froze as the quiet click of a pistol's cocking hammer sounded just behind his ear.

9 - The Battle of Mosleyhead

6 kilometres east of Mosleyhead, Brazak West
August 8th

Leo cried out as a burly man in black pulled him along by his ear. 'Lemme go, flak-tard!'

'Shud'up!' the oafish man barked back, dragging him onto the bridge.

'Admiral Zhukov,' he said as they arrived, 'look what Derrik found sneakin' around the drive room...'

Leo was thrust forward. He glared up at the admiral. The old man had a leathery, battle-scarred face and regarded the boy with a steady gaze.

'I see,' the admiral said. 'What's your name, son?'

'Leo.'

'What are you doing on my ship?'

Leo's mind stumbled. He had been expecting abuse or punishment, not level questions. He was slow to think of a reply.

'I wanna fight the Ganzies!' he said after a moment's thought.

'He's just a kid!' the burly man protested.

'Really, Midshipman Torril? I hadn't noticed.' The admiral kept his gaze on Leo.

'I'm no kid!' Leo said. 'I'm sixteen years old!'

'Heck of a squirt for sixteen...' Torril remarked.

'You could at least be realistic if you're going to lie about your age.' The admiral sighed, eyes scanning the room. 'Look, lad, we don't have the time or resources to send you home. So you might as well be of use here. We need every pair of hands in the coming battle, or we're all going to the Understorm.'

Torril looked horrified. 'Admiral Zhukov, sir...?'

'Midshipman, do you think this boy could load shells?'

Torril squinted at the boy. 'Doubt it. Sir, I don't even think he'd be able to lift 'em.'

Zhukov made a dismissive hand wave. 'A round is ten kilos. That's a family-sized tank o' Pure. You ever lugged your family's water back from market, lad?'

Leo nodded eagerly. 'Yes, sir!'

'Good.' Zhukov turned to the midshipman. 'See to it that the boy is well looked after. He's a broadsider. For now at any rate.'

Torril looked as if he was about to say something, but thought better of it and gave a nod. 'Sir.'

'Admiral!' one of the crew said abruptly. 'We have visual contact with the Ganzabi.'

'Signal the fleet: All Stop.'

'Aye, sir! All Stop!' the craftsman replied, cranking the helm throttle lever with a rattle. The speed gauge slid back to the centre, and from beneath them came the sound of shunting steel and whirring chains. 'Fleet standing by, sir.'

Zhukov turned to Torril and Leo. 'Now... I have much to attend to. Kindly get to work, both of you.'

Both Torril and Leo saluted and hurried out of the door.

Torril took Leo to his broadside team on J deck. He introduced Leo gruffly to the other operators. The gun's crew consisted of three in all: Okwin, who armed shells from the conveyor; Torril, who did the loading of the shells into the breech; and Anatali, who aimed the gun-sights with an array of levers and cranks.

Torril was grouchy, but the others seemed easygoing. Okwin was built like an iron bridge, with fair hair and a docile nature. Anatali was a skinny waif of a woman with a face half hidden beneath a heavy set of gunner's goggles and a leather cap, from which her long black hair slipped out and over her shoulders.

Leo's job, he discovered, would be to pass shells to Okwin and clear away spare casings and debris. There was a chute for junk metal, which Leo was instructed to throw every scrap he found into. It would be melted in the ship's reactor into its base elements.

The shells fired by the *Municipal*'s broadside batteries were heavy, solid things the size of a man's thigh, and weighed as though they were full of water. Anatali informed him that they were made in the Foundry, the mysterious factory deep within the ship, from little more than scrap metal and phenomenal amounts of energy. This way, she said, a ship could have vast stocks of ammunition simply by recycling the majority of its energy and matter.

'So, you clear on what you gotta do?' Anatali said. 'You're a slug monkey, basically!'

Leo frowned. 'A what?'

'That's someone who's job is to carry and supply ammunition to their comrades.' Anatali was sitting in a small seat attached to the side of the gun, one knee thrown over the other casually and a cigarette in one hand. She seemed nicer than Torril, certainly, but she did seem the kind of woman that enjoyed having subordinates perhaps a little too much.

The gunnery chief came wandering down the open corridor along which the gunner teams were stationed. As he passed, he glanced at Anatali and snapped, 'Nat, put that flakkin' fag out. Live rounds on deck.'

She stuck out her tongue after he'd walked on, but she stubbed the cigarette against the side of the gun barrel and tossed it into the sky.

Kiy assessed his situation. He had been in worse in the past. At least this time he was neither blindfolded nor gagged. He wasn't dangling over open sky, bleeding from a gunshot wound or precariously close to a spinning megaprop engine. He wasn't even bound at all, in fact— though confiscation of his bag, with the sling inside, had effectively chained him to the ship for the time being.

The pistol that had been pointed at his head had been held by a nervous teenager on his first flight out of Ganzabar. Luckily, the situation had been swiftly defused by the ship's commanding officer, a thirty-something captain by the name of Bayor, whose arrival had prevented Kiy from losing a decent portion of his cranium.

Though Captain Bayor had brought the situation under control, he hadn't been all that interested in dealing with

Kiy. From what Kiy had overheard, most of the ship's crew had been hurriedly thrown together from reserves in Capula, and it was well under recommended operating capacity. Figuring Kiy to be some partisan that snuck aboard at Brudor, the captain had elected to shut him in one of the empty cabins until they could figure out what to do with him.

Getting his satchel back would be his first priority, Kiy decided—at least, once he got himself out of the locked cabin. It was a makeshift arrangement, nothing compared to the typical calibre of brigs he'd had to slip out of in the past. He was just waiting patiently for the right cue.

Something belowdecks shifted with a clunk, and the hum of the engines lowered ever so slightly in tone. Kiy stepped to the porthole and strained to see ahead. He could pick out the shapes of a fleet sat opposite the one he travelled with. The Brazakker Home Fleet.

Ganzabar was ready to engage.

Kiy turned back to the interior, eyeing a large trunk sat at the foot of the double-berth. It probably weighed near half as much as him, but it might suffice. He stooped to empty it, and when he found it to be locked, he gave it a disgruntled kick for good measure. But when he attempted to lift it, he was surprised by how much lighter it was than it appeared.

He hefted it up to the window, then proceeded to use it as a ram until the fixture gave way. The round plate was whipped into the sky and the wind roared into the room like an eager, wild animal. Kiy dropped the trunk, gripped the edge of the torn opening and eased himself out through the gap.

Outside the ship, he placed his feet on a thin rim that followed the hull below the window. Gripping a rail that ran parallel above, he edged along the metal skin of the vessel. Dread crept over him. He was used to doing this with a sling as his backup, but without it... he was one bad slip from oblivion. There could be no mistakes today.

Then again, he thought, *that's exactly what I ought not to think.* After all, he'd done this dozens of times with the 'safety net' of the sling and had never needed it. All it would take was the nervousness of over-thinking and—

His foot slipped from the ledge just momentarily, enough to give him a sharp jab of adrenalin. Scrambling back onto the rim, he remained still for a moment, his hands gripping the rail tightly.

Up ahead, the path promised an easier route: a gantry with a doorway back into the ship's interior. He began to move again, more carefully than before. But as he neared the gantry, the ship began banking towards the side he clung to. Alarmingly, he felt his weight shift backward, away from his foothold. Another few degrees and he'd come loose.

He took his feet off the rim and hung by his hands. He swung his body to the side, away from the gantry. The strain was near unbearable, but it was only for a second...

Swinging back the other way, he leapt from the handholds and grabbed on to the gantry's railing posts, his legs flailing. Summoning a final burst of strength, he pulled himself up and climbed over them, collapsing onto the metal gantry plate with relief.

'This is too much like hard work without a sling,' he muttered.

'We're moving,' Okwin said, like an old tree noting a sunrise. Sure enough, Leo could hear the engines rumbling and the *Municipal* appeared to be advancing.

'Are we attacking them yet?' Leo said expectantly.

'That's what I like!' Anatali gave a whoop. 'A kid who can't wait to kill some Ganzies!'

The reverberating voice of the Deck Officer came over the PA. 'Gunners to battle stations,' said the metallic voice. 'All hands, prepare to engage.'

The Brazakker vessels formed a long line formation, hanging in the sky opposite their foes. The countless ships of Ganzabar's fleet had drawn up in a line also. The opposing fleet seemed significantly heavier.

On both sides, the colossal metal behemoths began to move forward. The movement was sporadic at first, then the whole sky was in motion, a multitude of mighty engines thundering into life with whines and deep hums. The two broad lines edged towards each other with murderous intent, like some colossal maw clamping shut.

Around the advancing flagship *Municipal*, the Home Fleet spread across the sky in a defiant line of slender shapes. The forward long-range guns of the *Altair* and the *Valyan Night* opened up on the Ganzabi lines. Explosions punctured the sky in violent bursts of smoke and flame.

A hollow boom sounded not far off the *Municipal*'s starboard, making Leo flinch. 'They firin' at us?'

Anatali shot him a grin of amusement. 'Yep. That's live rounds, boy!'

Leo watched Okwin lug a fresh round as though it weighed nothing. Okwin primed it, carefully swivelling the upper section anti-clockwise and pulling the top outward slightly, then he passed it to Torril, who slid it into the breech. Torril swung the lid shut, and the view out of the gun's large open aiming hole filled with the dark shadow of a Ganzabi warship.

'Target Patriot, zero-eight-seven, range four hundred. Stand by...' came the officer's voice. Anatali swung the barrel towards the heart of the mighty iron beast, turning the crank furiously to achieve the angle advised by her instruments and dials. She gave Torril a thumbs-up without looking away from her sights.

The order came over the speakers. '*Fire!*'

Torril gave the firing mechanism a rough yank and covered his ears. Leo had copied the others and had already clamped his hands over his. A heartbeat later, the cannon gave a deafening boom. No sound before this had ever been so loud as to be uncomfortable while his hands were still firm over his ears. The huge barrel, twice a man's height, flew backwards with the recoil, and Leo, his eyes seared by the muzzle flash, felt the whole deck of the airship rumble. The heavy casing of the spent shell flew from the breech and rolled along the deck. He fought to keep the next shell pressed between his knees without falling over.

Across the gap, the enemy airship shuddered in a ripple of fireballs as the shells found their marks. No sooner than the impacts hit the enemy ship, several enemy cannons fired in return. There was a whistling, and then a crunching sound as the shells met the starboard side of the *Municipal*. Leo toppled backwards, using his own body to cushion the shell's fall. The shells shouldn't be volatile until primed by Okwin, but they made him jittery all the same.

There was a yell and the sound of an explosion as one of the gun crews a few down from them took a direct hit.

Okwin lifted Leo to his feet with a single crane-like limb, then took the shell from him and began to prepare it. Leo gathered his balance and his bearings. The progression would clearly be needing him soon, so he stooped to grab the spent casing and hurried to the ammunition conveyor. He tossed the spent casing into the furnace chute, shaking his hands at the uncomfortable heat of the metal. On the conveyor was a fresh shell from the Foundry, which he heaved up into his arms. He turned and began to stumble back to the gun, more hits rocking the ship and causing him to sway with every other step.

Okwin took the warhead out of his hands just as Anatali yelled and the cannon fired again. They continued firing shell after shell as the *Municipal* circled the enemy ship. It was backbreaking work. But Leo soon found his pace, and thoughts of Feodora filled his mind with a desperate desire to see Ganzabar burn.

Finally, a terrific flash and a massive explosion sent the enemy ship drifting down in flames, to whoops and cheers across the deck. Leo gave a sigh of relief and leant against a bulkhead. A moment's respite was welcome.

Another volley of shells detonated along the starboard side of the *Pious Son*, gouging two holes in her hull. Inside, Kiy rounded a corner and passed the broken gaps. He burst through the doors at the end of the corridor, finding himself in the mess hall. He found his satchel among a heap of bags and clothing, where it had been tossed after his apprehension. A quick fumble brought relief as he found his sling still undiscovered inside. He slipped it onto his arm at the sound of footsteps beyond the opposite door.

The man that emerged was in great hurry and almost fell over backwards when he saw the sling pointed at him. He froze, raising his hands.

'Relax, it's not a gun.' Kiy gave a quick grin.

The Ganzabi man frowned. 'What?'

'It does hurt, though.'

The sling's clamp thunked satisfyingly into the man's chest, knocking him back through the doorway to the floor. Kiy retracted it and darted out of the room back the way he came, towards the holes in the hull. A bullet ricocheted from the wall, hopelessly off the mark, and Kiy's feet slid on the floor plates as he sharply veered to the left, leaping through one of the holes and out into the sky.

The raw elements ripped at his face and clothes as he tumbled through the turbulent air. Around him, the battle raged full tilt. Ships were firing, smoking, drifting and sinking. The noise was terrific, like being in the heart of a thunderstorm. Kiy weighed his targets and locked and fired the clamp on a nearby Ganzabi ship within moments.

He reeled himself in, swinging in a smooth half circle towards the Brazak battle line. It wasn't the first time he'd found himself dangling from a scarred ship in the middle of firefight, but the size of this battle was unprecedented. He'd never seen so many ships gathered in one place before, much less firing on one another.

Ahead, he recognised the unmistakable outline of the flagship of Brazak West. Hopefully he could reach Leo in time, though it looked like his options for extraction might be rapidly dwindling.

All around Leo were the mighty thuds of the ship's guns firing and the clangs of shells popping out and bouncing to the deck like dropped pans. To add misery to chaos, a

Justice-class Ganzabi battleship was hammering shots into the starboard side of the *Municipal*, accompanied by wailing shells from the enemy artillery frigate some way behind it.

White points of light impacted ferociously, sending hot fragments and deadly shrapnel in all directions. A woman loading the gun adjacent to Leo's fell to the deck with a scream, a metal shard the size of an axe embedded in her thigh.

Another explosion shook the deck above, and Leo kept his arms firmly wrapped around the precious shell he was carrying back to the gun. Prior to battle, when he'd asked Anatali why the shell conveyor was so far from the gun itself, she'd made an explosive gesture with her hands. The true implications of what she'd meant were only now coming to light; despite a number of successive hits, they had not suffered a direct hit to the ammunition conveyor. Apparently such a thing, unlikely as it was, would take out the entire side of the deck, if not the whole ship.

Leo was utterly exhausted. The shells seemed to be getting heavier and the run to and fro was fraught with danger, requiring a constant vigilance that was as draining mentally as it was physically. The din of battle hammered his senses, battered his sanity. War seemed all the more real, all the more terrifying, with each person he saw cut down by shells and shrapnel.

Suddenly, with a bang and a blinding flash, he was knocked backwards, and his shell rolled onto the deck with a clatter. Leo looked up to see that Anatali had been thrown clear of the cannon. A shell must have hit the rim around the gunhole opening.

Then he saw Torril, lying motionless. The deck heaved as the airship banked, and Torril rolled over limply. His face was bloodied and motionless.

'Torril!' Leo shouted.

'Shyut!' Anatali got to her feet shakily. Without skipping a beat, she turned to Leo and stared at him with her fiery eyes. 'You! Take over.'

Leo stared back in horror. 'W-what?'

'You were paying attention to what he did, right?'

Leo nodded nervously. He'd watched Torril fire a shell every twenty seconds or so for much of the last hour. It looked simple enough.

'Good boy.' Then she grappled with the sights of the gun again.

Okwin handed Leo a live shell, and with trepidation Leo slung the rear cover of the cannon breech to one side and slid the shell in awkwardly. He wound the cover shut as Anatali adjusted the trajectory for one of the enemy corvettes.

'Fire!' Anatali yelled, shielding her ears.

Leo yanked at the firing mechanism, but it didn't go all the way. He gave it another tug as hard as he could, then again. Suddenly his ears were blown out by an immense boom as the cannon fired. Leo was dazed by the noise, clutching his head and falling backwards.

When he got his bearings, he realised Anatali was shouting something at him. He tried to tell her he couldn't hear, but he couldn't hear if he was actually saying it. She kept talking, but his ears took a few moments to figure out how to hear things again.

'We did it!' she was saying. 'We got 'em!'

Leo stared out the gunhole in disbelief. The stricken corvette was listing to one side, then rolled over as its weight-balancing flipped into reverse. A cheer sounded across the gun deck at the sight of it.

Kiy lept over the railing of the *Municipal*'s rear observation promenade and hurried along its debris-strewn deck. Two Ganzabi cruisers, having downed the *Azkarya* and the *Lunastasia*, were now concentrating fire on the Brazak flagship. The cloudgazer ducked behind a bulkhead as a section of the outer deck shattered, sending shrapnel flying. Darting out, he swung over the gap with the sling, then sprinted to a door at the end of the deck. The deck seemed to heave downward as the airship slid into a twenty-degree nosedive, trying to outmanoeuvre its opponents. Kiy had to steady himself on a handrail as he descended into the dark catacombs of the ship's engineering decks. Twenty degrees feels like walking on a wall when you're standing on it.

'Shyut,' he muttered. *Leo could be anywhere on this ship, and it doesn't have long left at this rate.*

That wasn't the only problem, either. Even if he could find the damn kid, he still wasn't sure how he was gonna get off the *Municipal*. Brazak West's forces were looking ever more outgunned, and he wasn't optimistic about trying another Ganzabi ship. It would be even worse if they found out who he was. After all, he was wanted in Ganzabar for at least fifteen offences, on top of his numerous counts of international piracy. *Cross that bridge when I come to it*, he thought. First he had to find Leo.

The boy couldn't have lasted long on board without discovery. The captain would have either put him in the brig or, more likely for a Brazakker captain, put him to work. He was too small to bolster the marines and too inexperienced to be of any use to the engineers. There was really only one place he could be useful, and that was servant work with the gunnery crews.

Kiy ran for the stairs. 'You'd better be on the port side, kid.'

A cluster of shells from the enemy battleship slammed into the *Municipal* as its broadside opened up. The *Municipal* banked hard to escape, and dead bodies slid and tumbled. Okwin misplaced his footing and tipped backwards, rolling awkwardly several times before hitting the wall with a thud. Leo grabbed the breech lockwheel of the cannon to stop himself falling the same way, and Anatali held on to the targeting instruments, apparently weighing little enough to hang on to dials and gauges without breaking them off. The ship shuddered violently, the deep thrumming klaxon echoing around them. Then, gradually, the turn subsided, and Leo hurried over to Okwin.

'He's unconscious!'

'Ya think?' Anatali straightened her black tunic. 'You bring me the shells and prime 'em, I'll load and fire. Go, boy, hurry it up!'

The deck rumbled, then jolted.

'That doesn't sound good,' Anatali said ominously.

There was a loud *ping* as a small lead shot ricocheted off a nearby bulkhead. Anatali spun around to see Ganzabi troops pouring into the far end of D Deck. Several of the gunners had pulled pistols, but they were being overwhelmed.

'Attention all hands!' The voice of Admiral Zhukov came over the ship's speaker. 'Enemy troops boarding, starboard side!'

'Now they tell us!' Anatali pulled Leo by the collar to shelter behind a bulkhead.

Leo curled up against the wall and put his head on his knees. He tried to think of Feodora. What would she do? Nothing came to him. *I'd bet she'd be braver than me. She was always brave.*

The thunder of Ganzabi carbines was followed by the sounds of shots whistling by. Anatali fumbled at a storage case on the wall and took out a somewhat old-fashioned percussion musket, the kind used in the Old Nezzu War. She also took out a ready-loaded pistol and tucked it into the trousers of her uniform. She offered a second to Leo.

'On your feet, Midshipman.'

'I wanna go home,' Leo said weakly. He hated how he sounded, but it was the truth. He didn't want this anymore.

'On your flakking *feet!*' She grabbed his hair and wrenched his head back. His eyes were soaked with tears.

'You wanna go home?' she yelled in his face. 'Well you're gonna have to go through those tin-head Ganzies!' She indicated the far end of the deck beyond the bulkhead. 'Now take this.' She thrust the pistol into his hand.

Leo took it miserably. It was a simple, one-shot percussion pistol, but he'd never even seen a real one before, let alone learned how to use it.

Anatali placed the butt of her musket on the deck and fed a bullet into the end of the barrel, using the rod to ram it in. Taking a percussion cap from a pouch on her belt, she slid it into the slot on the breech. Then she took swift, careful aim from their cover at the huddle of marines heading towards them. She fired, cursed, then stepped back to load the musket again.

Leo peered around the corner. At least ten Ganzabi marines were pushing their way up the gunnery deck, impaling or shooting anyone who stood before them. Leo sank back behind the bulkhead, staring at the pistol in his shaking hand. He wanted to help. He had said he wanted to fight Ganzies, and he'd meant it. But his body wouldn't listen. It had been easier when they were on the other side of the sky.

Anatali fired around the corner again, then backed away and dropped the musket. Enemy troops rounded the bulkhead. She pulled out the pistol at her belt and fired a shot, wounding one of the two advancing on her, but the other lunged with his bayonet. Leo cried out as the end of the bayonet erupted from Anatali's back. She crumpled to the deck in front of him, dark red pooling beneath her.

With an angry shout, Leo pointed his pistol at the man who had stabbed her. He pulled the trigger, and the pistol kicked back with an angry bang—but nothing happened.

The marine looked at Leo. Leo's hands shook violently, and he dropped the pistol to the deck.

The Ganzabi raised his bayonet. 'Even using children now...' he muttered with disdain.

Suddenly the weapon flew out of the Ganzabi's grasp, smacked another Ganzabi in the face, and continued up to the ceiling. Leo looked up to see the rifle in the grip of a cloudgazer squatting on the support girders above them.

Kiy smiled, then propelled the weapon at another marine with the sling's clamp. It struck him in the head with a sickening crunch.

The Ganzabi soildiers were still assimilating this unexpected assault as Kiy leapt down, landing on a marine and knocking him to the deck. Kiy levelled his sling at a man running towards him, bayonet raised. The clamp hit him square in the jaw, throwing him flat onto his back.

Without reeling the clamp in, Kiy whipped it back to connect with the chest of another marine who was about to fire. Then he whirled the clamp in an arc, ducking as it passed over him, breaking the nose of yet another marine.

Three remaining Ganzabi marines aimed their rifles, then fired in a thunderous volley. But no sooner had they aimed than Kiy was whisked upwards by the sling, and the bullets hit the wall where he'd been. He landed behind the marines and incapacitated them with precision strikes of the clamp.

Leo gaped at the dozen Ganzabi laying dazed or unconscious around the deck.

Kiy grabbed him by the coat and moved to drag him away.

'Kiy, that was amazing! What're you doing here?'

'You there!' came a rough, choked voice. Anatali had sat up, her chest covered in blood, looking at Kiy with steely eyes. 'Who the heck are you?'

'I'm just here for the boy,' Kiy replied.

'You gonna kill these bastards?' she spluttered, motioning towards the wounded and unconscious Ganzabi.

'I believe that's your job.'

Anatli made a guttural grunt of contempt, then took a broken-off bayonet from the deck, crawled over to one of the less-wounded marines and plunged the shard into him. The man fell still.

Leo looked away. 'Kiy... did Ma send you?'

'Hennie did.'

Leo gazed out of the gun port at the airship battle still raging around them. 'How are we gonna get out of here?'

'There's no escape, even for a cloudgazer,' Anatali spat as she clawed her way over to another marine and ended his life with a grisly stab.

Kiy looked out across the sky at the ships exchanging fire. Smoke poured from the belly of the *Municipal*, bleeding into the sky. A group of Ganzabi ships were closing in, their forward guns firing stars that jolted the ship with horrible crunches. And in the distance, a mighty flash preceded the sinking, shattered form of the *Amnesty*. The Brazakker fleet could not take much more of this.

Anatali continued to silence the rest of the marines. The final one was coming around and fought back, pushing the bayonet shard away, but Anatali crawled on top of him and, in their weakened states, it was gravity that won out. Her weight was little, but it was enough to push the blade slowly into his chest, and he writhed a beat before finally falling still.

Leo kept his back to the gruesome scene, cringing at each awful, wet sound. 'I'm sorry,' he said.

Kiy turned to the boy. 'What?'

'For dragging you into this. I wanted to fight. I never thought it was... it was...'

'Anything like this?' Anatali coughed bitterly, still lying on the dead marine. Her path around the gun deck had left a long smear of blood; it was unclear just how much of it was her own. It was a miracle she was alive at all.

'You wanted to avenge Feodora?' Kiy asked.

'And make Ma proud. I guess,' Leo admitted, feeling his words were stupid.

Anatali managed a dark grin, slipping aside onto the deck. 'Well, you done a damn fine job for your first day, Midshipman.'

'Thank you, ma'am,' Leo replied glumly.

'But now I think... we're going down.' Anatali's expression relaxed as she tipped her head back against a bulkhead. 'Ganzabi are callous in battle, but even they... even they don't shoot ships they intend to capture. They've decided to down us, and I don't reckon we've got any guns left to dispute that.'

'There must be something we can do! What about life rafts?' Leo asked.

'Life rafts?' Anatali gave a laugh that, with a splutter, became a wet cough. 'This in't the Red Star Line, kid.'

Kiy exhaled. 'We can use floatpacks. Ganzies will probably pick us up, but I don't see any other options at this point.'

'But, Anatali!' Leo objected. 'We can't just leave her like this.'

Anatali smiled, blood smeared across her face. 'Don't you worry about me,' she said. 'Do what you got to. I've played my part.' She slumped with exhaustion. 'Da'vanya, Leo.'

Leo watched as her eyes glazed over. She was already gone, but he felt he ought to return the gesture anyway. 'Da'vanya,' he whispered.

Shouts down the hall were cut short by an impact that reverberated through the ship. Leo felt a queasy feeling in his stomach.

'Kiy...'

'I know, we're starting to sink.' Kiy's expression remained fierce, as though the idea annoyed him more than it frightened him. 'Come on—there's not much time.'

They hurried down the corridor to where a ripped-open gunhole displayed the full epic panorama of sky, streaked with vapour trails from skyfighters and missiles. Pockets of smoke pitted the blue vastness, and charged liquid sprayed from the Antimass tanks. Some Antimass-charged ship fragments rose upwards slowly, like floating seeds from a garden. The remaining Brazakker ships were in poor shape, and badly outgunned by the imposing angular Ganzabi, but they still held on desperately.

Kiy searched again for a friendly vessel within range of the sling, but they were all just too far away to risk it. The *Municipal* had evidently been drawn away from the main line as it tried to evade its attackers. They were running out of altitude and options.

Then a huge gleaming silver shape burst from the thick cloud below. It was elegant and flowing, all curves and circles, embellished with gold lines. The craft was the size of a battleship, but it moved with the swooping grace of a bird. It was smooth and featureless where one would have expected many of a normal craft's features to be. A golden triangular emblem adorned its side.

'What in the Understorm is that?' Leo asked, gaping.

Kiy squinted at the ethereal shape. He'd never seen the craft before, but he knew the sigil. 'Azrune.'

The ship slid past the *Municipal* with a mechanical whine like nothing Leo had ever heard before—like the scream of a jet turbine had been subdued to a whisper and whoosh of air. The sleek craft positioned itself between the *Municipal* and the three approaching Ganzabi ships, then came to an unnaturally abrupt stop.

'Well, not what I was planning on, but this will do.'

Kiy grabbed Leo's arm and leaped out into the sky. The boy's surprised scream was snatched away by the wind.

10 - Azrune's Arrival

Battle of Mosleyhead

Orange lights rippled around the white room, tracing organic curves and smooth forms. In the centre stood a tall man, his feet shoulder-width apart and his hands clasped behind his back. His skin was the colour of cocoa, his chest like a sheet of iron, and his head as bald as a moon.

Huge, sweeping windows displayed the Mosleyhead battlefield. A dozen or so wounded Brazak West airships were clustered to the left, some smoking, many with visible scars. On the right, the thirty-something Ganzabi airships had broken off and seemed to be weighing up the new arrival.

'I think it's time we put a stop to this,' the tall man said, half to himself. His voice was soft, but with a deep and commanding quality to it.

'Attention, unidentified vessel!' came a transmission over shortwave—a male Ganzabi accent with overtones of self-righteous outrage. 'You are entering a war zone, in violation of international laws of neutrality. Leave at once, or you may be fired upon.'

The tall man placed a hand either side of the podium in front of him, leaning forward. 'This is Supreme Commander Mesthpura of the *Akron*, flagship of the First Navy. We are here to retrieve stolen property of the Azrunite government. Your cooperation in returning it will ensure your well-being.'

The shortwave crackled.

'Now hear this, Azrunite ship *Akron*.' The voice sounded impatient, and pronounced the *Akron*'s name with contempt. 'Ships of the Ganzabar Federation take orders from President Carrick and not a damn soul besides. Vacate this battle zone immediately. This does not concern you.'

Commander Mesthpura's expression became grim. 'Do not try my patience. Once again, I strongly recommend you cooperate with us, or you will face the consequences.'

'Your arrogance is misplaced, Azrunite,' came the Ganzabi reply. 'We will not end this battle because of your pathetic meddling. There may have been a time when the world was forced to your will, but that time has ended. Your myths cannot silence our freedom.'

'Stand down now, Ganzabi,' Mesthpura warned. 'We wish to commence investigations, but we will respond if provoked.'

'The only thing you're going to do is eat your words, Azrunite.' There was a spike of static, then the radio was silent.

Kiy swung back and forth from the underbelly of the *Municipal* in huge arcs, Leo's arms wrapped tightly around his shoulders. The *Akron* suddenly fired up and came about, heading away from them.

'Wow, did you see that!' Leo exclaimed over the rushing wind.

Kiy didn't respond; his attention was completely focused on the Azrunite ship ahead. This wasn't going to be an easy shot to make.

He felt out along the cable of the sling, sensing the gigantic momentum of the *Municipal*, which was listing to starboard and gradually sinking, its final Antimass systems failing. His eyes traced the swift movement of the Azrunite battleship, which was headed towards the Ganzabi ships ahead. He shifted his weight to lengthen the swing back as much as possible, then they swung forward again, passing beneath the *Municipal* towards the *Akron*. Leo cried out as the sky seemed to swallow them.

With a deft whip of his arm, Kiy disengaged the clamp and lashed it around to fly towards the *Akron*. With their forward momentum and the lightning-fast speed of the sling, the clamp raced across the void. Still, it seemed to go on forever as Kiy and Leo fell.

Then the cable tightened and began to reel them in towards the Azrunite airship. As it did, they slid to the rear of it, being pulled along behind as the ship began to move towards the Ganzabi. Leo's eyes went wide as the ship grew massive before them, each of its subtle, geometric details coming into view. It was an incredible work of art, whatever else it might be.

As they neared the last few hundred metres, Kiy shouted over the rush of air, 'Brace yourself!'

Neither was sure what happened next, or quite how, but there was a jolt and everything spun. They met the upper surface of the Azrunite ship and rolled, and the next thing Leo knew he was clinging instinctively to a dual antenna.

They were on top of the ship, in a recessed circle of hull which contained an array of complex aerials and dishes. Kiy had smashed through some kind of ceramic half-sphere, and Leo realised the antenna he was resting on had been bent crooked.

Kiy attempted to stand, then fell in agony. He looked down at his leg to see the sickening white of bone protruding. The injury made him dizzy, and he swayed, trying to steady himself enough to sit upright.

Leo untangled himself and stepped over to help him.

'You okay?' Leo said over the wind.

'Fine,' Kiy managed, not nearly as confident as he'd intended. Even moving his leg was excruciating.

It was then that Leo heard a mechanical humming noise. The source of the noise emerged from the misty, cloud-heavy air quite suddenly, like a little round ghost of metal and plastic. It was a hovering device, apparently without engines, about the size of a child and unmarked but for occasional bumps and antennae. An orange light in its centre blinked at them.

Then there was a bright flash, and neither of them remembered anything further.

The lead Ganzabi ship swung around to face the Azrunite arrival and fired on it with its dorsal cannons. But as the shots reached the *Akron*, they inexplicably swerved aside and detonated harmlessly in the air. The sleek ship retaliated immediately, firing a stream of gleaming bluish pulses that tore straight through the side of one of the small Ganzabi escorts, turning it into an exploding wave of debris.

Swooping to port, the Azrunite ship then began tearing into the leading Patriot-class ship approaching the Brazakker line. The Ganzabi opponent swerved, billowing smoke, while its escorts swept around it and lay down a torrent of fire in the *Akron*'s direction. But again, the Azrunite ship was undamaged; with a fleeting blink of blue sparks, each shot veered way off target.

The *Akron* fired on a Ganzabi ship passing the opposite way, ripping it in two. The ship's central reactor shattered with a monumental crack and the vessel was consumed in a brilliant flash of white light.

A few more shots from the *Akron* was all it took before Ganzabi ships began to turn away and slide off towards the horizon, some crooked, others burning, a few reduced to limping skeletal remains of once-proud warships. The *Akron* quietly took up position beside the Brazak fleet, unscathed.

Nearby Brazakker ships had scrambled craft to evacuate the sinking *Municipal*, although it was now so fragmented and sinking so quickly that even the rescue ships were forced to break off and allow the remainder of the *Municipal* to tumble to the Understorm, along with those unfortunate souls still trapped on board. The surviving ships retreated to the newly appointed fleet leader, the *Galliant*.

All eyes were on the mysterious Azrunite battleship that most likely had just saved them all.

11 - Laronor

Laronor
August 9ᵗʰ

Hennie felt she must've been travelling for days. The aged transport plane she now rode was perhaps the fourth or fifth she'd boarded since leaving Brudor behind; she wasn't really sure. The floril that Kiy had given her had allowed her to wrangle short hops between cities, but Laronor was located far to the north of Brudor, in the industrial heartland of the country's airspace, and it had taken a while to get there.

Relieved that the transport was drawing close to her destination at last, she craned her neck around the small pigtailed girl in the window seat to get a better view of the city. The girl was bobbing around with excitement, but finally the girl's mother, in the seat directly behind, told her to sit still, and Hennie caught her first glance of Laronor.

The city slowly emerged from the mist and clouds of a dreary day. It seemed at least partly responsible for the fog, with its countless chimneys and factory towers churning out smoke. The city was much larger than any Hennie had ever seen, a bustling metropolis sprawling across the sky, urban grandeur on a scale she'd never dreamt possible.

'What's dat?' The little girl prodded the window.

Even Hennie was familiar with this one: a twin-spired building, each rectangular tower having three clock faces and an ornate bronzed gyroscope on its crest.

'That's the Admiralty,' Hennie said.

'Amurally!' the little girl repeated. Hennie smiled, thinking of little Ainu, then felt a pang of homesickness. She tried to think about something else.

There was a groan as the transport plane extended its flaps. They shuddered and swayed through pockets of high pressure, then finally the runway came up to meet them with a jolt, and the rumbling of the wheels died down.

It was some time before Hennie disembarked and was back on solid floatrock, but when she did, she left the aerodrome, took a large elevator down to the main street level and eagerly stepped out into the bustle.

Towers stretched up, disappearing into the clouds dozens of storeys above. She'd never seen constructs so vast, and she gazed up at them in wonder. It was one thing to see them from the air, but quite another to stand at their feet. Huge walls of brick were dotted with posters proclaiming slogans. Most were written in Azbuka, the common tongue, but some of them were in a language Hennie didn't even recognize. An antiquated, torn flag of Great Brazak was draped on a windowless brick wall. It was evidently a relic of the Liberation War, as underneath it was a defiant declaration of solidarity: 'ONE BRAZAK'.

Crowds busied the base of the elevator, but Hennie spotted an official waiting by a sign that read, 'Refugee Information'. She approached him nervously.

'Hi—'

'Hey luv, welcome to Laronor,' the attendant said. 'Follow Kirkov Prospekt, you'll get to the cabletram station; take a tram to Voxton, then follow the signs to the Farrow Shelters.'

'Um, thanks,' Hennie said, 'but I'm looking for a man named Miles Rathbone—'

'Just follow the prospekt, that way, please. Thank you,' the man said with bureaucratic brusqueness.

Hennie made a face of mild irritation, wondering if he was likely to have his job usurped by the sign he was holding. But she figured a good rest and a drink would not be far, and she found a smile for the man.

She stepped out onto the edge of the prospekt. She had never seen one with walkways so wide and busy, or lined with such a colourful plenitude of shopfronts, including a particularly brash lit sign for an Apteka. Down the centre of the prospekt was a channel of open sky through which countless autocabs shuffled in queues going in both directions.

She set off the way she'd been instructed. The walkway around her heaved with people: pale faces under flat caps, dark-skinned men in white hats, and swarms of young girls dressed in yellow and blue frocks. A tall man in a waistcoat and tails—probably a Franner, Hennie thought—tipped his top hat to Hennie politely as she walked by. She wandered past a group of scruffy boys selling papers from a pushcart, one of them doing an impressive one-handed handstand. Something bumped her back, and she wheeled about with a murmured apology as a grumpy old sweeper plodded past with a whirring and clacking device that gobbled up dirt into a metal cylinder. The air was moist and cool, and the cobbles of the road glistened with recent rain.

The scene captivated her, but she became aware she probably looked like a simpleton, twirling around like a spinning top.

Just then, a sound enveloped the city like a clap of thunder. The massive twin clock towers of the Admiralty boomed a regal quintet of chimes, declaring three in the afternoon. It was then that she saw it. In fact, she wondered how she'd missed it.

Behind the great clock faces, hanging in the upper skies like one of the moons, was an island. Islands in cities were generally of a similar elevation to each other for convenience, but its higher altitude alone was not what caught Hennie's eye. It also had a massive gun barrel protruding from it. It was hard to tell from here exactly how big it was, but it looked simply enormous.

She realised her jaw had gone slack, and she concentrated on the road ahead. *Better press on*, she thought.

When she reached the end of the prospekt, she ascended a great wide sheet of steps to the tram station platforms. The tram car was suspended from a trio of thick cables that stretched across the gulf to the nearest floatrock district. She'd barely stepped on amongst the bustle when the attendant clacked the door shut and blew a whistle. The tram lurched into motion, throwing her ungracefully into her seat. The car accelerated smoothly and descended past a cluster of high-rise apartments on a lower island.

As she rode, Hennie thought about Kiy and about her little brother, out there among the battleships. In her mind she saw the deck of Feo's ship again, the *Lykomin*. Only this time, Kiy and Leo stood with her on the deck, Kiy was dragging Leo along by the sleeve, and Feo's eyes were wide with panic. Explosions erupted along the skin of the craft, catching up to them.

Hennie shook the image away, trying to put her mind elsewhere.

The sky was just featureless white, with distant islands and buildings fading into the murk. As the tram made its way towards Voxton, the isle behind her seemed to fade out of existence. The stretch between the islands was a colossal chasm in comparison to the occasional small crossings of Brudor.

Finally, the tram arrived at Voxton. Compared to the urban neatness of Kirkov, it was immediately apparent just how weathered and run-down this place was. The walkways and brick structures felt claustrophobic and ancient.

Hennie and the other passengers disembarked and walked up a set of stone steps to a heavily crowded alley. The walkways became a labyrinth of twists and turns, but she pressed on with optimism, assured that the way she was going just felt right, but she was annoyed that she couldn't find a single sign or official to help confirm it.

But soon she realised the walkways had gotten increasingly desolate. She must have taken an odd turn. It couldn't be this far from the tram station, surely? There was nothing for it but to backtrack. Yet when she tried, she realised with nervous panic that she was only getting more lost. Streets twisted tighter, alleys narrowed, and the sky could be seen nowhere but above. The sensation was strange and claustrophobic.

Perhaps it was just that the situation was making her paranoid... but she also had the feeling someone was following her. At first she dismissed the thought as silly, but then she felt more certain of it. She hurried along, but when the passageway she was following came to an abrupt end, she realised she had no choice but to turn and face them. Perhaps it was just someone else who was equally lost.

'Excuse me.' She spoke as she turned, then jumped when she saw that not one, but two men stood behind her. One was very tall, with a hooked nose and beady eyes, while the other was shorter, but still wiry thin, and very old. They both smelled like a poultry factory.

"'Ello there, lovely. Need some help?' the shorter one said.

Hennie didn't like the look in his eye. She wanted to scream, but they must have seen it in her face.

'No need to tweet, little bird. You might have a slip-up.' The short man gave her a piercing glare that made her pulse race. She wished she could fly away.

'I'm a refugee, I'm just looking for the Farrow camp,' she said.

'Oh, well then!' the man replied, his tone mockingly friendly. 'We'll tell you the way. But you got to pay.' He chuckled, his grin missing a few teeth.

'No thanks,' she replied. 'I'll find it myself.'

The tall one moved around to one side of her, while the shorter one circled the other way. Hennie tried to back away so that they didn't surround her, but she was backing into a dead end.

'You don't seem to understand,' the tall man said, his voice a deep rumble. 'The price in't optional.'

Hennie swallowed.

The taller man lunged for her, but she leapt back, and his hands grabbed her bag instead. As she wrestled with him over it, the short man grabbed her waist from behind. She swung a heel up between his legs, and a cry of pain confirmed her accuracy. As he released her, her grip on the bag slipped, and the taller man fell backwards with it. Seeing her chance, Hennie bolted away.

She ran along twisting passageways between old and crooked residences, trying to find someone, anyone who could help her. She cursed the thieves, cursed this stupid place, cursed her damn self for being so dumb as to just wander off on her own in a city she knew nothing about. They'd seen her for the dupe she was. She hated them, wanted to go back and rip them apart but...

She stopped. *The bag.*

Everything had been in that bag. The details of Miles Rathbone, her money, her food and belongings.

Her radio.

She wanted to make it not true. She loved that radio, loved it so much.

And now, like everything in her life, it was gone.

She couldn't help herself. She sat heavily on a backdoor step and began to weep. They might hear her and find her here, but all of a sudden, that didn't seem to matter. *Let them find me. I don't care. They've taken everything.*

Looking back the way she'd come, a courageous thought came to her: she could go back and retrieve her bag. She couldn't think how to do it, but...

No, that was stupid. They were gone. At least they hadn't taken her life; for that she had to be thankful. Like her mother always said, 'Things are just things and more things can be bought.' But that radio...

The thought broke her heart. *But what can I do?*

She had to find the camp. Maybe someone there could help her get her things back. It would be okay.

Standing solemnly, she pushed on down the desolate alley, moving towards the sounds of people. Eventually she found a street, that intersected a major thoroughfare where a sign read 'Klepta Prospekt'. Another, much more temporary sign pointed the way to 'Farrow Refugee Compound'. She went in that direction, feeling immediately relieved. Things might turn out alright, after all.

Yet she was unready for the scene of woe that met her as she stepped through the gates of the compound. Huddles of people, wretched-looking things with miserable faces, sat about doing very little at all. Some went to and fro with bowls or cups, all of them empty. A pair of boys burst through a pile of wood and junk, in hot pursuit of a small black feline.

'Do you have any food, darlin'?' a woman asked as Hennie passed.

Hennie shook her head. *Do I look like I have anything at all?* she thought bitterly.

She wandered through the desolation, trying to look like she wasn't hopelessly lost, trying to look like she could handle herself. The wind tugged her pinafore from side to side as she walked. It felt a lot colder than it had on her arrival, and she realised glumly that she didn't even have a coat in the City of Winter.

Finally she stopped and sat, confessing inwardly that she just wasn't sure where to go anymore. Without her things she felt even more lost and alone, adrift in the clouds without a ship or floatrock. Just a tatter of paper at the mercy of the winds.

She'd sat for what felt like hours when her attention was caught by a cheer. She raised her head and struggled to see over several tents to a warm orange glow, from whence came a voice, loud and jolly in a sea of melancholy—the voice of a man who had something to sell. It wasn't a sound she trusted much, but it was lively and intriguing, and she went to investigate.

She found the man on a ramshackle stage inside a tent. He was a large, round man, in smart clothes, though dirtied by the black soot of industry. He rubbed his greasy hands together as he spoke, and his big round eyes held a glint of excitement. A small crowd had gathered around him, some looking sceptical, others curious or even eager. Hennie drew up behind the audience.

'... dark, difficult times. Your government has abandoned you, I mean... look! We are a wealthy country. We shouldn't be cowerin' in hovels like this.'

There was a shout of approval and a ripple of nods.

'Now let me just say this: I am not offering you charity. You don't want that. We're Brazakkers, right?'

There was a loud chorus of 'Yeah!'

'You want to work for your keep: a good job, a stable job. Most of you have had to give up yer homes. Well, believe me, Laronor can be home to anyone. I have rooms for hundreds, and I need workers for the war effort! Who will step up? Who will make their family proud?'

With a surge of enthusiasm, the crowd pressed forward, all attempting to be first to the signup sheet. The man grinned, looking over the people, mostly downtrodden working men and women in their more youthful years.

Hennie was pushed forward by the eager surge and began to edge away. The man's gaze picked her out at that instant.

'Hey, you there, the young lass!'

Hennie froze. 'Me?'

'Yes! You.' He grinned, looking like a cartoon in such dreary surroundings. The rest of the throng continued signing their names, assisted by several attendants. 'How old are ya, lass?'

'Uh, ah...' She felt taken aback by the question. 'Sixteen, sir.'

'Sixteen!' he cried. 'And a fine, able young woman you look. How would you like to make a living for your family for the war effort?'

Hennie imagined her mother's voice in her head, pleading not to lose another child to the wretched Ganzies.

'I'm not gonna sign up to fight,' Hennie said.

'Whoa whoa whoa whoa...' The man took a step back, raising his palms defensively. 'Don't get the wrong idea, now. All this is local work, safe as bakin', ya get me?' He clasped his hands together. 'If the young lady is interested?'

Hennie deliberated a moment. 'As long as it i'nt making hats.'

The man laughed hard and slapped his belly. 'Ah, brilliant. Hats. Love it. Listen.' He stepped over to her. 'I'm looking for bar staff, right, at the Worker's Hammer, a lively place over in Zoxeth. Reckon you'd be perfect.'

She regarded him carefully. 'Maybe. What's in it for me?'

'You won't be here,' he said, motioning to the compound.

Hennie looked around her. She had no money, no spare clothes, no food and no idea where to find Miles Rathbone. It was hardly a choice.

She turned back to him and grimaced. 'You got a deal.'

Kiy awoke to find himself lying on a large, austere bed, someplace bright and warm. He immediately felt for the sling on his arm, but it was gone. He struggled to remember where he was, then visions of the floating mechanical device with the glowing orange light came to him.

The foreign ship. They must be captive on it.

He got to his feet, and pain shot up through his leg to remind him of his injury. But when he looked down at it, he felt some relief that it wasn't as bad as he thought. It was dressed, clean, and he could actually stand on it, if only tentatively.

He looked around. The room was like a small dormitory, although Kiy had never seen anything quite like it. The walls were mostly flat and featureless, just off-white metallic surfaces with sweeping gold lines running along them. Where they met the floor and ceiling, they curved into them. A desk jutted out beneath a large gold-rimmed window, with some sort of gravity-defying ornament sat on it. And on an empty table beside the bed was his sling.

He frowned, stepping up to it. It simply lay there, as though he'd taken it off just before going to sleep. Perhaps he had; he still couldn't remember how he'd got here. He took it and slotted it onto his right arm, which made him feel a little better. But the question bothered him: why would they leave his sling right next to him?

The room had only one door—a sliding door with a small groove-handle sunken into it. Kiy pulled the handle sideways, and the door slid open without a sound. He jumped back in alarm and raised his sling when he saw the figure standing in the doorway.

She was of a short, slight build, with chin-length dark hair, a round face and a petite nose. She wore a short navy blue jacket, a short skirt and black boots with white leg-warmers. Overall, her uniform was minimalistic; silver plates on her shoulders perhaps suggested some sort of rank.

'Oh. You're awake,' she said, hands on her waist.

Kiy swallowed. He felt he should by this point have launched the sling's grapple to meet her temple and be halfway down the corridor, but he'd frozen up the moment he saw her; he couldn't say why. Because she was unarmed? Unthreatening? Undeniably pretty? That last notion bothered him the most.

'Who are you?'

'Officer Elzie Kerowan,' she said. 'Lower the grapple, please. We wouldn't want you shooting off because you got excited.'

Something about her tone made Kiy feel hugely foolish. He decided to comply.

Officer Kerowan made a slight tip of her head to indicate he should follow, and she led him down a beautiful carpeted corridor. Large windows with golden trim ran along the length of it, making the space inside bright and airy. It felt nothing like a warship.

After walking silently through several long corridors, they entered an elevator that took them up several levels. The doors slid open, and Kiy found himself walking onto what had to be the bridge. The glass displays glowing with yellow numerals, the banks of lights and lit readouts, all of it was in stark contrast to the glass dials, switches, plugs and levers of Brazakker ships.

'Welcome.' The voice belonged to a tall, bald, dark-skinned man. He wore a long, heavy coat in navy blue that went to his knees and was fastened by a column of a dozen buttons on his right. 'I'm Commander Julius Mestphura. You're aboard the Wingstar-class battleship *Akron*. I hope you find it comfortable and informative.'

'Informative?' Kiy said, looking around.

The commander smiled. 'There is always something to be learned by another point of view.'

'What do you mean?'

'Every ship and culture is a point of view to the observant.'

Kiy's expression became severe. 'Where's Leo?'

'The boy? He's fine. You are looking very well too, considering the state you arrived in. I hear you'll be making a full recovery.'

Kiy glanced at the bandaged injury as the Azrunite commander continued.

'Allow me to indulge an Azrunite custom: I'd like to introduce you to my crew. My first officer and trusted confidante,' he indicated the slim, handsome young man stood beside him, 'Mr Lor Gatista.'

First Officer Gatista greeted Kiy formally. He had long blond hair swept back with a wide clasp, and a face of fine, precise features. His body was sinuous, displaying a minimalism and precision that seemed to match his calculating expression—as well as much of the Azrunite elegance that surrounded him.

Mestphura gestured to the bony-looking old man at the helm. 'This is Tempus Maroni Kaj'aku, our craftsman; incidentally, the highest ranking Maroni in the First Navy.'

'A pleasure,' Kaj'aku said.

Kiy realised that the bone-thin figure was not a man at all. He had pale grey skin, almost greenish. A long nose and two black, iris-less eyes peered from beneath his hood. His uniform— a heavy robe that mostly concealed his appearance—was easily the most unique among the bridge crew.

Mestphura anticipated Kiy's question. 'Maroni are slender humanoids living mainly in western Azrune. They were almost wiped out elsewhere. By mankind, as you might expect.'

Although he'd heard of them, Kiy had never actually seen a Maroni in the flesh. He could see why they might be shunned. With his slightly short and hunched form, he looked the sort of individual society would mistrust.

'And here is Miss Tamalin Raldotya, comms officer,' Mestphura said. A woman with long, pitch-black hair and skin like porcelain gave a polite bow, keeping her bright blue eyes fixed on Kiy. With her freckled complexion and surname, Kiy saw the Valyan in her right away.

'And of course, you've already met Miss Elzie Kerowan,' Mestphura finished.

Kerowan gave Kiy only a fleeting glance.

'Quite the eclectic crew you've got,' Kiy said. 'But if you don't mind, I'd like to see Leo now.'

Mestphura nodded. 'Very well. I shall have him sent up to greet you. We have much to discuss in the meantime, however. Shall we?' He extended a hand to a door at the rear of the bridge.

Kiy followed the commander into what appeared to be a small meeting room. His need to confirm Leo's well-being was pressing, but he felt he'd have more luck if he appeased the Azrunites. They were often said to be a capricious sort of people, but rarely ever malevolent.

Azrune was unique among the nations of Azimuth. Of all the hyper-advanced technology from the Gold Age—over a thousand years ago—nearly all of it outside of Azrune's borders had sunk to the Understorm in the many wars since. Yet somehow, within Azrune, that technology survived. Some said it was because Azrune never changes. Some said it was because they remained neutral in every conflict and ignored just about all requests for aid, whether it be from oppression, poverty or tyranny. They were a deeply habitual people, some might even say backward. It was a curious irony that they should also be the most technologically advanced in the world. And after all these years of insulating themselves from world politics, it seemed more than a little odd for them to suddenly intervene in a war. And it was clear from the engagement that their prior avoidance of battle was certainly not due to weakness. Gold Age technology lived up to its legendary reputation.

The commander's chamber was dominated by a large, curved window. The view it provided was the kind of breathtaking, unbroken panorama one might expect on a luxury cruise ship. Elsewhere, countless pictures of proud birds, mostly exotic birds of prey, adorned the walls.

Kiy sat down while the commander poured a drink for them both.

'So, Kiy is it?' Mestphura asked, handing him a glass.

'Yes. Kiy Tanthar.' Kiy felt he was being treated like an ambassador. It didn't seem fitting to treat someone who'd broken into your ship with such polite reverence.

'Tanthar?' Mestphura mulled the name. 'Any relation to the captain of the *Dawnstar*?'

Kiy gave a wary glance. 'You know a lot about Brazakker history considering you never involved yourselves with it.'

'The ambush at Nantez was an infamous battle in the Liberation War,' Mestphura said evenly.

'It wasn't a battle,' Kiy snapped. 'It was a massacre.' He stopped, aware that he was all too close to ranting. It was surprising that Mestphura even knew of the incident; how could Kiy have expected him to know it well? 'Captain Tanthar was my mother. Both she and my father went down with that ship.'

Mestphura nodded. 'I am sorry to hear of your loss.'

Kiy looked into his glass. It was sleek, slender, minimal, exquisitely formed—like everything on board this ship. The bright light from the window reflected through its prisms and crystals, causing it to glitter. The sparkling peach-coloured drink within it tasted like Pure, but with a hint of strawberries.

'Why do you care?' he said eventually.

Mestphura looked out at the view. 'Are you referring to your family history, or our intervention at Mosleyhead?'

Kiy gave him a sideways look. 'You seem to know about me already. So let's start with why you're in Brazak West. You've got me curious.'

'The answer is the same either way. Compassion.'

'Compassion?' Kiy spat the word out.

'Yes.' Mestphura sipped at his drink.

'Is that something you just found out about? Finally reached 'C' in the Crystal Archive?'

The Crystal Archive, said to be the great store of all human knowledge, was a colossal databank in Nubylon, at the heart of Azrune. However, it was a well-known fact that the ability to access the data has been lost at some point over the many millennia since the Gold Age. It was said that Azrunite scholars had so far been able to reclaim little more than five percent of it.

Mestphura smiled at the joke. 'I understand if you feel Azrune has turned a blind eye to the injustices of the world. But we are not without our reasons, and I am just one commander. Only the future I can change.'

'This is your own initiative?'

'All actions of an Azrunite commander are their own initiative, Mr Tanthar.'

'That's not really what I meant.'

'To a greater degree than you might expect, even. The hierarchy here is different to what you are used to. I cannot explain it without going into lengthy detail. Suffice to say that this is definitely an intervention by Azrune with the aim of ceasing war. That is all you need to know, in truth.'

'Yeah, well... forgive me if I don't buy it as being that simple.'

'As you wish.'

Kiy swirled the liquid in the glass. 'So, when will you let us go?'

'Let you go?' Mestphura gave an amused smile. 'I do not like to think of you as a prisoner—merely a guest that I must inevitably impose upon somewhat.' He frowned briefly. 'You see, you have left me with a problem.'

'Oh?'

'That sling of yours,' he said. 'Clamping to the antenna, not to mention the subsequent... *rampaging* over the array, has damaged our navigation system and broken the transponder. Our equipment here is very sensitive to such things. This has left us with impaired navigation.'

'Are you serious?' Kiy suppressed a laugh. 'A hyper-advanced battleship like this, sailing blind, because I bent an antenna?'

'If you want to think of it like that, you may. Your very... *specific* choice of entry has impaired our ability to tell where we are. Perhaps the Ganzabi should consider using cable-guided people as missiles should our paths cross again?' He looked amused. He finished the drink with a long, slow swig, then set it down. 'Mr Tanthar, in my country there is a custom whereby a host will meet every last need of a guest, and in return the guest customarily offers a single favour, typically the solving of a problem.'

'And this extends to prisoners?'

'I wonder if it might.' Mestphura looked thoughtful. 'You see, we can return to port to replace our guidance system, but it will cost us valuable time. You look well travelled, and I would assume your type know this area well. I would like you to be our consultant navigator for the duration of this voyage.'

Kiy wondered what he meant by 'your type', but he assumed that his sling gave him away as a bandit of some sort, at the very least. Cloudgazers were outlawed entirely in Azrune—but then, the rules of a culture do not always extend to its armies.

'You won't be on duty so much; rather, available for information. The bulk of our navigation is handled by calputer.'

'By calputer?' Kiy frowned. 'It must be a machine the size of a skyfighter.'

'It is actually much bigger, though it does much, much more than navigation,' Mestphura said. 'But I digress. This is my request; do it and I will consider it repayment for your trespassing and the resulting damage to my ship. When our mission is through, you may leave. I trust you will agree this is fair?'

Kiy considered using the sling to escape, but there didn't appear to be any ships in the vicinity anymore. And in any case, he appreciated that at least Leo would be safe aboard the most advanced airship in the world. He'd just have to delay getting back to Hennie until they got close to a settlement. He gave an assenting nod.

'Good.' Mestphura motioned to the door. 'A crewmember will lead you back to your quarters, where Leo will be waiting. At nineteen hundred hours, I'd like to you to meet Miss Kerowan on the bridge; she will brief you on all you need to know.'

Kiy stood, then stopped, turning to the commander. 'What about the boy? You'll release him too?'

Mestphura templed his fingers. 'He is free to leave when you do.'

'When your mission is complete? How long is that?'

Mestophura smiled. 'One step at a time, Mr Tanthar.'

The cloudgazer left the room without another word.

Mestphura waited for the door to shut behind Kiy, then he leant over to the sleek Pulsegraph beside his desk. The device sent encoded messages via Transpulse, in secure packets of binary bursts. He slid out the typing pad, a slender metal slab with forty or so lettered keys, and as he typed his message, it came up on the glass plate screen.

|| ACQUIRED CLOUDGAZER STOP

Hamel cursed, clutching the flight stick. His view was hazy and clouded by the smoke coming off his fighter's engine, shrouding the cockpit. His Dragonfly monoplane was barely flying, having been riddled with holes and lost several vital parts. Say what you like about the durability of the Dragonfly, he thought, but this baby was really going the distance. Things wouldn't be so bad really, except he didn't know where he was.

Of course, Flight Sergeant Hamel Jerome, of Ganzabar's proud seven-fifty-sixth squadron, would never have said he was lost—merely that he was temporarily unsure of his position.

The plane shuddered periodically, and he suspected an oil leak. Any minute the damn thing would seize up and he'd be making a one-way trip to the Understorm. But there was hope: a strange, bleak kind of hope. In the distance ahead, he could make out the shapes of a city. It was odds and evens as to whether it was hostile Brazak West or friendly East. Actually, he'd been shot up deep in West airspace, so the odds weren't nearly so favourable as that.

He hoped the city was Valyagrad, which had been secured for Ganzabar by a recent push, but if it was, he'd expect to have picked up transmissions on the squadron's band of VHF by now. Perhaps he was completely off track and the city was Laronor, in which case he was in big trouble. Laronor was perhaps the second most strategically significant enemy location after the capital. It was likely to be heavily fortified, and it was not the sort of place an injured Ganzabi pilot could ditch a fighter without causing a ruckus. But he had little choice but to try.

Whatever city it was, they might have already seen him. He hadn't spotted any interception craft though, and the visibility was pretty poor just below mean city level. If he could just slink below the street line, there was a chance he could avoid detection until he was about to ditch.

A shadow enveloped him and his entire plane. He looked up to see the massive bulk of an airship passing overhead slowly, its numerous propellers churning. He was about to say one last prayer when he realised it was only a passenger liner. It continued on its course, apparently not even noticing him.

A large cloud stood ahead of him, and he edged into it, trying to hold the same heading. The cockpit was entombed in a featureless universe of light grey.

Then the mist of the cumulus parted and he saw a bundle of small islands ahead, extending out from a set of bridges on the fringes of the settlement. They looked quiet and simple, with no apparent air defences, although there could easily be some nearby. With a grunt of determination, he banked the damaged plane towards them and trimmed the controls again as the power of the engine gradually bled away. He pulled up, gaining height and moving boldly out of the mist to hold a hundred metres or so higher than the houses ahead.

Suddenly there was a loud snap, and Hamel felt the controls change. He was pretty sure he'd just lost something important, but exactly what he couldn't be sure. Looking over his shoulder shed no light on the matter, and besides, there wasn't anything he could do about it now. Just a little closer, he thought.

Finally, with a terrible shrinking hum and a feeble clatter, the engine gave out. The propeller slowed and, much to Hamel's distress, his airspeed needle dropped. He pitched the plane down further to try and reclaim some speed, lining up on the long jetty at the end of the street ahead. *Come on.* Just a few hundred left and he'd be over floatrock.

Then he saw a group of people in the street below. They had come out of their houses to stare at the fighter coming right for them.

'No!' Hamel yelled. 'Fools! Get out of the way!'

As though some heard him, several turned and began to run. But their reaction was slow. They weren't going to clear the road in time. Hamel made a split second decision. He did what seemed like the only human thing.

He wrenched back on the control stick, and the plane swooped upwards again, missing the crowded jetty. As it did, the right wing stalled and slipped sideways, throwing the plane into a cartwheel. The tail met a chimney, shattering it in a cloud of masonry. The rest of the craft spun over the rooftops before tumbling down and lodging in a terraced roof.

The noise was terrific; stone and metal erupted, turning brick and balconies into spinning fragments. Parts of the skyfighter flew apart in a spectacular plume of metal shards and mutilated components. The entire area was covered in a grey shroud of dust. As the noise of the impact died away, the tinkle of falling glass from broken windows could be heard.

Hamel blinked to steady his vision. The first thing he noticed was that he wasn't in a plane anymore; he was in a tree. By some good fortune, he'd somehow survived the worst crash of his life. Even so, he was dazed, winded and bleeding, and his ankle was agony to move. He was pretty sure a rib was broken, and his right arm throbbed. But he was alive, by some miracle, Gnost be thanked.

He rolled to look over his shoulder. Several houses down, a roof had a huge chunk taken out of it. A wing protruded from the hole, and smoke was pouring into the sky. If that didn't attract attention, he didn't know what would.

'Gotta get out of here,' he muttered to himself, pushing himself from the tree onto the slanted roof beside him. His ankle cried out in protest, but he steadied himself by gritting his teeth and chanting profanities. He fought his way to the end of the roof and slipped down onto a walkway just below the edge. His legs gave out under him.

Some way off he could hear voices calling to each other. Alarm, surprise. Co-ordinating, organised voices and a rabble of yells. He couldn't make out what they were saying, but it didn't sound good.

The closest house was boarded up. In fact, so were a lot of the houses on this street. Hamel picked himself up—

motivated by the sound of footsteps coming closer—and smashed the door open with his shoulder.

Inside, he found darkness. He elbowed the door shut behind him.

14 - Need For A Cloudgazer

Nezzu Strait
August 13th

Elzie Kerowan stood expectantly with her hands on her hips. Of all the stupid ideas in her time, teaching some illiterate Laro mercenary how to do navigation (on a ship that navigated itself) was up there. But he was to be taught. She groaned inwardly just thinking about it.

The Brazakker strode into the room casually, still wearing those filthy trousers and that worn-out shirt and duster. Typical pirate. Typical cloudgazer.

He paused, clearly trying to recall her name. 'Hi. Ka... -ren, was it?'

'Kerowan. Elzie Kerowan.'

'Right! I'm Kiy.'

'Last name, if you please. And that's ma'am to you, by the way.'

'Oh, right. Well it's Tanthar, then. *Marm*,' he said, mimicking the long 'a' of her Azrunite accent.

Did he think he was being funny? 'Let's get on with this, shall we?'

'Yep.'

'Navigation, right...' She stood at the navigation console. Where to start? Unlike the table, maps, compasses and slide rules of Brazakker warships, Azrune's ships had glass screens with light displays. Calputers did most of it. Best to start with similarities.

'Take a look at this. Do you recognise it?' She pointed to the dot with characters underneath and two numbers appended below them.

'Our position. Altitude and bearing,' he replied, clearly guessing.

'A good start. Perhaps you're not as dumb as you look.' *And he doesn't look that dumb, truth be fair.* She cleared her throat. 'You're familiar with Wind Shift?'

'Probably.' He shrugged.

'Probably? I thought Mestphura said you had navigation schooling?'

'Years ago, from my father. He was a navigator. I will admit it's been a while, but perhaps you should just explain to be sure?'

She sighed. This was ridiculous. Her voice took on the tone of a textbook. 'Wind Shift is the effect of the winds gradually altering the positions of all cities in Azimuth. To configure waypoint paths, we use the transponder signals of cities, in relation to a central reference point. Which is...?'

'Nubylon, capital of Azrune.'

'Correct. See, you did know, you're just an idyat.'

'No, I just like the sound of your teacher voice,' he said with a slight smile.

Sky be damned, is he flirting now?

'Just pay attention.' She looked back at the displays.

'Right, right.'

She went over the means of getting navigational information out of the central calputer, and the systems on the *Akron*'s bridge to utilise that information. When he probed for technical details, she explained them with academic clarity.

'You sure know a lot about all this,' he observed. 'I thought there was no navigator on the *Akron*.'

'We're not one-dimensional people, you know,' she retorted. 'You don't get through Solar Harp Academy without taking an interest.'

'Oh, of course. To be academy-educated. I dream of it.'

His tone was so dry, Elzie couldn't figure if he was mocking her or genuinely meant it.

'What does this do?' He motioned to an obscure switch in the corner of the panel.

'Ah! Don't press that! That engages the jump system.'

'The what?'

'Forget it,' she said. 'Just don't press it. Ever.'

'Right.'

'Anyway, I think that's everything.' She cocked her head to one side. 'You got all that?' *Because I'm not going through it again.*

'Yeah yeah, sure.'

'Good. You'll be requested as needed.'

'Sure thing, *marm*.'

She twitched, but ignored the dig. Leaving him, she stepped out onto the forward promenade, a curved balcony deck that stretched out just below the bridge.

At the fore, Commander Mestphura stood watching the shifting white shapes of clouds passing under them. She approached him with deliberate steps.

'Sir.'

Mestphura didn't look round. 'Miss Kerowan.'

'Tanthar has been briefed on the job. He seems capable, even navigation-educated to a point.'

'Excellent.'

Not really. 'Sir, I must ask a question.'

'Fire away.'

She looked to one side, her lips pouting. 'What are we doing out here?'

The question hung. Mestphura seemed to be thinking, although Elzie felt he could just as easily be leaving her to flounder. Finally, he said, 'Kerowan, have you been to Brazak West before?'

Elzie shook her head, her bobbed hair flying in the wind. 'No, sir, I have not.'

'Strange, is it not? We rarely leave the borders of our own airspace, even to a place as relatively close as this.'

'We're here for the sights?' Elzie frowned.

Mestphura shook his head. 'No, it's just that sometimes we forget our insularity. Did you know Brazak West is renowned as a haven for mercenaries?'

'Yes,' she responded mechanically. 'And therefore I suppose it isn't surprising for one to encounter a— *cloudgazer*.' She spoke as if the very word might carry disease.

'I am developing the impression that you disapprove of having a cloudgazer aboard,' Mestphura said evenly.

She paused a little too long before saying, 'Not at all, sir.'

The commander gave a wry smile. 'You can be frank with me, Miss Kerowan. You know that.'

Elzie sighed. 'What makes a cloudgazer, sir?'

Mestphura met her gaze silently.

'Just a sling,' she continued, her frustration spilling over. 'A tool. An ancient relic. A mere grapple hook is all it takes. They are nothing more than glorified pirates, hooligans and thieves. They have no order, no code. They aren't even... they're no more a group than people of a particular eye colour, or born of one month. You simply cannot trust their professionalism. Sir.'

The Azrunite commander seemed to consider this. 'But by that point, is distrust of them any more grounded than fearing a man's character for the colour of his skin?'

She frowned at that. 'No, there is a difference. Cloudgazers all have one thing in common: they have stolen something.'

Mestphura seemed to take the point. 'I suppose. But slings can be inherited.'

'From outlaws!' she insisted. 'There are no *true* cloudgazers anymore.'

'There is always a possibility that dealing with mercenaries such as cloudgazers will not be in our favour.' Mestphura's body stiffened, and his expression hardened. 'But that is not our concern. Instructions have been issued, and were quite clear.'

Elzie was taken aback. 'The Ministry?'

Mestphura nodded. 'I messaged Nubylon when the pair arrived. They seemed to be expecting something of the sort. I was surprised to receive enthusiastic instructions to hire him. As you might well imagine.'

Elzie frowned, taking the information in. Cloudgazers were forbidden in Azrune, but perhaps that law didn't extend to ships at sea. Still, it was unclear what the First Navy would want with a vagrant like Kiy. 'I just don't see how anything good can come of such a partnership, sir.'

'That,' Mestphura said warmly, 'is why neither you nor I belong in the Peace Ministry.'

She raised one eyebrow quizzically. 'Do you even know where they're going with all this?'

'Even if I knew their intentions, I doubt I would be at liberty to disclose such information, Miss Kerowan,' Mestphura said with a hint of amusement.

She grunted, disappointed. Ever a disciple of technology, the one thing she resented being deprived of above all was information.

'Miss Kerowan,' Mestphura said as he watched the birds in front of the *Akron* perform silent, swooping turns. 'I understand your sentiment. Nevertheless, I will require your complete support.'

Elzie shot him a sharp look. 'Yes... of course, sir.'

'Good.' The commander nodded almost regally. 'I know I can depend on you to trust in my judgement.'

She tipped her head in acknowledgement. Mestphura had a demeanour that commanded respect, but he was not usually so stuffy, so official. She was pretty certain there was something weighing heavy on his mind. But she could also sense that he would say nothing more on the matter.

'Very good, sir,' she said. 'I will get back to the hangar.'

'Indeed. Don't let me keep you from your duties.' He gave a smile then assumed a look of meditation.

'As you say.' Elzie clasped her hands in front of her and bowed slightly, then hurried off towards the lower decks.

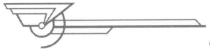

15 - Advance Motion

Nubylon
August 16th

'Ganzabar have declared war on us.'

The Proctor looked up from his book. 'Really? Well, I mean, that isn't terribly surprising.'

'Something of a formality, after the *Akron*'s actions, I suppose,' Prime Minister Tendrassi said. She stood beside him with one hand on her hip, wearing a smart, form-fitted suit that was padded and starched, a single-piece garment except for the shoulder-padded jacket over it, all in white, trimmed in light blue.

The Proctor was wearing the same as the day before, and every other day for as long as she'd known him. 'I'm sure they weren't expecting a fight from this old-timer.' He paused a moment in reflection. 'They've just forgotten. They think us weak because we're peaceful.' With an amused look he rose from his seat, placed his book on the throne, and stepped to the window. 'I think it's our move.'

'What did you have in mind, Proctor?'

'Humour my solicitude, Madam Prime Minister. What colour is peace?'

She said the first thing that came to her head; that always seemed to be the best way to talk to the Proctor. 'White?'

He nodded, looking at the sleeve of his tunic. 'Agreed.'

She looked at her own and thought of Azrune's gleaming white ships. 'We are a peaceful people,' she said.

The Proctor half shrugged, looking listless. 'All peoples are peaceful; it is the tyrants and despots who lead them that are not so.' He looked at his palms with a troubled gaze.

'Ganzabar is a militant culture,' Tendrassi countered. 'They thrive on conflict... weapons... politics. One in three own firearms. Naval service is compulsory for five years.

And you know the old Ganzabi navy motto: "Contest, not victory, is the keystone of Honour."'

'Propwash,' the Proctor said stubbornly.

One of the more bizarre aspects of being around the Proctor, Tendrassi thought, was that he made her feel as though she were talking to a grumpy old man inside the head of a child.

'Social differences, maybe,' she admitted. 'But nonetheless, the Ganzabi profit hugely from warfare. In the past sixty years, they have grown their borders twicefold, all through war.'

'Statistics. I already know statistics.' He pressed the button to open the glass door to the balcony. It slid aside silently, and they walked out into the morning air. 'People are just people. Trust me, Madam Prime Minister. I have watched people for a very, very long time.'

She gave a gracious, light bow. 'Your counsel is always the highest of wisdom, Proctor.'

'It is something to keep in our minds, you see.' He took out a pipe and lit it. She always had to fight back an urge to grin at the sight of what appeared to be a small boy with a pipe. 'What is the current situation at Mosleyhead?' he asked.

'The main Ganzabi fleet has withdrawn to the Nezzu Strait. There are large numbers of ships attacking Brazak West elsewhere, though. Unofficially, they're also pissed off that the *Akron* attacked them before a declaration was made. I felt tempted to point out that it was somewhat reminiscent of their own actions on several occasions. In any case, Commander Mestphura would never have attacked without providing adequate warning.'

The Proctor puffed. 'I do enjoy these pebble-ripple returns. Indeed, Julius isn't the kind for hot-headed impulse. I believe the Ganzabi offered to make this difficult for us.'

'Also, we pointed out that we signed a mutual protection pact with Brazak West four years ago, agreeing to assist in their defence.' She eyed the Proctor curiously. 'I am still not sure how you pulled that off, considering that, to my knowledge, my predecessor enacted no such agreement.

But the records of all parties check out, and all the documents are there. I will concede, it must have been low-profile.'

'It was more of a back-track than a back-stage,' the Proctor said dismissively. 'But the important thing is that we are now able to move elbows. The Erewhon class is the priority here; the war is a useful excuse to go through the wardrobe and look for answers.'

'Yes, Proctor.' She feigned comprehension.

'Good. Then we can continue. And I'm to understand the *Akron* has enlisted their cloudgazer? Most fruituitous.'

'Yes, Proctor.' She hardly noticed anymore when the Proctor made up words. 'They encountered the criminal during the battle there. I still have no idea how you saw that coming.'

'Keeping true to tampering,' he said. 'The old folks, they all keep in touch.'

The Prime Minister nodded. She was used to the Proctor's archaic, cryptic way of speaking. Sometimes she even thought she was beginning to understand it a little. 'I shall send orders to the *Akron* directly, to work with the Brazakkers in rooting out the target.'

'A good plan, but, in light of our earlier discussion, I'd rather we didn't embroil the wren in the butter.' The Proctor stared a moment, then shook his head. 'No, better they search alone. Start with Minataway. I will notify them of my findings when relevant.'

'Y-yes. Of course.' She had often wondered how the Proctor knew impossible details or events that were yet to happen. Like nearly all Azrunites, Prime Minister Tendrassi didn't believe in psychics, mystics, supernatural deities or other such nonsense. Which meant the Proctor, whatever he was, was a *scientific* phenomenon. Explainable... somehow. She just never could figure out *how*. A study of the Proctor would be about the only scientific taboo in all Azrune. But even if it weren't, she would never condone such a thing; it would be deeply disrespectful of an individual who was like a father to the nation.

'Are we at terminus, Madam Prime Minister?' the Proctor said, puffing on the pipe.

'Yes, that is all. I shall dispatch the *Akron* to begin searching Minataway at once.'

'Very good.' He leant on the balcony. 'Splendid advance motion, all of it.'

16 - Plan Of Attack

Molisk, Brazak West
August 18ᵗʰ

Airship engines and lifting mechanisms hummed and thrummed, and the walkways of Molisk trembled as gigantic shadows swallowed them. Small stones rattled across the metal gantries, windows beat on their panes, and flower pots fell from perches against steel balconies. Those few residents remaining in the ruins of the town watched fearfully from slitted doors or hid beneath kitchen tables.

All around, the Ganzabi fleet slowly penetrated the airspace of Molisk, unopposed. Dozens upon dozens of vessels hung over the settlement, menacingly silhouetted oblongs that looked like a swarm of swords, sounded like a thunderstorm, and cast monolithic shadows across the little roof terraces and clumps of floatrock.

Hovering barges, like little open-top boxes with Repulsor engines, slid from the bellies of the larger ships. Each barge was crowded with Ganzabi marines, their heads protruding above the sides like bottles in crates. As the transports spiraled down towards the landing parks and walkways, an authoritative Ganzabi voice boomed over the loudspeakers.

'Attention. Attention. This settlement is now controlled by the Federation of Ganzabar. You are required to comply or lethal force may be used. Attention...'

At the crest of the fleet, looming over the town hall's central clock tower, was the battlecruiser *Grace of Gnost*. Veteran of the Merchant Wars, it was some eight hundred metres long and bristled with cannons, funnels and engines.

Atop the ship's central tower, below the bridge deck, was the captain's quarters. Inside, Admiral Moller sat mulling over the combat reports that had been handed to him.

So Azrune wanted to join the fray too? Well, that was fine by him. High brass had flown off the handle at this sudden foreign intervention, but Moller could hardly care less about the Azrunites. The more the merrier, as far as he was concerned. He commanded the military forces of the greatest country in the world. The entire Lystrata Commonwealth, with Sultan Deyderriş and all his little Mush'kas, could be opposing him for all the difference it would make. One Azrunite ship didn't matter. Ganzabi honour was forged in joining of battle without fear. It was moulded by righteousness, faith and the innate liberty of the Ganzabar Way. Whether your enemy was vanquished on this day was not important; Gnost would see to it that they be defeated in the end. What *was* important was being on the right side, and fighting for it.

Moller had always thought of Brazak West's separation from the Federation as a missed opportunity. Brazak East had shown that integration into Ganzabar was not impossible. Yet the western Brazakkers remained enslaved to their oppressive regimes of state-controlled lives. So terribly downtrod. So tragically mistreated.

Today was a day to celebrate, then. Having assembled the Armada and having subdued resistance on the southern border, they were now prepared for a full-scale pacification of Brazak West. They would silence this threat before it had a chance to grow truly dangerous. Their compatriots at Mosleyhead had been less successful in drawing off and shattering the New Brazak Navy—no thanks to the Azrunites—but he had dispatched the countess to lure them out of the way, and she had persuaded him she could take care of that little problem. So long as she was back in time to uphold the Plan, he didn't much care what she did.

His fleet had paused here at Molisk to consolidate their control of the area. Teams of Ganzabi marines had been sent on 'collection duty': descending to the streets to gather the young and able-bodied, who would be taken to the Federation, where they would be put to effective use—and just as importantly, where they would not be in position to form any kind of partisan resistance.

With the nearby Brazakker forces licking their wounds, they were not likely to encounter any further trouble here. As such, Moller had decided to retire to his office.

But now one of his crew entered and requested his attention.

'Yes?' Moller answered, his nose still in papers.

'Admiral, we have decoded a transponder signal, using the captured information recovered this morning. Three hundred ninety kilometres on bearing three-two-zero.'

'And?'

'Sir, it's a Gundar.'

Moller finally looked up. 'Good.' He set the documents aside and took a long look out the window.

The cities of Azimuth were not static things; little in the world was, sitting as it was on a shifting sea of flowing air currents. Countries remained very much where they were *relative* to each other, but the exact locations of cities and stations fluxed every day. It was only their respective transponders, beaming Transpulse codes to identify themselves, that made navigation feasible. However, in a state of war, nations no longer shared transponder decoders —and to complicate matters, they often shifted cities and installations around to throw off their enemy. Thus the layout of their opponent's airspace was a hazy game of guesses until intelligence could be gleaned.

Moller rose and led the way up a spiral of metal stairs and onto the main bridge deck. 'As soon as the collections are complete, I want us to set a course for the Gundar.'

'Very well, sir,' The comms officer replied rigidly.

'A celebration is in order, I think,' Moller said. 'Ensign Jace, I'd like some preparations made for a toast tonight, in the officers' hall. To the victory of Ganzabar!'

The young man to his side nodded quickly and dashed away.

Moller addressed the room with a jovial grin. 'Friends! We shall dine in Risely by the end of the month!'

There was a cheer of agreement from the officers.

The stout man at the helm looked at the admiral sincerely. 'Is it true what they say about the Gundar, sir?'

Moller nodded, slowly at first then fervently as he found his outrage. 'Indeed, Gannoway, indeed it is. Let me tell you about Brazak West's new so-called "defensive cannons".'

The attentions of the other crew on the bridge were drawn to his tone.

'The Gundar is a fortress of an installation. Each cannon is over ninety metres in length, and its shells, the size of small skyfighters, impart all the force of a reactor explosion. The name "Gundar" refers to both its ability to shoot and its range. You see, it uses radar to track and hit targets, and it can hit a target hundreds, even thousands of kilometres away.' He swept a look around the room dramatically. 'That's right. Our cities, our very homes, are all in range of these deadly weapons. And that is why we will ensure they're destroyed before they can be used.'

'They're not yet operational, sir?' asked his first officer, Lieutenant Fredson.

'We have reason to believe they will be capable of firing in the next few months. Hence our mission is simple: capture the Gundars. Their evil ends here.' Moller paused for oratory effect. 'We once tried to show them the good of the Ganzabar Way, but they turned their backs on us. So be it. But we will not allow the sword to be pointed at our throats!'

Moller looked around triumphantly as the bridge gave a hearty cheer.

17 - On The Move

Nezzu Strait
August 25th

Kiy looked around the bridge. At the moment, he felt only one, overwhelming emotion: boredom. Time passed slowly aboard the *Akron*. Kiy could not remember when they'd come aboard, and he'd given up trying to find the ship's timekeeping displays or pestering the crew. But it had to have been a week, at least.

He'd initially forgotten the names of the officers on the bridge, but as he worked with them, he re-learned them, and they became familiar—though the people themselves remained mostly distant. He was an outsider, and in any case a cloudgazer. Elzie in particular still looked at him like a stowaway.

Leo, on the other hand, was really fitting into life on the ship. He'd gotten something of a special place among the crew, almost like a mascot. He was shown the remote controls for the Azrunite guns ('so high-tech!'), was used as an 'assistant mechanic' (holding tools, usually) and even had a brief go as craftsman, during which he pulled levers for a whole thirty seconds.

Poor lad, probably thinks this is what life on a ship is like. And yet, perhaps he was not so naïve, Kiy thought. The kid had spent a day on the *Municipal*, after all, which was enough to teach him what the navy was like for most of his countrymen.

But Kiy was restless. Brazak West was still at war, and Hennie and her family were still out there in the line of fire. Meanwhile the *Akron* was flying drunken zig-zags across western Nezzu, and he knew of at least three calls for assistance from the Brazakkers that had been ignored by the Azrunite ship. He should have guessed Azrunite 'compassion' wouldn't last long. He hoped the fleet hadn't been counting on it.

Mestphura appeared on the bridge beside Kiy, snapping him from his reverie. 'New orders just in. Can you direct us to Minataway, Mr Tanthar?'

The Borderlands? Kiy thought. 'Of course.'

'Punch it in.'

The destination was simple enough, but the motive had him confused. Minataway had once been the central expanse of Great Brazak. It wasn't particularly pleasant, so the settlements had moved out of it after independence: Ganzabar wanted to keep East, and West wanted a buffer zone. Since then, East, stimulated by Ganzabar's ferocious economy, had become greatly affluent, yet at the same time, it had grown ever more firmly under the Ganzabi thumb.

However, Brazak East had been dormant in the war so far. The Eastern Brazakkers wouldn't be keen on fighting their Western counterparts, but then again, Ganzabar was too savvy to lose their support by pressing such an action. More likely Ganzabar would simply disseminate how all this mess was Brazak West's fault, further illustrating the superiority of the Ganzabar Way.

Which raised the question: If the Brazakkers weren't fighting for Minataway, and the Ganzabi weren't either, then what was Azrune doing there?

Kiy brought up the console's display and input a series of waypoints. There was no local information to identify surroundings, but it wasn't too hard matching the dots.

'Plotted,' he confirmed.

Elzie walked up behind him and pointed to a switch. 'If you hit that, the directional information will be relayed to everyone else's displays.'

Kiy did so. 'Neat. These things are smarter than people.'

'Speak for yourself,' she said, continuing past.

'Coming to heading zero-four-five,' Kaj'aku announced. 'Altitude six-six-fifty.'

'Engage at high cruise,' Mestphura said.

Kaj'aku pushed two throttle levers smoothly forward. The ship's engines emitted a deep hum followed by a high pitched whine that swelled gracefully as it pulled away.

'Commander, Transpulse from the Brazakkers. Marshall Saratov is requesting allied ships to assist defence of Tovstok.'

Mestphura looked troubled as he replied, 'I will speak with him. Gatista, you have command.'

'Yes, sir.'

The *Akron* turned smoothly to the east and accelerated away, its large turbines crying out across the sky with a whooshing thrum. On the forward promenade deck, overhanging the prow of the airship, Leo Litvyak sat watching the clouds pass beneath his feet. Occasionally the ship would carve through the large, woolly white of the cumulus and everything would be engulfed in fog. Then moments later, the cloud would pass and the morning sun would reappear in a limitless blue expanse.

Leo knew that, somewhere beneath the blanket of white thousands of metres below them, somewhere in the bowels of the world, was the fabled Understorm: the lowest level of clouds. And nobody really knew what was below that. Anything that ventured there was ripped to shreds by the wind, debris and lightning. He knew the fates of those on the ships that sank down into that maelstrom. He wondered if Feodora was one of them. One thing he was sure of though: his big sis wouldn't go down without a fight.

Leo thought about home sometimes. Olya popped into his mind often. He wished she were here to argue about things and call him a mug head. And of course he thought of Hennie, Almay, Naki, Ainu, his mother. Even Father. He missed them all terribly when he sat and thought about things.

He'd like to think he wasn't stupid. He knew before he set out that war wasn't going to be all banners and roses. But even the constant warning from adults who thought they knew better could not have prepared him for what he'd seen on the *Municipal*.

An image of Anatali seemed to be forever engraved on his mind: her closing her eyes in grim acceptance, the chest of her uniform wet with blood. She had been ready to give her life. Could he have ever said the same?

'Hey, you that Brazakker kid?' came a jolly, deep voice.

Leo looked over his shoulder at a man who looked barely out of his teens. He was well built and muscular with a bronze tan and curly, close-cropped, light brown hair. He wore a yellow flightsuit with a panel fixed to his chest, from which a cluster of cables led into a chunky collar.

'Don't be shy, little buddy.' The man grinned, slapping a friendly hand on Leo's shoulder. 'The name's Marc. Marc Nareem. What's yours?'

'Uh, Leo.'

'Ulleo? Well good!' Marc beamed. 'Man, I love your Brazakker names, they're crazy.'

Leo laughed awkwardly. 'Ahm. Yeah.'

Marc leant an elbow on the rail. 'How you finding the *Akron*?'

'I like it. Hey, what're those for?' Leo indicated the devices fixed to the front of Marc's jumpsuit.

'I plug myself into the kitchen cookers, mate!' Marc laughed. 'Nah, I'm a pilot, y'see. It's for pilot stuff. Oxygen, radio... stuff.' He waved his hands excitedly.

'Oh, right,' Leo said, still staring at the device.

'You ever flown a skyfighter?'

'No. I'm too young.'

Marc looked confused, but his enthusiasm quickly overcame it. 'Best kind of freedom there is, mate! We fly Foxtails here.' He shot a look at Leo. 'They're Brazakker planes! You've seen 'em, right?'

'Yeah...' Leo made a face. 'Wait—why do you fly our planes? I thought Azrune was the most advanced country ever?'

Marc laughed hard. 'Ah, something like that, mate, yeah! 'Tween you and me, it's probably 'cause our fighters belong in museums. So, anyhow. Gonna ask if you wanted to try it sometime.'

'What? I can't fly a skyfighter!' Leo said.

'Well, not a real one. I mean, not yet. But y'know, we got a little room in the back. Big enough for a quick ride, easy.'

Leo's eyes lit up.

'How's that sound, kiddo?'

'Really?'

"'Course.' Marc turned and headed for the steps at the other side of the deck. 'Come by the hangar some time. Elzie's down with it.'

'Miss Kerowan?'

'Yeah, she's the flight captain,' Marc said, turning before he descended. 'Leads Lancet Squadron.'

Leo was amazed. 'Oh. I had no idea.'

'You didn't think she just went about nursing people back to health, did you?'

What is he talking about? 'Uh, I guess.'

'Anyway, got to run or I'll be late again. Later, Ulleo!'

Marc gave a wave before disappearing down the stairs with huge strides.

18 - Jerra

Laronor
September 4th

Zoxeth, the industrial core of Laronor, was in full swing
on a warm September evening. Hennie emerged from the
pub wearily, rubbing her hands on her filthy pinafore. It
had been less than a month she'd been working in Laronor,
but it already felt like a lifetime spent a slave to the
Worker's Hammer.

She walked down the street sluggishly, limbs and feet
aching from a hard day of physical work. Making hats had
never been this exhausting. The Hammer was
claustrophobic and noisy, full of rowdy men and
demanding women. It was always busy, at least whenever
Hennie was there, and so unruly.

Today, some blockhead from the mills at Alderney had
groped her while she was serving the table. She'd
immediately gone to complain to Aleece, head of the bar
staff.

'Sorry, that's life, chucks,' Aleece had said, though not
unkindly, then carried on wiping down the counter.

'Oh, it's tough bein' pretty, eh,' quipped Maroj, an older
woman on staff. Another of the barmaids had then
interjected that it must be nice living a simple life in the
south, 'where you just complain to get your own way'.

Recalling it all made Hennie feel angry, so she pushed
the whole event from her mind. She tried to appreciate the
night air, which seemed laden with anticipation, but to
Hennie the promise was dulled and hollow. She *felt* the
excitement should be there, but in its place she found only
a grim anxiety.

Thinking back, she remembered the late second-summer
evenings in Brudor, when she would go to the fayre on the
Common with her sisters and brother. She remembered
how one year, Feo had danced with a tall blond boy with

the most beautiful eyes. They'd had a falling-out over him shortly after. He'd been eighteen anyway—too old for either of them—and nothing could have come of it. But now the thought of having been angry at Feo stung Hennie to the heart. She wished she could take back everything bad she'd ever said to her. She would never have said any of those things if she'd known her sister wouldn't be here today.

Official news of the *Lykomin*'s demise had reached her not long after she began working at the Hammer. She had been serving a table of ship hands, and overheard them describing the *Lykomin*'s grisly destruction. To their credit, they were sympathetic to her flood of tears, and on learning of her sister's death Aleece had given her ten minutes' peace around the back to 'sort her thoughts'. They were alright, Hennie figured, the maids and patrons of the Hammer. Well, some of them.

The fat man that had hired her—a fellow by the name of Presber—was a slave-driver, but somehow he had managed to keep her from losing all patience with him. Every time she complained about something, he had an excuse. Every shortcoming was met with an apology and a flakey promise. He'd even convinced her to work extra hours, promising more than twice what he'd actually paid her so far. But she was still yet to see anything of the remainder, she cursed inwardly.

She imagined Feo, a lieutenant of the New Brazak Navy, looking on her sister now. What would she think? Standing there in her fine black uniform, looking down at her little sister and seeing a hopeless serving girl. *Sorry to disappoint you, sis*, she thought. *I could never be a worthy Litvyak.* Tears threatened her eyes and she threw the thought aside angrily.

She thrust her hands deeper into the pockets of her overcoat and marched on towards Waltov. She'd tried several times to recall Kiy's paper instructions from memory, but it was no good—the only thing she could remember was that Miles Rathbone's address was in Waltov. It turned out Waltov wasn't much of a detour from her walk to the Hammer and back, so she'd decided to make it part of her commute. She wasn't really sure why;

she didn't even know what Miles looked like. What did she expect, that Miles would be walking around holding a sign with her name on it? It was too hopeless to call it a plan, but it made her feel better to at least try *something*.

As she crossed over the bridge into the district, she gazed down between the two floatrock islands. Some way down, a small airship slid along the path of the chasm, passing over another craft coming the opposite way. The wind whipped past, tugging at her coat and dress, but she found her gaze stubbornly fixed on the ships in the distance.

'OOWww!'

The cry came from out of sight, on the far side of the bridge. It was followed a squeal, and the sound of a scuffle.

'Just give it 'ere!'

'No!'

Hurrying to investigate, Hennie rounded a corner to find a group about her own age fighting with each other. Or, not so much with each other; it was more that three of them were beating the fourth up.

'Give it!' said the biggest of the three, a pale girl with black hair clawed back into a tight ponytail.

The victim, also a girl but considerably shorter than the first and far more delicate, struggled in the arm-lock of a tall boy. The other attacker, a stocky boy, snatched a small silk bag from the victim's hand. But she still had hold of it, and the little purse ripped. A shower of a dozen or so coins clattered onto the walkway, most bouncing out of sight or through the gaps in the railings.

The tall boy let go of his victim, who scrambled after the bouncing coins to the obvious amusement of the rest. The pale girl reached out and grabbed the young girl by the collar of her beautiful yellow dress, stretching it with a little rip.

'Sorry, Jerra,' she said mockingly, as the smaller girl fought to free herself. 'You can't 'ave those. Your family's got enough, I think.'

Hennie reached her boiling point. Without thinking, she ran up and threw a punch. She didn't really aim it, it just sort of ended up meeting the tall girl's face. The girl recoiled in pain and surprise, letting go of the younger girl and holding a hand over her bloodied nose.

The others stopped and stared at Hennie, unsure what to think. She was not the biggest, toughest or strongest girl her age. But as she stood glaring, her feet apart and fists clenched, she did her best to look formidable.

The two boys moved towards Hennie menacingly.

'Whu der flok ure you?' the tall girl said, clutching a bleeding nose.

'None of yer damn business!' Hennie snapped.

'You wer' the one who flakkin' butt in, here!' the smaller boy said, his voice thin and whiney.

Hennie lashed out, knocking his glasses off his face. He backed away and began to cry.

'Not so fun when it's someone bigger than you, is it?' Hennie yelled. 'Go, on, get out of here!'

The shorter boy ran off whimpering, and the larger went after him. Only the black-haired girl remained, fixing Hennie with a bitter gaze.

'Ou'll be sorry fur dis,' she said, then went off after the other two.

Hennie watched them go, then turned to the younger girl. She was a little older than Olya, not much younger than Hennie. She was still trying to recover the coins that had been scattered across the walkway and beyond.

'You okay?' Hennie asked.

'Oh.' She looked up. 'Um. Yes. I must express my thanks to you for doing that. You're very valiant.'

Hennie shrugged. ''S'okay. I'm Hennie.' She thrust out a grubby hand.

'Jerra Lightlock,' She extended a gloved hand to meet Hennie's. 'It's a pleasure to meet you, Miss.'

'Pleased to meetcha, too.' Hennie grinned heartily, shaking Jerra's hand with an enthusiasm the girl was clearly unused to.

Hennie couldn't help but notice how beautiful and elaborate Jerra's clothes were: a fine yellow dress, neatly matched shoes and delicate lace gloves. Next to Hennie, she almost looked like a little baroness, albeit a slightly grotty one.

'You alright?' Hennie said after a pause.

Jerra looked around dejectedly.

Hennie saw the small ripped purse and bit her lip. 'Oh...' She looked around. 'Hey, don't worry; I'll help you find 'em.'

'Really?' Jerra looked almost confused.

'''Course!'

They scoured the walkway in the diminishing light, managing to find another twelve floril before being forced to give up the rest.

'Thank you, Hennie,' Jerra said. 'I have to be going now, though. Father will worry.'

'No trouble,' Hennie replied. 'I'm sorry we couldn't find it all.'

'That's okay,' Jerra said, brightening. 'It's... well, the work is more important than the pay, I suppose. I work for that factory there, you see.' She motioned to the large munitions factory on the island Hennie had just crossed from.

'Wow, really? Uh—I mean, you don't look like a factory worker. I mean—sorry.'

'That's alright,' Jerra said. 'It's in order to assist the war effort. My family is comfortable, but Mother believes we should join the fight. I... well, it does not agree with my constitution. So, I work.'

Hennie raised a brow. 'You're too young to fight, aren't you?'

'Well, yes, but... they begin rifles training at fifteen, you know.'

Hennie went wide-eyed. 'You're fifteen?'

'Not yet. But, very soon. I would have joined this year.'

Hennie gave her a skeptical appraisal. She looked a little scrawny for infantry, but then again, Hennie imagined the infantry weren't being too picky right now.

Jerra looked over her shoulder. 'I hope they don't give you trouble because of me.'

Hennie shrugged. 'I wouldn't worry about it. Maybe we could walk together; they might leave us alone.'

'Yes, good idea.' Jerra smiled a little. 'Arispas'ba, Hennie.'

'That's alright, no need to be so polite!' Hennie laughed as she fell into step alongside her new friend. 'But I gotta say, I think you might want to start wearing a plainer dress. That one is gettin' ruined...'

They continued to talk until their paths forked, then said their goodbyes. Jerra disappeared up a grand-looking avenue lined with trees, while Hennie crossed into the catacombs of Voxton.

Hennie looked with an air of depression upon the run-down building that was her new home. Little had she known the rooms Presber offered would be right around the corner from the slummy camp she had hoped to leave behind. It was a rough area, and Hennie'd had her share of troubles on her way to and from the Hammer in the small hours.

Tucked away in a dim corner alley was the entrance to her one-room apartment. The view wasn't bad, she would admit; beyond the mesh of power wires and the next line of rooftops, she could make out the elevated harbour gantries of Southport. The elegant shapes of passenger airships came in and out of the airways, and beyond them the curve of the floating dock platform was set against an azure sky.

But if her view was acceptable, her room was bleak. At night it was often cold and drafty. Damp and soot had accumulated like a wet shadow slowly encroaching on the walls. Things would crawl and slither in the corners, and the plaster was cracked and broken in so many places that she felt eyes on her all the time. The cold copper basin in one corner was all she had for bathing, and a rotten sink was so filthy she used it as little as she could possibly manage. Occasional swells of odour from the block's drainage system exploded up from the grating outside, like a silent, invisible flood of putrid fragrance.

She hated it.

She dwelt on how much she hated it as she stared out over the harbour, through the little cracked window. Meeting Jerra had lifted her spirits a little; she was the closest thing to a friend Hennie had known since leaving Brudor. But the atmosphere of her room instantly dragged her back down.

She wondered if she'd ever see her Ma again. Every time she had gone to government officials, the army, or whoever, nobody had been able to help her. No-one knew where her mother was, or who might tell her. Nor did anyone know who Miles Rathbone was—but then, why would they? This was a huge city, with so many people. Even Kiy would never find her here. And the war could go on for years. How long would she have to go on like this? She felt so completely lost. Lost and, most of all, alone.

It wasn't until her eyes caught on the small calendar fixed to the wall by the stove that it hit her: her seventeenth birthday was yesterday. She'd worked so long and hard at the Hammer she'd completely forgotten about it. It was silly, but she felt that of all the things to happen, this was the most unbearable.

She curled up on the ratty chair and watched the dust floating through the light from the room's single naked bulb. She remembered the way Kiy had always described the city: vibrant and egalitarian, a place of sophistication and wonder. Laronor was a place where he'd always felt like *himself*, he'd said. It was a place where the people's hospitality was always there—'they're a blunt sort but they're good people'. And they'll look after you, y'know.

Her eyes welled up. 'You flakking idyat.' She sobbed into her knees.

19 - Details

Minataway
September 12th

The graceful prow of the *Akron* cut through the thickening clouds, which had grown darker and murkier as they approached the tempestuous skies of Minataway. Swaths of rain raked across the empty exterior decks in angry waves, but inside, Kiy and Leo watched from the cosiness of the ship's dining hall. It was a curiously simple place, missing the tall ceilings and lavish furniture of luxury liners, yet too aesthetically comfortable to feel like a ship's mess.

'Weather's gotten real wet,' Leo said.

'Mmmn.' Kiy sat opposite him, sipping from a mug.

Leo turned to him. 'So, uh, where we goin'?'

'Special mission,' Kiy said, evoking a frown, then added, 'I don't understand it myself, kid.'

'Well,' Leo said tiredly, 'what's the destination? You can't pretend you don't know that. That's what they're keeping you for, right?'

'I'm not so sure anymore,' Kiy said thoughtfully. 'I think maybe there's more to it than that. Navigation seems pretty easy with this system. Even without local knowledge they can interrogate nav transponders and local control towers, especially now they have clearance.'

'I don't know what that means, Kiy, but you still haven't told me where we're going.'

Kiy threw him a sarcastic glance. 'New Frander.'

'Really?'

'Don't be daft, lad. We're going to Minataway.'

'Where's Minataway?'

Kiy took another sip. 'Borderlands. Brazak East—well, nearly.'

'Brazak East? Why there?'

Kiy shrugged. 'My sentiment exactly, kiddo. I think only that Mestphura guy knows—'

'Oh, hey,' Leo interrupted, 'check it out.'

Kiy turned to see that Elzie was getting food from the expansive buffet spread.

'Man. She is serious totty,' Leo said, staring at her as he took a bite from his sandwich.

'I doubt you even know what that means. Anyway, she's a bit old for you.' Kiy watched her a few moments, then returned to reading an Azrunite operations manual.

'I think *you're* a bit old for *her*,' Leo sneered.

'Pretty sure we're the same age, short-top,' Kiy shot back. 'Though she's not my type.'

'She seems nice to me.'

'You should try looking at her face.'

Leo turned red. 'What are you talkin' about?'

'Typical one-track mind of a thirteen-year-old boy. I mean, what colour are her eyes?'

'Um... blue?'

'Brown. Almost black, in fact.'

Leo laughed. 'You're just saying that.'

'Take a look yourself. I rest my case,' Kiy said, cocking his head at a diagram with markedly greater interest than he was giving the conversation at hand.

'Why don't you like her, anyhow?'

'Not so much that.' Kiy flicked a page in his manual. 'It's more about the fact that she's got something against me. No idea what—probably just a distrust of cloudgazers. That's typical of arrogant highbred moderates with dull lives.' He gulped the last of his coffee, then glanced out the window. 'I suppose I shouldn't be surprised, but I kinda expected better from an Azrunite. They're supposed to be tolerant—'

'Depends who we're tolerating.'

Kiy realised Elzie was standing beside their table. He wondered how much she had heard.

'Oh? Who don't you tolerate?' he enquired indifferently, paging through the operations manual.

'You know...' she said with mock casual thought. 'Pirates, thieves, murderers... scum, I guess.'

'Scum?' Kiy swirled the word around his mouth. 'And me without my needle moustache.'

'Kiy isn't scum,' Leo said.

'I didn't say he was.'

'You didn't, no.' Kiy gave her a glance, then carried on reading.

Elzie's eyes narrowed. 'You got a problem with me, Cloudgazer?' When Kiy didn't respond, she became visibly annoyed. 'Hey! I'm talking to you.'

Kiy looked up at her. 'Sorry, what? I was a million miles away.'

'Ugh!' She clenched her fist in frustration. Her drink tipped off the tray and splashed across the floor. She marched out of the room without so much as a glance back.

Leo watched her go. 'Man, you got a way with women, Kiy.'

Kiy glanced down at the spillage. 'She didn't even clean it up.'

'You were right, though,' Leo said. 'Her eyes are dark, alright.'

Kiy eyed him carefully. 'That's what I said.'

Leo grinned. 'So I was thinkin'... what colour are Mother's eyes? Do you know?'

'What?'

'You heard me. C'mon, Captain Details, you've known us long enough.'

Kiy slapped the manual shut and regarded Leo suspiciously. 'Green.'

'Wrong. Hazel,' Leo said smugly.

'That's hardly a fair comparison.'

'Oh, what? Someone you've been working with for a year, compared to someone you just met? Sure.'

Kiy leant back in his chair. 'I fail to see your point here.'

'She might not like you much, but you definitely like her.'

Kiy looked unimpressed. 'What? You were paying attention just now?'

Leo laughed. 'Whatever Kiy.' He leaned over with a grin. 'You know, I could talk to her. I could tell her you like her...'

'Knock it off.' Kiy looked out the window, then back at Leo, who was smiling smugly.

'Man, who's the thirteen-year-old boy now?' Leo said.

'That's still you.' Kiy started to resume reading, then stood abruptly. 'I'm gonna get some air.'

'It's raining.'

'I'm waterproof.'

Leo watched him leave, then sat back and ate his food with a smile.

The downpour intensified. The *Akron*'s starboard observation deck was awash with sheets of rain, blowing in in waves. Kiy stood at the rail, the water soaking him through. His hair was dripping wet and pressed down to his forehead.

The back of his skull ached. He reached up to stroke the scar there gingerly. The pain always resurfaced when his mind was in turmoil, and the memories it brought up only made things worse.

It felt like a lifetime ago.

20 - Old Wounds

Nantez, Occupied Brazak West
March 1ˢᵗ, 9315
Fourteen years ago

A plane weaved gracefully through the air. From behind, the intersection of wing and tail cut a crosshair that lined up against the long dark shape of an airship dead ahead of it.

Clink.

The glider torpedo fell away from the fuselage, and the fighter-bomber pulled away. The torpedo tipped forward as it dived, seeming to free-fall in slow motion.

Shwaaaa-clunk.

Glider wings flicked out of the torpedo's sides and it levelled off, flying straight like a gull riding thermals.

Getting closer.

Sailing in.

Flying in.

Screaming in.

The impact was just one in another volley of projectiles to rock the *Dawnstar*. On the bridge, a panel of gauges crashed to the deck with the sound of shattering glass.

Captain Tatyana Tanthar gripped the deck rail as the floor beneath her heaved. 'What have we got left, Eugene?'

The man next to her answered as first officer. 'We've got less than half our guns and one turbine still operational.' Then, as husband, he added, 'Honey, the kids—'

'Kiy is with Julene; they're headed for a plane.' The ship shook again, and there was a grinding noise from below. 'Darling, I really thought we could have...'

Eugene moved closer. 'I know. But don't worry. They'll be okay.'

'I love you.'

Running, running, running. Feet hitting the deck, as fast as they would go. He clutched his little sister in his arms, a tiny three-year-old, bawling to the noise of the klaxons and the grumbling of bombs hitting the ship. The air, thick with smoke, was red with the strobing alert lights.

'Easy, Julene,' Kiy said soothingly. 'Mum 'n' dad are coming soon, everything's gonna be fine.' He was only twelve, but his parents had entrusted him with keeping Julene safe. And he'd make sure of that—whatever it took.

An explosion tore into the ship a deck above, and a big chunk of the ceiling crashed down right in front of them. Kiy just managed to dodge it, pulling Julene down the corridor, surrounded by fires and crumbling bulkheads.

He burst through a thick hatch into the hangar area. It was a large open space filled with deck crew desperately attending to an assortment of fighter planes. Kiy weaved through the chaos of fuel pipes and stepladders to the escape plane that was waiting for them.

He ran up the ramp and slumped into a seat, Julene on his lap.

She pawed at the small round window. 'Mommmmeee.'

'Mummy's comin',' Kiy assured her. 'They're comin' soon.'

'MOMMMMEEE!' she bawled.

Seconds ticked by. In his mind, Kiy saw them running through the corridors towards the escape plane, and willed them to run faster. *C'mon, Mum. C'mon, Dad.* He tried not to fidget or give Julene the impression anything was wrong.

The roar of engines grew and the plane lurched forward, wheeling around to face the hangar opening. This wasn't right. Where were his parents?

'Stop the plane!' he called out, but went unanswered.

Then, with a sickening pull, they surged forward and swooped out of the hangar, leaving the *Dawnstar* behind. Banking away from the ship's rear, they dived, accelerating sharply.

Behind them, the carrier began to disintegrate. Small white explosions like bursting bubbles appeared all down the length of its great majestic hull. They were barely a kilometre away when the *Dawnstar* was enveloped in a blinding flash. Its reactor had exploded, and it splintered into a thousand shards that sank into the morning clouds.

'No...' The word came from Kiy's lips, but it was as if someone else had spoken it. Nothing seemed real. The sound of Julene's crying was a million miles away. She couldn't know what had happened, but at the same time she must have sensed that something was terribly wrong. He wanted to tell her it would all be okay, but the words wouldn't come. He could only sit and stare blankly at the drifting fragments of his parents' ship, trying to think desperately of some way it could be untrue.

Gotta keep calm. They're okay. They were somewhere else, they got out, and they're okay. They're okay.

He took his little sister into his arms and hugged her tightly.

He lost track of time, until darkness engulfed them. It took him a moment to realise they had docked in an airship hangar. Hadn't his parents said the plane would take them to Laronor?

'What... what's going on?'

Nobody answered. He didn't like this.

The main hatch opened with a clunk, and a group of Ganzabi marines stormed into the compartment. Shock stunned him into compliance at first; only when one of the marines took hold of Julene and started to carry her off did he snap to his senses.

'No! Stop! Let her go!' Kiy yelled. He struggled against the guard escorting him.

Julene cried out, her big blue eyes pleading with Kiy as she disappeared from his view. Kiy would never forget that look, her blond curls framing an expression of confusion, desperation, panic.

It was the last time he ever saw his sister.

Then one of the soldiers addressed the man in blue. Kiy knew, even back then, that the man in blue was important.

'Captain Moller, sir. The plane is clear.'

'The pilot?' the man in blue asked.

'Shot evading capture, sir.'

'Very good. Impound the boy on the *Isenbard*. The girl is to travel with Madam Armix.'

Kiy thrashed angrily against his captors, prompting another soldier to demand he sit still. Kiy spat at him. The soldier retaliated by swinging the butt of his rifle around and clubbing Kiy on the back of the head.

Then there was nothing else to remember.

21 - Flying Foxtails

Minataway
September 12th 9329

Kiy gingerly ran his finger along the scar on the back of his head. Scarcely a day went by that he didn't think of Julene, out there, lost in the skies. Sometimes he dreamt of finding her; sometimes he dreamt of the moment when they took her. In some of the dreams he could fight them, do something, stop it happening. But then he'd awake, reality would return, and it would hurt all over again.

She was still alive; of that he felt certain. Perhaps she was living in Ganzabar, or she'd been sold to the slave markets of Lystrata. He would give just about anything to know. She'd be nearly grown up by now, about Hennie's age. He imagined what she might look like, what she would say if she saw him. Would she even recognise him?

His eyelids flickered against the wind and rain. Thick grey cloud surrounded the *Akron* like mist. He wasn't sure how long he'd been out on the observation deck, but it felt like hours. The rain had soaked him to the bone and the wind had chilled him through, but in the cold Kiy always found a strange familiarity, a kind of calm peace.

He caught sight of a ripple some way off ahead of the ship, to port. It was as though the air was being distorted, like the haze over a heater, or a runway during a hot summer day.

Then part of the cloud shimmered, and for the blink of an eye, rain bounced from some unnaturally straight surface; but just as soon as the pattern formed, it dissipated. Kiy shook the water from his face with irritation. Was he hallucinating now?

No—there it was again. For less than a second, the shape in the rain looked like a ship.

Kiy rushed along the gantry and leapt up a flight of stairs, crossing to portside. He ran down several long hallways, bumping past a junior officer with a glowing glass device in his hand. Bursting out of the opposite side of the ship, he stared intently over the side rail. After a moment, the shape in the rain appeared again, shifting and flickering, then vanished once more.

Kiy ran back inside, up to the next deck, and to the bridge.

'Mr Tanthar,' Mestphura said, eyeing Kiy's dripping clothes. 'Is everything alright?'

Kiy blinked, willing his eyes to focus on the blurs outside. He swept a wet fringe from his forehead. 'I saw...'

Mestphura followed Kiy's gaze. He scanned the sky for several seconds, then said, 'I don't see anything.'

Kiy searched the horizon, looking for the distortion in the air. He thought he caught sight of it again, but the raindrops on the windows blurred his view and made him uncertain. He groaned inwardly. He was going to sound delusional if he tried to explain.

'Sorry, Commander.' He paused. 'I just... I could have sworn I saw an Ealvin Hawk. I think it must have flown on. My apologies for the distraction.'

Mestphura looked delighted. 'Not at all, Mr Tanthar. The Ealvin Hawk would be a truly wondrous sight in these parts —in this weather, especially. I had not thought you a man so driven by nature.'

Kiy nodded pleasantly, recalling Mestphura's quarters. *You can tell a lot about a man by the way he decorates his surroundings.*

The Azrunite commander returned to the centre of the bridge, and Kiy slipped out into the rain again. He studied the horizon closely, his hands into his pockets. If there was something out there, the *Akron* would be able to see it, he figured. Nothing could hide from this damn ship. And yet...

He descended the exterior steps to the main deck level. He decided to wander the length of the ship, as he often did when his time was his own. It was an enormous craft, but the actual habitable parts didn't go that far. Most of it was a solid, inaccessible mass, encased in layers of automation. It was like a big organic creature, a bird of glass and steel, being steered by a small host of human riders. The crew complement was less than a hundred, on a ship the size of the *Municipal*.

As he entered the aircraft storage area, he noticed Leo talking with a few other crewmembers. Kiy hovered out of sight, eavesdropping on the conversation.

'So how about today?'

Officer Kerowan regarded Leo with her small smile. 'Yeah, he can fly with us. We're not doing anything dangerous.'

'Prikolnah. Wicked cool.' Marc Nareem grinned at Leo. 'You ready then, little buddy?'

'Man, am I ever!'

'We'll be doing a training exercise: difficult weather flying,' Elzie explained. 'It's easy going, we're just taking advantage of the poor visibility for some practice.' She threw a sideways glance at Marc. 'Having you in the back will maybe stop Marc here from dickin' around so much.'

'Hey!' Marc said indignantly. 'I'll have you know I intend to dick around just as much as usual.'

Elzie handed Leo a yellow flight suit and gave them both a salute, which Marc returned sharply and Leo returned clumsily. She chuckled at the sight and then turned for the door. When she saw Kiy, the smile subsided, and she continued past him without a word.

Kiy approached Leo and Marc. 'So,' he said, looking at the flight suit in Leo's arms. 'You're going out in a skyfighter.'

'Yeah,' Leo said. 'Why, aren't I allowed?' It sound more like a challenge than a question.

Kiy wanted to tell him he wasn't. He couldn't bear the thought of anything going wrong, because he couldn't bear the thought of returning to Hennie and her mother to tell them Leo wasn't coming home. But Kiy was nothing if not a risk-taker. He'd feel a hypocrite to bar Leo simply because it might be dangerous.

He shrugged. 'Fine with me.'

Leo looked to Marc. 'Marc, this is Kiy. He works for my Ma sometimes.'

'Kiy, huh?' Marc offered a firm handshake. 'Nice to meet ya, pal.'

Kiy shook Marc's hand rigidly.

Marc explained the manoeuvres they would be doing, while Leo climbed into his flight suit. The Azrunite helped the boy clip the smooth white metal attachments in place as he talked.

'So, there's room for both of you in one?' Kiy asked.

'Yep!' Leo chirped. 'They're Foxtails, Kiy.'

'Foxtails? You fly Brazakker planes?'

'Azrunite versions, but yeah, that's the dealio,' Marc said. Kiy could tell Marc had a passion for such things.

The Azrunite led them through to the aircraft storage area. 'The Foxtail's a damn fine flier to begin with,' He told them. 'But our special variants have some serious kit to push them to the next level.'

A large rack of planes were suspended from the roof of the tall compartment by crane arms. Kiy scarcely recognised them as Foxtail duplanes. Each one sat in a steel cradle, immaculate and shiny in white with gold trim, their glossy paintwork shining in the cold fluorescent light of the fighter bay. These planes were far removed from the brazen, worn workhorses of Brazak West; they were like show models of a vehicle he'd never seen new.

The Foxtail was a fairly short plane with a generous wingspan. It had two engine pods, one on either wing, each one sporting triple-blade propeller engines and vertical fins. The wings crossed through the fuselage towards the back end, with a canard at the front for pitch control. But unlike the Foxtails Kiy was used to, these featured a number of strange attachments and additions.

'Bet you're wondering what this is.' Marc motioned to a bulky but smooth and curvy device fixed to either side of the fuselage behind the pilot. It had a ribbed form, as though it contained a coil.

'Some sort of air conditioning?' Kiy ventured.

Marc laughed. 'Ha! Nope, this... is a mag-shield generator.'

Leo gave an incredulous look.

'Yep, that's right,' Marc said. 'These things are shielded from bullets.'

'No way!' Leo gaped.

'Yeah way!' Marc said with pride. 'Using super strong magnetic... uh.' He looked at it. 'Actually, I gotta be honest, I don't really know how they work. Ask Zi.'

'Zi?' Leo asked.

'Elzie.' Marc seemed to be hit by a thought. 'Man... don't know what's gotten into her lately, y'know. She's a sweetheart usually, when she gets to know you. Been a bit... skiffy lately.'

Leo glanced knowingly at Kiy.

'But anyway,' Marc continued, 'she's been flying skyfighters her whole life. Can talk to machines like nobody else.'

Kiy frowned. 'Talk to machines?'

'Calputers. She knows about Gold Age tech. She could tell you loads about this stuff. All I know about the shield thing is, it pushes off anything but a perfect hit. A lot like the *Akron*'s one.' He leant casually against the plane. 'Unfortunately we ain't got fusion reactors on a skyfighter, so you can't keep it on all the time. Couple of seconds, tops.'

Leo nodded attentively.

'And this thing here,' Marc continued around the craft, 'is what we call the Pivot Break.' He tapped a fixture on the underside that ran almost from nose to tail. It was punctuated by black rectangles and had the awkward look of an implant.

'What does that do?' Leo said.

'Uses gryos and a quick burst of Repulsors to turn on the spot.' Marc flashed a cocky grin. 'Not easy to do, and, man! It throws you about a lot. But, ah... pretty good fun.'

'Turns on the spot?' Kiy asked. The Foxtail was already renowned for its manouevreability. He could scarcely envision why someone would put such a thing on a plane that almost turned on a floril anyway.

'Airman Nareem is the only one in the squadron able to pull off a successful one-eighty reversal,' Elzie said, striding across the hangar towards them. She had changed into her yellow flightsuit like the others. 'The process runs contrary to a plane's design and makes them near-impossible to control. He's probably my best flyer.'

'Naw!' Marc laughed. 'You're jus' sayin'.'

'You won't be pulling off anything like that today, will you?' Kiy asked.

'Jeez, Kiy!' Leo complained.

'Not likely,' Elzie replied flatly, inspecting the plane with a glass pad on her forearm. 'Marc, you're in the way, you lug. I can't see the pitot tube.'

Marc stepped aside sheepishly.

As Elzie checked out the duplane, other pilots started entering the fighter bay and checking their own planes. Marc waved Leo over to the craft beside Elzie's and slapped a big hand on the nose-cone.

'This beauty is mine,' he said, turning to Leo. 'Hop in.'

Leo eagerly climbed the stepladder and scrambled into the rear of the cockpit. There was no seat as such, just a small padded area behind the pilot.

Kiy watched Elzie as she slid open the canopy of her own plane and climbed into her cockpit. She glanced over at him, then looked away as though he wasn't there.

'Comfy, sport?' Marc asked Leo. From the stepladder, he handed Leo a harness and fixed him down in the back. Leo gave Kiy a grin and a wave.

Kiy couldn't help but smile back. He remembered the first time his father had put him in the seat of a plane. He'd never been so scared in his life. Never again, he'd sworn. And yet, here he was getting from place to place on the end of a glorified piece of string attached to a magnet. He couldn't quite say why aerofoil craft made him uncomfortable. Childhood experiences can be odd that way.

A crewman came over and politely told him he would need to step back behind the black and yellow stripes. Kiy nodded and moved to the corner of the bay.

'Clear!' Elzie yelled. She fired up the magnetos and her craft's twin Mithron engines roared to life. The rest of the squadron followed suit, and from across the storage bay could be heard the hums of pistons and the roars of spinning blades slapping at the air. The noise was incredible. Eight aircraft, each with a pair of V12 engines, singing in a mechanical chorus.

The wall through to the main airstrip began to fold away, and the cradles smoothly slid across the ceiling-rails, carrying their planes over the deck. As they passed into the larger hangar area, they swivelled around and lined up on the runway. At either end were wide openings leading outside, although currently the rear entrance was meshed with a bracing grid formed by thick white straps.

Kiy watched the aircraft form up. When the forward doors slid open, the engines of the skyfighters roared louder. Kiy could feel the wind rushing through the hangar, in through the front doors and out the back, and eight planes now hummed in the slipstream. He watched in fascination as the cradles released in quick succession and each fighter leapt out into the sky.

Inside Marc's skyfighter, the second from last in the lineup, Leo gripped the seat in front of him with anticipation. There was a dull clunk as the latch released them and Marc throttled the engines to full power. The fighter pounced forward, and a tremendous force of acceleration threw Leo to the back of the little compartment. Around him the hangar vanished, and he was suddenly out in the grey skies, droplets gathering on the canopy.

The plane banked gently, moving to join the staggered column of skyfighters assembling in formation off the *Akron*'s port side. Leo craned his neck in wonder at the view. Marc glanced over his shoulder and grinned. He twisted the plane around in a victory roll, and the world spun on demand.

'How 'bout that, eh, fella?' he said over the headset.

'Prikolnah!' Leo yelled back with a grin.

22 - A Loyal Soldier

Laronor
September 14th

The Worker's Hammer heaved with more patrons than Hennie could care to count, the cramped bar area compressing them into a solid mass of people. It was hot—the stifling, moist heat of nearly a hundred active bodies—and the stench of dried lager was everywhere. Cups clattered and plates clanked, and chattering voices rose with the booming laughter of men and shrieks and giggles of women.

Hennie weaved between tables hurriedly, carrying a tray of empty glasses. As she placed the tray on the bar, she caught the gaze of a man sat in the corner. It wasn't the first time she'd caught him looking at her tonight, but as before, he quickly looked away, staring instead into his drink. He was really making that one drink last.

'Three Puff Guineas and a Vodstok for fourteen!' Aleece called merrily, dumping the drinks on Hennie's tray. The thick-handled glasses of the Puff Guineas spilled more alcohol onto the tray.

Hennie looked at them with exhaustion on her face. 'Gotcha,' she said to no-one, as Aleece had already disappeared back into the kitchen.

Hennie hurried for table fourteen—though there wasn't really much hurrying in an establishment like the Hammer. It was more a constant stream of excusings and apologies as she forced her way through the crowd.

Suddenly a large man beside her stood up quickly, catapulting her tray into the air. Drinks went flying, at least a half dozen people got wet, and glasses shattered against the floor.

'Stupid slooka!'
'Watch where you're going!'
'Look at this jacket, it's ruined!'

Angry voices jeered at her, and she felt her face redden. It wasn't even her fault—but she dared not say that aloud. Instead she tried to apologise to the angry patrons, but of course they were indifferent to her words.

'I reckon she owes us a night's drinks!'

'Yeah, and the rest!' There were laughs at that.

Hennie's expression soured. *Just you try it.*

'Cut the girl some slack,' came a voice with an exotic accent—Valyan, perhaps. Or maybe Brazak East.

'What's it got to do with you?' one of the angry patrons growled.

'I'm just sayin'! Jeez, lighten up, you drunk.' The voice was impatient and condescending at the same time. Hennie finally saw the man behind it: it was the same man who had been gazing over his glass at her for hours. He was wiry and toned, with a trim survival physique, but no prizefighter. And by the way he was dressed, he was either a homeless bum or doing a fantastic job of impersonating one.

'You wanna take this outside?' the angry man said.

Hennie felt her throat tighten, and hoped Aleece would hurry up and make an appearance before things got any more uncomfortable.

The man in the corner looked away dismissively. 'You aren't even worth the trouble.'

Fury glowed on the face of the burly patron. He was heavy and thick-limbed, with a large feral beard—a merchant crewman, judging by the slack trousers and baggy shirt with dark waistcoat. 'Oh, no trouble at all! Laying you out would be a breeze, you half-pint little eastern hen.'

The man in the corner glared back. 'You wanna say that to my face?'

The angry patron lunged. The wiry man dodged to one side and threw his table forward, catching the patron on the knee and causing him to stumble. Immediately four of the angry patron's friends launched themselves at the wiry man. After that, everything became a blur.

Hennie yelled at them to stop, but the room was now so loud she couldn't even hear herself. There were cheers and cries, shrieking from one of the girls, and the action was hard to follow.

Then Aleece appeared. Her high-pitched, almighty yell rose above the din, and with that, it was all over. The angry deckhands backed off. The wiry homeless man was sprawled on the floor, dripping blood and crawling slowly.

'Who started this?' Aleece demanded, holding a huge knife from the kitchen. She was terrifying when she had to be, Hennie thought.

People backed away from the five deckhands.

'Alright, you five, ged'out. Now! This ain't a place for fightin'.' Aleece waved the knife at them.

Grumbling, the deckhands left, one of them throwing his empty glass to the floor. The sound of the splintering glass made Hennie flinch. The Hammer had gone quieter than she'd ever heard it.

'You too.' Aleece had her other hand on her hip, stood over the battered and bleeding homeless man. 'Ged'out.'

'Aleece, it's alright. He was just trying to stick up for me,' Hennie said, stepping forward. She was unsure of the homeless man at best, but she couldn't help but feel kinda sorry for the poor guy.

Aleece's mouth twisted. 'Fine. Then take him roun' back and get him cleaned up. You got five minutes, chucks.'

'Yeah, can we get our order please?' came a woman's voice impatiently.

Hennie shot the woman a sour look, then took the bleeding man by the shoulders and led him through to the kitchens. She sat him in a quiet spot near the back doors and began to run some soap and water. Fetching ice from the pantry, she wrapped some in a cloth towel and instructed him to place it against the swelling bruise on his forehead.

'Thanks,' he said gruffly.

'No problem. Guess I owe you thanks as well.'

He shrugged.

'What's your name?'

'Karak.'

'Hennie. Nice to meet you.' She began to sponge blood off his arm. 'That was very brave, what you did.'

'The guy was dissin' me,' Karak said. 'He had it coming.'

Hennie grinned to herself. 'A lesson he won't soon forget.'

'So I got a few scratches in the process.'

She squinted at him. She still couldn't place that accent. 'Where is it that you're from?'

He sighed. 'I'm a southerner. My parents were Capridori, so, yeah, I gotta funny accent. Big flakkin' deal.'

'Sorry, I didn't mean to sound like I was accusing you of anything.'

'Sure.'

She wrung out the sponge into a basin, trying to ignore the bright crimson that turned the water to a thin red soup. 'I'm from the south too, you know.'

Karak didn't respond. She figured he didn't want to talk about it, so she changed the subject. 'So, what do you do?'

'Nothing.'

She dabbed the wound again. 'Do you have anywhere to go?'

He considered the question. 'Not really.'

Hennie went quiet. She was unsure what to say to that. She felt she ought to offer him something, but she didn't have anything to give.

Karak seemed to read her thoughts. 'It's okay. You don't have to put a roof over me. I can get by.'

'No, it's okay,' Hennie started to say, then stopped herself. She wanted to help, but she'd learned her lesson about being too trusting in the city. Maybe Jerra could help. 'Listen, I'll see what I can do.'

'Much obliged. I ain't a begging man, you must understand.' At the look she made, he frowned. 'Oh, I'm sure they all say that, all the bums that come in here on their knees.'

'I can't say that they do.' Hennie dabbed disinfectant onto his cuts.

'I was a military man, once.' He barely flinched as the anti-septic seared each wound. 'I've been out of work for some time.'

'Really?' Hennie couldn't help but imagine Feo roaming the city, down on her luck. How could a nation cast aside someone who would have laid down their life for it? It infuriated her. 'You deserve better, Karak. And you'll get it, I'll see to that.'

'Thank you, Hennie.' He leant back, eyes closed, and for the first time, he smiled.

23 - Danger Uncovered

Minataway
September 15th

Kiy watched Marc's plane swoop up into the sky, closely followed by Elzie's fighter. They became hazy shapes in the moist grey clouds. As he watched Elzie climb, he wondered what was going on in that woman's mind. Marc had said she was acting up. Maybe it wasn't him at all, he mused. It could be something else entirely. Had he judged her too harshly?

'Beautiful machines, aren't they?' Gatista stood beside him.

Not really, Kiy thought. 'Yeah.'

They were in a glass-like bubble that jutted out of the airship, providing a grand view of the spectacle. And a dry one, too, although the rain had died down to a barely noticeable drizzle.

'Used to fly them myself. Not these days though.' Kiy didn't think Gatista looked particularly old, but he was certainly older than the fresh-faced young men and women that had climbed into the planes.

'I try to avoid it wherever possible,' Kiy admitted. 'Not a fan of 'foils.'

'The Aerofoil is the purest form of flight,' Gatista said. 'Older than the stars of the night sky. Repulsors may push for a moment; Antimass can suspend a huge ship; even floatrock is just delaying the inevitable. As far as nature's concerned, it's all about the wing. Just look at the birds.'

He motioned to the gulls flying alongside the ship, gracefully swooping from side to side.

'Wings aren't much good if they stop,' Kiy said.

Gatista shrugged. 'They're good for those that don't do much stopping, then.' He let the words linger a moment, then stepped back into the main ship.

Aboard Marc's fighter, Leo relished in the swaying, jerking, twisting flightpath. He watched the rest of the squadron, then looked over at the *Akron*. As it started to pass into the rear view, a series of bright flashes exploded across it.

'Wow!' he cried out. 'Were those real?'

'What's that?' Marc said.

'The *Akron*! Look, there they are again.'

'What?' Marc looked over his shoulder, and his eyes went wide. 'Shyut!'

He wrenched the plane suddenly to the side and began to make a tight turn. Leo gripped the handles on either side of him, letting out a yelp of both excitement and fear. He suddenly felt much heavier, as though his arms weighed more than the massive cannon shells on the *Municipal*.

'Lancet One, did you catch those hits on *Akron*? Copy.' Marc's tone had changed instantly to one of uncharacteristic professionalism.

'Confirmed, Lancet Two,' Elzie's voice came over the comm. 'What in the moons was that?'

'Heck if I know.'

Kiy picked himself up and gathered his senses. It took him a moment to figure out where he was. There was something hauntingly familiar about the place. It was an awful place, from long ago. Only... it was different somehow.

The deep warbling klaxon of a Brazakker warship was replaced with a piercing, short 'whoop' sound that repeated like an anxious heartbeat. Pulsing neon blocks of light, arranged along the line where the walls met the ceiling, washed the corridors in a vivid orange.

The Akron. *That's right. I'm on the* Akron.

He raced to the bridge, climbing the outer stairway and almost leaping through the outer door into the bridge section.

'—and perform a full visual check,' Mestphura was saying sternly. 'There is clearly something out there that our systems cannot detect.'

The crewman who'd recieved the instruction disappeared into the elevator towards the engine room.

Kiy asked, 'Did something hit us?'

'Unclear,' Mestphura said. 'Possibly fire from a stealth ship.'

Stealth ship? Mestphura seemed to know what that was, so Kiy decided to shut up and observe.

The ship shuddered again, which worried Kiy. To him, the *Akron* had seemed untouchable. But Mestphura didn't even change his stance: gazing straight ahead, feet shoulder-width apart, hands locked behind his back. It was as though he were a part of the ship itself.

'Another near hit,' Gatista said. 'Targeting, see if you can track the source.'

'We have something out there alright,' Raldotya reported from the comms station. 'Shots came from zero-two-five. Elevation, approximately ten degrees minus.'

Mestphura nodded. 'Descend one hundred fifty.'

Kaj'aku nodded and slid the appropriate levers into place.

'Sir, Lancet Squadron witnessed the hits, and they are attempting to identify the target,' Raldotya said. 'No visual contact.'

'Very well. Kaj'aku, hold our heading. We want them to think we still don't know where they are. Gatista, prepare dorsal cannons to fire as soon as we identify the flashpoint.'

'Yes, Commander.'

The *Akron* continued to drift along, waiting for its mysterious attacker to make the next move. They didn't have to wait long. There was a shimmer to the starboard side, followed by a volley of shots that narrowly missed the bow.

'Target sighted!'

'Fire!' Mestphura boomed.

The *Akron*'s guns fired at the shimmer. The bridge crew watched the tracers as the shells whistled away and shrank out of sight.

'Negative hit, sir.'

'Commander, the mag deflector—' Raldotya said. 'It's powering down.'

'Why?'

'I don't know. Diagnostic checks out okay, it—it just started the shutdown sequence for no reason.' There was a hint of alarm in Raldotya's voice. 'Sir, it's not responding.'

Mestphura frowned. 'Gatista, go see what you can do.' He turned to Kiy. 'I'd like you to lend him a hand, Mr Tanthar.'

Kiy was about to protest that he knew next to nothing about engineering, least of all when it came to Azrunite mag thingy-flaks. But they probably would need all the hands they could get, skilled or otherwise, so he followed Gatista to the elevator.

They descended half a dozen decks, then hurried down a corridor to a chamber deep within the ship—the Power Plant.

The first thing that struck Kiy about the Power Plant was the complete absence of crew. A Brazakker ship's plant was a steaming hot reactor room filled with dozens of engineers busily tweaking valves and levers, keeping the reactor at optimum efficiency. But this was a completely different kind of engine. Sleek organic panels encased all the workings, and displays quietly conveyed information that, apparently, nobody needed to read. The centre of the room was dominated by a large torus, clad in a plated metallic sheath. Dozens of conduits snaked out from it, many of them with segments like windows. The conduit interiors glowed a luminous light blue.

'It should be possible to override the mag shield from here.' Gatista hit a switch, and a console rose from the floor.

'What do you want me to do?'

'Open that panel there and detach the three blue cables.'

As Kiy headed to the panel, the ship took another hit. A crunching sound was followed by a grumble in the deck.

'We'd better move fast. We're going to start taking serious damage if we can't get the mag deflector back,' Gatista said, punching codes into the console.

Some way out from the ship, Lancet Squadron dived towards the latest sighting of the enemy. Judging by the pattern of shots, the enemy vessel appeared to be circling the *Akron* at a distance of about a kilometre. Visibility was way better than that, yet Lancet couldn't spot it. It didn't add up.

Elzie radioed the *Akron* with her observation.

'Copy that, Lancet One,' Raldotya said over the shortwave. 'We believe they're using some sort of advanced camouflage, rendering them invisible.'

'Say again, *Akron*. Confirm: invisible?'

'Affirm, Lancet One.'

Elzie disengaged the radio and pulled into a steep turn. 'Well, shyut.'

The duplanes swooped down and levelled off parallel to the *Akron* about half a kilometre out. Elzie scanned the horizon for any sign of the enemy, while the rest of the squadron did the same.

Inside Marc's fighter, Leo turned to watch the rear of the canopy, deciding that Marc probably had the front covered. A bright flash caught his eye.

'Marc!'

Marc looked over his shoulder just in time to catch the second muzzle flash.

'Elzie, five o'clock!'

Elzie snapped around to see the fading shimmer. 'Copy that. *Akron*, we have sighting one-eight-zero, abeam starboard at one kay.'

On the *Akron*'s bridge, Raldotya gave a nod. 'Copy that, Lancet One.' She tapped the bearing into the navigation computer, cross-referencing it with the *Akron*'s lookout reports.

'Position triangulated. Enemy craft is orbiting us one point three kilometres approximate. Extrapolating current position: one-six-five.'

'Excellent work,' Mestphura said. 'Kaj'aku, bring us about to starboard.'

'Aye, Commander.'

Mestphura turned to the gunnery intercom and snatched the handset from its hold. 'Attention starboard broadside gunner: prepare to fire on bearing one-six-zero, elevation forty-three degrees.'

'Standing by!' the gunner reported back.

As the *Akron* swung around, her starboard guns lit up in a furious blaze. The whistling shells curved high, then fell, several exploding in puffs of black smoke and flame. But where they struck, the air shimmered and shook—until finally the form of a long and graceful airship appeared. It was gleaming white, with light blue and gold trim.

In Lancet Squadron, Elzie's eyes widened. There was no mistaking: it was an Azrunite ship.

'Commander...' she said into the radio.

'We see it, Lancet Squadron,' Mestphura responded. 'Engage the enemy ship immediately.'

'Clarify! Craft is Azrunite vessel,' Elzie said urgently.

'Noted, Lieutenant. Engage.'

Elzie paused only a moment, allowing the unknown ship to grow bigger in her sights. Then she said, 'Wilco. Lancet Squadron, engage.'

Marc's protest came over her radio at once. 'But it's—'

'Battle orders, Lancet Two!' she snapped back.

The duplanes screeched across the sky, closing in fast on the hostile ship.

Ahead of them, four columns of flame shot up from the slender craft. Elzie stared for only a heartbeat before she realised what they were.

'Anti-ship missiles!' she cried.

'Lancet Squadron,' Raldotya called over the crackling shortwave, 'the mag deflector is still not working. Repeat: we have *no* mag deflector. You must take down those missiles!'

'Copy!' Elzie replied, her heart pounding. 'Squadron, break and intercept! *Now!* Go go go!'

The colossal rockets veered off in four different directions, all of them taking parabolic arcs that would steer them progressively towards the *Akron*.

'Sir!' Raldotya turned to Mestphura on the bridge.

'I see them,' he replied quickly. 'Kaj'aku, turn on three-five-five, full speed!'

'The target is leaving the combat area. Sir,' Raldotya gestured with frustration, 'they're getting away...'

'Never mind the target. Evade those missiles, or we're all going to the Understorm.'

Elzie pulled back on the control column, and her Foxtail went into a steep climb towards the highest of the incoming devices. The airframe shuddered with the tremendous turbulence generated by the rocket motors of the huge anti-ship missile. The missile had started slowly but was quickly accelerating; she knew she had only a couple of seconds at best before it exceeded her maximum speed at such a high climb rate.

She led the crosshair of her Morzer cannon a dozen metres ahead of the missile, and squeezed the trigger. The guns rumbled, and what felt like an agonising amount of time passed as the rounds flew out to meet their target.

Then a shot found its mark, and the engine of the warhead caught fire. Elzie wrenched the plane to one side as the missile exploded in an enormous fireball, throwing her about the cockpit like a stone in a can.

Gatista was starting to lose patience with the system diagnostic. There didn't seem to be anything mechanically wrong, the system just refused to activate the deflector—on the grounds that it simply didn't want to.

The voice of Mestphura came over the speaker in the reactor chamber. 'Attention, Drive Room. We've got three anti-ship missiles incoming, so you've got about sixty seconds to get that deflector working.'

'Isn't there a way of turning these damn things on manually?' Kiy asked. 'You know, like an actual lever?'

Gatista shook his head. 'No—well, we could bypass the starter and hit the deflector power switch directly. But that's not safe to use.'

'Did you not just hear that thing about us getting blown to Hadnar?' Kiy said.

'It's not that simple. The switch is located on the underside. Only accessible via a maintenance ramp in drydock.'

'Well why didn't you say so?' Kiy took his sling from his backpack and slipped it onto his arm. 'What's it look like?'

Gatista squinted. 'Large grey circle, red pullswitch... hang on, what are you doing?'

'Some maintenance,' Kiy said, running out of the chamber.

Lancets Four and Five dodged both ways as the second missile exploded between them in a mighty plume of flame and smoke. Marc was tracking the missile closest to the *Akron*, coming up fast in the opposite direction to him.

'Hold on to something, Leo,' he called. 'We're gonna do a pivot.'

'Oh, crap.' Leo gripped the handholds on either side of him.

The missile came headlong towards them, looking like a small black disc with a bright halo of thick smoke and an orange glow. Leo panicked, thinking they would hit it—but at the last second Marc jerked the plane sideways and pulled the handle on the Pivot Break.

A sophisticated array of flaps and slats extended as the fighter pirouetted and spun to face the opposite direction. Leo felt like the world had just toppled on its axis. His stomach wanted to heave its contents across the compartment, so he clamped his hands over his mouth just in case. They seemed to be hanging in midair, motionless, as the missile thundered past from behind, right into the skyfighter's sights.

Marc pulled the trigger, and glowing tracers spat into the warhead's fuselage, detonating it in a spectacular cloud of debris and fire.

The plane stalled and dipped, and Marc throttled it back up to cruising speed.

Leo whooped. 'That. Was. *Amazing!*'

Marc laughed. 'Alright, we got em all!'

'That was the last one?' Elzie said, diving through a layer of rain-swept cloud.

'You hit one, Taiko and Nirma got the other, and I just hit one.'

'Marc, that's *three*! Who taught you maths?'

'Shyut.'

'Lancet Three, missile sighted, four hundred from *Akron*!'

Marc spotted it and slammed the power to maximum, cursing. He was still the only one in Lancet Squadron close enough to the *Akron*, and even he looked too far to intercept in time.

'Come on, girl. Run faster. You can catch it,' he muttered assuringly to his Foxtail. The missile crossed his view, closing with the *Akron*, but it was beyond the maximum range of his cannons for even a pot shot. He willed the plane to go faster. He felt like he was flying through crude oil.

The trail of smoke that was the missile got closer and closer to the *Akron* until it seemed right on top of it. Marc couldn't bring himself to watch.

With a flash of blue energy, the missile abruptly flung itself downwards as though it had forgotten what it came for. It dived into the sky another few hundred metres then seemed to stop in midair. Marc stared in disbelief as the warhead became a little circle with a flaming halo.

'What the—'

By the time he realised what was happening, it was too late. Damn! How many times had Elzie told him? Constant bearing, constant danger.

He flicked the duplane away, but the missile was already on top of them. A fraction of a second later the warhead detonated.

Beneath the belly of the Azrunite airship, Kiy hung from an opened access panel, from which he had pulled down a red circuit breaker. He watched the missile curve back the way it had come, then explode into a fantastic fireball.

Relief washed over him, and he almost relaxed to the point of letting go and drifting down into the clouds. That had been way too close. The mag deflector had got the damn thing, but not a moment too soon.

It was then he noticed an object trailing smoke from the wave of the explosion, spiraling downward. It was a Foxtail —and it was in trouble. A sickening dread swelled in Kiy's stomach as the plane plunged into the thick rainclouds below and out of sight.

24 - Karak's Plight

Laronor
September 18th

Grumbling black clouds swathed Laronor in heavy rain, the wind ploughing it across rooftiles and walkways in sporadic gusts. Water came down relentlessly, channelled along gutters, piped this way and that, gushing over the edges of paths and out of overflow tanks, falling into a mist as it disappeared into the endless sky.

Droplets on the windows glinted in the warm light emanating from the Worker's Hammer. The pub sat on the corner of two large intersecting prospekts that were empty but for a scruffy man selling newspapers from a wheeled stand, a little canopy giving him meagre shelter.

Inside the Hammer, the raindrops sounded a cosy, muffled beat, and the establishment's usual rancour was only a busy background chatter. At a table in the corner, Hennie sat opposite Karak, sipping on a mug of hot chocolate as he sipped a beer. The grey, misty view outside was warped by the countless sliding, meandering drops on the pane.

'You do me a great kindness, Hennie,' Karak said.

Hennie blushed. 'That's alright. It's nice to have company on a break now and then.'

He leant back, resting his elbows on the long back of the seat. 'You have any soldiers in the family?'

'My older sister. And my Aunt Lydia was a famous fighter pilot in the war.' She gave a self-conscious smile, playing with a strand of hair. 'Um, the other war, now, I guess.'

'Lydia Litvyak? That does ring a bell.' Karak tipped his glass. 'Well, here's to them. May they have many a proud battle!' He took a long swig.

'Yeah.' Hennie chewed her lip. 'My sister was killed a few weeks ago, when Ganzabar sank the *Lykomin*.'

'Oh,' Karak said to his beer. 'I'm sorry, I didn't realise.'

'It's okay. I used to fall apart every time I thought of her, but she died protecting us all from the Ganzabi. I should be thankful for that.'

Karak looked eager to change the subject. 'It's a good vocation. I'd do anything to go back to it.'

'How'd you end up on the streets anyway? You look fighting fit.'

Karak caught the phrase with a sly look, and Hennie flushed red.

'Not a pretty story,' Karak said. 'I won't go into it. There was some corruption high up, and I got the boot for it. Suffice to say my military career was over and I've been struggling to find work since.'

'That's terrible.'

'Oh, but I do miss a rifle in my hands. Might as well be lame, you know. It'd be the same difference.'

'Well,' Hennie said, 'perhaps you could work for the Militsya.'

'Law enforcement, huh?' Karak looked amused. 'I don't think I'd have any better luck. The corruption ran high.' He took a few large gulps of his beer, then sat in thought. His eyes darted towards the other patrons, but all of them were engaged in their own noisy conversations, oblivious to them.

'I've heard that,' Hennie said to fill the pause. She watched Karak with a kind of nervous fascination.

Finally he took a breath and leant in close. She could smell the beer on his breath. 'I do know how I could get my old job back,' he said. 'Although... I'll need your help.'

'Me? How?'

'You seen that big station in the upper sky? The one to the south?'

'Yeah, I have,' Hennie said, intrigued. 'It's a Gundar, right?'

'That's right. A huge defensive installation, part fortress and part mega-cannon. Ninety-metre barrel, calibre the size of an autocab...' He took another swig. 'That's where it happened. If I can get back there, I—I might be able to set things straight.'

'I don't know how to get there.'

'Hennie!' Karak said, his voice suddenly impassioned. 'You're a tough girl! You can do something like this, I can tell. You've got it in you.'

She blushed. 'So if you just get back to the Gundar, you can fix your career?'

'I'll be able to make my family proud again,' he assured her.

Hennie hesitated, then gave him a firm nod. 'Alright. I'll help if I can.'

'Thank you.' Karak bowed his head gratefully. 'You're an angel.'

'It's the least I can do,' Hennie replied, standing up. 'Anyway, I have to go. Gotta start my shift.'

'Of course. Adyu, Hennie.'

Hennie managed an awkward wave, then made her way back to the bar.

25 - Hold Back

Wirral Drift Defensive Installation,
65 kilometres from Laronor
September 23rd

A multitude of angular shapes slithered like daggers through the clear, cloudless blue. The Ganzabi fleet drew closer to a cluster of structures set upon layered metal platforms.

On the bridge of the *Grace of Gnost*, Admiral Moller surveyed the defences he was up against. The situation for the Brazakkers of the Wirral Drift outpost looked hopeless. Moller's fleet numbered over fifty major ships, while only a few light escorts protected the installation.

'Fleet in position, sir,' Lieutenant Fredson said. 'What are your orders?'

Moller rubbed the bottom of his chin with a thumb. 'I want *Fourth Nexus* and *Faithful Servant* to engage the two escorts.'

'And the platform?'

'They will have abandoned it by now. There's no way they can hold off this fleet. They aren't suicidal.'

'Very well, sir.' Fredson began tapping out the orders over the Transpulse.

Shortly after he'd sent the message, six smaller ships broke away from the main formation in two groups, filing one behind the other.

'Forgive me, sir,' Fredson said, watching them go. 'But is a three-to-one ratio over our enemies not pushing the boundaries of what is honourable?'

Moller half shrugged. 'It is on the limits of honour—you are quite correct.' He looked down his nose at the distant enemy group. 'But do not mistake me for the countess.'

'My apologies,' Fredson said.

The debacle with the *Lykomin* had brought on mixed feelings amongst the Ganzabi Navy. For the most part it had brought the morale boost that always comes with a crushing victory—but the countess's methods for that victory had been weak and decadent. Outnumbering and outgunning their lone, lightly escorted opponent by over six to one, she had swept them away mercilessly. The *Lykomin* was reported to have refused surrender before she sank with all hands. That had kept Naval Command happy with the outcome, but there was just no honour without a fair (or at least partially favoured) fight. And then there was her cowardly new ship...

Suddenly the guns on the Brazakker platform opened up on *Nexus* and *Faithful*, which turned to evade despite the shots flying wide. As they broke formation, the defender ships leapt forward with hit-and-run attacks, isolating the slower Ganzabi vessels so as to concentrate fire on them. The foremost of the Ganzabi ships lit up with flame and pulled away from the fray.

'Perhaps they're stupider than we thought,' Fredson said.

'Or smarter,' Moller murmured icily. It wasn't like Brazakkers, taking a stand here at Wirral Drift with so little to offer. Still, the Armada was getting closer to Risley with each day, and was probably just a hundred kilometres from the nearest Gundar. Perhaps it was all they had left to buy time.

'You see, we must exercise caution against these Brazakkers,' Moller said as they watched their ships put some distance between themselves and the platform. 'We are not dealing with the simple, honest peasants of Lystrata anymore. These northfolk are sly and knavish. They will sooner burn a city and fall back, than clutch on their floatrock while we take shots. You might think such cowardice would allow us to defeat them more easily, but in truth, their calculating tenacity only makes them more dangerous.'

'So therefore, remaining on the platform only proves their own weak desperation,' Fredson surmised.

'Perhaps. But it does mean we will need to reconsider our attack plan. A frontal assault on that platform could be costly, despite being a certain victory. We need to ensure we retain ample ships to attack the Gundar.'

The admiral watched the fort carefully. Floatrock installations generally supported much greater mass, enabling them to carry more weapons and heavy fortifications. The downside was that they were a huge effort to position anywhere.

'We can take it,' Fredson said, his eyes narrowing. 'We have the ships, and they are superior to our enemy's.'

Ah, the arrogance of youth, Moller thought, not without some nostalgia. Lieutenant Fredson was no older than thirty, a promising student and something of a protégé. But this was his first actual tour of duty, compared to Moller's six. He had much to learn.

'You miss the point.' Moller made no effort to coat his chiding. 'We need the ships, and the supplies, in order to be successful at Laronor. We've met with stronger resistance than we anticipated, and the fleet is already down to two-thirds strength after the fiasco at Mosleyhead.'

Fredson hung his head a little. 'Forgive me, sir. I cannot help but be a patriot.'

'A patriot is not a fool who gets his fleet sunk,' Moller said evenly. 'He is a man who makes his country great. But for you there is still time to learn. Don't be hesitant to voice your opinion with me, Fredson.'

'Yes, sir.'

A tall young man strode up to Moller and saluted. 'Sir.'

'Yes?' Moller didn't look round.

'The Countess de Saufon reports that she is luring the Azrunites to the Beyer Fields, with the Fourth Fleet moving into position.'

What is she playing at? Moller gritted his teeth in irritation. He was trying to conduct a serious military operation, but was lumbered with an unreliable noble more interested in frocks than fleets. Enough was enough; she needed to understand her place. After all, few things were as unsettling and dangerous as an unruly woman.

'Get on the Transpulse and command her to return to formation. She's taken too long. We are losing the initiative.'

'Admiral, if I may be so bold,' Fredson offered. 'If we were to capture the *Akron*, it would give us a far more powerful advantage than anything the Brazakkers can pull together in the next few days. With the *Akron*, our victory would be more than likely—it would be overwhelming.'

Moller hmmed.

'Just think,' Fredson splayed his fingers enthusiastically, 'a Gold Age, Wingstar-class battleship.' He let the thought sink in. 'You taught me that nothing in this world is invincible, sir. But I believe the *Akron* is the next best thing.'

'And how do you suppose the countess will take it?'

'She has a way of getting things she wants,' Fredson said with a smirk.

Moller nodded grimly. 'She does, at that. Very well, Mr Fredson.' He looked at the tall messenger. 'Ensign, belay that last order. Tell her I want progress reports, and she is not to spend any longer than three days. Then she is to return to formation.'

'Of course, sir.' The man saluted and left.

Fredson watched him go, then turned to the admiral. 'What about the fleet orders, sir?'

Moller cleared his throat, straightening. 'The fleet is to hold back.'

26 - Bella

Laronor
September 29th

Hennie and Jerra met the following evening outside the Empire Arms factory in Voxton. Hennie told Jerra about what had happened at the Worker's Hammer with Karak.

'Anyway, he wants me to take him to the Gundar,' Hennie said.

Jerra balked. 'The Gundar? How?'

'Sky knows. Wish there was something I could do.'

Jerra shook her head pityingly. 'Poor soul. It does not seem right to me, Hennie, that we treat our soldiers with such ill care. Perhaps you could ask my father—'

'Heeey!' a melodic young man's voice called. 'How are we today, Jerra m'lovely?'

She smiled shyly. 'Oh, hello Sput.'

The owner of the voice was a young man, maybe a year or two older than Hennie, and he regarded her with a keen look. 'This her, pet?'

'Yes.'

Sput winked at Hennie with a cheeky grin. 'Heard what ya did, heard what ya did. Liked it very much—Hennie, was it?'

Hennie eyed the young man, who was buzzing around them like some human-sized fly. 'Yeah—what do you want?'

'Oh, nothing, nothing. I'm a talker. Like to talk. Like to sing, but that's another story.'

Hennie wasn't sure what to make of this young man, but he was obviously acquainted enough with Jerra that he didn't seem a threat. 'What are you talking about? What did I... "do"?'

The boy chuckled. 'Ah, you socked Big Bella, right in the face. 'S'why I think I'm gonna like ya.'

'Okay...'

'You must be new round this part o' town. Laronor's a fine city, y'know. Gem o' all the Brazaks. But it can be kinda rough, 'specially round our way.'

'I'm surprised you're still breathin',' Hennie remarked. Jerra smiled.

'Oh, I'm no trouble-stirrer, Hennie-me-lovely. I'm a gentleman. A gentleman's gentleman. Oh, a lady's gentleman too, of course. Oh! But that goes without saying.'

Hennie folded her arms, hoping to make a point.

'So I guess what I was gonna say was, you ever considered joining the infantry? We could use a brave soul like yourself.'

'Not a chance,' Hennie said. 'I couldn't do that to my mother.'

'Fair enough, m'lovely, fair enough. But what about the Reserve?'

'The what?'

'You've 'eard of it, right? The Laronor Reserve. They need ev'ry able and fit lad 'n' lass who can carry a Bluebell and knows how to shoot.'

'Sky's sake!' Hennie rolled her eyes. 'How many times... I don't want to fight in this damn war.'

'Nor do I, dear Hennie,' Jerra interjected. 'But should Ganzabar attack, they will not likely heed such protestations. I profess, I too am a member of the Reserve.'

'You... you are?' Hennie was dumbstruck.

Jerra nodded. 'I'll not stand idle while the Ganzabi violate my home. I shall not look for trouble, but if they come here, I shall be ready.'

Sput nodded. 'Unlike us, the Reserves only fight the enemy when they trespass on our isles.'

Hennie considered. What Jerra said seemed sensible enough. And the more Hennie thought about it, the more she felt vulnerable at the notion of being just another unarmed civilian at the mercy of invading foreigners. After what they had done to Feo, no way was she letting them walk over her.

'Okay, Sput,' she said. 'Where do I sign?'

It was the end of the week before they saw Big Bella again. She loomed out of the shadows of the evening streets, this time accompanied by a gang of five teenagers armed with sharp sticks and bits of pipe, none older than Hennie herself. By the time she had become aware of the gang's approach, they had mostly surrounded her and Jerra.

'Turn around and walk home your separate ways or yer gonna regret it,' Big Bella said, hands on her hips. There was a big plaster on her nose, and Hennie spotted the boy with the black eye she'd dished out. Neither looked like they'd give her an easy time for it.

Jerra shrank back. Hennie could see her impulse to run, and no doubt Bella could see it too.

What would Kiy do in this situation? The image of him with the tomato came back to her. *Never give your opponent the opportunity for an easy victory*. Yes, running was the *worst* thing to do. If she and Jerra split up and ran, they would each be alone.

'Flak you,' Hennie said loudly, bracing her stance. 'We're not stupid.'

Bella snorted. 'Yer don't look like it.'

'We're not afraid of you.' Hennie narrowed her eyes.

'Yer need to understand who's in charge,' Bella said. 'Yer do what I flakkin' tell ya round 'ere.'

'I don't think so,' Hennie replied boldly. She really hoped Jerra was looking braver than she felt herself. 'Sure, you could fight us. Maybe you'll beat us. But we'll hurt you. We'll *really* hurt one of you.' She eyed the short boy with glasses. 'The one we hurt could be you. How bad do you wanna get hurt today?'

Bella laughed. 'You think you're flakkin' scary, like? Who the flak d'ya think y'are? Stupid slooka.'

Don't back down, Hennie thought. Hennie's mother always maintained that bullies were cowards at heart. Maybe that wasn't always true, but Kiy, too, had often said that most battles were fought on intimidation. Besides, Hennie didn't have a whole lot of options.

'You know I can hurt you.' She clenched her fists. 'And those two know I *will*.' She pointed at the two boys she'd seen off last time they met.

Bella thrust a finger at her. 'Right, I'm gonna show this southern flakwit a thing or two. If Shorty tries anythin'— deck 'er.'

Hennie steeled herself as Bella strode towards her ominously. She sensed Jerra backing away behind her. Seemed it would be just the two of them.

Bella lunged, and Hennie found herself on her back, trying to throw the taller girl off her. She'd only ever been in one real fight, years ago in school, and it had been a tame affair. This was different; Bella's fighting style was visceral, raw and unbounded. She landed blows with street malice and savvy forethought.

Bella's fist knocked the wind out of her, then she pressed the side of Hennie's face to the walkway. Hennie grasped for the bigger girl's hair, then wrenched at it. Bella rolled off with a yelp, and Hennie scrambled up. She threw a punch, but Bella pushed her arm aside and hit her square in the jaw. Hennie stumbled back in a daze.

Bella grabbed Hennie's hair and pulled her closer so she could deliver a knee to the ribs. Hennie winced with the pain, but steeled herself for a second blow. As it came, she grabbed Bella's leg and threw her own weight forward. Bella fell back, with Hennie landing on top of her.

Hennie was about to strike again, but seeing Bella on the ground and looking in serious pain, Hennie faltered. Bella seized the opportunity. She lashed out suddenly, drawing blood and sending Hennie spinning.

Hennie blinked to steady her vision. She was lying on her front, rising slowly to a knee. The next thing she knew, her head was wrenched back by the hair, and Bella had her in an armlock.

'I'm gonna break yer flakkin' head open,' she hissed.

'No, stop!' Jerra called out. 'Please...' She began to rush in, but Bella's friends pounced, and a scuffle erupted.

Bella tugged harder on Hennie's hair. 'I'm gonna make yer sorry y'were ever born...' She pulled Hennie's arm back until she cried out in pain.

BLAM.

The thunder of the gunshot startled her so much that Hennie didn't even recognise it at first. For one moment of terror, she thought Bella had shot her in the back, and she wondered why she couldn't feel it. Then Bella let go, and Hennie fell forward onto her palms.

Looking up, she saw the tall figure standing beside them: a man with dark straight hair and a neat beard, both tinged with grey. In his right hand he held a military-issue revolver, now pointed at the sky, barrel smoking.

'Even at a time like now, Brazakkers just can't help but fight each other,' he sighed, lowering the weapon.

'What the flakkin' hadnar—' Bella began.

The man swiftly levelled the long pistol at Bella, holding it outstretched with one hand as though it weighed nothing. It was a heavy iron piece, chipped and worn dark by years of good use, but it still had a certain grace about it. 'Isabella Mortan, I've heard so very much about the trouble you've been stirring lately.'

She stared down the barrel uneasily.

'So I suggest,' he continued, 'that you take your grief elsewhere. If I hear another yap of trouble because of you, you'll be on a Lystratan workship quicker than cholera. Understood?'

Bella nodded quickly, then turned on the spot and scurried away, suddenly looking like little more than a frightened child.

Hennie watched her go with something resembling sympathy. Then she turned back to the man. 'Who are you, and what are you doing pointing guns at kids?'

'Neither of you heard me the two times I called you to stop, which is reason enough for a warning shot. In any case, she would have smashed your brains on the walkway, given the chance.' The man stroked grey whiskers. 'Or perhaps you'd prefer I call her back and she can finish up while we just stand here?'

It was only then Hennie noticed the other three armed men standing some metres away to the left and right. All of them wore the uniform of the Militsiya—a grey tunic with orange shoulder straps and a dull-blue cloak.

'No, sir,' she said at last.

The rest of Bella's lot had run as soon as the Militsiya arrived, leaving just her and Jerra. While Hennie was steeped in cuts and bruises, Jerra appeared to have got away with little more than messy hair and a few rips at the hem of her dress. Evidently, Bella's cronies weren't as dangerous as Bella herself.

'It's pretty clear to me who started this ruckus, so you can both stop looking so bashful,' the man said. Then he turned to Jerra. 'Jerra, what did I tell you?'

Jerra was looking at her feet. 'I know: just avoid her. I'm sorry, Father. It was not easy.'

Hennie raised her eyebrows. So *that's* why they were here. She'd thought the Militsiya's appearance was overkill for a teenage brawl. Then again, she felt Bella might honestly have killed her given half a chance.

The Militsiya man gave a deep sigh, regarding his daughter with an expression that wasn't so much angry as disappointed. 'Sky help you when your mother finds out, child.'

Jerra said nothing.

Hennie looked at the man carefully. 'So you're Jerra's father.'

He holstered the pistol and nodded. 'Sergeant Edwark Rathbone, Laronor Militsiya.'

Rathbone? Jerra had said her surname was Lightlock. Hennie looked at the man carefully. 'Did you say 'Rathbone'?'

He regarded her from head to foot. 'I did indeed. Why do you ask?'

Of course. She remembered now. It was the way of Svalic culture, more common in the north: women kept their surnames after marriage and the children took their mother's. Hennie's mother had once told her about this when explaining why her grandparents had different surnames.

'Do you know a Miles Rathbone?' she asked tentatively.

Edwark raised an eyebrow. 'My brother. Why?' He lay a gentle hand on Jerra's shoulder and took a careful look over her face and limbs for injuries.

Hennie could hardly believe it. A relative. Finally—this was the lucky break she needed. 'Kiy Tanthar sent me here,' she blurted.

Edwark looked at her as though she'd spoken in a foreign tongue. 'I don't recall anyone by that name.'

'Oh. He said your brother Miles might be able to help me.'

Edwark's expression went grim. 'Would that he were still here, perhaps. Miles is missing—presumed dead. At least, according to those who tally the corpses and count the shells.'

'Oh.' Hennie's fortunes plummeted again. 'I'm sorry to hear that.'

'He's a merchant airship captain,' Jerra offered.

Edwark gave an affirming grunt. 'I believe he used to serve with a Tatyana Tanthar back in the old occupation years, now I think on it. He's got his own ship; but strictly cargo these days.'

Hennie considered his choice of words. 'You reckon he's still alive?' she asked.

Edwark half smiled. 'I've got a feeling he's still hanging on somewhere out there, but I couldn't tell you where. It'd be just like him. Though—wishful thinking of the family is something I see every day.' He paused. 'Can't do a damn thing about it, either way.'

Hennie sighed. 'I see.' *What am I supposed to do now?*

'Don't look so down, Hennie. Why were you looking for my uncle?' Jerra asked.

Hennie shook her head sadly. 'My home was in Brudor, but I can't go back. I needed somewhere safe where Kiy can find me, so I—'

'Well then.' Edwark stood, satisfied Jerra had escaped unharmed. 'Why don't you stay with us?'

Jerra smiled. 'Indeed! It is the least we could do.'

Hennie couldn't believe it. It was as though she had become a hundred times lighter. Just the notion of not having to go back to that damp apartment made her spirit soar. 'Really?'

Rathbone's expression warmed. 'Come on, join us for dinner tonight. Roast duck and dumplings.'

'That sounds... amazing.' Hennie's stomach growled at the prospect. She felt like she hadn't eaten in a century.

27 - Pursuit

Minataway
September 15th

'Sir, may I have a word?' Elzie Kerowan strode onto the bridge, fresh from the hangar, her chin-length dark hair messy and her complexion pinkened.

Mestphura appraised her calmly. 'Very well. Come through.'

They entered his office at the rear of the command tower. Kerowan paced the room while Mestphura looked out the window patiently.

Finally she stopped and stared at him. 'Alright. So. What in Hadnar's name is going on here?'

'Would you like to phrase that a little more precisely, Miss Kerowan?' Mestphura said tersely.

'Was that an Azrunite ship that fired on us?'

'It appeared to be.'

Kerowan sighed irritably. 'Permission to speak openly, sir.'

'Denied.' He scratched an eyebrow.

She looked affronted. 'Sir... I don't understand. Why are you covering this up?'

'I am not covering anything, Miss Kerowan. I am merely enforcing discipline on my ship, which presently seems to be greatly needed. Now perhaps if you calm down a little, we might be able to discuss this.'

She took a deep breath. 'Sir, I saw the markings on the vessel before she retreated. I already know its name.' Leaning on the railing that ran beneath the window, she watched the clouds shrink from view as the *Akron* sped past. 'And I think you do too.'

'Are you insinuating that I am keeping details of this mission to myself?' Mestphura sounded more amused than angry. His apparent indifference infuriated her sometimes.

'It's the *Postremo*!' she said, hands held out in exasperation. She waited for a response, but got none. 'What are the honest chances that transfer to this remote region, shortly after the 'loss' of the *Postremo* prototype, is just a staggering co-incidence?'

Mestphura sighed and took a seat at his desk. 'And where is this going?'

She stopped to think. 'Well, the Peace Ministry didn't lose the *Postremo* in an accident; it was taken. And we're here to get it back. But I still don't see the need for you to keep me and the other officers out of the loop, sir. We're your council.'

On that she was right. The complex relationship between an Azrunite commander and their officers was something that few outside the First Navy understood. It was an unwritten code, a kind of symbiosis of trust. Elzie felt a strain on that trust right now, and she didn't like it at all.

'I understand your feelings on this,' Mestphura said. 'I am not fond of having things this way either. But I have my orders. And despite our code, orders must be adhered to first and foremost.'

'So you *have* been keeping this from us.'

Mestphura didn't reply. She tried to wait patiently, but she didn't last very long. Mestphura could out-silence anyone she knew. She let out a grunt of frustration. 'Alright, I don't need to be told what I already know.'

There was a knock on the door.

'Enter,' Mestphura said.

The door slid aside and Officer Raldotya stepped in.

'Yes?' Mestphura said.

Raldotya gave a slight bow, her long black hair falling forward. 'Update on the target. Enemy ship appears to be somewhat damaged and is retreating to an area of dense storm clouds to the south. According to Mr Tanthar, it is known as the Beyer Fields and is highly treacherous.'

'Very well. Set a course to intercept,' Mestphura said. 'Oh, and Officer Raldotya?'

'Yes, Commander?'

'The ship's identity is now known to be the *Postremo*. Miss Kerowan got a look at it herself.'

Raldotya's eyes went wide, and Elzie was taken aback. 'Y-yes. I did.'

Raldotya nodded. 'Very good, then. I'll request that Kaj'aku get us underway immediately.'

'Excellent.' Mestphura interlocked his fingers. 'Miss Raldotya, please call the officers in as soon as you have done so. I would like to brief everyone on our situation.'

'As you say.' Raldotya nodded dutifully and left, the door sliding shut behind her.

Elzie was unsure what to say, so it was Mestphura who broke the silence. 'I think we could all use a little more information on this than we've been given. Don't you agree?'

Elzie saluted. 'As you say.'

The *Akron* sped across the windy expanse of Minataway. The clouds were clumpy and tinged with red, their undersides flattened and frayed in patches of rainy mist.

The officers had gathered in Mestphura's office for debriefing. Mestphura had been explaining how the mag deflector had been brought back on-line.

'The power test switch? But isn't that external? Skydock-use only?' she exclaimed.

'Kiy got to it using that sling of his,' Gatista said, motioning to the cloudgazer, who had sat in silence for the entire meeting.

Elzie's mouth hung open, then she looked away, cheeks burning. Kiy felt the expression should have given him satisfaction, but such gratification escaped him now.

'Perhaps you should elucidate on the situation regarding Marc and our young guest,' Mestphura said.

Elzie composed herself. 'It was right after the mag came back. The missile that was headed for the ship was so deep in the field, it reversed course sharply—and detonated close to Marc's Foxtail. The plane took some damage from the blast, then lost altitude. We lost visual with them shortly afterwards. We can't get so much as a transponder signal now.'

Mestphura massaged his forehead. 'I was afraid of such. You know we can't spare the time for even a brief search pattern while we still have a trace on the *Postremo*.'

'So we're not even going to try looking for them?' Kiy said in a hollow voice.

'It's not that simple!' Elzie snapped. 'In any case, Marc won't be looking for us. He'll use that nut of his to figure out the rough direction of the last settlement we passed and head that way. If we searched for each other, we could both be going in circles, what with weather like this. They should have a good six hours' fuel on board, and they both have Floatpacks; that will see them to... where was it, Tovstok?'

'Which was in Ganzabi hands,' Kiy pointed out.

'It's still better than falling to the Understorm, Mr Tanthar,' Raldotya offered softly.

'Believe me, Cloudgazer, I would love to be out there looking for them,' Elzie said. 'Marc is one of mine, too, you know. But there's no use. The *Akron* can see much farther than us, especially in this vis; we only have our eyes. And I won't risk losing another plane.'

'If they survived the explosion—which would seem very possible—there is a good chance both Marc and your young friend Leo are alive,' Mestphura said.

'That's if the Ganzies don't break his head open when he lands.' Kiy grimaced. 'I can't expect an Azrunite to understand, but believe me, Ganzabar's military hospitality isn't something you forget.'

The faces around the room met his glower with looks ranging from indignation to pity. There was an awkward silence, but it was broken by Mestphura. 'As I've said, we can't keep the ship here on account of a single missing fighter, not in light of our critical mission. What do you expect me to do?'

Kiy drummed his fingers in thought. The idea of letting go of Leo, after coming this far, was unthinkable. To see Hennie's face and have to tell her what happened... She had put all her trust and hopes in him, and he wasn't about to give up. But Mestphura was right.

He let out an exasperated sigh. 'Nothing.'

With that he stood and left the room. He heard the whispers from behind him, but he wasn't interested in what a few coddled Azrunites had to say. They must think this was still like the old days of the Nimbus Wars, but the world had changed. The Gold Age was hundreds of years ago. Life was different now; warfare was different. Honour still existed, but it meant less and less. In Ganzabar it was viewed more as a quota to be met than as real respect. Just a cold check-box on an antiquated list, its meaning long forgotten.

But then, what did he know about honour either? He'd grown up in the occupation years, lived through the Liberation War. Subjugation, strife and double-crosses defined his youth. All he knew of honour was in the stories his mother used to tell. Perhaps the Azrunites were the only ones who really knew about honour anymore.

Kiy returned to his quarters and sat down heavily, watching the clouds pass by as the ship sped on in pursuit of its quarry. The wispy structures, sliding along through a reddened sky, were a soothing sight. But try as he might, he couldn't lay his troubles to rest.

Shouldn't have let him go up in that damn skyfighter, he thought, even though he knew full well he couldn't have stopped him. *Sky be damned. Should have got off the ship earlier.*

So many ifs and should'ves, but none of it mattered now. He just had to figure out what to do with the present. Leo was out there somewhere. If he was alive, he was most likely trapped in an enemy-held city, preparing to be packed onto a ship bound for the prisons of Ganzabar.

Kiy had to stop that from happening.

No airship truly sleeps, at least not in flight. There are always things to be done, be it on lookout, running the engine or operating the helm. But all the automation on Azrunite vessels made the *Akron* eerily quiet at night, with only the bridge crew and the odd sentry awake. Which was why, as Kiy left his quarters, he supposed there was little need to be discreet; there wasn't a soul around, and no sound but the steady hum of the engines.

Even with the lights dimmed, the corridors of the *Akron* were still brighter than a Brazakker warship ever was. As he passed a row of windows, he glanced out into the night, but saw only a darkly tinted reflection of the corridor. He took a lift down several floors, then walked across the desolate storage hangar and entered the fighter bay. As he passed by rows of dormant Foxtails, hanging from their cradles, he was incredulous that he still hadn't seen anyone.

He stopped and regarded one of the planes. He had no idea where to start in getting it launched. He'd flown an aerofoil before; that part was doable. But activating the launch arm had him confounded. He glanced around, looking for something he could fly. Something fast. Guns would be optional. After all, he was no fighter pilot; if fighters engaged him, he would likely come off dead whether armed or not.

He wondered whether or not the *Akron* would try to track him down. Likely not. Lancet Squadron would have a hard time finding him, at least for the hour or two until dawn. And if they slowed to search, they'd jeopardise their pursuit of the *Postremo*.

He passed through into the main hangar; its outer doors were closed against the wind beyond. In one corner, two interlocking doors formed an ellipsoid doorway. Kiy tapped the button beside to open it, and the doors slid away from each other. Inside the bay beyond sat an elegant-looking aerofoil craft.

He walked around the aircraft approvingly. It was perfect. Two large engines and modest cabin size, indicating it was probably some kind of nippy personnel shuttle. He pulled open the hatch and climbed inside, familiarising himself with the controls. He hadn't flown in a long while, and in any case the Azrunite displays were queer and foreign. At first they seemed overly simplified, missing important readouts and controls, until he found the switch to activate the flight panel, and then the panel was filled with glowing yellow letters, sliders and lines. It was overwhelming, but he soon identified the basics and was confident he could at least take off. As for landing... well, that was generally optional for a cloudgazer.

All that was left was to open the hangar doors. Doing so would probably set off an alarm, but that was fine—he'd be long gone before they could do a thing about it.

He got out and walked to the controller's room in one corner of the main hanger. He looked around the switches and buttons on the wall, trying to find something that might be the door release mechanism.

'It's here.'

The voice was quiet, conversational, and so unexpected that Kiy spun around and nearly lost his balance. At first he thought he was seeing a ghost, then he registered that the figure was Mestphura, sat beside the door with his leg crossed over one knee and his fingers templed. He nodded to a large switch on his left.

'Mestphura?' Kiy took a moment to set his senses straight. 'How did you know I'd be here?'

Mestphura made an innocent face. 'I think we all knew, Kiy.'

Kiy had to concede that was probably true. 'Alright, maybe. But how long have you been here? All night?'

'Of course not. The ship alerted me,' Mestphura said casually.

'The ship...?' Kiy repeated uneasily. He knew the *Akron* was advanced, but he'd clearly underestimated it. He had the sudden sensation of being watched from everywhere, and he had to fight the reflex to survey the walls for cameras or recorders. That was always the thing with Gold Age technology: you could never see it, it was just *there*.

'So,' Kiy said, eyeing the commander defensively. 'You've come here to stop me?'

Mestphura shrugged. 'You can leave if you like. As I said, the switch is right there. But if it would do you any good, don't you think I would have agreed to it in the first place? What will you do when you get there and you've found them? Just fly home?'

Kiy started to speak, then stopped. He had planned to ditch the plane altogether. He wasn't sure how he'd get Leo out. That seemed to be a recurring problem with these rescue missions. He made a mental note to stick to delivering things in future; it was far less problematic.

'I could use a Ganzabi ship,' Kiy said.

'Take over a ship?' Mestphura looked entertained by the concept. 'Have you ever done that before?'

Kiy looked away. He felt like a foolish child, scolded by his parents. 'No.'

Mestphura hmmed, then went quiet, looking out into the hangar.

'But there's a first time for everything,' Kiy said, almost to himself.

'Can you think of a way to operate it, with only three people, well enough to overcome the Ganzabi fleet attempting to stop you?'

Kiy exhaled. He was right. It was not incredibly likely that a skeleton crew of two men and a boy could even get a gunboat going well enough to move, let alone fly it well enough to evade the Armada.

'Fine.' Kiy relented. 'Have it your way. I'll stay. But I'm leaving at the next port we pass.'

'So be it.'

Kiy walked towards the door.

'Oh, one more thing, Mr Tanthar,' Mestphura said.

The cloudgazer turned to look at him.

'If you ever do steal one of my planes, I will blast you out of the skies. Nothing personal.'

Kiy wasn't sure if the commander was joking, but he decided he didn't much want to find out. 'Understood.'

28 - Bluebell

Waltov Barracks, Laronor
October 9th

Gunfire erupted from the leftmost rank of rifles to the right. The sound clattered around the yard like a kid banging a stick along a railing, but Hennie was growing accustomed to the volume and no longer reached to cover her ears, only flinching slightly when the rifles fired.

The Laronor Reserves had been drilling the technique all morning: fire while advancing forward. Rathbone had confided to Hennie that they were no infantry, but they'd been working on their shooting by adding drill practice to their resumé. They'd need all the help that could be mustered when the invasion came. They were the last line of defence, after all.

Invasion seemed to be all anybody talked about these days. It was Brudor all over again. Hennie wondered what would happen if Laronor fell to the enemy. Would there be another airlift, just run away again? Run away to another city, keep on running until there was no more Brazak West? Then what? Flee to the USK?

The USK hadn't moved in support of Brazak West as they had before. Officially, this was because intervention was still being hotly debated by the Senate in New Frander, but the rumours of economical motives persisted. Either way, Hennie wasn't holding out for a ticket west.

She'd asked Rathbone what they might do if the worst was to happen, but he'd simply told her Laronor wasn't going anywhere. She wished she could find assurance in that. She knew he meant what he said. But if Ganzabar had a fleet that could end the world, what good were his intentions?

'Lighten up, lass. End of the world might never happen,' Rathbone said, eyes fixed on the troops.

'I'm sorry. I don't mean to be gloomy.'

'Don't apologise; smile,' he replied warmly.

She watched the Reserves take aim. The guns rumbled again, sending two dozen smoke plumes into the cold morning air. The rank that had fired then crouched onto a knee as the line behind stepped forward through the gaps and took aim. The next few shots were much more sporadic, as the formation got out of drill.

Rathbone blew his whistle, bringing an end to the firing. 'Enough! Return to start positions. Let's try that one again, only this time pay a little more attention.'

Hennie stole a glance at him. He was a hard-featured man, but with a fatherly gentleness. She hadn't known him all that long, but he seemed ready to help anyone. Perhaps a simple transport was not such an audacious thing to ask, she thought.

'Mr Rathbone,' she started, but at the same time he blew the whistle again and the guns roared over her voice. There were a few moments of firing, then Rathbone sprang forward, blowing his whistle several times.

'No, no! For the last time, Stratz, have a cartridge on hand! What good is deft handwork without organisation?'

As he walked out onto the compound, Hennie remained on the sideline. She let out a weary breath. *What good is standing here in the cold when I can't even ask the question I want to ask?*

Jerra stepped up next to her. The girl's attention was on her father, who was giving in-depth instructions. 'How are they?' she asked.

'Not great,' Hennie admitted.

They watched Rathbone adjusting the posture of one of the Reservists, posing with rifle in firing stance. Jerra's eyes betrayed a deep concern. 'I worry about Ganzabar coming here, Hennie. I really do.'

'It'll be okay. Laronor's gonna be fine,' Hennie said, surprising herself with the cheeriness in her voice.

Jerra seemed lifted by that. 'Well, we've seen them off in the past. I dare say we could do it again.'

'Damn right. I'd take them on myself, but...' She trailed off. She felt like all she ever did was make excuses.

Jerra put a lace-gloved hand on Hennie's forearm. 'On that subject, I think we'd better start your training, Hennie.'

'My training?'

Jerra nodded. 'Follow me.'

'Wait, you're coming too?'

'I'm your instructor,' the younger girl said, leading on. 'There's a shortage right now, so Father asked if I could teach you what I know.'

To one side of the training grounds was a spacious yard, deserted but for a series of targets scattered about. Several rifles were propped against a tall luftwood box on which the initials Б.Г.И were stamped beneath a red star.

'I'm going to show you how to use the Bluebell,' Jerra said, picking up one of the rifles. She looked quite peculiar holding it while wearing a beautiful green gown and lace gloves, and with her hair in plaits.

Hennie took up another Bluebell, turning it over in her hands. She'd never even seen one before. Its heaviness surprised her. 'I've never fired a gun,' she said, as though disclaiming herself of any expectations.

'This is a firearm,' Jerra corrected, although in a tone that was entirely polite and scholarly. 'A gun is a weapon fired by a ship.'

'Oh,' Hennie said, still staring at her rifle. 'How do you... I mean, you don't seem the fighting type. How do you know about all this?'

Jerra considered. 'I should confess that I never had the intention to join the Naval Infantry. Mother wished it so, but I'm not very good at—well, it's complicated.' She hefted the rifle up, then smoothly cocked the lever forward and slid a round into the chamber with practiced fingers. 'But. I can shoot. I'm just...'

Hennie watched her in polite silence as her thoughts ticked on.

'It's a little embarrassing, but...' Jerra looked at the rifle. 'I'm scared of blood, Hennie. The sight of it makes me feel like I'm going to be sick. My own blood most especially.' She raised the sights of the weapon to the target across the yard as she talked. 'Once, as a little girl, I was running in the yard. I fell and tore my knee on the paving stones. I remember seeing it, then felt this dreadful panic. I passed out...' She stopped dead, her face blank, and lowered the weapon again.

'It's okay.'

'No, Hennie. It is not. It is greatly foolish,' she said miserably. Then she raised the rifle back up and aimed again. Hennie put her hands on her ears as Jerra squeezed the trigger, and there was a booming crack. The smoke lingered before the wind took it, and Hennie strained to see the marks on the target. It was difficult to tell how Jerra had done; there were already at least two dozen marks present.

'There's nothing wrong with being scared of blood, Jerra,' Hennie said quietly. 'Not everyone is a soldier. That's how it ought to be.'

'Mother says girls should serve on ships.' Jerra shoved the rifle's loading lever down, hinging it in half and ejecting the spent casing. 'It is the noble thing.'

Hennie knew of the Brazakker, and particularly Svalic, tradition of sending at least one daughter to join the Navy. She supposed it could be hard when there was *only* one daughter. And in her own case, harder still with one less daughter. She doubted her Ma would be as keen on the tradition as Mrs Lightlock.

'Serving on a ship is one thing, but the infantry?' she said. "Ought to leave it up to the boys. I don't want to go sticking bayonets in people.'

'Ships are boarded,' Jerra said.

Hennie found she could hardly argue with that.

'My dear Hennie, did I ever tell you,' Jerra turned to her, 'what I actually want to be?'

'No, what?'

Jerra looked almost surprised at her own answer. 'A schoolteacher.'

Hennie smiled. 'Well then... continue the lesson.'

Jerra grinned at that.

They spent the next few hours going through the use of Brazak West's infantry rifle, the Empire Arms Bluebell, which Jerra built at the factory where she worked. She explained that it was a self-cocking, lever-operated breech-loading cartridge rifle, although Hennie didn't know what any of that actually meant. Nevertheless, by the time they were done, she could at least get a shot on the target board from twenty paces, if not all that near the centre.

'You're pretty good for a beginner, Hennie.' Jerra said as they placed their rifles down.

'Nice of you to say, but I don't reckon I'm cut out for this.'

Jerra pondered. 'I think you have the fighting spirit; I can sense it about you. You had it when you stepped up against Bella.'

Hennie hadn't forgotten. 'Guess so, but I don't think I could shoot anyone.' She looked across the training field at the target. It wasn't very human-like.

'I think what's important is that you channel the fighting spirit,' Jerra mused. 'If someone is trying to hurt you and the people you care about, should it not be justified that we use force to stop them?'

'Yeah, tell you what: if the Ganzies come paradin' around here, then I'll be havin' the fighting spirit.'

Jerra gave a nod. 'On that, Hennie, we are both agreed.'

'Jerra, sweetheart,' Rathbone called from across the yard, at the archway leading outside. 'Can you tell that brother of yours to try and make it to dinner? Auntie Maenis will be over.'

'Yes, Father.'

Hennie frowned at her. 'You have a brother?'

Jerra picked up her bag. 'He's not very sociable.'

'No kidding, if I haven't met him before now.'

'Spends almost all his time at his workshop. Come on, I'll introduce you to him.'

As they neared home, they turned down a narrow walkway to a small clump of isolated floatrock behind Jerra's house. It seemed in a world of its own, with only a single structure on it: an open hangar big enough to house a small skyfighter.

There was a crash and tinker of falling metal from inside the hangar, and Hennie looked at her friend curiously.

'That's my brother,' Jerra said. 'Busy as ever, it would seem.'

Inside was a young man crouched beside a large machine. He was either tightening or loosening something as they walked up to him.

'Hi, Miran,' Jerra said.

The boy looked round, startled. He looked a little older than Leo. The likeness to his father was striking. 'Oh. Hi, sis.' He turned back to his work.

'This is Hennie. She's a friend that's been staying with us.'

'Hello, Miran.' Hennie cocked her head, trying to see what he was up to. 'I don't think I've seen you around the house before.'

Jerra shrugged. 'He practically lives out here.'

'What's that you're working on?' Hennie asked sweetly.

'The diheds for my repulsor rig. Turbine jacked okay this morning but the ramscoop still won't link to the auxillary output and I'm getting polarity mis-alignment every time the graviton deflector fluctuates.'

Hennie mulled that over. 'So you're making some sort of ship? That's cool.'

'A small one, but yeah, basically.' He turned to look at Hennie properly for the first time. 'It is?'

'Heck yeah,' Hennie replied.

Jerra looked bashful. 'I'm afraid I'm clueless when it comes to this sort of thing.'

'She in't wrong,' Miran remarked as he began to dig through a toolbox.

'You got a name for it?' Hennie said.

'Mygos,' Miran replied, fishing out a screwdriver.

'Oh, like the moon?'

'Like the Valyan god of redemption.'

Hennie raised her eyebrows. 'Oh. How close is it to flyin'?'

'It flies already. Just got to get it staying the right way up.'

Hennie chuckled, then saw Miran wasn't laughing and cleared her throat awkwardly. 'Ah.'

Miran continued, 'Diheds, you see.'

'Diheds?'

'Dihedrals. They're the little thrusters on the side that keep it stable and stop it rollin', but this one's being a pain in the props.'

'Don't you need one on both sides?' Hennie said tentatively, looking at the mess of parts and deducing it looked a little one-sided.

'S'posed to.' He rapped a small component with the screwdriver. 'But that's a real good one. Got it off this Azrunite. Would get another, but 'twas the only one. I've jigged it to do the job o' two, but it's just too unpredictable when I do that.' He sighed.

'Maybe you should get another one.'

Miran gave her a dismissive look. 'Don't think so. A Tripoint DF8? You'd 'ave t'go to Nubylon to find another.'

'DF8,' Hennie repeated. 'I'll ask around. If there's another one this side of Nezzu, I'll bet someone at the Hammer knows.'

'Huh, really?' Miran stared at her a moment, then turned back to the dihedral and began fiddling again.

'Sure. Leave it to me, Miran,' Hennie said confidently.

Jerra smiled at her brother. 'That's a kind offer. Say thank you, Miran.'

The boy went a deep red and looked down shyly, mumbling thanks and something about not being a baby.

'Also, Father wants you to attend dinner,' Jerra added.

'Can't,' Miran replied. 'Too busy.'

There was a pause as Jerra fidgeted. 'Auntie Maenis is coming. Father was quite insistent.'

Miran gave a long sigh. 'Well, I guess the Sky has spoken.'

That seemed to satisfy his sister. 'We'll meet you there in half an hour. Come on, Hennie.'

The two of them left the workshop, the sky dimming around them.

'That's so kind of you to offer to help my little brother like that,' Jerra said once they were out of earshot.

''S'okay.'

Jerra walked on without a word, then glanced up at the darkening sky. 'You're not going to involve him in this effort to reach the Gundar, are you?'

'I admit I'd thought about it. But that's not why I'm helping him.'

'Please don't bring him into this, Hennie. It could be very dangerous. Promise me.'

Hennie looked up at the ominous installation hanging above the edge of the city like another moon. 'I promise.'

The cell was pitch black, broken only at irregular intervals by the blinding white, cold lights of the corridor whenever the door was opened. He knew there were at least another dozen in his cell, moving around in the dark, closed space, and never far enough for him to not be pressing against some nameless body. Putrid smells assailed the senses, and the air hung thick and stale. There was no conversation, and the only sounds in the cell were the moans of its occupants and the low hum of the ship.

Kiy lost track of time in that place. He wished for anything and everything. He prayed to the Sky to deliver escape. Mostly he wished his mum and dad knew he were here. They must be out there somewhere; they could rescue him and Julene. Oh, Julene, poor little Julene. He begged for her to be someplace better, someplace with at least light and a bed and maybe even food. The thought of her in this was unbearable.

Suddenly the cold light appeared to burn the darkness away. A thick arm reached in and plucked Kiy out of the stench, then all was too bright to see. His feet barely supported him, but he tried to walk all the same.

His ears were his only eyes. After some time, a sound approached them—a howling, ghostly roar. Fear ran through his veins, but he refused to let it take him. *Don't show fear.*

He realised the roar was stationary and it was he who was moving towards it. The air began to stir and felt cooler, and then it hit him in a moment of clarity:

It's the outside. They're going to throw me overboard.

He tried not to panic, but the thought pounded at his mind and his legs went weak under him. He stumbled, then was hoisted back up and carried on marching. Beside him a deep voice grumbled something. He tried to speak out—to protest or beg, he couldn't decide—but his throat was dry and cracked and wouldn't work.

His vision improved to where he could just make out the rough shapes moving around him, but all was still a blur. A bright, bright blur.

Finally, he was brought to a stop before a wide, white square. The wind howled at him from it.

'You failed her,' a man's voice said.

Kiy tried to say something. He tried to yell at the voice, cry that it wasn't true. His voice sounded like a mumble. His blood was pulsing too loudly in his ears.

Then the arm wrenched him forward, and Kiy fell through the white into a blinding universe of light. His stomach seemed to leave him a second, and everything around him was rushing, freezing. Wet mist ripped at his blind face, and the wind shrieked at him cruelly as he tumbled, spinning like thrown litter, swirling into the bright abyss.

And for a moment his mind calmed. Was this what it had meant all along? Had he returned to the Sky?

He awoke with a start at the sound of a knock. It took a moment for his brain to get up to speed and figure out where he was. He was in his quarters on the *Akron*, lying on top of the sheets of his bunk. The present came back in fits and slivers.

The knock at the door came again. He sat up, gathering himself, and bid them to enter.

Officer Kerowan stepped in, regarding him with concerned eyes. He was unsure what to say. In all honesty, she was the last person he'd expected to see walk into his quarters.

'Come with me,' she said. 'Mestphura wants us on the bridge.'

Curious, he followed her out of the room and down the hallway. Storm clouds surrounded the *Akron*, although they were at a distance and the air was clear of rain. Yet the air had an electric quality to it that prodded the primal brain, hinting that a storm was just waiting to happen.

When they arrived on the bridge, Mestphura stood in the centre of the room, his hands clasped behind his back and his feet firmly planted. He didn't acknowledge Kiy as he usually did, but stared straight ahead.

Kiy followed his gaze. Beyond the grand bridge windows, a sleek white ship, smaller than the *Akron*, sat about a kilometre ahead. It had swooping lines, gold and light blue trim, and a delicate narrow frame. Two large protrusions, above and below, resembled curved masts—and indeed, each drew a large canopy like a sail. But these sails didn't appear to be for catching the wind; they were fixed in place and ran lengthwise. As their fabric caught the light, a pattern of tesselating hexagons shimmered across it.

'What is it?' Kiy asked.

Elzie was mesmerised. 'The *Postremo*.'

'Why are they just sitting there?' Kiy asked.

'The Adaptive Camoflauge appears to be damaged and inoperative,' Raldotya said, her eyes darting from her display to the view.

'And we outgun them,' Gatista added. 'Especially this close.'

'Distance?' Mestphura called.

'Five hundred,' Gatista answered.

Kiy chewed his lip. *Stinks of a trap*, he thought.

Mestphura shifted uneasily, clearly having similar thoughts. 'Keep an eye on them. I want us ready on the trigger if they so much as blink.'

'All guns standing by,' Gatista said, studying his readout panel.

A screen, much like the sleek displays around them, folded out from the bridge's ceiling and blinkered a moment before displaying the colour blue. Then the image jumped and adjusted, and a picture of a woman appeared. To Kiy's amazement, the image of the woman was moving and smiling as though she were a person actually sitting there.

And then she began talking.

'Surprised, Commander Mestphura?' she said provocatively.

'No.'

'I'll bet you didn't expect someone like me to be on your fancy intership comm system.' She laughed. She was reclining lazily on a chair identical to the one that sat behind Mestphura—the chair he almost never used. She had one leg hung over the armrest, and her slitted skirt had fallen away to show smooth caramel skin. She spoke with a thick West Ganzabi accent. 'Ya know what I reckon? You think I'm some halfwit child that wun't know what a comm-system was if I tripped on it, right?'

'Who are you?' Mestphura said flatly.

'Oh yeah, I should just back up a little. Allow me to introduce myself.' She stretched her arms grandly with a performer's smile. 'I am the Countess de Saufon. And this'—she gestured her surroundings—'is the *Postremo*. I thought I might just... borrow it a li'l while. As you weren't using it.' She looked at her nails. 'You really shouldn't leave your things lying around like that.'

'I have not ever served on the *Postremo*, Countess, nor does it belong to me,' Mestphura replied. Kiy knew Mestphura wouldn't be taking her words literally, but he was playing the straight man.

'Oh, but of course you haven't.' She had a theatrical way of speaking that Kiy found annoying. 'You aren't a very popular man right now with the Peace Ministry.'

'Putting your tangential claims to one side,' Mestphura said, his deep voice betraying some measure of frustration, 'and on behalf of said Peace Ministry, you are required to surrender the *Postremo* immediately.'

'Oh,' she said lightly. 'No, I don't think so. Why'd I do a thing like that, anyways?'

'If you do not surrender it, we will be forced to destroy it.'

She shook her head. 'Oh, now that would be so unpleasant, wouldn't it? Only, you're not gonna do that. You have orders specifically *not* to. She's precious, I know. So don't lie.' She grinned smugly, then suddenly added, as though she'd almost forgotten: 'Liars are bad in bed, y'know.'

The countess seemed to be trying to test Mestphura's patience. Kiy didn't imagine such a thing was possible, but if there existed a person who could succeed, they could be looking at her.

'I have no orders prohibiting the destruction of the *Postremo*,' Mestphura replied. 'Better to lose it than let you continue rampaging around the Brazaks.'

The woman laughed—a wicked and shrill sound made all the worse by the distorted medium that carried it. 'Silly little man. You think this is about raiding Brazak West for treasure? Oh, dear. Such a small view of the world. I expected more intelligence from the great Mestphura.'

'Whatever you expected, you'd be wrong to think we'd strike a deal with someone like you.'

She coiled like a snake on the little screen, all venom and malice. 'I see now you're nothing more than a pawn for your masters. A shame; I could have made you a happy man, Mestphura.'

'Idle talk and hollow threats are not intimidating to me, Countess, and I have no interest in offers of wealth,' Mestphura said evenly. 'Your attitude of disrespect will only make things more unpleasant for you.'

'Is that so?' she said with mock hurt. 'I am so very afraid right now, Commander.' She flashed a wide grin.

Raldotya spoke up. 'Sir, the camoflauge—'

The ship's shape had begun to warp, as though it were an image passing a misshapen mirror.

'Fire!' Mestphura shouted, and slammed a button to close the intercom system. The sound of the countess's laugh was cut off as the screen disappeared back into the ceiling.

'The guns won't fire!' Gatista wrestled with the firing controls. 'They're still initialising... I don't understand!'

Mestphura scowled. 'Sky and Moons!'

Beyond the prow, the *Postremo* vanished, the light from it splintering into all its component colours before fading.

'Commander, numerous enemy vessels are emerging from the surrounding clouds!'

'She's led us into a trap,' Elzie said, her face pale.

'All hands to battle stations. Power up the mag. And get those damn guns online, now!' Mestphura ordered, his self-reprimand written on his face. They had known the *Postremo* was up to something, yet he had let that vile woman talk on.

The shrill, repeating *whoop* of the Azrunite klaxon rang out, and the ship's interiors shifted to pulsing orange.

'Commander,' Raldotya said, 'we have sightings of Justice, Patriot, Principal and Brimstone classes.'

'Guns are still not responding,' Gatista added.

Mestphura templed his fingers. 'Mr Kaj'aku, any chance we can outrun these ships?'

'We can try, Commander. But we're likely to get seriously damaged in the attempt; they'll likely catch up.' If the notion put fear in him, he didn't show it.

'Commander,' Elzie said, 'we could make a Jump out.'

Mestphura appeared to consider the notion for a split second before dismissing it. 'That has every chance of leaving us helpless and will most likely get us captured. I cannot risk that happening, even if the alternative is our sinking. We must evade until the guns are back online. Then we concentrate firepower on one ship at a time— reduce their numbers.'

A rumble echoed around them. Kiy was unsure if it was thunder in the storm clouds or enemy cannons.

'Very well,' Gatista said, flicking a row of switches. 'I'm attempting to shut down the dorsal guns, might be able to get some response out of them afresh...'

As the bridge swelled to a flurry of activity, Elzie darted out. Kiy followed, catching up with her in the corridor.

'Where are you going?'

'To the hangar, to get my squadron in the air.' She gave him an odd look as they strode. 'What, did you think I can't step without Mestphura giving the direct order? I know my job.'

He kept pace with her as she hurried on. 'Not at all. Hierarchy is something I pretty much ignore anyway.'

'Good,' she said patronisingly. 'You can start by ignoring everything you're supposed to do and let the professionals do it.'

'It would kill you to be civil, wouldn't it?'

'Civil to those without civilisation, perhaps.' She barged past him and passed through a bulkhead door, then slammed it shut in his face.

Kiy stood staring at it, unsure what to do. *Why am I even still here?* He ought to be out finding Leo, not stuck here, caught in a feud that had nothing to do with him, marooned on a ship that didn't need him. He decided to head to his quarters and fetch his sling; it was time to get off this crazy boat.

He returned to his cabin and slid the door shut. Once he'd placed the sling on his arm, he felt much better. He was pondering where to start, listening to the quiet humming of the ship, when it occurred to him that something wasn't right. Even on the sophisticated Azrunite ship, he ought to have been able to hear the battle. At least some vibrations, at any rate. But instead, there was only an uneasy quietness. Even the klaxon had stopped.

Then all went black.

Kiy was quickly at full alertness. A hint of visibility came from a few pulsing lights on a panel that controlled the cabin temperature, and he blinked his eyes to help them adjust. Listening carefully, he heard occasional rumbles and distant muffled noises that could have been shouts.

He felt his way to the door, but it failed to budge. His fingers traced the frame, looking for a gap, but the seal was flush. Cursing, he felt underneath the panel beside it. Surely there was some kind of manual release? Coming upon a handle, he gave it a tug, and the door came loose. Kiy had to drag it aside to get through.

Rows of glowing dots—emergency lighting, apparently—illuminated the edges of the floor in the corridor. As Kiy stepped out of his quarters, he definitely heard a scream from the deck above. His mind already knew what was happening, and it chilled him.

They were being boarded.

He ran down the corridor. When he reached an intersection, he pressed himself flush against the wall and peered around the corner. The crossing passage was deserted in either direction. But the sounds of fighting were clear now, descending from the higher decks: small arms fire, yells and intermittent explosives. *Damn fool Mestphura*, Kiy thought. *How did we get boarded so quickly? These Azrunites have no idea how to fight a battle, truly.*

He passed a bank of robots recessed into the wall—the same kind that had greeted him when he first arrived. Gatista had later explained that they were Gold Age security drones. Hovering on tiny Repulsor motors, they were autonomous enough to find and incapacitate intruders. So why were they still fixed into their mounts on the wall? Why wasn't the ship security system fighting back?

Something had gone terribly wrong for the Azrunites.

Kiy reached an elevator, but it just sat dumbly when he tried to get a response out of it. He dashed through an exterior door, thinking to take the stairway to the higher deck, but had to dart back behind the door when a group of heavy footsteps began to make their way down. Kiy ran back down the corridor, thinking to take the exterior stairs at the opposite side of the ship, but there were shouting Ganzabi voices from that direction too. So he turned again, heading aft.

The corridor soon became a gantry across a spacious room at least two stories tall, filled with machinery. Kiy vaulted over the rail of the gantry, then used the sling to pull himself in underneath it. He hung there, as close as he could, listening to his blood pound through his ears.

Just when he was beginning to think he was being overly cautious, he heard the sound of dozens of boots clanking on the metal walkway. They grew closer, then passed right overhead before shrinking away into quiet.

Kiy waited until they were definitely out of the room before daring to breathe again.

At least a quarter hour passed before Kiy was confident the activity had died down enough for him to move around. He pulled himself up onto the gantry and stood, exhaling with relief.

His ears immediately perked to a shuffling sound. He turned, his eyes going wide as he came face to face with a Ganzabi marine standing in the doorway.

The marine raised his rifle to fire. Kiy lashed the sling's clamp at him like a whip, knocking the weapon from his hands, and the Ganzabi stumbled backward. The marine turned and ran in blind panic, and Kiy leapt after him. If the Ganzabi got the chance to tell anyone there was a cloudgazer aboard, Kiy wouldn't be around for very long.

Kiy made the corner and fired the sling again, catching the man's feet and toppling him face-first. He reeled in the cable, the marine flailing and clawing at the floor, until he had him at his feet.

The man rolled over and held up his palms as Kiy pointed his revolver at him. 'I give in! I give in! Don't kill me!'

Kiy regarded him pitifully. He looked a little overweight, with a shabby uniform and ill-fitting helmet. *Ganzabar's Finest, eh*? But there was a hundred thousand Ganzabi soldiers; he conceded they couldn't all look like the ones on the posters.

'What's going on here?' Kiy said icily.

'We've taken the ship!' the marine said hurriedly. 'You're the only one left. There isn't a chance, Azrunite. Give yourself in. If I'm alive, they'll be kind to you.'

Kiy's eyes narrowed. '*Kind* to me?'

'That is,' he corrected, seeing the bitterness in Kiy's eyes, 'they might let you live.'

Kiy was almost amused. 'You're threatening me?'

'No! Please, I didn't mean it that way. But it's for... it's for the good of us both.'

'And now you're telling me what's in my best interests.' Kiy raised an eyebrow.

'No! I—'

'Relax, I'm not going to kill you.' Kiy waved the revolver casually. 'Not so long as you do what I tell you, anyhow. You seem like a sensible guy, not into heroics or anything. That right?'

The man nodded.

'Good man. Do what I say, I promise you'll live. Now, perhaps you'd like to tell me where the *Akron*'s crew are?'

'I don't know.'

Kiy hit him with the butt of his pistol.

'Ow! Shyut, I don't, I swear! They're still on the ship, that's all I know. Probably waiting transfer.'

Still on the ship? Well, there was still hope of getting out of this mess. Perhaps. 'You got a radio?' Kiy asked.

The marine nodded.

'I want you to radio and ask for the prisoners' location.'

The marine deliberated a moment—a moment that Kiy ended by cocking his weapon and aiming it at the man's head.

'Alright, alright! What do I tell them? They'll want to know why.'

'Tell them you have another prisoner to bring in. And no tricks. I'm just a merc that wants to be on his way. Standing against me is a pointless way to die.'

'But why—'

'Now.' Kiy poked him with the pistol.

The man nodded nervously. He removed his backpack and activated the bulky radio handset.

Kiy watched him make the transmission suspiciously, half-expecting him to try something. And if he did? Kiy didn't know if he could even shoot the man. He'd never intentionally killed anyone. Of course, there had been times when his actions had contributed to someone's death, but still, he found the notion of simply shooting a man in the head disturbing.

The voice on the other end of the line returned with a crackle. 'Copy. Bring them to the rear hangar. We're rounding them up here.'

'Will do, sir,' the marine replied.

Kiy made the gesture of a cut across the neck.

'Over,' the marine added, his voice cracking slightly. Kiy hoped the man on the other end hadn't noticed anything out of place.

'Good work,' Kiy said. 'Now I need your uniform.'

'You're joking.'

Kiy gave him a hard look.

'Okay, you're not joking.' The marine removed his chestplate, tunic, trousers and boots. He stood awkwardly in his thermal-wear as Kiy piled up his belongings.

'Now let's move it.' Kiy marched the man down the corridor, stopping only to take a padded jacket from the wall, then directing the marine through a doorway to the walkway along the side of the ship.

'Wait! Where are we going?'

Kiy ignored the question. 'Put this on.'

The marine did so.

'You know what it is?' Kiy asked.

'Life chute...' the man said uneasily.

'You pull the red cord and it deploys a float, keeping you aloft for anything up to ninety days.'

The man's eyes widened in fear. 'But—'

'Think fast.'

Kiy gave him a hard shove, throwing him over the sleek handrail. The wind tore away his cry as he tumbled into the clouds passing below.

Kiy figured he probably had only ten or twenty minutes before they recovered the marine and word of a cloudgazer running loose on the ship got out. He wasn't too fond of time limits, but this was the best he could come up with. *Short of shooting the guy and dumping the body overboard, like most mercs would have done*, he reminded himself grimly.

He found himself wishing Elzie were here, if only to prove a point.

30 - Rathbone Manor

Waltov, Laronor
October 10th

The house Jerra lived in was called Rathbone Manor, as Hennie was reminded by a lamplit sign beside the entrance bridge. Situated on its own modest floatrock isle, amidst clusters of affluent homes in Waltov, it was the largest building Hennie had ever visited that was for only one family. Two stories high and at least four times that in width and depth, it had a traditional grand appearance, with twelve-paned glass windows and pillars flanking the front door.

Hennie was staying in one of the upstairs guest bedrooms. It was lavish compared to just about anything, let alone that dreadful tenancy in Voxton. She still hadn't figured out what the Rathbones used most of the house for. At first she thought Jerra had a really big family, but prior to meeting Miran she hadn't seen any siblings at all.

'Father's family are very comfortable. The Rathbones have a long history in this city, you see,' Jerra told her as they ate dinner, although she was being coy about it and was talking underneath a much noisier conversation between her mother and aunt. 'Father is perhaps less so; he is more a man of good work than good wealth, as they say.'

Hennie nodded, taking a sip of her drink without breaking her attention. Most nights they drank First-Grade Pure (she never knew water could taste so good), but tonight they were drinking wine. She put it down to the company.

Miran had eventually joined them at the table and sat in a thundercloud the whole time. He barely touched his food.

'How's the ship, son?' his father asked as he finished the last of his vegetables.

'Fine.' Miran stared at his plate.

'Still tinkering, are we?' His Auntie Maenis beamed. She was a plumper, more senior mirror of Jerra's mother. 'I tell you, Doyrie,' she said, 'that boy's been a tinker all his life, has he not?'

Mrs Lightlock simply nodded, glanced briefly at her son, then resumed talking with Maenis on a previous subject.

'Like you'd know,' Miran muttered, though the remark went ignored by the elder end of the table.

Hennie changed the subject. 'This gull is delicious.'

'It's pheasant, my dear,' Mrs Lightlock corrected her woodenly.

'Oh. I've never had pheasant.' Hennie swallowed and averted her eyes, her cheeks burning.

Jerra cleared her throat. 'Father,' she said, 'Hennie was hoping to visit the Gundar. Have you any idea how to get there?'

Edwark removed something from his teeth, placed it on the side of his plate, then looked at Hennie sympathetically. 'Well, it's a fascinating place, but I'm afraid they won't let you go there. I'm sure we could fix you up with a little sightseeing fly-by sometime, though.'

'They say it can hit an airship from twenty kilometres,' Miran interjected moodily, 'but the range is effectively unlimited.'

Hennie was surprised to hear him speak again. 'So it will defend us from the Ganzies?'

'Not single-handedly,' Edwark said with half a smile, 'but it'll certainly help.'

Miran frowned. 'What's to stop the government using it as a superweapon? Shooting hundreds, even thousands of kilometres... it could be used on other cities.'

Edwark looked aghast. 'Nonsense. And quite impractical, I'm sure.'

Miran sniffed obstinately. 'Bet it could be done.'

'Son, even if yer could—and that's a big if—you couldn't aim it, not over a distance like that. That's the kind of maths only... well, only an Azrunite calputer could do something like that. I bet even that workshop of yours doesn't have one o' them.'

As the table fell quiet, Hennie pondered the notion. The ability to strike a foreign city with a terrible weapon that spelt instant death without warning... It was chilling to contemplate a world where such a thing existed.

Miran persisted. 'What if somebody had an Azrunite calputer and—'

'They're huge, son.' Edwark was starting to show impatience. 'The size of rooms. You don't just find them in bars.'

Miran rolled his eyes, then got up and left the table. Edwark looked as though he meant to respond, but seemed to think better of it and went back to picking at the remains of his pheasant.

Hennie sank into her own cloud of thoughts. Could the Gundar really be a doomsday weapon? She tried to put the idea out of her mind. The last thing she needed right now was more troubles to dwell on.

31 - Fortitude

A Ganzabi warship,
somewhere near Tovstok

Finally the guard brought water and something to eat, although it reminded Leo of the stale, plain biscuits his Nan had always offered whenever they visited. He never would have eaten those had he actually been given anything else as an alternative, and it was much the same here. The biscuits were hard and slightly salted, but his stomach had rioted for hours, and he was simply glad to have something to put it to rest.

As he ate, he found himself recounting how they'd gotten here. 'Here' being some brig cell on the Ganzabi cruiser *Fortitude*. After the missile exploded right on top of them, everything had been a blur. The world had spun around, and Leo had slipped out of consciousness. Marc later told him he'd only taken twenty or thirty seconds to pull out of the spin, but by that point they were deep in cloud. The radio was smashed, along with most of the electrics, and the screen was pitted with cracks and dents. By some miracle the other essentials were still in working order. They climbed back up to altitude, but couldn't find the *Akron*. So Marc took a compass heading for Tovstok and ploughed on through miserable weather.

Things had looked hopeful for a bit, but as soon as the cloud began to clear and they approached the city, they were intercepted by the looming shadow of a Ganzabi warship. Realising a fight would be a one-sided story, Marc had flashed his lights in a distress pattern, and the Ganzies had responded with a docking order in pulse code.

Marc had then dumped the Pivot Break and mag shield, to prevent them being captured. It was standard procedure in imminent capture; a single switch beneath an orange cover dropped all the precious Gold Age technology into the Understorm.

As the Ganzabi cruiser approached, Leo had argued a death in combat would be the proper thing to do, but Marc clearly found the notion horrific; he'd made it clear surrender was the only sane option. Leo had panicked then, recounting what Kiy had told him about how Ganzabi handle prisoners. The thought of exploding in a fireball seemed vastly more appealing.

'They won't hurt us, kid,' Marc had replied, as the shadow of the rear hangar loomed over them. The cockpit was thrown into darkness punctuated only by the glowing yellow glyphs on the instrument panel. 'We're prisoners of war.'

'It's not like that!' Leo protested. 'They don't play by the rules in Ganzabar.'

'Nobody's gonna hurt you. Trust me, man.'

Both of them had been partially right. Upon landing, the guards had shocked Marc. He'd been dragged from the cockpit, beaten with rifle butts and kicked repeatedly. Leo had been ready for a struggle and had gotten his fair share of bruises for it. But as soon as the commanding officer arrived, the violence evaporated and they were escorted to their cell without further incident. Treatment from then on had been far more humane than Leo had expected.

'I guess...' he reflected, chewing on the biscuit, 'this could be worse.'

'It's flakkin' rubbish, mate,' Marc lamented. 'These biscuits taste like floatrock.'

'How'd you know? You ever eaten floatrock before?'

'Yeah. Makes your willy stand up.'

Leo made a face as though working something out, until Marc interrupted. 'I'm pullin' your leg. Don't go tryin' it.'

'I know! I'm not stupid...' Leo replied defensively.

They lapsed into quiet, though only because they were eating. Marc seemed to be the kind of person that couldn't abide silence, always trying to spark up a new subject to talk about. Leo kept the conversation going as well as he could, but as the hours had passed by, sometimes there was nothing more to say. They had talked about Brudor, the Litvyak family, life before the war. Leo had told Marc about his mother and sisters, and how his sister Feo had been an officer on a ship, just like Elzie was.

Now Marc asked, 'What's the deal between Elzie and your mate Kiy?'

'What do you mean?' Leo looked uncertain. 'They aren't at it or anything.'

Marc laughed. 'They aren't at it! Ah man, the stuff you come out with, it's genius.'

There was a loud bang on the door and an incomprehensible mutter outside.

'Ooh, stop having fun, you're supposed to be in prison,' Marc said in a parody Ganzabi accent.

Leo chuckled. Marc somehow made the world feel less dangerous. 'So how do we escape from this place?'

'Gee, I dunno. Hadn't thought about it.'

'What?'

'I don't really know where to go from here,' Marc admitted. 'I've never done anything like this before.'

'Great.' Leo sank his chin into his palm.

'This war business is kinda new to me.'

'Yeah—that's one thing I've been wondering...' said Leo, his gaze drifting. 'If Azrune is never at war, where'd you learn to fight and fly like that? You guys must all be total greeners.'

'Technically, I guess we are.' Marc shrugged. 'We don't get caught up in battles like the Ganzabi or you Brazakkers.'

'I'm only thirteen.'

'And you've still been in as many battles as me,' Marc pointed out. 'Nah, all we've got to keep our skills up is training.'

'That's it?'

'Well yeah, but it's not like anything you've ever seen, believe me. I seen training, New-Age-style, and... they ain't bad or anything, but it's really a totally different level. I ain't talking cut-outs on firing ranges, hovering targets and dummy cargo ships. Back home, we have this chair thing you sit inside, right? And there's these screens you wear over your eyes that make it like you're really there.'

Leo looked at him, his face betraying equal parts curiosity and scepticism.

'Simulated Reality, they call it,' said Marc. 'Gyros make the g-forces feel like you're in a real plane, they plug you in so you can see it, feel it, touch and taste it—'

A metal clank interrupted Marc, and the door to the cell swung open. Three guards entered. Two of them took hold of Marc by the shoulders.

'Captain wants to speak to you,' the third said gruffly as they dragged Marc to his feet.

'Excuse me but, uh, we were havin' a conversation—'

'Quiet!'

Leo smiled to himself at Marc's defiance. But as the door groaned shut and the sound of footsteps echoed away outside, it felt a lot colder in the room.

32 - Countess

The Postremo, *captain's quarters*
October 12th

'My lady,' said the squat man at the door, announcing his presence.

The Countess de Saufon sighed at the interruption. She could deny him audience again, but he might actually have something important to say for once. 'Yes, Talot?'

The man glanced around uneasily, as if overwhelmed by the lavish extravagence surrounding him. Prior to being the personal cabin of the countess, the captain's quarters of the *Postremo* had been quite different: too plain for her taste, all geometric Azrunite shapes and boring colours. She had since adorned it with rich rugs and tapestries of red and blue velvet, and great hanging chandeliers that cocooned glittering crystal bulbs. The desk had been replaced with her personal dresser, covered in candles and a thousand little fragrant bottles and jars. The bed had been stripped of its mediocrity and given only the very finest satin sheets and thick Gawker-feather pillows.

Talot eyed her reclining decadently on her imported Lystratan-leather couch, plucking red olives from a porcelain bowl. Her face was pretty—the kind of stunning beauty that drove her admirers near to madness, with the slight almond shape to her eyes and the petite nose belaying her Aquitano heritage. Almost at the end of her teens, she had a slight but curvaceous physique. Long, straight hair of pale blond draped her bare shoulders, and piercing blue eyes seemed to glare at a world that didn't meet their standards.

He regained his composure and bowed. 'I am pleased to report that the *Akron* has been captured completely intact.'

She perked up like a giddy child. 'Oh, marvellous! Tell me, Talot, did you get to see the look on that Mestphura's face?'

Talot looked uneasy. 'Um, I... wasn't there personally, ma'am, but—'

'Oh, delightful,' she interrupted. 'Was there anything further to add?'

Talot swallowed. She had a deeply intense, self-assured glare that made him sweat under the collar, and she seemed to almost wriggle with comfort in her seat. 'The admiral has requested ah... an update on our situation and a return to the fleet immediately.'

'We're on the way for the, like, millionth time. Gosh, so impatient...'

Talot cleared his throat. 'Yes. Also, Captain Isikel would like to know your ETA for the inspection.'

'Inspection?' She stared with blank hostility.

'Uh... that you requested? Before we move on... you know how these military types so like their schedules—'

'Oh, of the *Akron*, yes. But geez, Talot. Don't you know it's rude to rush a lady?' Her expression softened and she stood and gave a swirl, her dress wheeling about her like a flower going into bloom. 'When I see the *Akron*, I want to look my best. So, I was wonderin' what to wear. I'm thinking something different. Something... special.'

She stepped towards her wardrobe: a mighty row of greywood cabinets with tall mirrors on their doors, engraved by Aquitano sculptors with elaborate swirls and flourishes.

'Yes, of course, my lady.' Talot nodded dutifully. 'I shall have your maids sent through immediately.'

The countess threw up a dismissive hand. 'Leave them be. I don't need their fussin' today.'

'Very well, my lady.'

'Nor yours. Now shoo, shoo.'

Talot left hurriedly with another bow, the door sliding shut behind him.

The countess slipped the thin silk cardigan off her shoulders, then strode across the room. 'It seems that your Cracking is almost worth killing for.' She opened one of the drawers of her dresser and rummaged for jewelry.

'Of course it is, dear lady.' From behind one of her dressing screens, a slender man emerged with a wide grin.

He wore a long white robe, trimmed in blue and gold lines. His dark hair was short and spiked, lending an electric quality to his smile.

'And you, Grabe, are worth your weight in gold.' She smiled at him wickedly. She strode to her vanity screen and gently removed her corset, keeping her naked back to the man on the far side of her room.

Grabe flexed his metallic digits. They were hinged with fine joints and had small glowing lines running across them. 'I am glad I can please you, my lady.'

'Oh, you can at that.' She turned fractionally, but not enough for him to enjoy it. 'And you'll be rewarded, believe me.' She began to sift through the dresses in the wardrobe.

He stepped up behind her quickly, sliding his arms around her and cupping her bare breasts. 'All I ask for is you, my sweet Saufette.'

She sighed. 'Yeah, but that ain't what I'm talkin' about.' The feel of metal fingers on her skin sent goosebumps through her body every time. But there were more pressing matters.

'Then what do you mean?' he protested.

'I said I'd make you a million floril, didn't I?' She smiled under a long-lashed, heavy-lidded gaze.

He chuckled. 'Oh, let us not cheapen our time with talk of money.' He took a step after her.

She pulled away from him, crossing the room with a long ornate dress pressed against her chest, measuring it up in the multitude of wardrobe mirrors. 'But business comes before pleasure. Take a look over there.' She motioned to a large device on the other side of the room, just one of many antiques littered about her quarters.

'What is it?' he asked.

'Some old Gold Age thing,' she explained, watching as he approached it with fascination. 'It can turn a lump of waste matter into solid gold.'

His eyes gleamed. 'Transmutation...?' he said in awe.

'Yes. Go on, take a look. I know you wanna.'

He stepped up to the huge machine, a lime green metallic circle set on stepped cylinders making a set of concentric steps. Around the circumference was an assortment of bulky metal parts that appeared to be hinged to it. He stepped up curiously into the middle and looked down at the glass plate in the centre, which emanated a gentle blue glow.

'Is this where the magic happens, my lady?'

'Yes.' She stepped closer, still holding the dress over her bare upper body, a gown of the most illustrious shade of gold. Gold. Indeed, gold seemed fitting.

'What can we try it on?' he asked eagerly.

She smiled venomously and dropped the dress aside. 'You.'

His eyes lingered on her for too long. By the time he realised what she meant, her hand had moved. The metal segments around the circle swung upwards and encased him in a thick metal cocoon. The sides were heavy overlapping curves, forming a vertically elongated sphere, the metal thick and muffling. Only a small window on one side broke the shell's form. Grabe threw himself against it, banging his palms desperately. She could see him yelling, but only the slight thud of his hands could be heard.

'What's wrong? I said I'd make you a million floril,' she said innocently, pressing a sequence of glowing keys.

As she watched, he began to writhe, his atoms being transformed gradually. She looked away and continued to dress as the shuddering device did its work.

The machine gave a jolt and a whine—and then it was done. The walls came away like segments of a tangerine, falling back to the floor around the circle. In the centre of the glass plate was a crisp gold statue of Grabe on his knees, fists balled against his temples and mouth wide with anguish. A ghostly blue light from beneath the glass lit his face, twisted in his final moment.

The countess adjusted her dress—a long gold gown with fine lacing around the chest and a low cut on the back—along with long satin gloves of deep blood red and a small jacket of red velvet trimmed in gold. Then she appraised Grabe with her hands on her hips. It was a shame, she thought; he'd been fun, and highly useful, but it was better this way. The *Akron* and the *Postremo* were well enough for her uses. He was a traitor to the Azrunite people; it would have been merely a matter of time before he betrayed her as well.

She moved to a panel on the wall and held the intercom button. 'Mr Talot, I think I've found my outfit. Tell Captain Isikel I'm on my way.' She looked back at Grabe. 'Oh, and I have a new ornament. Can you find somewhere to put it?'

33 - Jump

Akron, the Beyer Fields
October 12th

The electrical hum of the fence was the only sound in the hangar. Several of the crew sat about in sullen silence in a small, temporary brig, just one of many. Two Ganzabi marines stood guard, one by an alarm, one by the brig's gate.

Elzie looked up as another Ganzabi approached the man standing guard at their gate. There was a murmur and a nod at first, but then the two soldiers seemed to disagree. The one at the gate protested, while the man who had arrived waved a warning finger. She bent towards the humming fence, straining to hear, but their voices were too low and far.

The man at the gate spat on the ground. Elzie felt a surge of revulsion; she wanted to go over and push his face into it. How dare he spit in her hangar, disgusting savage! But Mestphura had been clear: there was to be no trouble. Trouble meant casualties, and there was no use in those. Not now.

It had all been a complete disaster. No sooner had she run into the hangar, to get the squadron in the air, than the place had gone dark. All power, all defenses, offline and unresponsive. And nobody had the slightest idea why.

And the next thing they knew, the place filled with Ganzabi marines. Without the automated defence system, it took only a matter of minutes before they were all over the ship, and Mestphura told them all to go quietly. She'd gotten to see firsthand what Kiy had described mockingly as 'Ganzabi hospitality', and when one of them groped at Raldotya, Elzie had struck out hard enough to draw blood. His compatriots had subsequently beat the same back from her, she recalled, gingerly touching the gash on her brow and her bruised jaw.

Her attention returned to the two talking Ganzabi, who had now raised their voices slightly. She could begin to make out what they were saying.

'I tell you, this is my watch and I ain't budgin'!'

'You wanna get the captain angry? You're to report for cargo extraction duty—'

'Go flak yourself, yer jus' tryin' to get out of stackin' crates.' The guard shoved the other soldier away.

The man raised his palms defensively. 'Alright, fine, no need to get short, man. Tell you what, I'll trade you something.' The light fell on his face, and she caught a glimpse of a sly smile under the heavy brow of the helmet. There was something about it...

The soldier slid off a bulky backpack and undid it, while the guard looked on. Elzie could see the guard lean in eagerly. The soldier rummaged through the contents of his pack.

'Well?' the guard said impatiently. 'What is it?'

'Look.'

As the guard leant in, the man pulled his arm from his pack—but with a bulky metal device now attached to it. She recognised it straight away.

Kiy's sling connected with the guard's face, making a wet thunk and sending him sprawling back, blood dripping from his nose. The second Ganzabi in the hangar, who was stood beside an alarm, took only a second to gawp before he realised what he had to do. But he wasn't quite fast enough; Kiy fired the sling, and the clamp took the marine's feet out from under him. He fell with a clang and his helmet hit the hangar floor.

Kiy removed his marine helmet, freeing his messy hair and looking across the occupants of the cell. His eyes met hers a moment, but he made no show of recognition.

'Nicely done, Cloudgazer,' Gatista said, standing up.

'Thanks.' Kiy smiled.

Raldotya also got to her feet. 'Where did you learn such a convincing Ganzabi accent?'

'Oh, I spent some time down there, years back...' He went to push open the gate. There was a sudden crack, then the hum of the electrical grid cut off abruptly. No sooner had it done so than the box hooked up to it began blaring an angry, rattling siren.

'Shut it off!' someone called out.

Kiy whirled around and slammed the clamp of the sling into it, tipping it backward. It hit the floor with a heavy thud, a shatter of glass, and the death throes of electrical sparks.

There was a quiet moment, then a voice came over the radio in Kiy's pack. 'What's going on? All stations, report.'

'Shyut,' Gatista muttered.

A flurry of voices began to exchange confusing and increasingly worried checks over the radio.

'Now what?' Elzie looked at Gatista.

'Once the Ganzabi catch on to our escape, we'll have a whole battalion of marines descending on us,' he said. 'If we're to do this, we're going to need to clear them out completely to take the ship back.'

'What if they just shoot the *Akron* down?' Kiy asked.

Gatista shook his head. 'They clearly want it. They won't do that. Unless we try to escape.'

'Uh... that's also a problem?' Kiy pointed out.

'Don't worry about it for now,' the first officer replied, looking at Elzie tellingly. 'Elzie, we're gonna need a leap of faith. The rest of us will keep them occupied.'

She looked at Kiy uncertainly for a moment, then nodded, determination setting into her face. 'Tanthar, can you get me past the Ganzabi to the bridge?'

Kiy raised an eyebrow. 'Do I look like an army?'

'That sling is army enough, it would seem,' she said, stepping out of the defeated electrical fence.

'Well, I'm pretty sure I can get you there. But then what?'

'Leave that to us.' She shot a knowing glance at Gatista before setting off at a run.

Kiy followed her along small side corridors and lesser-used paths, and they worked their way up towards the bridge. On an exterior walkway, she stopped at a door that led to a long corridor. At the far end, two Ganzabi stood with rifles at their hips, talking casually.

'Show us your magic,' Elzie said.

Kiy threw a doubtful look. 'If we start a firefight, they'll all descend on our location, and we'll never get past them. We'll have to go round them.'

'That'll take too long.'

'Not if we go under the ship.'

She gave him a reluctant look, then nodded. 'You really mean it, don't you?'

'Are you one of these girls that's got a problem with being carried?'

She rolled her eyes. 'Fine, very well. Take hold of my waist. Enjoy.'

Kiy snorted. 'Don't lose sight of yourself. You can flap if you prefer.'

'You can get flakked.'

'You are such a moody—'

The sound of boots approached. Kiy grabbed her and leapt over the rail.

She stifled a yell as her stomach was left behind, and the pair tumbled down into the open sky. Kiy extended his free arm, she heard the clunk of the sling, and the fall became a sideways motion, moving them towards the bow of the ship. They swung back up, onto another platform. The entire swing had taken just a few seconds in all.

Elzie stumbled as Kiy let her go.

Kiy took a cautious glance around. 'It's clear, let's go.'

'Alright...' Elzie agreed breathlessly. 'Just stop spinning the ship for a second and I'll be right there.'

The quietness on the bridge shattered as they burst in. At the helm stood a portly man with small glasses, who nearly fell over when he saw them. The officer at Raldotya's post was a tall man with a hooked nose; his narrow eyes betrayed a look of fear. Only the commanding officer remained composed, and even she appeared young and inexperienced.

The craftsman ran from the room immediately, but the tall comms officer ran at Kiy—who overpowered him easily, dealing a swift blow with the sling. Elzie darted to a panel tucked away behind the engine readout consoles, but as she wrenched it open she heard the click of a pistol cocking.

'Not another step,' the Ganzabi captain said, her percussion pistol trained on Elzie with a professional two-handed grip.

Elzie slowly withdrew from the panel, raising her hands.

Kiy's finger itched to move, the tall hook-nose man unconscious at his feet. He could knock the pistol from the woman's hands with the sling, no doubt. But could he do it before she shot Elzie? Risking one's own life on a gambit was one thing, but risking someone else's life was something else altogether. And his revolver sat foolishly holstered on his thigh.

'Now what?' The Ganzabi officer stared at Kiy defiantly. She was slim and petite, with long blond hair and a small, upturned nose. Her cool blue eyes seemed to quiver as she glared. 'You expect to just fly out of here? Are you stupid?'

Kiy's eyes flicked to the door on hearing distant shouts. He could have sworn there was a rifle shot as well. Should the Ganzabi arrive in force, it would all be over. His gaze turned to Elzie, and his eyes met hers. Her face seemed to have similar thoughts beneath. Just waiting for a moment to act.

Kiy saw her before she moved, almost as though the signal in her brain were a visible pulse. He raised the sling and fired it.

The clamp hit the captain's weapon as she fired. There was a flash of bright sparks where the bullet ricocheted off the control panel, just a hair's width from where Elzie had been. As Kiy had moved to fire, she had thrown herself aside onto a red lever.

The repeated whoop of the alarm was now blaring, and the deck lighting shifted to a pulsing orange. The Ganzabi's pistol spun across the deck, and her pupils shrank to pinpricks as she stared at Kiy. He whipped his revolver from its holster to point it at her.

Elzie dragged herself back to her feet by the lever handle. 'If *we* can't have her... *no-one* will.'

An automated voice on the ship's PA system commenced a countdown. Three minutes.

Kiy baulked. *Surely she didn't?*

The Ganzabi woman was incredulous. 'You're insane!' Her stare lingered on Kiy, then she looked at Elzie. 'Reverse it! Now!'

'That's not possible,' Elzie told her coldly.

Kiy looked at Elzie uneasily. Had she truly lost her mind? He tried not to let his reservations show in his face, but the Ganzabi woman clearly saw his emotions.

'That's right, Cloudgazer,' she said, pronouncing it like it was a dirty word. 'You've doomed yourself.'

Kiy refused to believe Elzie would commit a ship-wide suicide. Azrunites were far too rational for such notions. Or so he'd always thought.

'The *Akron* cannot be allowed to fall into Ganzabar's hands. Our lives are not near so important,' Elzie declared.

Kiy felt a lump in his throat. He'd never have dreamt Elzie could be so fanatical.

The Ganzabi woman snatched a mouthpiece from a radio system set into the ceiling. She spoke over the ship's PA system. 'This is Captain Isikel. All hands, abandon ship. Self-destruct has been activated by insurgents. Repeat, evacuate immediately. All prisoners to remain on board, on penalty of death.' She kept her eyes on Kiy as she set the mouthpiece back.

'Kiy, what are you waiting for?' Elzie said. 'Shoot her.'

Isikel took several steps back towards the angular arch leading out the rear of the bridge. 'You know we won't let you escape from this exploding tomb you've made for yourselves.' She gave a smile of mock-politeness, then ran from the room.

Kiy lowered the pistol.

Elzie narrowed her eyes. 'You can't shoot women, can you?'

'I don't find it easy to shoot *anyone*, damn you.' He shoved the revolver back in its holster. 'But, well, my sister...'

Elzie looked the way Isikel had gone. 'Your sister—?'

'Forget it. Just every time I see a young, slightly Laro-looking Ganzabi woman, my brain makes connections where there are none.' He gave her a dry look. 'Don't worry, I promise next time to blow her brains out.'

'Right,' Elzie said uncertainly.

'Now,' Kiy said, 'care to explain what the flak you're doing?'

'What do you mean?'

'This self-destruct countdown. Even if you reverse the mechanism after they leave, they'll just pound us to pieces.'

'I wasn't bluffing; this system is not reversible,' Elzie said. 'But don't worry. Trust me.'

'Trust you?'

She threw him a smile that hinted mischief; he found it both intoxicating and inarguable. 'I know you're not used to that idea,' she told him, hitting several small switches, 'but this will work. You know that Azrunites don't believe in any of that going-down-with-the-ship crap. We've just got to make some preparations.'

'Like what? Nuclear-proof pants?'

'The ship will seal itself airtight in two minutes and ten seconds,' Elzie said. 'We need to be sure we're inside by then.'

'Wouldn't want to miss the fireworks.'

On the bridge of the *Postremo*, the Countess de Saufon strode in confidently, sat down, and gazed over the *Akron*. Dozens of troop transports were hurriedly breaking off from the boarding points, swarming back towards her fleet, causing her serene countenance to evaporate.

'What is all this?' she said angrily. 'Get me Captain Isikel at once.'

'Miss Saufon,' said Commander Mofkan, her most senior officer, on her right, 'Captain Isikel reported that the Azrunites have initiated the self-destruct.'

The countess gaped, then she put her hands on her hips and pouted like a spoilt child. 'But I wanted it! How dare they! Turn it off, *right now!*'

'The process is not reversible, my lady. It is designed to prevent the technology falling into the wrong hands.'

She smirked at that, stroking the arms of her chair as though they might purr. 'Well, you don't say.'

Mofkan grimaced. Now that she'd gone and 'misplaced' their Cracker, there wasn't much chance of overriding a self-destruct this time.

She shrugged and looked out at the ship again. 'Oh well, who cares. Take us to whatever a safe distance is, and we'll shoot them like fowl if they try to 'bandon ship.'

'Yes, Miss Saufon.'

She smiled to herself wickedly. 'Actually, that sounds kinda fun after all. Talot, fetch me a glass of Sharooza...'

Mestphura was visibly relieved to be on his bridge again, and didn't seem the least bit bothered that Elzie had just initiated the destruction of the ship to which it was attached.

Kiy watched Elzie as she referred back and forth between a set of switches and a large label of instructions on the inside of a cabinet door. This was not something she was used to operating, that much he could tell. She was removing plugs from sockets on one side and criss-crossing the leads over to a bank of plugs on the other with a mixed degree of certainty. Perhaps there *was* an override, and she was just being a bitch again.

It seemed most of the crew had managed to stay in one piece, no doubt thanks to Mestphura's order to come quietly. A few had been killed in the boarding, and a few more in the subsequent chaos of the escape from the brig, but were it not for the imminent destruction of the ship—now only thirty seconds away—Kiy figured they would all be doing rather well, all things considered.

Up and down the length of the craft, hatches were being secured by members of *Akron*'s crew. The Ganzabi barges had all left, although several incapacitated marines had been left on board to go down with the ship.

On the rear of the vessel, the hull parted, exposing a dark cavity within the rear engine section. Plates folded back to reveal slender grey tubes extending backwards. There were perhaps five or six, each one as big as a town's grain silo. They were not noticed by the retreating boarding barges, nor by the Ganzabi war vessels that had backed off to a sensible distance. As the insides of the cylinders glowed and hissed, an ignitor device spat sparks into the growing furnace.

Aboard the bridge, they could feel the deck rumble as if the world itself were trembling.

'This is one heck of a bluff,' Kiy muttered. 'I hope you know how to turn it off.'

'Critical heat levels in ten,' Gatista said.

Mestphura watched a screen of readouts. The bridge hung on his next word. 'Initiate in six.'

Elzie turned to Kiy and spoke quickly. 'Okay, now you remember that button I said never to press?'

'Four.'

Kiy eyed it. 'Yeah?'

'Three.'

'Press it now!'

'Two.'

Kiy swivelled and jammed the button.

The deafening roar and shudder of acceleration drowned out the last of Gatista's countdown. Elzie stumbled, grabbing hold of Kiy's coat as the deck was wrenched out from underneath them. Acceleration took them, a kind Kiy had never known before. It was like the kickback of a turbo in a skyfighter, but applied to the scale of a city. The deck shook, the consoles shuddered and his ears roared. Around him, the crew were gripping anything they could. Outside the forward windows, the horizon dipped down out of view. Kiy's mouth fell open as they passed through an entire sheet of clouds, followed a few seconds later by the higher, wispy clouds. Gradually the deep blue of the sky took over the view, darkening from aqua to a rich velvet as the ship thundered on.

The Countess de Saufon's lips were pursed and eyes alight as she watched the *Akron* rise up faster and faster. Its rear was obscured by a flare as bright as the sun, and it left behind a column of smoke that was so vast it obscured half the fleet. She watched the roaring craft curve upwards in a progressively steeper angle, almost vertical now, climbing like a missile.

'Shoot it! Why is nobody *shooting* at it?' she said, then overturned her own question with an angry yell. 'I thought you said it was going to self-destruct!'

Mofkan sweated. 'Miss Saufon, Captain Isikel reported—'

'I don't care! I said *shoot it!*'

Talot cowered. 'It's out of range already, my lady.'

She stood a moment, trembling in anger, then threw down her cocktail against the deck in a shatter of fine crystal.

The ship seemed to be getting ever quicker, and the view gave Kiy a strange sensation. He was sure the ship was now almost vertical, yet he still stood on the deck, holding on to the console. Then he saw the fringes at the top of the view lighten, and with even greater confusion he realised they had inverted. Why was he not crumpled on the ceiling?

The sound of the Jump engine had changed also. It was not so much a roar anymore, but a rumble in the deck and the bulkheads. Even the rushing air around them seemed to be getting quieter. Were they slowing down?

Suddenly, Kiy noticed he could see a star. He blinked. Another one! And yet it was midafternoon. He stared in fascination as the deep velvet gave way to almost black and more stars appeared. The sky was turning to night before his very eyes.

Finally the view from the forward windows showed complete darkness but for the stars that now awoke in their thousands. He'd never seen so many before. The roar was gone, replaced by an eerie silence. The horizon was above him, still bright like day, and ever so slightly curved. It struck a mesmerising contrast with the black night sky they were now sailing in, and which stretched out below.

They were somewhere far above the entire world, upside down in the night. Kiy couldn't make sense of it.

'Oxygen levels: perfect,' Elzie said, watching her console intently. She looked at the others with a broadening grin. 'We did it.'

'All systems still running normal. It... works. After all these years.' Gatista stared out at the surreal new sky.

'Indeed. It is truly remarkable,' Mestphura said. The view was silent, graceful, and both stunningly beautiful and strangely frightening.

'Where are we?' Kiy asked.

Elzie walked to the window. Kiy stepped up beside her, looking down and wondering if he was actually looking 'up', into the countless stars. Elzie was transfixed beside him, her reflection in the window like a beautiful ghost looking in at her, lost in an endless night. He shook the poetic image out of his head.

'We are... well...' she began, 'I know the theory behind all this, but it is a little fantastic...'

'If this reading is to be believed,' Kaj'aku said, 'we have zero airspeed, yet transponders indicate a change in position that is astronomical. I'd estimate something like... twenty-three times the speed of sound.'

Gatista whistled.

'How are such speeds even possible?' Kiy asked.

'It's because we're so high, there is basically no air,' Elzie said, animated with excitement. 'And as such, no air resistance. Our top speed is determined only by our thrust.'

'No air?' Kiy repeated. 'How high is that? The highest an airship has ever been is about thirty or forty thousand, isn't it? Then Antimass dwindles.'

'There's still air there, although not much,' Elzie said. 'But we didn't get here with Antimass. We got here on fusion rocket motors. "Here" being on the order of a hundred thousand, maybe more.' She smiled.

Kiy decided he liked her smile. 'So at this speed, how long before we reach... uh, wherever it is we're going?'

'Nubylon, capital of Azrune, is where the Jump returns us. Our ETA is,' she glanced at the display, 'about fourteen minutes.'

Kiy realised his mouth had fallen open. He made a conscious effort to close it. 'So... you bluffed them into thinking this Jump thing was the self-destruct?' He frowned. 'Why didn't you tell me that's what you were going to do?'

'Because,' she said deliberately, 'I needed to be sure you'd act right. You thought I'd really done it, and that Ganzabi saw it in your face.' She started back towards her station.

Kiy exhaled tersely. 'You've got some nerve. Any other cloudgazer would have clubbed you and gone over to the Ganzies.'

She turned and gave him that smile again. 'I know.'

The Ganzabi Armada

Leo had seen some big ships these past months, but nothing measured up to the enormous monster looming out of the clouds ahead. He sat beside Marc on a small aerofoil shuttle, a specially arranged transport to take them off ship. Two guards and a pilot were its only other occupants. Marc had been comatose since coming back from his 'chat' on the *Fortitude*.

Since leaving the ship that had captured them, they'd travelled for most of the day. Kiy used to say you watch the sun when lost by day, and the stars when lost by night. By the sun, Leo reckoned they were going north, but that didn't add up. Why would they be heading for the front lines, and not back to deepest Ganzabar? He decided he must have got the direction wrong somehow.

As they approached the Ganzabi battleship, Leo realised just how vast it was. It was a bulbous, swollen and irregular thing, like some bloated cattle beast from the parks in a ranch town. Only traces remained of the strong angles and unhassled surface that made a ship look Ganzabi. It was overladen with every type of upgrade and attachment conceivable: guns, armour plates, scanners, radars, transpulse masts, secondary armour plates, additional power generators, auxiliary ramscoops. The result was an appearance almost cancerous—an ugly, overloaded, overpowered amalgamation. Leo was unsure what this new ship would have in store for them, but he was afraid of it.

All around, the sky was a brilliant blue, but the clouds were clumped heavily, ensnaring the ships around them. The shuttle interior flickered as the craft passed in and out of cloud. It made Leo feel drowsy.

The plane banked slightly, smoothly coming around to the rear of the battleship, where massive hangar openings jutted out in various places. A long runway strip extended from the opening ahead of them, and the craft made a whirring grumble as the flaps were deployed.

Leo strained to listen to the pilot's calls over the shortwave, but he was sitting too far back. In any case, the two guards in between him and the pilot were talking loudly with each other. He had tried to eavesdrop on their conversation earlier, but had given up when it became clear they were simply talking about women.

Marc stirred a little, then opened his eyes lazily.

'You okay?' Leo said quietly, as the guards carried on chatting.

The Azrunite stared at him for a few moments, then his eyes wandered the cabin. They were bound to chairs by wrist and ankle. Beyond the guards was a thick mesh of wire obscuring the cockpit.

'Where are we?' Marc asked in a low, groggy voice.

'Don't know, but we're landing on a Ganzie battleship. Some kind of transfer.'

Marc tried to focus. 'Moller.'

'What?'

'Did you get a look at the ship?'

'Yeah.'

'What's it look like?'

'Looks like a fish that ate too much.'

Marc's face cracked stiffly into a smile. 'That'll be the one. The *Grace of Gnost*, flagship of Admiral Moller's fleet.'

'The invasion fleet? So we *are* north?' Leo looked out at the dozens of other ships that hung dormant around them, but just then the sky vanished, replaced by the darkness of the hangar. Beneath them, the rumble of the wheels appeared, then quickly tailed off.

'Reckon so,' Marc said, keeping his voice a croaking whisper.

The craft halted smoothly and the two guards turned to them.

'Alright, come on guys,' one of them said. He seemed a fairly simple fellow, jovial and business-like, but Leo resisted the urge to like him. He was a filthy Ganzie, after all.

The other marine was a dark-skinned Meedish and generally spoke less. He began to remove Leo carefully. 'Mac, these cuffs are too big for the kid.'

'They'll be fine. Little flakker's probably scared to move anyway, ain't that right?' The first looked at Leo.

Leo played the part. Better they believed that, he figured.

The pair of prisoners were escorted out. The two Ganzabi with them wore faded blue uniforms and carried stubby firearms. They approached a slim, hard-faced woman at the hangar exit. She eyed them with a sharp, hawk-like gaze and an aura of self-importance.

'Yes?'

'Prisoners to see Admiral Moller, ma'am,' the ensign at Marc's right announced.

She motioned to the passage behind her. 'Take them to cell one-three-six on K deck.'

'Ma'am, with all due respect, these were transferred as high priority and—'

'The admiral ain't got time for talkin' to boys and cowards. You will take them to the cell on K deck or so help me Gnost. Do I make myself perfectly clear?'

'Yes, ma'am!' The ensign straightened and saluted.

She stepped back to allow them to pass, then the two Ganzabi led Leo and Marc down the hall to a connecting corridor.

As they made their way through the endless corridors of the gigantic vessel, Leo sized up every possible situation that might lead to an escape. They passed marines and engineers and cooks; sometimes crowds of people would push past them going the other way. Trolleys met and crossed their path. Most of the corridors looked to have been overhauled with miles of new cables and ducts, and switch-boxes, steel tubes and tanks entangled almost every room. Leo had never known a ship with so many hiding places. All he needed was a distraction.

Leo could not believe his eyes when a group of oddly dressed performers rounded the corner. The lead lady wore a large, elaborate hat covered in red and blue feathers and a dress laced in gold and inlaid with precious stones. Her two dozen female dancers wore next to nothing at all, and looked to have been picked from some kind of perfection factory. There was a gangly man with his face painted purple, two fat men carrying a massive horned instrument, and a man only a metre high wearing a laughing mask. It was all Leo could do not to be distracted himself.

'Ow!'

'Hey, come back here!'

A kick of the shins, a barge of the shoulders, and Leo was stumbling through the solid mass of dancers and clowns. There were barked yells and curses, sounds of confusion and a clang that was either metal hitting metal or a gunshot ricochet. Leo pulled hard at his wrists and managed to wriggle out of the clumsy great iron hoops, chucking them over the side of a gantry into a deep chasm of interlocking machinery. They clattered a few times on the way down, the sound reverberating as though it were bouncing off all corners of the ship.

He ran as fast as he could down a flight of steps, turning every corner he saw. He could hear his pursuers lagging behind, then he launched himself up off a rail and grabbed onto a thick duct running the ceiling. Pulling himself up onto it, safely in shadow, he crept along into a dark passage where a dozen pipes came together. The shouts and hurried steps died away as Leo pushed deeper into the steel labyrinth.

His heart was racing. A part of him felt invincible. Here he was, on the enemy's flagship, and he'd escaped them. They must feel pretty stupid. He was momentarily overwhelmed with triumphant elation. Yet gradually, little thoughts started to trouble him. What to do now? He was still trapped on the enemy's ship. He could hide, but for how long? He had no supplies. They would find him eventually. He had to do something.

As he wandered the endless, deserted tubes, he began formulating a plan.

'What do you mean, "He ran away"?'

The Ganzabi marine had gone pale even before the verbal barrage from the brig officer, a lean, muscular man with mid-length greasy hair and beady eyes. Anger had given the man an almost comical cherry-red complexion, and his glare looked as though it could melt bulkheads.

Marc watched as the marine tried to explain how the Victory Parade Troupe had enabled the boy's escape, but the officer was having none of it.

The man at the desk spoke up. 'So there were two, but now there is only one?' He looked as though he had been born with a clipboard in one hand.

'We will bring in the boy, too,' the marine said. 'If we can just sign in this prisoner—'

'I'm afraid I can't permit that,' the man said officiously. 'The papers must be re-submitted.'

'Forget the boy, he's not important,' the brig officer said. 'Security Chief Carver has more *competent* men looking for him now.'

'I could go look for him, if you like,' Marc said casually.

'Shut up, Azrunite!'

The heavy door to the lifts slid open and a stoutly built bald man strode in with an air of importance. The Ganzabi men hushed. Marc looked round indifferently.

'Mr Rahl, sir,' the brig officer said. They all gave a salute.

'Officer Greyhem,' Rahl said with a look of disdain. 'The admiral wants to see the prisoners.'

Greyhem hesitated. 'Well, sir, there's been a... minor problem.'

35 - The First Nation

Nubylon

The capital city of Azrune was a wondrous sight from a distance, but up close it was of its own class entirely. White, curving walkways snaked through towering buildings capped with elegant arcs, graceful spires and geometric pinnacles.

The *Akron* slid along the harbour edge smoothly before approaching the massive circular doors of the hangar building. Kiy had never seen anything of such vast proportions; it dwarfed even the huge Admiralty of Laronor, which itself had a hangar large enough to enclose a battleship.

But as they slid through the opening, Kiy saw a void that seemed big enough to house an entire navy. It was black inside, forming a strange artificial night. The space was so immense that he couldn't quite make out the floor. A multitude of sleek white ships were scattered around at various levels, although he couldn't tell if they were small or distant, such was the confusion in his sense of scale. Some were attached to gantries, metal cranes and hover platforms, while others slid along silently through the artificial sky. He felt pretty sure that the *Akron* was still the largest of them all. Whenever they got close enough to see the people standing on the walkways and decks, their eyes were always on the great flagship.

When the *Akron* arrived at its docking space, Kiy withdrew from the observation deck and made his way back to his cabin. He had spent too long on the ship, he'd decided, and it was time he moved on. He had to find Leo—and he'd have to start all over again, too. He wondered if he should go to Laronor first and seek out Hennie, just to make sure she'd got there okay. It felt like another life when he'd last seen her.

But that plan was no good. He couldn't go to Hennie empty-handed, or at least unknowing of Leo's fate. He shook away morbid thoughts of what he might say to Hennie should he find out Leo was dead. And even if Leo was still alive, Kiy wasn't sure where to start. It could take years to track him down. The thought had been wearing on his mind, grinding it down over hours and days until he felt unable to think straight.

There was a polite knock, and Gatista entered.

'Commander Mestphura has asked for your company in this evening's gathering, celebrating the *Akron*'s safe return. All officers will be in attendance.'

Kiy made himself busy collecting his few belongings. 'I was planning on leaving.'

'He was... quite insistent,' Gatista said with some amusement. 'But then he's not the only one. We're all indebted to you for what you did back there in the Beyer Fields. We would very much be honoured to have you join us this evening.' He watched Kiy as though weighing him up. 'Elzie will accompany you. She's on her way with something smart for you to wear.'

Kiy hummed. He had always wanted to see the legendary city of Nubylon, ever since he was a child. And if he left now, he might never come back again; Azrune wasn't the easiest place to find yourself in. That Elzie would also be there suddenly made for a strangely enticing prospect. There were still a lot of questions in his mind about that woman. One evening wouldn't hurt.

'Alright. Thanks Gatista,' he said.

Gatista gave a courteous Azrunite salute-nod—a slight bow and turn of the head—then left the room.

When Elzie appeared later, Kiy almost didn't recognise her. She was garbed in brilliant white, with a long poncho that had rectangular slits subtracted from it. Tall white boots reached her knees, and a short skirt blended into a layered tunic, with oversized sleeves that concealed her hands. The hems and collars were embellished with angular shapes in gold and azure. Her hair was restyled from a simplistic bob to an intricately pinned and braided work of art.

In her arms, she held a bundle of clothes looking to be of much the same style, which she handed over to Kiy.

'Your smart dress,' she said. 'To make you look less of a bum.'

'Eh, anything's possible,' Kiy remarked with a smile.

Elzie seemed to be inspecting every detail of the room besides him. 'You really wanna come?' she asked.

'I guess. Why not?'

She shrugged, watching him from the corner of her eye. 'Just figured your type might get bored, is all.'

'My type? As in, a cloudgazer?'

'Oh, and you should probably avoid referring to yourself as that until you leave,' she said. 'Cloudgazers are illegal here, as you probably know.'

'I am quite aware of my profession's legal borders,' Kiy said drily.

She made a slight grunt, then looked at him expectantly.

'So...' he began, as though waiting for her to get the idea, 'can I get a little privacy?'

'What do you mean?' she said. 'Just swap clothes. We don't have all day.'

Kiy made the sound of clearing his throat. 'Where I come from, taking your trousers off is kinda something you do in private.'

There was a pause as Elzie went to say something, then her face lit up in recognition. 'Oh. Oh! Right. I see.' She blushed. Kiy had never seen her do that before, and for a moment she seemed very girlish. 'Sorry, didn't mean to offend. I'll wait outside.' She retreated through the door.

When Kiy emerged from the cabin some minutes later, he inspected his appearance uncertainly. In contrast to the outfit Elzie was wearing, his had turned out to be a simpler one-piece robe that went right down to his feet, with long baggy sleeves that swallowed his hands. He felt somewhat ridiculous in it, but he figured that every country had its styles. He probably looked quite dapper here. Well, perhaps.

Elzie appraised him, then went on ahead. 'Follow me.'

Nervousness lumped in his throat. He couldn't figure why; he rarely got nervous. He'd chased airships amid exploding shells and had felt more at ease than this. Etiquette was sometimes more intimidating than battlefields.

They met Mesthura at the gantry onto the dock, gowned in formal white much like Kiy's.

'Ah, Kiy. Glad you're able to join us,' he said, a broad and hearty smile making his face much warmer than Kiy was used to.

'A pleasure, sir.'

'You can forget about ranks this evening, Kiy. We shall be off duty. Think of this as our way of thanks. I only ask that you use an alias while here. For this evening, you are Klaus Omwell.'

Kiy nodded. 'If it pleases you.'

'Where's this shindig happening, anyway?' Elzie said.

'Tyloria Hotel,' Mesthura replied. 'Gatista and the others will meet us there a little later.'

'The Tyloria?' Elzie repeated uneasily.

Mesthura frowned. 'Yes, why?'

'Nothing,' she said. 'I mean, other than... it's in Amutep, right under the nose of the Domestic Ministry, and Kiy—'

'—will be fine,' Mesthura interrupted. 'Nobody knows he's a cloudgazer without his sling. And they don't need to go asking.'

'Don't worry about me,' Kiy said. 'I can blend.'

Elzie seemed sceptical, but relented.

The commander led them down the corridor from the dock. It was the cleanest and brightest corridor Kiy had ever seen in a harbour's hangar. At the far end they emerged onto a wide landing area with open sky around them. Nuzzled to one side of the platform was a grand-looking autocab, which they boarded. It gave a loud click and, with a purring hum, accelerated towards the urban core.

'Quite a city,' Kiy remarked, hoping to loosen the conversation a little. It wasn't untrue: he found what he saw captivating. Lithe skyscrapers stood proudly aloft on their cylindrical floatrock foundations. The late afternoon sun glittered off wide discs of clear water, pouring over at their edges into reservoirs and fountains and circumnavigated by smooth white walkways and paths. Massive, gracefully thin trees lined the boulevards, reaching up higher than the masts of a battleship. The streets seemed quiet, relaxed, and sparse compared to any other city Kiy had seen—near-desolate for a capital.

'Have you ever been to Nubylon?' Mestphura queried.

'No.' Kiy had never gone to Azrune at all, but then few outside of it ever did. He wouldn't normally have let such a thing stop him, but there was little work for a cloudgazer in Azrune anyway. It was a place that generally kept to itself, had next to zero crime and a high standard of living. Add to that a law against plying one's trade, and it wasn't so appealing a destination, however wondrous it might be.

'It is possibly the oldest city in the world,' Elzie said woodenly. Her hands sat one atop the other on her lap, her legs crossed. She watched the city sliding silently past as she spoke. 'Even the *Akron* doesn't compare. And that's at least seven hundred years old.'

Seven hundred? Kiy wondered how something that old could still fly. And not only fly, but fly better than anything built today. The Gold Age had indeed been built to last. Too bad the age itself had not.

'It's said,' Elzie began, 'that during the height of the Gold Age, there were no nations. There was a global union of all the people of Azimuth, and Nubylon was their capital.' She shrugged almost to herself. 'The ancient meaning of the word Azrune is "world union".'

'Of course,' Mestphura interjected with a smile, 'that's probably just something we embellished for ourselves, to make us feel better about having little say anymore.'

The autocab slid up to a monolithic rectangular building that seemed to be made entirely of glass and tapered to its summit. A white, organic-shaped canopy like a gull's wing formed a graceful curve over the path leading into the building's entrance, a tall triangular archway. Kiy stepped out and looked up at the imposing lines of the arch at the end of a long strip of carpet.

A grey-robed attendant greeted them and led them through. They proceeded through a labyrinth of corridors to a spacious lounge with tall, gold-rimmed windows. The room was filled with dozens of people all dressed in formal white gowns. Percussion pulsed around the room like a swaying heartbeat, with lyrics and instruments that were foreign to Kiy's ears. Behind the music, conversations thronged.

'Ah, the great Julius Mestphura!' cried the raucous voice of a jolly great Aquitano man with a fiercely untamed beard and terrific eyebrows.

'Minister Alamando.' Mestphura grinned warmly as the man strode up to them. 'I trust you're well.'

'That I am! And dear Elzie! Perhaps you will treat us to another fine display of dance this evening?'

Elzie slanted her mouth. 'I'm not sure if it's a good time —'

'Splendid! We're looking forward to it!' Alamando's voice was a crescendo. 'Everything has been terribly drab around here recently. The other ministers pace about miserably, mulling on the predicament we're in, hoping for some news from the Navy. Then—you just fall out of the sky! Ha-haaah!'

'Not with good news, alas,' Mestphura admitted. 'The *Postremo* is in Ganzabar's hands.'

Alamando looked as though he'd just sat on something painful. 'That is unfortunate. But it's far from over, is it not? I'm told there's little in the way of repairs or resupply before the *Akron* is ready to resume the search—' It was then that he noticed Kiy. He appraised him with sudden gravitas. 'I don't believe we've met, sir.'

'Klaus,' Kiy said simply.

'He's a Brazakker,' Elzie put in. 'And a rude one, at that.'

'A friend of Elzie's. Visiting Nubylon for the first time,' Mestphura explained, eyeing Elzie sharply.

'Ah, well met, Klaus,' Alamando replied. 'I hope you enjoy the evening's entertainment.'

An older gentleman approached them. He looked past sixty but physically fit, with a scholarly quality to his features and healthy tint to his weathered skin. His head was marginally less bald than Mestphura's, ringed by a wispy barricade of grey hair around the back.

'Welcome back, Mestphura,' the man said as he joined them.

'Good to be back,' Mestphura replied, then looked to Kiy and Elzie. 'This is Donneroque, Supreme Commander of the *Horizon*.'

The old officer made a polite bow to the group. 'I apologise, but I must briefly steal Mr Mestphura from your company.'

'Of course,' Elzie responded politely.

Mestphura gave them a formal nod of parting, then followed Donneroque to an elevator.

'I wonder what all that was about,' Elzie said.

Alamando looked dismissive. 'Probably about the dirt in the papers lately. Oh, I won't bore you with it. I'm sure Mestphura can do that.' He brightened. 'Dancing beats work, that's what I always say.'

'No dancing until I get a drink. Where's a drone when you need one?' She turned. 'What'll it be, Mr Alamando?'

'Dram, my dear.' He beamed.

'Klaus?'

'Vodstok for me, thanks.'

Elzie disappeared into the mass of people, and Alamando engaged Kiy in the sort of conversation one encounters at formal parties. Kiy tried to maintain it so as not to draw attention to himself, but he found his mind distracted by Elzie's recent change of behaviour. It took the swirling shapes and colours of a group of five energetic female dancers to draw his mind back to the present.

They stood on an elevated stage on the far side of the hall. In the centre of them was a pretty, chestnut-haired woman of probably no more than twenty, with a dazzling smile. She was tapping her foot and swaying in time as the musicians began a new song. A wave of approval went up as she slid into the dance. Her hips swayed side to side, a whip-like motion oscillating her body back and forth. She slowly revolved on the spot, her hands twirling, and the twist seemed to follow up her arm. Then the dance changed —a kind of hop in time to the complex rattle of darbuka drums. She pivoted on one foot, then the other, as though drawing circles on the floor with her toe. Then the dance changed again, becoming a kind of slink to either side as she made graceful arcs with her arms, the long sleeves of her tunic drawing intricate loops.

'Aren't they magnificent?' Alamando said. 'The Skyliners. Finest dancers in Azrune, if you ask me. You have bhangra in Brazak West?'

'Mmn?'

Alamando could see Kiy wasn't quite taking it in. 'A Beyjuk tradition, I believe, though a staple of any Azrunite celebration. Elzie has quite the talent for it.'

'Seems to be a multi-talented girl, that one,' Kiy remarked.

'Indeed,' Alamando said, his eyes following the Skyliners' performance. 'A graduate of Solar Harp academy, expert in calputers, one of the best pilots in the service and exquisite on her feet. You're a lucky fellow.'

Kiy realised what he meant and fumbled with his words. 'We're not... I mean, I—'

Alamando laughed boisterously. 'Relax, I was kidding you! That would be absurd, of course.'

Kiy humoured him with a grudging smile as Elzie reappeared. Alamando greeted her warmly, receiving his drink. 'My dear Miss Kerowan, you are too kind.'

She smiled, handing a short glass of colourless liquid to Kiy. 'Thank you, Mr Alamando. Are we still without our fair commander?'

'I imagine he may be a little while,' Alamando replied, then gave the two of them grave glances. 'The leak has caused quite a stir, I'd say.'

'Leak?' Elzie repeated.

Alamando managed to look sheepish. 'It's been all over the press since yesterday morning. Insider information claims that the Navy have lost a top secret prototype.' His gaze was continually drawn to the dancers, to whom he gave an admiring smile. 'I doubt this will change the *Akron*'s mission, whatever that may be, but it seems you chose a good time to drop by.'

Elzie looked ill, and Kiy felt himself becoming self-conscious. Talk about work was perilously close to talk about his identity. And Elzie seemed far more disturbed by this than he'd expected.

'Any idea what the Ministry are going to do about it?' she asked after an anxious pause.

'Wring their hands some more, I would imagine,' Alamando quipped.

'I should go and find Mestphura,' she said abruptly, then excused herself.

Kiy made to follow, but she turned and muttered, 'Mingle.'

He frowned, but remained put as she disappeared from the room. The dancers came to the end of their set and a wave of applause surged around him.

The dwindling evening light flooded through tall windows, stretching across the bare, spacious office of Minister Gorder, who stood in deep thought, his hands clasped behind his back. A portly man in his twilight years, he was shorter than the two commanders who stood with equally regal composure opposite him: Mestphura and Donneroque.

'The war is over,' Gorder declared. 'Tomorrow the prime minister is calling an emergency meeting to vote on Azrune's withdrawl from the conflict. Given the recent political climate, I very much doubt there will be any debate to speak of.'

'The *Postremo* is still unrecovered,' Mestphura protested.

'That is your own failing, although it is a national problem.' Gorder's stern eyes showed hints of sympathy. 'You must understand, Mestphura, that I cannot wait for the *Akron* to be made ready before resuming the search. That's why Donneroque is here; in two hours the *Horizon* will sail for Brazak West. The *Akron* is to resupply and await further orders.'

'If the war is over,' Mestphura said, 'the *Horizon*'s presence in the combat zone will surely incite international incident.'

'We will strive to maintain a low profile,' Donneroque assured.

'No doubt,' Mestphura said. 'But even with a capable commander at the helm, the *Horizon* will be spotted sooner or later. What do you propose to do then?'

'You may not be aware,' Gorder told him, 'but since the disappearance of the prototype, the *Horizon* has been fitted with an optical camouflage matrix not unlike the *Postremo*'s. While it doesn't allow it to stay permanently concealed, it does permit it short periods of invisibility. I have every confidence that we shall avoid further embarrassments with the task in Commander Donneroque's capable hands.'

Donneroque shifted uncomfortably. He didn't seem keen on being exemplified as Mestphura's replacement.

'What of the *Akron*?' Mestphura ventured.

The Minister rubbed his neck, looking out of the window. 'That remains to be seen, Commander Mestphura. I will have you mobilised again as soon as I can.'

'Supreme Commander Mestphura? I'm sorry, but he's still not returned from the Ministry,' A young male assistant was telling Elzie as Kiy stepped into the quiet lounge.

'Can you please tell him Officer Kerowan needs to speak with him? It's been almost an hour.'

The assistant nodded and disappeared into an elevator.

Elzie then noticed Kiy. 'What are you doing here?'

'I thought I'd come see what was keeping you.'

'You're like a lost dog,' she chided.

'Being abandoned at a foreign political function is not my idea of a good time,' Kiy said. 'Where are Gatista and the others, anyway?'

'They should be here somewhere.' She glanced around before eyeing him and sighing. 'Have you been walking around all this time with your collar flat?'

'I guess.'

She leant in and fussed at it. Once she'd got it flared up right, she showed a hint of satisfaction before her expression fell and she sat down heavily on one of the couches. The room was some way from the main function hall and the music couldn't be made out, but there was an ambient tune with plucked strings and gentle beat playing within the room itself. It reminded Kiy of the jazz bars in the USK, though he saw no band. The music seemed to be coming from a recording, although the fidelity of it was indistinguishable from the real thing.

'You alright?' he said.

Her eyes lowered, and it took her a moment to find the words she meant to say. 'You shouldn't have come.'

There was an uneasy pause. 'Why not?'

She didn't seem sure. 'If anyone finds out...'

'They won't. And Mestphura doesn't seem to think there's a problem.'

'He's not the most orthodox of men, Kiy.'

'Why are you so worried?' He sat beside her.

'You don't understand,' she said tiredly. 'This isn't the world you're used to. There are ways. They'll find you.'

Kiy nodded. 'Yes, I'm sure there are, here.' His arm twitched involuntarily. He tried to discreetly rub the spasm away without drawing attention to it. 'I almost left too, you know. Tonight.'

'Yeah? Then why didn't you?'

He glanced at her, thinking she probably hadn't meant to sound so harsh, but her face was dour and her eyes cold, and whatever was holding her gaze was beyond the room. He looked back at the floor. 'Sky knows.'

'I tried to warn you not to come,' she said, although it wasn't clear whether she was trying to convince him or herself.

'Pretty lame attempt.'

'What?' She turned and glared at him. 'You're the idyat here!'

He gave her a hint of a smile. 'You just didn't want me to go, did you?'

'Oh, believe me,' she rolled her eyes, 'I can't want that enough.'

'I don't believe you.' He leant forward.

She looked away, though there was a trace of amusement in her face. 'You're insufferable.'

With a beep and a whoosh, the doors of the elevator opened. Both of them turned and stood, expecting to see Mestphura. Instead, a lithe feminine figure stepped forward, wearing a skin-tight grey bodysuit armoured in vital places with white plates that looked like polished ceramic. The upper half of her face was hidden by a sleek helmet of the same material. She raised her arm, at the end of which was a dark, bulky device tipped with a shiny, stubby barrel.

Instinct took over and Kiy dived to one side. A projectile whistled through the air and shattered something behind him.

Kiy heard Elzie yell out as he rolled back to his feet, pulling back the gown to reveal his sling, which he slid his arm into in one fluid motion. He fired it through the doorway, out of the room.

Elzie started to shout something, but he was already flying through the arch on the end of the cable. He hit the ground again just outside the room, on the indoor balcony of a large atrium, leapt over the balcony, and used the sling to cross the gap to the far side.

As he started off down the corridor, he heard a thud behind him. Whirling around, he saw the figure had landed just behind him. His eyes widened, and the word 'how' had begun to form on his lips, then he ducked as she fired again. A dark blur passed over his head. He darted down a side corridor.

He threw himself into a full sprint as questions assailed his mind. Who was she? How did she cross the atrium so quickly? She couldn't be a cloudgazer; *surely not here*.

He was about to reach the far end of the corridor, which ended at a tall window, when the window exploded in a shower of glass and another helmeted figure landed in front of Kiy, crouched on one knee. Kiy clumsily changed direction and barged through a door to his left, into a spacious room with a long dining table neatly set. As he vaulted it, he could hear the footsteps of at least two people behind him. There was an open window at the far side, and he leaped through it into the sky.

As he tumbled down through the wind, he felt a measure of relief. He'd made it. What, for many, would be the most terrifying plummet of their lives was to him a wonderfully liberating turn of events, thanks to the sling. He raised it up and fired the clamp at a nearby tower, then pulled himself in over a smooth arc. He kept the momentum going as he reached the tower, flipping over and landing neatly on a maintenance balcony.

He straightened up and brushed off his coat sleeves. *Now to get out of this crazy city*, he thought. The question was, how? Probably best to distance himself from the *Akron* and her crew, just in case—

A blunt object hit him hard between the shoulder blades. He cried out in pain, stumbling forward. Managing to stay on his feet, he spun around and grabbed a railing for support.

The masked white-plated woman was just a few strides away, walking towards him with calm, bold steps. To either side of her, figures wearing the same kind of outfit, both male, landed lightly.

'Who the flak are you?' Kiy backed away.

The woman pointed and fired her wrist device. Kiy leapt, his sling taking him upwards as it attached to a beam overhead. But this time the masked woman saw it coming and whipped her arm back. The cable that had shot from her device recoiled, wrapped around Kiy's leg and pulled taut. He was forced to release his own under the strain, and crashed down.

The woman's cable snapped back into the device on her wrist with a sound like a cane cutting the air. Kiy dragged himself back onto his feet as she approached, just in time to block a savage and precise kick from an armoured shin.

One of the other faceless figures appeared behind him and delivered a lightning-fast kick to the back. As Kiy fell forward, the woman's knee swung in and knocked the wind right out of his lungs. She hit him on the temple with blinding force, then he was lying on his back, pinned there, her foot to his chest.

He had the most curious sensation: ghostly wandering shapes at the back of his retinas swam into view, circling over him like curious gulls. The colour of everything faded into grey, and his focus was pulled away into the distance. His head throbbed, and everything dwindled into night.

Skybay, Nubylon
October 13ᵗʰ

'Sentinels?' Mestphura repeated.

Elzie nodded, though she could scarcely believe it herself. She hadn't seen them for long; in a blink Kiy was gone, the Sentinel right behind him. She had tried to follow them, but it was as though they had wings. When she'd lost sight of them, she'd feared for the worst. All searches for Kiy had turned up blank, and the classified nature of his presence forced Mestphura to settle for waiting.

It wasn't until morning that the Domestic Ministry had confirmed that Sentinels had apprehended a man of Kiy's description. Elzie had come straight to Mestphura's apartment to inform him.

He dressed hurriedly, cursing his own judgement. 'I don't understand how they tracked him so quickly. Even with the *Postremo* declassified, Domestic had no knowledge on Tanthar.'

Elzie just shook her head.

'I'm going over there to speak with them. I'd like you to accompany me.'

'As you say,' she responded meekly.

They caught an autocab back to the Amutep district. Mestphura barely waited for the machine to settle outside the Domestic Ministry before he was out and striding up the steps. Elzie had to jog to keep up with him. As they entered the Domestic Ministry's grand lobby, with its spotless polished floor tiles and sweeping gold panelling that divided every wall into distinct upper and lower styles, a long-limbed, slightly crooked old man greeted them coldly.

'Julius Mestphura. I thought we might see you our way.'

'Magistrate Wolming,' Mestphura acknowledged, regarding the boney, hawk-nosed man in front of him without enthusiasm. The magistrate was the head of his Ministry and the most senior official of his jurisdiction, which was that of the interior affairs and security of Azrune. And Wolming had clearly been expecting them, despite the early hour.

Mestphura drew himself up. 'We have reason to believe your Sentinels have mistaken a friend of ours for someone else.'

'Oh?' The magistrate seemed uninterested.

'Yes,' Mestphura said firmly. 'A man named Klaus Omwell.'

Wolming gave Mestphura a hard glance, but assented. 'Very well. Follow me.'

Mestphura walked alongside the magistrate while Elzie trailed behind. They entered an elevator that shot up through a glass tube, from which they could see the open interior of the building. Balconies looked out over an indoor garden, and a graceful fountain sprayed a plume up several storeys.

The lift stopped some floors from the top, and they made their way to a series of secluded rooms with smooth rounded doorways without handles. The magistrate stood before one of them expectantly, then the door slid aside.

Inside, Kiy lay on a simple bed, seemingly asleep. The room had a single window, looking out onto the building's warmly lit central column. Sunlight filtering down from above was so diffused it became a soft yellowish glow.

'This is the man?' the magistrate asked.

Mestphura nodded. 'I would wish to speak with him.'

'I'm afraid that won't be possible, Commander,' the magistrate said, emotionless. 'He's not regained consciousness since we took him in.'

'What in Sky's name did you do to him, man?' Mestphura said.

Elzie stepped up to the cloudgazer and leaned over him. Aside from a bruised swell on his forehead, he appeared otherwise unharmed.

'He'll be alright, in time,' the magistrate said. 'It seems he took a blow to the head during his evasion of capture. We will be transferring him to Goldstar Hospital, but I'm afraid we must continue to detain him.' He made a beckoning gesture off to his left. 'He was carrying this.'

One of the magistrate's aides, who had apparently been standing in the corner discreetly all this time, passed Kiy's sling to Mestphura.

Mestphura kept any telling reaction from his eyes. Elzie kept her eyes averted altogether.

'Commander,' Magistrate Wolming said gravely, 'surely this is some mistake? A man of your stature would not associate with a cloudgazer.'

'I've always believed it required more than holding a hammer to be considered a carpenter, sir. Or perhaps you would now consider me a cloudgazer?' Mestphura said with almost scholarly contemplation. He matched the magistrate's glare before handing the sling back to the aide, who scurried back.

The magistrate sneered. 'So we are to believe he was holding it for someone else?'

'What evidence have you that he used it?' Mestphura enquired. 'Possession of a sling is not in itself a criminal offence.'

The magistrate made a sly, conceited expression that on kinder features might have been called a smile. 'Call in Constable Kaezuur,' he said to his aide, although his eyes remained on Mestphura and Elzie.

The assistant left the room for several moments. Then the door slid open, and Elzie did a double-take in spite of herself.

The woman who entered wore smooth white armour on various points of her body; the rest was covered only by a smooth second skin of grey fabric that hugged her athletic shape. Her head above the mouth was masked by a sleek visor-helmet such that only her pursed lips, a smooth chin and a tuft of blond hair at the back were discernible. Still, judging by the set of her mouth, her expression seemed stiff and uncompromising. Elzie imagined that under that helmet she might be glaring at them coldly, so she did her best to glare back.

'Constable Kaezuur, did the incapacitated use this tool during your encounter with him?' the magistrate asked.

The Sentinel gave a single, mechanical nod.

'I see. Tell me, was he accompanied?'

Another wordless nod.

'Interesting.' The magistrate appeared troubled, although he clearly already knew the answers to all his questions. 'Are any of the individuals present in this room?'

The Sentinel thrust a gloved finger at Elzie.

The magistrate looked at Elzie smugly. 'Thank you, Kaezuur. That will be all.'

The constable turned and left the room as silently as she'd entered.

Mestphura had his arms folded and was starting at Magistrate Wolming testily. 'I will have you know that were it not for this man, the *Akron* would not have returned to Nubylon at all. He is to receive the utmost care and, upon recovery, he is to be released.'

The magistrate glowered. 'You dare command me, Mr Mestphura?'

'No. This is simply what you will be forced to do. You can mark my words in stone, Magistrate Wolming.'

'Perhaps it would be more fitting to save them for the cabinet, Mr Mestphura.'

Mestphura met the old man's gaze. 'What?'

'The emergency meeting, at which these infringements will be discussed further, and which you will be required to attend.'

Mestphura was riled. 'For what purpose?'

'To discuss you and your Ministry's misconduct, I should imagine.' The magistrate smiled politely, though he could not keep the smugness from his lips. 'I will see you there, I am sure.'

'That you will,' Mestphura said with contempt, then turned and left. Elzie hurried after him.

As they reached the elevator, she began to speak urgently. 'Sir, I need to talk with you—'

'It will have to wait, Miss Kerowan,' Mestphura replied as they stepped in. 'We cannot discuss matters here.'

She obliged grudgingly.

Mestphura led the way as they left the Domestic Ministry. But when they stepped outside, they found a trio of Navy officers waiting for them.

'Commander Mestphura, the Peace Ministry requests your presence at the prime minister's emergency meeting,' a tall woman informed him.

'So I hear,' Mestphura said.

The five took a waiting autocab to Central, the core district of Nubylon, and set down outside the Circular Palace. Mestphura, Elzie and their accompaniment of Navy officers went through the grand entrance and into a bubble-like elevator that ascended smoothly into a glass tube before making its way through the ancient structure. Its path became horizontal for some time, then swung upwards. When it reached the top of the tube, it slowed and stopped without so much as a sound to declare its journey complete.

The group exited into a tall hallway adorned with smooth white panels and gold edges. The styling was much like the *Akron*: elegant geometry, circles and rectangles with segments added and subtracted in a mathematically precise manner. Clean, concise, almost clinical in its sterility. At the end of the passage was a set of tall glass doors. The Navy woman leading them stopped, and they waited a while. Beyond the doors, the meeting seemed already to be underway.

Finally, a short Meedish man with long black hair came through the door and gave a silent nod to the Navy woman. She motioned for Mestphura and Elzie to enter the hall.

The auditorium inside was vast. Elzie followed Mestphura's lead and sat down on a bench. Once they'd done so, the Head of the Board, who sat at the front of the room, tapped a gavel lightly, and the chatter died down.

'Now, if I can call attention to the Supreme Commander of the *Akron*, in attendance: Commander Julius Mestphura.'

He tapped the block again. Elzie tried to relax in her seat, but found it awkward. The bench seemed designed to be uncomfortable on purpose.

'First,' a woman nearby stood to speak, 'would the Board please recognise that what we are dealing with here is a bypassing of democracy?'

'Hear!' There was a ripple of voices in favour, along with heckling.

The Head called them to order. 'I would kindly ask the Culture Representative of Halcyon to remain seated and we will deal with her issues in due course.' His eyes fell on Mestphura. 'Supreme Commander Mestphura. You are aware of the criticism brought against you by the people of the First Nation?'

Mestphura didn't so much as blink. 'Perhaps you can elucidate, sir.'

The Head seemed mildly put out. 'We will not go into detail here, but suffice to say that there is strong public disapproval of the *Akron*'s intervention at the Battle of Mosleyhead. While we understand that you were acting on instructions of the Proctor, we must also regard that, as a Supreme Commander, you are permitted to make moral judgement calls fitting the circumstances. Azrune has no quarrel with Ganzabar, as you well know.'

'If the Board may permit me to speak—'

'In time, Commander Mestphura. Our current concern is the missing Erehwon class prototype, recently declassified as the *Postremo*. Recovering it has been your primary assignment. In what way does this mission require inciting a war?'

'Well, madams and sirs, I can assure you that these two issues are one. It is no co-incidence that Ganzabar invaded Brazak West almost immediately after the advanced Erehwon prototype was stolen. Ganzabar is now in possession of it and seeks to—'

One of the ministers interrupted. 'The commander makes baseless accusations against neutral powers.'

There was a wave of angry whispers.

'Order!' cried the Head.

'Said "neutral power" has fired on us on no less than three occasions,' Mestphura said drily.

The objecting minister raised a finger. 'Was this before, or after, you fired upon them, Commander?'

'Order, please!' The Head banged the gavel. 'Domestic Representative of Solar Harp, please refrain from questions at this time.'

'Regarding that question,' Mestphura said, 'Ganzabar's aggression was in response to our request that it break off from its invasion, which itself is a blatant violation of the Junders Treaty.'

The Head leaned forward, peering down his spectacles disapprovingly. 'How Ganzabar breaks the rules set with lesser nations is none of our concern. Need I remind you that your presence in the engagement between Ganzabar and Brazak West was in violation of our sacred duty to neutrality in all conflicts.'

'Sirs.' Elzie spoke up fiercely. Mestphura looked around, surprised to hear her speak. 'Article 18, Section 3 of Unation Law specifies that diplomatic ships are not considered trespassing within a battle zone. As the *Akron* is Azrune's flagship, it may be considered of diplomatic status in neutrality situations, as per Article 21.'

That sent up a ruckus of heckles and jibes. Diplomatic ship? What, a battleship is now a diplomatic envoy? Flagship or not, it's propwash. Nonsense, rubbish. Have her removed. Order!

The gavel was banged another three times.

'Order! Please do not interrupt the proceedings unless you have been recognised by the Board,' the Head said to Elzie, then straightened his spectacles and investigated the screen set into the table in front of him. 'Now, if we can get back to the issue at hand, namely of the *Akron*'s actions in recovering the *Postremo*.' He frowned, looking down at Mestphura. 'Do you deny allegations that you have enlisted the services of a pirate?'

'I don't follow,' said Mestphura blandly.

'The... cloudgazer,' the Head said irritably.

'I should clarify, good sir. There is no criminal on board my ship, nor has there ever been,' Mestphura said. Elzie tried not to betray her surprise, but she caught herself with a fleeting smile when she realised Mestphura had no intention of lying. He just had his own view on things.

'Then these can be nothing more than rumours.' The Head nodded. 'I understand you have recruited a new member of crew during this assignment, however?'

Mestphura paused for a heatbeat. 'I have in employ a temporary navigation consultant. Due to damage sustained by our navigational systems.'

'Damage which he himself had caused with a sling. Is that correct?'

Mestphura stared. It was suddenly all very clear. They knew the facts; they knew everything. They just wanted him to stand up here and say, 'Yeah, I hired a cloudgazer.'

The Head continued. 'It must also not have escaped your notice that this "expert" is one Kiy Tanthar, wanted for at least seventeen infringements of Unation Law and forty-two counts of Piracy Without Marque by the Federal Government of Ganzabar. It would appear you are guilty not only of conspiring with known pirates, but also deception in the presence of the Most Honour'd Board.'

'I will not be called a liar,' Mestphura growled. 'And Mr Tanthar is not a pirate.'

'In any case,' the Head said, beginning to collate the items on his desk, 'I regret to inform you that the *Akron*'s flight commission is suspended while an investigation committee looks into the full extent of this infringement.'

Mestphura said nothing. He looked past the Board at a woman sitting in shadow to one side. They seemed to exchange a glance before she broke it.

'This meeting is suspended until tomorrow, when the Domestic Ministry shall present their evidence. Please withhold questions until then. Commander Mestphura, Officer Kerowan: you are dismissed but must remain in dock.' The Head brought the gathering to a close with a final tap of the gavel.

A roar of voices arose as several dozen stood and began to make their way out. The woman across the room got up and left through a side door, and Mestphura stormed after her. Elzie went to follow, but two officials stepped forward and took her by the arms.

'Officer Kerowan, come with us, please.'

Some way behind the prime minister, two luftwood doors were flung open and Mestphura came striding down the hallway. There was something frightening about the man when he moved with such impetus, a usually gentle giant steaming forward, anger boiling beneath the surface.

'All I want is an explanation,' he boomed.

Prime Minister Tendrassi spun quickly, throwing the long fabric of her cloak and tunic outward like a ball gown. 'I did what I could, Mestphura.'

'Those jackals out there are your own government!'

'And like me, they answer to the people,' she said. 'And the people say no. You can't imagine how *hard* the people are saying no.'

'Oh? I don't remember there being such opposition when the recovery plan was pulsed to the *Akron*.'

She shook her head sadly. 'People sit up and take notice of things when they are presented on a plate by the media. And following a leak of information, everything has changed. This situation is not politically sustainable.'

'The press don't run the country. You do.'

'Do you really think so?' she said with an ironic smile. 'No, I simply do what I must to meet the demands of our people. That is ultimately all any fair leader can do.'

'Propwash. You can convince them. And anyway, isn't it about time Azrune stopped avoiding everything and started actually using what it has to help make the world a better place?'

'Mestphura, you are so terribly naïve!' She seemed almost amused. 'What right have I to impose my will on another nation? To impress my own vision of justice on world affairs?'

'You were elected to!' Mestphura said, exasperated. 'They need you to show them why this war must be stopped.

We've watched Ganzabar throw its weight around for decades.'

'The Brazakkers are not without fault here. They have as much of the blame in the Junders Incident.'

'That isn't the point. They're not the ones who decided to launch a full scale invasion on the other. If they did, we should be right there stopping them. I know the press care about nothing more than selling copies of the most dramatically embellished truth they can get away with. But government is different; you have to make a moral choice.'

'No, Mestphura, we don't. Moral choices do not belong in politics.' She straightened. 'They will not ensure the stability of government. Democracy does.'

Mestphura looked away bitterly. 'Forgive me if I feel betrayed.'

She paused. 'Mestphura, if this is betrayal, then it's not by me. That would be the officer who gave the press classified information in the first place.'

Mestphura realised what she meant. He felt as though a bullet had just punctured his chest. He'd just assumed the pulse had been intercepted. But a deliberate breach by someone on the *Akron*?

He started to speak, but he was at a loss for words.

'I'm sorry, Mestphura,' she said gently.

A slow tapping of small footsteps approached. Prime Minister Tendrassi looked up, but Mestphura just stared ahead blankly.

'Come now, Julius,' said a genderless voice, finally drawing Mestphura's attention. 'You look as though the world will end, my friend.'

'Proctor...' Mestphura tried to regain his composure.

The Proctor stepped up to them. 'Correctly identified. I have not seen you in over eight thousand four hundred and three hours, Julius.'

'And I have not seen you beyond the Palace Crest, ever,' Mestphura said, raising his eyebrows. 'What brings you here?'

'I do mostly as I please. Azrune would not be here today were it not so,' he said factually. 'I ask that you don't feel anger against Ms Tendrassi here. She is in a difficult situation. The Peace Ministry itself has few if any options after the information leak.'

'I refuse to believe there is a crewman aboard my ship in whom I cannot place complete trust. Let alone one senior enough to have done this,' Mestphura said.

'I wish I could make it not so, but the leak was traced to the *Akron*,' the Proctor said sadly. 'I, too, cannot imagine an officer of yours in discontent.'

Mestphura's expression sharpened. Everything suddenly made sense. He was beginning to boil with anger as he made to leave.

'Mestphura,' the Proctor said, his words halting the commander momentarily. 'I have witnessed countless times, such as now, where all seems chaos. This will work itself out. Do not be like the thunder, Julius. Be like the breeze.'

Mestphura lingered, saying nothing, then continued out the door.

37 - Goldstar

Tolisto, Nubylon
October 23rd

When he came to, Kiy felt surprisingly clear-headed. He sat up slowly and methodically took note of his surroundings. Another Azrunite room—again, it was more hotel-room-without-a-door-handle than cell. The bed sheets were a brilliant white and a short cream carpet covered the floor. The walls were smooth and bright, the ceiling dotted with small round lights, and more light poured in through a large spotless window.

He had memories of pain in his head, a pain that made him nauseated just recalling it. The ghost of an ache went through his spine, but it was barely a discomfort. He'd had a sensation like this before, the last time he'd been treated to Azrunite medicine. It was like waking up to find your injuries were only nightmares but your body was still not quite convinced.

He got up, only realising he was naked when the sheet left him bare. His clothes weren't anywhere to be seen, so he grudgingly returned to the sheets and tried to collect his thoughts.

The last he could remember, he was with Elzie in that lobby. They'd been having some sort of argument. Had she tried to kill him? No, that was ridiculous...

Ah, yes, he thought. It was *them*.

They were like cloudgazers, in a country where bearers of the sling were outlawed. But they moved with grace and finesse that seemed beyond human. Their movements were calculating and pre-emptive to the point where they may as well have been psychic. He'd never known anything like them. What *were* they?

The door slid open with a whisper. Hushed voices came from beyond the opening, and Kiy quickly lay back down and feigned unconsciousness, hoping to hear a careless word or two.

'Mr Tanthar,' came a woman's gentle voice.

He lay still a moment longer.

'Someone here to see you.'

'You can get up,' a familiar deep voice said. 'We know you're awake.'

He opened his eyes to see who was talking. A neatly dressed woman with red hair in a ponytail looked over him carefully. Beside her stood Mestphura, his brow furrowed.

'How are you feeling, Mr Tanthar?' the woman asked.

'Where am I?'

'Goldstar Hospital. You hit your head,' she said softly.

Mestphura nodded. 'What's the last thing you remember, Mr Tanthar?'

He sat up against a pillow grimly. 'That acrobatic bitch with a sling knocking me out.'

The red-haired woman seemed taken aback, but the commander merely nodded. 'His memory appears to be fine. Leave us, if you please, Doctor.'

She lingered a moment, then relented. 'As you say.' She gave a slight bow and left.

'Mestphura, kindly explain what the flak is going on.'

'They know what you are,' he said grimly. 'And they're not giving you back.'

'Who's they?'

'The Domestic Ministry.' Mestphura put his hands behind his back and gazed out of the window. 'There was a leak of the *Akron*'s mission details, and now politicians have gotten involved. The wrong sort of politicians. *Akron*'s flight commission has been suspended, and you're in the loving custody of the DM. Two armed guards are beyond that door.'

Kiy let out a single, bittersweet laugh. 'Sounds great. What's the bad news?'

Mestphura shook his head. 'Mr Tanthar. We owe you a great debt. Your services to the First Nation are not forgotten. We will work to resolve this mess.'

'Well, that's something,' Kiy said blandly. Then he was struck by a thought. 'Is Elzie okay?'

'Miss Kerowan?'

Kiy nodded. He felt it odd he should address her less formally than Mestphura, who'd known her so much longer. 'She was with me when those sling-wearers attacked.'

Mestphura stared outside, his expression grim. 'She's fine.'

Kiy eyed him carefully. *Why does he seem so disgruntled by that? h*e thought, but then he had the feeling they were probably under surveillance and his words would be cryptic and guarded.

'So what's going to happen to me?' he enquired.

Mestphura considered the question. 'We will see to it that you get released. We—'

'Mr Mestphura?'

The commander turned. It was the doctor, at the door again. 'I'm sorry, but the minister insists that you have to leave now.'

Mestphura accepted with a nod. 'It appears my time here is up. Have hope, Kiy. We shall resolve this.' He followed the doctor out, and the door slid shut, leaving only the eerie silence of floatrock.

It was dark outside the next time the door opened. Kiy turned to it sharply, having almost forgotten it was a door at all. A small boy wearing a white tunic stepped in, eyeing Kiy curiously. Kiy frowned at him, craning his neck to see if anyone else had come in already. But there was no-one, just this young boy, staring with deep dark eyes. The door slid shut again.

'How did you get in here?' Kiy asked slowly.

'I walked through the doorway.'

Kiy blinked. 'No—I mean, who are you? You're not just some random kid. Are you?'

'Correct.' The boy unfurled his palms. 'I am the Proctor.'

Kiy watched uncertainly. He'd heard of the Proctor, the figurehead leader of Azrune since the Gold Age, but he'd never known what appearance to expect. Nor was he sure what to believe in this place. The kid could be making a fool of him.

'Alright, then. If you are, prove it.'

The boy looked offended. 'How?'

Kiy paused to think. Ask him something a child wouldn't know, he thought. 'How does floatrock work?'

The boy didn't seem the least bit fazed. 'A graviton-dissonant crystalline matrix that effectively anchors itself within a gravity well, with a resistive force proportional to the mass of the crystal, by disrupting—'

'Okay,' Kiy interrupted, holding up a palm, 'I get it now. You're some kinda kid genius that they rope into being figurehead for the day? No—let me guess—a king that found the elixir of eternal life? Or just an elaborate hoax?'

'None of these things,' the boy replied, looking confused by the notion. 'I'm just the Proctor.'

'Right.'

'And I owe you an apology, Cloudgazer Tanthar.'

'Wait, what?'

The Proctor tilted his head. 'Five months ago, a top secret prototype airship was stolen from our naval base at Irokwai. Somehow all of our defences were shut down and bypassed, and the perpetrators were able to remove the craft without even alerting the base. Shortly before the incident, one of our greatest Machine Talkers, Grabe Narvyl, went missing, presumably kidnapped. Narvyl was one of the few people capable of remotely overcoming the security and defences at the Irokwai facility, a process called Cracking. It became clear that whoever had the ship had Narvyl as well.'

'I don't see how this is relevant to me,' Kiy said.

The Proctor held up a forefinger. 'I'm coming to that, but I think it's important for you to understand the gravity of this situation.'

Kiy smirked. 'It's a good hint that things are getting pretty insane when you're arrested by sling-wielding acrobats, on the orders of a child who happens to lead the most pacifist nation in the Seven Skies.'

The Proctor raised an eyebrow. 'A child? Oh... yes, I see.' He looked over himself, then continued. 'No, not as such. This is simply the only functional frame. My options are like bowls and spoons.' Kiy felt a question hesitate at his lips, but the Proctor continued, 'That's why I wanted to apologise. I did not order this confinement—only your acquisition.'

'Acquisition?'

'The *Akron* came across you by chance, but it was dice play. In war, it is only a matter of cycles before the cloudgazers come to the fore. The only thing unexpected was just how quickly you apparited. I heard your sling and told them to follow. That's how this mess got started.'

Kiy's face went blank. 'Not sure I follow. Are you saying you found me by chance, on purpose?'

'Only yes,' the Proctor said. 'The *Akron*'s task was to recover the *Postremo*, which in itself is not impossible with our means. But we also want Narvyl back, and for that we needed... someone of your talents.'

'Didn't go to plan, I guess?'

'A plan that cannot be broken is merely a step,' the Proctor noted. 'Even I can only control so much in this world.'

'Why didn't you just employ an Azrunite to do it?'

'An Azrunite cloudgazer?' The Proctor looked amused by the idea. 'Do you think, based on where you are now, that such an individual would liaise with her government?'

Kiy frowned. 'Why did you even outlaw the sling?'

'Ah, you were not always taboo, Cloudgazer Tanthar. Back then cloudgazers were... different. Not the vagrants of today.' He made an apologetic gesture. 'I do not hold the mistakes of the many against the merits of the few. But Azrune is a true democracy, you see. The majority make it what it is; we just wrap laws up to sell them with words. And that is how we find ourselves here.'

'Country's crazy, is what it is.'

Proctor smiled fondly. 'Much as all are.'

'What about the ones that attacked me? The armoured ones in white,' Kiy said. He'd met a handful of cloudgazers over the years, but those Azrunites sure were something else.

'Ah, the Sentinels.' The Proctor shifted uncomfortably. 'Were it that simple. While they do not use a sling—they are equipped with an inferior imitation, the hook—there is a bigger problem. I'm sure, to those on the outside, a nation can seem like one single thing. It is not. You see, the Sentinels are under the jurisdiction of the Domestic Ministry, a facet of our administration aggressively concerned with internal affairs. Where matters concern the outside, they seem to believe nothing to be important. Even the imminent attack on Laronor, where my sources tell me —'

'Wait!' Kiy's eyes widened. 'What's happening in Laronor?'

'Ganzabar's Armada is advancing on Laronor as we speak, maybe no more than a few cycles away. If they take it, I fear we may all be in grave danger.' He looked at the floor as though distracted by it.

'Why?'

'The Gundar. I think I know what our foe is up to, but I hope I'm wrong.'

'I have to get out of here,' Kiy said.

'Patience, Cloudgazer Tanthar. Your opportunity will come. I cannot directly obstruct the Domestic Ministry.'

Kiy sighed. 'You can't help me?'

'I never said quite such as that.' The Proctor gave a sly grin. 'There's no requirement to keep you here. I shall set about the conditions for your escape. Unfortunately, I cannot gurantee it will be without resistance from elsewhere...' He had a distant, uncomfortable look that passed as quickly as it came. 'But I have every confidence in you.'

And with that, the Proctor gave a small bow and departed. The doors swished closed behind him.

'Some pants would have been helpful,' Kiy muttered in the silence.

38 - Reserve

Snow had fallen heavily the previous night, covering every rooftop and open walkway with a layer thick enough to sink a thumb into. Water erupting from the drains had frozen like a spiky sculpture of a single, blurred moment, and the usual bustle of the city seemed to have frozen along with it. Only the occasional greatcoat-clad gentleman or fur-wrapped lady disturbed the fresh snow with their footprints. Word going around was that Second Winter was setting in early; it was still mid-October. Some claimed that Mother Winter had come to watch over the Brazak people and drive back the invaders. It was at least true that a prompt winter was a good thing for the Brazakkers, who were ever more adapted to the icy weather than their southern adversaries.

Hennie walked in childlike strides along Skyview Prospekt, one of the main thoroughfares through Voxton: two large walkways with a corridor of sky between them that was forded by a bridge every fifty metres or so. Her new Bluebell rifle was slung over one shoulder, and her attention was fixed on the markings she was making in the snow.

Karak strode beside her with a more reserved gait. 'Snow seems a real novelty to you,' he observed, hands deep in his pockets for warmth.

''T'int that much, in truth,' Hennie countered. 'We get it in Brudor most winters, but I still love it. How about you? Didn't you say you were southern too?'

'Eastern. Rather not think about home, though,' he replied flatly.

'Oh.'

Now that the city was on high alert, Hennie had asked to join the street patrols. The reserves were too short to offer her a partner, so she'd convinced Mr Rathbone to allow Karak to tag along. Hennie was sure that if they saw combat, a real soldier would be handy to have around.

With the invasion fleet advancing every day, an eerie sense of doom had crept into the days. Few people talked, and when they did it was almost always about invasion. Ganzabar would be here soon, they said. Maybe tomorrow, maybe next week. Maybe their vanguards were already here —hence the patrols. Nobody knew how soon the battle would be, but the Wirral Drifts had been overrun and there was nothing standing between the enemy Armada and the city.

Several liners were docked in Southport, filling with crowds of civilians hoping to retreat further west. But unlike in Brudor, here those who wanted to flee seemed to be in the minority. Some citizens were even confident enough to say there wouldn't be any fighting at all in Laronor, but Hennie thought that was just crazy talk. Still, she'd decided to remain in the city with the rest. Sooner or later they'd run out of country to run to, anyway. Her host certainly showed no sign of faltering.

The admiralty's great clock towers boomed seven in the morning, some way off in the distance. The street should have been heaving on a Thursday, but it was almost desolate.

'Bang! I shot you.'

The declaration came from a young voice, probably less than ten, just up ahead.

'Yer never!'

Hennie saw a large group of children running about in the snow, playfighting. One was waving a—

'Stop!' she yelled. 'Hey! Give me that!'

She ran up to the bewildered child and swiped the percussion pistol from him with a scolding look. The children were all about the same age and stood to about Hennie's elbow. She felt like an adult as they all glared up at her.

'Giv'it back!' the young boy pouted.

'Yeah, we found it!' another complained.

'Where did you get this?' Hennie demanded.

'Flak you!' the kid spat, then darted away. Hennie followed for a few steps before realising the boy was far too quick for her, and the rest of them had scattered in all directions the moment she took up the chase. She was left standing in the silent snow, at the hub of a wide splay of footprints.

Karak caught up to her. 'What was that all about?'

Hennie showed him the old weapon. 'Just a couple o' toe-rags up to no good.'

'A Chenkov, huh? Haven't seen one of them in years. What were *they* doing with it?'

She tucked the pistol into the front of her pinafore. 'Sky knows.'

Karak took a glance around. 'Don't these kids have parents, for Gnost's sake?'

Hennie shook her head. 'It's a disgrace.'

They resumed their patrol, turning left after a few blocks to follow the route they'd been given.

'So. You a Gnostic?' she said after a while.

'What makes you say that?'

She thumbed over her shoulder. 'What you said back there. Didn't realise you were a Gnostic, is all.'

'Well... you never asked,' Karak replied.

She had to give him that.

She remained deep in thought for a while, absently walking as though on an imaginary tightrope, before answering. 'I guess it's not that unusual. We used to know a few Gnostics back home.'

'To tell the truth, I'm not all that great an example,' Karak said, his eyes scanning the sky. 'I mean... I believe, but—I haven't been to church for at least ten years.'

'Is that bad?' Hennie asked, genuinely.

He smiled at that. 'It's not considered ideal.'

Hennie suddenly noticed where she was. She found this happened from time to time in the city: she'd be walking down some totally unknown prospekt or avenue and suddenly find herself back in the heart of familiar territory without ever expecting it. 'Hey, we're right by Waltov,' she said. 'My host's family lives just up that way.'

'Didn't you say their kid was building an airship?' Karak said.

Hennie cursed herself for telling him about Miran. She had only mentioned it in passing, but it seemed like he could always find a way to bring it up again. He was clearly really interested in the Gundar, which made keeping her promise to Jerra all the harder. Next he'd be wanting to go see the damn thing.

'Do you think that'd be okay?' Karak asked.

Hennie realised she'd not been listening to what he was talking about and had missed the preface to the question. She didn't want to admit she hadn't been paying attention to him, though, so she said, 'Uh, yeah, I think so.'

'Great.' He grinned. 'I can meet you back here after your patrol is over.'

It gradually dawned on Hennie what she'd agreed to. She groaned inwardly and bit her lip so hard she thought she might draw blood.

39 - All Ahead Full

Wirral Drift Defensive Zone

The snow whirled around the Ganzabi fleet as they hung in formation a few miles from the Wirral Drift installation. It was still light, and visibility was good enough to make out the other ships in the fleet, but Moller knew it would soon get worse. October was drawing on, and a Brazak winter was a fearsome thing. Visibility became nigh on impossible, systems froze up, and any crew on exterior decks couldn't be out for long without risking life and frostbitten limb.

All the more angry it made him when the scouts returned with their report of the Brazakker gun platform they'd been delayed by. There had been no exterior activity, no movements or changes of any kind, yet as soon as ships approached, the guns fired, though off their marks. Moller smelled a rat.

And sure enough, once a detachment of marines had snuck into the installation, it had turned out to be deserted. The cannons had been hooked up to fire on proximity of incoming radar traces, using a messy system of hooks and cables all rigged to the communications switchboard. He was somewhat impressed, but no less furious.

Even worse, the remnants of the enemy fleet had evaded his mop-up operation and had regrouped at Laronor, no doubt thanks to the deteriorating weather. The city was looking ever more problematic. Moller watched the cursed snow falling softly past the observation windows of his office. They would surely need the *Akron* at this rate.

'Sir?'

He looked over his shoulder at Fredson, who had just leant in through the bulky doorway.

'The Azrunite prisoner transfer from the Fortitude is here, sir. You wished to see him?'

Moller frowned. 'Weren't there two?'

'The other is just a boy, and a Brazakker at any rate. He got free into the lower decks somewhere, Mr Carver has a team looking for him.'

The admiral shrugged dismissively. 'No matter, then. Though the useless idyats that lost the boy are to be dishonourably discharged.'

Fredson's face creased with sympathy. No greater blow could be dealt to a fighting man in the Ganzabi Navy than to be stripped of his honour and banished from service. Honour was what you joined for. If you left without it—or with even less than you started with—then it would be years wasted and families ruined. But Fredson could not fault his superior's judgement. Losing a mere boy was an embarrassment to the uniform. 'Very well, sir.'

'Bring the Azrunite in, then.' Moller made a beckoning nod.

'Aye, sir.'

The man shown in was tall and wide-shouldered, with a face that had gone unshaven. He was followed by Moller's security chief, Jayzon Carver, who was even taller and had the build of a man who sculpts his appearance at the cost of near everything else. They both sat, and the Azrunite slouched back, as though at a casual interview.

'My sources tell me your name is Marc Nareem, and you are a pilot from the *Akron*'s Lancet Squadron.'

Marc looked at him listlessly. 'Yeah?'

Moller narrowed his eyes. 'I want you to tell me everything you know. I want to know everything about the *Akron*: strengths, weaknesses, abilities, the works. If you co-operate, your fate will be agreeable. If you do not co-operate—well, you will in time. Mr Carver here has a lot of practice getting the unwilling to speak.'

Carver scowled at Marc, as though to prove the point.

'Sure, sounds easy enough,' Marc said nonchalantly, leaning back in the chair to get comfortable, despite his arms being bound together behind him.

There was an uncomfortable pause.

'Well?' asked the admiral.

'Oh, I don't know,' Marc said. 'Y'know how sometimes you know a thing so well, you think you can talk about it for hours, then when you have to say something you can't think of a damn thing?'

Moller and Carver exchanged a look.

'I mean, I just feel like a total prick, you know. Here you are, bringing me all this way, and I can't even think what to say—'

Marc was cut short as Carver swung his fist across the young man's face.

'Idyat,' Moller barked. 'Are you so stupid as to mock me, airman? I don't think you realise how serious a matter this is. Do you know who we are, son? We're going to get you to speak, by Gnost.'

Carver leant in and grabbed Marc by the hair, then swung his other fist into the Azrunite's chest. Marc doubled over, then straightened and looked at Moller almost in surprise. 'Okay, okay.'

Moller watched him expectantly. 'Now. Operational specifications.'

'It's, uh... shiny.'

'What?' Moller glared.

'The *Akron*. It's very shiny.'

Carver hit him again.

Marc winced, paused, then looked up. 'No, it actually is!'

The big man threw a punch that knocked Marc's head to the side.

'Ugh... and, um... the mess hall have burritos. There's this girl who runs it on the night shift—Marissa. She is... *so* fine —'

Carver yanked back Marc's head and drew a fist back as though to break his nose, but before he could strike, Moller shouted a syllable and he froze.

'Enough. It's clear we're going to need something a little more potent.' Moller templed his fingers.

The bulky security chief withdrew awkwardly, as though uncertain what to do with his hands.

The door burst open and Fredson leant in. 'Admiral Moller, sir.'

'What is it now?'

'Central Office, sir. There's a 'graph from the countess. The *Akron* escaped her trap. It was last seen headed for Nubylon... on a mesospheric trajectory.'

'Oh, man, I missed a Jump?' Marc lamented.

'Shut up!' Moller's eyes bulged and the veins in his neck swelled as he fought to contain his rage. That stupid, stupid, useless woman! She would cost them the campaign at this rate. Were she in his direct command, he'd have shamed and discharged her already, but it just wasn't something you could do when dealing with the president's own daughter.

'Have the fleet prepare to move out immediately,' he growled, pushing his way towards the door.

'What about the Rooner?' Carver grunted, motioning to Marc.

Moller barely glanced over his shoulder. 'Throw him overboard, for all I care.'

'Yes, sir.'

Moller and Fredson strode out, down the corridor towards the bridge.

'Is that really wise, sir?' Fredson said, once the room and Carver were beyond earshot.

'What?'

'Killing the prisoner. We may yet glean valuable information from him.'

'The *Akron* is gone, Fredson.' He stopped, uttering the words in hushed briskness. 'We have no reason to believe Azrune has any other ships in the Nezzu region. Their pitiful flagship has been sent cowering back to their capital. The First Nation are, as I have long suspected, no longer relevant.' He continued walking, then turned again as though remembering more of what he meant to say. 'It's about time I stopped being so forgiving to our enemies. Kill the pilot. And when you find him, kill the boy.'

'What about the countess?' Fredson asked. 'We will need her to make full use of the Gundar.'

The admiral almost roared. 'The countess be *damned*. She can shove that cowardly plan up that fancy little ass of hers. This is the finest collection of ships from the greatest nation in the world. We don't need that damned witch to take a city of vagrants. When she does get here, confiscate the damn ship and send her home, before she ruins everything.'

'Understood, sir.' Fredson nodded, then swiftly left to dispatch orders to the rest of the fleet.

The admiral strode to the bridge, where he raised his voice for all to hear.

'Comms, signal the fleet to fall in. Craftsman, set a course for Laronor. All ahead full.'

40 - Recovery

Tolisto, Nubylon

There was a muffled clunk. Kiy had the sensation of being woken by a gentle rocking of his shoulder, but when he sat up and looked around, there was nobody there. The lights had dimmed such that he could only just make out the walls and ceiling, but the room was assuredly empty.

'Go.'

The voice didn't startle him, despite not having any discernible origin, which he felt should have bothered him. He began to wonder if he'd heard it at all.

He slid off the bed and stood uncertainly, his senses returning as his brain awoke. He became aware that his naked form was probably being watched by someone, yet that didn't seem to bother him either.

Suddenly there was light. So bright that it was everything for a moment. Then his eyes adjusted and he saw that the door had opened.

'Now.'

This time the voice made him snap round to look over his shoulder. But again nobody was there. It could have been a woman's voice, or a boy's. It seemed familiar, as though he had once known it well but had forgotten to whom it belonged. Whoever it was, they sounded urgent, and he felt compelled to press on.

He took a sneak look past the door into the brightness beyond. There were no guards outside. There was nobody at all, in fact. The whole hospital seemed deserted. He ran out naked down the corridor, feeling insane but pushing on regardless. It had to be worse to remain imprisoned than to make a naked escape.

He slowed as he came to a lit sign, explaining the hospital sectors. The display changed suddenly to a single arrow. Kiy looked down the corridor it indicated, then took a run in that direction, his head feeling groggy. The corridor ended at a lift. The lift's display, too, suddenly changed: from a number showing floors to an exclamation mark surrounded by red. Kiy looked around just in time to see a nurse pushing a floating trolley around the corner, and managed to dart out of view. Once the nurse had passed, he looked up at the lift display again; it had reverted to showing floor numbers. They were decreasing.

When the compartment arrived and the doors slid open, it was empty. He slipped into it quickly and hit the button for the lowest floor. The doors slid closed with annoying slowness, and finally the lift began to move, the bright interior lights of the shaft outside passing downwards.

Wait, downwards? *The lift is going up*, he thought. He wondered if he was stumbling through a cascade of coincidences. He had the delirious feeling of being led.

At the top floor, the doors opened and he stepped out onto a silent and empty roof. It was flat, not the curved dome or spire of most other buildings he'd seen in Nubylon. Across a gap of dozens of metres, the far wing of the hospital was a sheet of glowing windows. The wind on his bare skin made him shiver. He began to wonder what he was doing here; it seemed like madness. Perhaps he was mentally unwell? Things weren't making much sense, after all. And it was almost as though he were watching it all happen to someone else.

Stumbling a little, he made his way to the edge of the roof and looked down over the sparkling lights of Nubylon. The sky below the hospital was a dark purple. His head swam. He stood staring down at the city until the lights began blurring. Afraid of falling, he backed away from the edge uncertainly.

It was then that he heard a sound. An oscillating, deep, artificial throbbing that grew quickly louder. He wondered how much of the throbbing was in his head.

A bright light engulfed him as a hovering craft flew up over the lip of the roof, shining a searchlight at him. The light froze him for only a moment, and then he was sprinting back towards the lift.

The craft swooped overhead, the lilac glow of its repulsor generators bathing him in light. It set down some way ahead in his path.

He stopped when he realised that the woman who had leapt off the machine and was running for him was Raldotya.

'Kiy, it's okay! Don't be alarmed.' She hurried over with a blanket in her hands. He could only stand dumbly, staring, as she put the blanket over his bare shoulders. 'You have to follow me, okay? We need to get you off the roof.'

Relief soothed him, returning feeling into his cold limbs. Raldotya took him back to the craft, her hands gripping his shoulders supportively. He clung tightly to the heavy blue blanket, more for assurance than warmth or dignity.

'Hold it!'

The sharp voice was instantly familiar, but he'd never heard that tone in it before. Kiy turned and frowned at the woman pointing an angular white revolver at the both of them.

'Stay out of this, Elzie,' Raldotya said, her grip on Kiy's shoulders tightening.

'I'm here to rescue him,' Elzie announced.

'He's free to go as he likes,' Raldotya called over the engines. 'You're the one pointing a gun at him.'

'I'm pointing it at you.'

Raldotya's eyes pleaded. 'Elzie!'

'Why don't you tell him where you're taking him, huh? Back down to his room, courtesy of the Domestic Ministry?'

Kiy felt more confused than angry. 'Is that true?'

Raldotya looked uncertain. 'No! The doctors just want him to be okay. We're trying to help him—'

'Don't listen to them!' Elzie shook the pistol angrily. 'Wolming has lied to them!' She glared at Raldotya. 'If you deliver him to the government, you will only be betraying him.'

'You betrayed him already!' Raldotya's anger flared.

Elzie's eyes narrowed. 'Kiy, I can get you out of Azrune. But you have to trust me.'

'Don't listen to her, Kiy.' Raldotya put herself between them. 'She got discharged from the *Akron*. She's rogue.'

'I have to get back to Laronor,' Kiy said, almost to himself.

'Then come with me,' Elzie repeated.

Kiy took a step towards her.

'What are you doing?' Raldotya said. 'Kiy, please, she's lying to you. She misled us all.'

Kiy took another step forward. 'I'm sorry, Raldotya. I have to leave.'

'Come on!' Elzie grabbed Kiy's wrist, then turned and ran. Somehow Kiy kept up with her, clutching at the large blanket with his free hand. He could hear shouts behind them and the sound of the craft firing up.

'Quick, in here!' Elzie said, dragging him down a short set of steps and through a doorway, her white revolver poised upright in her other hand.

They found themselves in a glass corridor that led to a dock of shuttles and luxury yachts. Elzie continued right past the ships to a wide metal chute. 'For laundry,' she explained, 'but it's the fastest way down—and the only way without being spotted. You go first. I'll be right behind you.'

Kiy shook his head, but he obediently climbed into the opening and let go.

The chute was nearly vertical. Kiy was accustomed to freefall, but not like this—in the darkness, in an enclosed space, with no idea what was below him. But after a gut-wrenching descent, he landed softly in a pile of linen and quickly rolled aside before Elzie came down after him. The two of them clambered off the pile, and Elzie once again took the lead.

They traveled along increasingly narrower and less aesthetic stairways and passages, then along hanging walkways beneath the hospital's underside.

All cities of Azimuth sat on clusters of floatrock. Because it was pumped from below and added in layers as the cluster of buildings grew, it took on an irregular shape on the underside. While the top was smooth and landscaped, the under-layers were laced with walkways, tubes and cables that were needed to connect power, water, access and so on from other sectors and islands. Some of the largest and least-regulated pipes in the system were the waste disposal pipes. They were also some of the most dangerous—prone to flush-outs into open sky and filled with foul fluids.

It was in the darkness of a waste tunnel that Kiy again remembered he was naked but for the blanket Raldotya had slung around him. The way ahead would have been black were it not for the piercing white beam from a small torch clipped onto Elzie's jacket sleeve.

'Can I please get some clothes at some point?' he asked.

Elzie smirked. 'I rather prefer it this way. If you give me any trouble, I can just whip the blanket off you.'

'You're a cruel, heartless woman.'

She laughed. 'I don't actually have any spare clothes, if you hadn't noticed.' She tugged at her sleeve demonstratively. 'You can borrow the skirt, I suppose.' As she shone the torch back, she noticed his uneasy expression. 'Oh, sorry. Bit funny about that kind of thing, eh?'

'Apart from the fact you're currently wearing it, that wouldn't... ah, be right,' he managed.

'I find it odd that such a thing concerns you at a time like now, anyway.' She stumbled as the tunnel descended into a foul-smelling liquid. 'Ugh. Be careful wading in this crap. Processors thin it to sludge, but there might be some nasty surprises in there.'

Kiy eyed it uneasily. 'Where are we, anyhow?'

She waded in further. 'We're somewhere under the Trocador Multiplex, in one of the waste tubes that connects us to the transit station. From there I'm hoping we can make a right turn to come out under the Circular Palace Gardens.'

'Why there?' Kiy tried not to think of what filth might be covering him up to his bare thighs.

'The Proctor is meeting us.'

'The Proctor? You didn't mention anything about that.'

'I didn't want to mention in front of Raldotya. He can't be known to help us. We're both renegades around here now.'

'Why you?'

She said nothing for a while, then finally, 'I don't want to talk about it.'

Kiy's curiosity was frustrating him, but her tone compelled him to change the subject. 'Why was Raldotya helping the Domestic Ministry anyway?'

'Sky knows,' Elzie answered irritably. 'They probably tricked her into fetching you. She's got a heart of gold, but she's so gullible. They knew you would trust her. Good thing I got there in time.'

They strode on in silence, the darkness warping time. Kiy couldn't say how long he'd been following her.

Suddenly, Elzie came out with a question. 'Tell me, Kiy... Why *did* you come with me? After everything Raldotya said?'

It caught him off guard. 'Uh, because you had a gun, and you dragged me?'

'No, I mean the real reason. You wouldn't have come unless you decided to, I am sure of that.'

He considered. 'Well, I figured you probably wouldn't kill me. So I wanted to see if you really could get me out of Azrune.'

She ran a hand through her hair. 'Sky knows how so foolish a man could be a cloudgazer and not be dead already.'

Kiy grinned. 'I'd like to think if anything, it explains how I find myself crawling around naked in a sewer.'

She laughed at that. 'Alright—I think this is our stop.'

They'd come to a ladder that ascended to a round opening. Elzie went up it first, and the two of them found themselves in the quiet, moonlit gardens of the Circular Palace.

'I need to wash,' Kiy complained.

'Not the time.'

'I can't meet your head of state smelling like a Porruck's anus.'

'We both do!'

'Can I help you?' came a third voice, startling them.

Kiy looked around to see a short fat man with slicked-back hair and his hands clasped together. He wore a neat burgundy velvet uniform of a kind Kiy had never seen before.

'Got a towel?' Kiy asked. It was the first thing that came to his mind.

'Kiy! That's the Gardens curator, not some bell drone,' Elzie scolded. She turned to address the round man. 'We're expecting the Proctor.'

'At this hour? That is highly irregular.' The curator sniffed. 'Besides, that will not be possible. I'm afraid the Proctor is unable to join you at this time.'

'What do you mean?' Elzie asked uneasily.

The curator looked mildly embarrassed. 'He's eating his breakfast.'

Elzie exchanged a look with Kiy. They didn't know what time it was, but considering the sun wasn't even up, it must have been before six in the morning.

'It's sort of urgent,' Elzie said.

'Very well, then.' The large man smiled politely. 'I shall go and let him know, but I don't think he will be able to see you today.' He walked away into a jungle of exotic, well-kept foliage.

Kiy decided to try washing his shins and feet in a fountain nearby, ignoring Elzie's looks of disdain. But he had hardly begun when they were both startled by the appearance of the Proctor, mere moments later.

'Proctor! Please forgive us; my colleague meant no offence,' Elzie said, dragging Kiy from the fountain.

'That's not a drama,' the Proctor said softly, carrying a large white box with gold trim. 'You must smell like a Porruck's anus after wading through those pipes.'

Kiy fought the urge to laugh. 'You were here the whole time, I suppose?'

The Proctor half shrugged. 'I have engineered this communication with the intention of exclusivity.' He stepped over a small wooden bridge arching over a trickling stream. The light of the moons caught the tumbling water in specks of white, seemingly distracting him. He then looked back at Kiy and Elzie.

'Do either of you know the full capabilities of Brazak West's Gundars?' he asked, setting the chest down beside them.

They shook their heads.

'It seems a great many people don't,' the Proctor noted. 'I mean, their theoretical limits, at least. Ganzabar seems to think they have near infinite range and can strike at cities hundreds of kilometres away.'

'I thought they were just defensive cannons,' Kiy said.

'Much as your government has stated repeatedly. An impasse,' the Proctor observed. 'It is clear to me what Brazak West created them for, and what their feasible limits are with the New Age tech that created them. However, I've run calculations, and it would seem that, as crazy as the Ganzabi idea sounds, it may actually be possible.'

'Shyut. You're kidding,' Kiy blurted.

'I categorically do not,' the Proctor said. 'If the trajectory was high enough and the muzzle velocity fast enough, then the thin air of the upper atmosphere may allow it to reach a speed necessary to hit a target well over a thousand kilometres away. Difficult, but deadly possible.' He paused. 'Hitting anything at that range would be nearly impossible with New Age thermionic valve target computation,' he added, then stared at them with sudden visceral glare. 'Gold Age calputers, on the other hand...'

'The *Postremo*.' Elzie's mouth fell open. 'But—they'd still need to know the location of what they're firing at.'

'And there is only one location in the world that is always broadcast to all...' the Proctor said.

The look of realisation on Elzie's face turned to one of horror. 'Nubylon.'

The Proctor gave a sombre nod.

'Funny.' Kiy shook his head. 'Suddenly Azrune's in danger and everybody cares.'

'Kiy,' Elzie said, 'it's not like that.'

'Oh, no,' the Proctor said. 'It is *precisely* like that. Azrune's safety is always my primary concern. If anyone was to obtain both a Gold Age calputer, such as the core of the *Postremo*, and one of Brazak West's Gundars, they would attain the ability to strike us from anywhere. I cannot allow that to happen.'

'Do we know that's what they have planned?' Elzie asked.

'Ganzabar has been attempting to crack the shell of Azrune for centuries; that much is a public secret. Even if this is not their plan, the fact that they will be capable of it is reason enough to mobilise against it coming to pass.'

Elzie ran her hand through her hair with a sigh. 'If you know all this, why is the government trying to end this war?'

'I am an advisor, Elzie.' The Proctor seemed terribly old for his looks all of a sudden. 'The outcome at Laronor may be the only thing that serves to convince them of the danger. Of course, by that point it will already be too late.'

Kiy grunted. 'I do despise politics. You seem more preoccupied with the excuse than the morality.'

The Proctor seemed ruffled at the thought. 'Do not mistake me. I know what must be done. That I may be able to leverage political support to do so is just icing on the table.' He paused, not noticing the bewildered looks his metaphor had evoked. 'That's why I'm going with the two of you to Laronor.'

'You are?' Kiy gaped.

'Indeed, without delay. We must prevent Ganzabar from capturing the Gundar at all costs.'

'How the flak are we supposed to do that?' Kiy said.

'We will decide when we arrive and can henceforsooth assess the situation better,' the Proctor replied.

'Just us?' Elzie asked uneasily.

'Sometimes a little push is all that's needed.' The Proctor nodded to himself, then flashed a smile. 'Of course, I'm working on a shove, as well.'

'I appreciate you freeing me, but I'm not much good to you without a sling,' Kiy said.

The Proctor held up a finger as though recalling something. He turned to the box he'd brought with him and handed it to Kiy. Inside, Kiy found a newly pressed dark blue Azrunite naval uniform—and his sling. He looked at the Proctor in amazement.

'You managed to get this back from the Domestic Ministry?'

The Proctor looked almost annoyed. 'Petty children. They have no appreciation for a work of art.'

'Thank you.' Kiy took it in his hands. He always felt better when the sling was with him.

'Did you still hear her voice?' the Proctor asked.

Kiy froze. 'What did you say?'

'Jan. You heard her even without the sling, didn't you? Its effects are somewhat residual.'

Kiy was dumbstruck. 'How...'

The Proctor made a dismissive gesture. 'That's an explanation for another time. Anyway, I wasn't able to get your clothes back, so please accept this uniform as compensation.'

'When do we leave?' Elzie asked.

'As soon as we can. We'll be taking my yacht. Come, follow me, it's the third flowerpot on the left.'

'Third flower...' Kiy repeated, confused. 'Can I at least get dressed?'

'You may do so once we're underway,' the Proctor insisted, and led on.

They proceeded down a spiral pathway lined with bushes. The third in a row of large round pots marked a concealed pathway leading to a sharp descent. They followed it to a massive hangar that dwarfed the small ship sat in the middle of it.

As they walked closer to the yacht, Kiy got a better sense of scale. The ship was more impressive up close—the grace and finesse of its Azrunite styling was unmistakable—but it was still very small for an airship. A Foxtail skyfighter was slung under the central body, held in the grasp of steel fingers.

'Hurry. We've not a Tuesday to lose.' The Proctor stepped up the gantry. 'The country is in peril.'

Elzie followed, with Kiy just behind. 'Country's crazy, is what it is,' Kiy muttered to himself.

The door slid shut behind them and the craft's engines began to whine.

41 - Gundar

Waltov, Laronor

'Miran... meet Karak.'

Hennie outstretched a hand on introducing Karak, which felt overly formal, but she was already feeling dissonant. While it was clear that the only reason Karak wanted to meet the kid was the prospect of reaching the Gundar, she wasn't sure why she was going along with it. She'd convinced herself that Karak had been wronged and deserved a break, a chance to get his life back. Now she was starting to wonder if she was just doing it because of his rugged good looks. *Shyut, I'm not even sure if I'm joking.*

Miran seemed excited to meet Karak though; Karak's interest in the Mygos no doubt fuelled a keen enthusiasm within the boy. '... This side doesn't have a support spar yet,' he was telling Karak. 'I have one right here, but fittin' the new Dihed that Hennie got me'—he flashed her a grin as he mentioned it—'took most of yesterday. A few calibrations and she'll be fit to fly.'

'I've never been out in a ship like that before,' Karak said wistfully.

'You should come! And Hennie, too.' He turned to her, looking adorable. Hennie's promise to Jerra was feeling ever closer to peril.

Karak grinned. 'That sounds like a great idea, kid.'

Hennie scratched her arm absently. 'What, uh, did you have in mind? Fly around the block or something?'

'How about to the Gundar?' Karak suggested.

'I don't think—' Hennie began, but Miran, in his excitement, cut her off.

'Flak yeah! That's an awesome idea. And—oh man, you're gonna love these—check out what I got, these are just what we need...' Miran turned to rummage in an open top box, tossing out various items. They looked like ship innards, but Hennie didn't recognise any of them.

'Aha! Here.' The boy presented a metal box with wires pouring from one side. It looked much like the rest of the junk he'd tossed out of the box and Hennie had to ask what it was.

'Military transponder,' Miran said, looking positively smug. 'You can look like military craft with this baby.'

'I'm not gonna even ask where you got that.' Karak laughed.

Hennie didn't like where this was going. 'How about we just... take a leisure spin and, um, visit the Gundar another time? I mean, it's a little far away...'

'It's only a kilometre or two!' Miran protested.

'And you've not tested the ship yet...' Hennie continued.

'Geez, Hennie!' Miran said. 'I thought you were cool, but now you're acting all girly. You don't have to come if you're too scared.'

That riled her. If the little brat had been there to see the bombs falling on Brudor, he might be able to tell her something about being afraid. 'I'm not scared of the stupid Gundar,' she snapped.

'Then that's all three of us in.' Karak had that big charismatic grin of his, but Hennie felt like she wanted to punch him right now.

'I'll go get the support spar so I can fix it on, then we can go.' Miran beamed, the animosity of a moment ago instantly cast aside in his excitement. He almost skidded out of the doorway.

Karak began to move as soon as Miran was gone. He climbed up onto the seat of the Mygos and flicked a switch. A whine from the magneto somewhere inside began to slowly rise in pitch.

'What are you doing?' Hennie hissed at him. 'Are you crazy?'

'It's too dangerous for a kid,' Karak said. He hit a row of switches and slid forward a lever shaped like an upturned 'U'. The ship slowly rose off the hangar floor. Hennie decided all that talk about not having ridden a small ship was probably propwash.

'Karak! Turn it off, right now.'

'You should stay too,' Karak told her. He began to slide the ship forwards, out of the doors.

'Oh no, no way.' She pulled herself up onto the side platform and sat down gracelessly in the second seat. The two of them mostly filled out the cockpit space, behind which was only a small baggage area anyway. 'I'd rather face the Gundar than Miran when he finds out you stole his baby.'

Karak clunked a lever down a notch, and Hennie heard a shunting sound followed by the propellers at the back spinning up. Karak smoothly throttled them out the hangar door.

The craft slid upwards, the rooftops of Waltov dropping away beneath them. Hennie crossed her legs as her stomach left her. Even at a hundred metres up or more, she dared not look back in case she could make out Miran's expression as she imagined it.

The thought of what they'd done made her feel disgusted with herself, but she was thankful she'd managed to at least hold her promise to keep Miran out of trouble. Of course, that was far from a comprehensive list of her worries.

'Didn't he say this thing was unfinished?' Hennie shouted to Karak.

'Support spars. Who needs 'em,' Karak quipped.

Hennie wasn't so sure about that, but Karak seemed to know what he was doing.

The craft climbed into the upper sky confidently, swinging around to the south until the Gundar was ahead and above them. Hennie could see Laronor stretch out beneath. From up here, the city looked a lot different from how she'd first seen it. She knew where places were, but it was more than that. It looked more like home, somehow.

Karak had plugged the military transponder into the dashboard and was playing with the dials on the front. The Mygos was by no means a fast ship, and it was a good ten minutes before they found themselves at the station's threshold.

'Okay, now what?' Hennie asked. She felt anxiety in every bone in her body. She couldn't get Miran's face out of her mind. 'We don't even know if there's enough fuel in it!'

'We're squawking Supply,' Karak said.

'I'm not squawking, I'm just pointing it out.'

Karak just laughed. 'No, the transponder. It means they probably won't even bother talking to us until we dock.' He tweaked another dial.

'So what's on this Gundar, anyway?' Hennie asked, her eyes weighing up the Gundar as it got closer.

'It'd be easier to explain once we're there,' Karak replied. His expression was set as he took hold of the controls to steer the craft smoothly to the right. As he did so it began to make a creaking shudder that raised Hennie's pulse.

'It's going to break...' She gripped his arm in fear.

'It'll be fine!' Karak said, although more in concentration than assurance.

As the Mygos straightened, the shudder stopped and Hennie felt like she could breathe again. What had possessed her to think this was even remotely a good idea?

A crackled voice rasped from the instrument panel. 'Morning there, Supply Alpha-Five, this is Gundar Tower.' It sounded like a cheery young man; the accent reminded Hennie of Kiy.

Karak looked at the radio as though it were a perilous warning light, then shot Hennie a look. 'You talk to them.'

'*Me?*'

'I'm busy here.'

Hennie leant forward to the talkpiece, holding her finger above a red button Miran had helpfully labelled with embossing tape. She hesitated, looking across at Karak with panic. 'What do I tell them?'

'Just say hi back, followed by "Supply Alpha-Five". Let's see what they want.'

Hennie held the button and went to speak, but found her voice had shrunk. 'H—hi there.'

She let go of the switch, then pressed it again to append a hurried 'Supply Alpha-Five' to her sentence. Her heart pounded. How was talking to someone so scary?

'Supply Alpha-Five, you're early,' the man on the radio said. 'But it's okay, things are quiet. Proceed to free dock, port west-side.'

Karak didn't take his eyes from dead ahead. 'Repeat that last part, plus our name.'

'Whose name? Mine?'

'No, "Supply Alpha-Five". That's what they're calling us.'

'Oh—right, right.' She leant closer to the panel again, pressed the talk button and stated the instruction back. As she completed it, she gave Karak a satisfied smile, but he seemed distracted.

They headed for the dock. It was deserted, of both people and ships. They slid the Mygos into a nook for a small airship, then made to disembark.

Now that the flight was over, Hennie's anxiety lessened and she felt a surge of excitement. She stepped out onto solid floatrock eagerly, thanking it for being there and trying not to think about the implications of having to return the same way.

'No sign of anyone,' she observed, looking about. 'This should be easy, right?'

'I should be fine. You ought to head on back now.'

Hennie shook her head. 'It's okay; I can just wait here if you like. I'll find someone we can talk to about your—'

She felt something hard poke her lower back and froze.

'I'm afraid this is going to be anything but easy,' Karak said. 'I'm sorry, Hennie.'

She turned to see him holding her Bluebell, and she slowly raised her hands.

Ganzabi Battleship Grace of Gnost

Through the grating at the end of the duct, Leo could make out someone entering the cell at long last.

He had been sure that before his escape the guard had said he and Marc were to be imprisoned in cell one-three-six on K deck. Well, truth be told, he'd thought it was cell one-six-three, but that cell had contained an old man with a ragged beard who looked as though he'd been there for an eternity. So then he figured it must be cell three-six-one, but that cell had held a feisty young dark-haired woman pacing and yelling abuse intermittently. He'd lingered to watch her with fascination and boyish curiosity. But then his mission had pulled him back and he'd resumed the search for his Azrunite friend.

Finally he'd tried one-three-six, tracing the pipes and ducts as noiselessly as a mouse might. The cell system, he had discerned, was laid out in a mostly logical manner, and it took just a little diligence to find the cell he was looking for.

It had now been at least a day since he'd escaped into the duct system. He'd figured how to syphon water off the vapour pipes with small checking valves that were nearly as shadowed and secluded as the system itself, but it took time and felt risky. Once or twice he'd heard voices, and mindful that they were on the lookout for him, he'd bolted before he could undo the tap. It wasn't a comfy existence, but he was consoled that the Ganzies were effectively looking for a needle in a haystack.

Still, upon finding cell one-three-six empty, he hadn't been sure what to do next. Which was why he was sitting glumly, trying to formulate a new plan, when the guards finally appeared at the cell doorway. And much to Leo's relief, they had Marc in tow.

He waited until they threw the Azrunite into the room and left, then he waited a minute more to be sure, before whispering.

'Marc. Psst.'

Marc looked up at the grating and squinted. 'Leo?'

'Yeah, I'm in the vent.'

'Nice one, kiddo.' Marc checked a glance around him. 'I think they're gone; should be safe to talk.'

'Where have you been? Have they been torturing you?'

'Only with boredom,' Marc joked, though a black eye and blood on his lip told the truth. 'Then they were meant to throw me overboard, but apparently they're behind on the paperwork.'

Leo made an anxious groan. Marc's indifference made him wonder sometimes if the Azrunite even understood what dying was. 'How are we gonna get out of here?'

'Getting me out of this cell would be a good start, I reckon,' the Azrunite answered jovially. 'Can you smash open that grating?'

The opening of Leo's vent was right in the middle of the high ceiling, too high for someone on the ground to reach, but from above it seemed as though it wouldn't put up a lot of resistance.

'I prob'ly could, but I bet it's alarmed,' Leo said after some thought.

'You sure?'

'Trust me, I've snooped around a lot of ships. And even if it wasn't, I can't pull you up from that far down, and you probably wouldn't fit in here.'

'You saying I'm fat?'

'Marc, be serious a sec!' Leo fought to keep his voice down.

'Alright, alright.' Marc relented. 'I've got an idea.'

'For real?'

'I think I know where they're gonna try and throw me over the side. We were just there, actually; got one of the paperpushers to thank for saving my skin. He informed them that they can't do it till they file an execution application! Crazy, innit? Anyway, it was on Q deck, towards aft, port side. They got a handy little lookout platform with a convenient gap in the handrail, for executions I guess. Hide nearby and distract them best you can. I'll do the rest.'

'What if they don't take you there?' Leo said miserably.

Marc seemed unbothered. 'It'll be fine, mate. I haven't got any other ideas anyhow.'

Leo was about to protest further when boots sounded on the walkway outside the cell. Two men arrived and escorted Marc from the room without a word.

'Am I going to get chucked over yet?' Marc asked them.

One of the marines slapped him on the back of the head. 'No talking!'

'Hypocrite.' Marc muttered.

Leo heard another slap as they marched him out of sight, then he began to scurry quickly back down the ventilation passage.

The wind was howling almost ceremoniously as the exterior door swung open to the Q deck observation gantry. The *Grace of Gnost* was approaching Laronor, and countless other ships were scattered about them. Wind and snowfall whipped at the uniforms of the two marines and Marc's yellow flight suit as they escorted him along the walkway. The gap in the rail was just up ahead.

'These Azrunites are such pussies, just giving in and accepting their death,' one of the marines said to the other over the noise of flapping clothing and whistling air.

The other nodded. 'Yeah, what's with that? Hey!' he said to Marc. 'You *do* know we're about to kill you, right?' Then he laughed.

They arrived at the point where the rail dipped into the floor, leaving a metre or so unbounded. Beyond the lip was nothing but the distant clouds far, far below.

'Say your prayers, Azrunite,' the first marine said mockingly. 'As if you even had any.'

The other laughed, then stopped abruptly and tumbled forward onto the walkway, his eyes rolling back in his head.

Behind him stood Leo, holding a length of metal pipe.

As the second marine made to grab the kid, he momentarily neglected his Azrunite prisoner. Marc's hands were bound in rope, and he looped his arms over the Ganzabi's head and pulled back, his bindings pressing against the man's throat. The man fought back furiously.

'Hit him!' Marc said through gritted teeth.

'I might hit you!' Leo protested.

The Ganzabi elbowed Marc hard, then threw his weight forward. Marc was thrown right over him, landing on his back on the deck. Leo swung as hard as he could at the Ganzie, but the marine dodged and grabbed the pipe. With a quick tug he'd wrestled it away, despite Leo pulling with all his strength.

Marc took the distraction as an opportunity and kicked out with both feet. His heels caught the marine at the ankle, knocking him back several steps. As he stumbled, his foot stepped just past the lip at the edge of the walkway—and he tumbled into the sky with a scream. The sound dwindled almost immediately, leaving only the wind.

Marc shuffled away from the opening, his hands still bound. Leo reached down to the Ganzabi that lay unconscious and pulled a combat knife from his belt, then sliced Marc's bindings.

'Cheers, Leo,' Marc said—but his smile turned to shock as Leo went to plunge the knife into the fallen marine's body.

'What?' Leo looked up at the stern eyes of the Azrunite. The boy's hand, and the knife within it, had been halted above the fallen soldier by Marc's firm grip.

'What in the name of Sky and Moons are you doing, kiddo? There's no need to kill him, he's already down!'

'It's what Anatali would have done,' Leo grunted, his arm trembling to fight Marc's strength.

'Shyut! I can't believe a kid like you has learned to think like that.'

'What about the guy you just pushed over?' Leo relented and pulled away from Marc's grip grudgingly. 'He's as good as dead. Who knows how horrible dying in the Understorm is. At least this guy wouldn't have known nothin'.'

Marc sighed. 'Leo, mate, it's not the point. Fight to incapacitate. If the enemy is no longer a threat, they're no longer the enemy. I know sometimes the only way to stop them leaves them dead, but that's not what we're trying to do. Yeah?'

Leo looked unsure. 'But he's still a threat. He might shoot a Brazakker tomorrow.'

The Azrunite turned away, wheeling open the door back into the ship. 'If we worry about stuff people *might* do,' he said, 'we may as well kill the whole damn world. Come on, let's get out of here.'

Leo looked at the fallen man one last time before pocketing the knife and following the Azrunite back inside.

43 - Hamel

Laronor Gundar, Brazak West

'W-wait...' Hennie stuttered.

'Hands where I can see them.' Karak's voice was sharp, his accent suddenly a much stronger Ganzabi tone.

She lifted her hands higher. 'I don't understand...'

He spoke quickly, as though it inconvenienced him. 'Two months ago, a Ganzabi pilot named Hamel Jerome crashed his plane in eastern Voxton. Now he wants to get home. So if you shut up and do as you're told, you don't need to get hurt.'

Hennie felt like she was going to be sick. 'The crashed Ganzie pilot? I thought they found him dead.'

'Wrong. They found a nameless soldier, down on his luck, lying dead in my flight suit.'

She began to tremble. Rage and fear entwined. 'You mean you...'

'Please, just shut up, Hennie. It would be a shame to put a bullet in that pretty little skull of yours, so why don't you stop talkin', huh?' He prodded her forward with the rifle. 'You insisted on coming along, but I can find my own way if you mess with me.'

Her lip curled, but she moved grudgingly. 'I'm not going to be your flakking hostage.'

'Is that so?'

'I won't let you,' she said. But her words were at odds with her actions as her feet carried her forward.

He smirked. 'You think you're gonna stop me? That's cute. Y'know, you actually turned out more resourceful than I thought. I was hoping for money, at best. But you're still just a kid. So don't do anything stupid, you hear? I don't want to have to shoot a kid.'

They arrived at a chain-link gate. Karak—*Hamel*, Hennie had to remind herself—went to push the gate forward but found it padlocked.

'Look, Hennie,' he began, his attention on the lock, 'I get it. You don't wanna betray your country; I sympathise. Well, I don't either. All I want is to get home.' He took a small length of wire from a breast pocket and attempted to pick the lock with it as he continued. 'If you were me, you'd understand. You don't know what it's like to be far away from home, never knowing if you'll ever see your family again.'

Hennie decided she certainly knew how that felt. But she wasn't about to let Ka—*Hamel* get into her head again. She wondered if the suspicious lack of a supply crew from their craft would raise an alarm back in the dock. She'd gone from hoping the Gundar's security was secretly flawed to hoping—begging—that they were paying attention.

'Heck, you'd probably do the same,' Hamel decided, keeping an eye on Hennie as he fiddled with the gate.

'I wouldn't kill someone for a uniform,' she replied angrily, 'or lie about who I was, or steal a little boy's airship —'

Hamel laughed derisively. 'Oh, spare me. You had plenty of chances to stop me. But now I'm Mr Big-Bad-Ganzie, suddenly you have a conscience.'

Hennie went quiet. She had to admit, she'd led him here. And would it really hurt anyone if she just let him get home?

She closed her eyes. 'Fine... if you promise to go and never come back.'

Hamel grinned as the lock on the gate was defeated. 'You're hardly in a position to bargain. But I promise you, as much as this has been fun, I won't be coming back. Not till I get another plane, anyhow.'

Something in his smile, the taunting in his eyes, made her instinctively pull back. But Hamel caught the intention and gripped her wrist firmly. She whipped back and pulled at him. He struggled, grabbing hold of her other arm to try and subdue her. She responded by sinking her teeth into his wrist.

Hamel let go with a curse and Hennie stumbled. She spun ungracefully and made to run with all the speed she could muster. But it was then she felt the heavy wood of a rifle butt hit her head, and she tumbled forward, falling abruptly still.

Hamel Jerome stared in rising panic at the lifeless girl sprawled in front of him. His cold fingers clenched the Bluebell, the instrument of her demise. *Damn you, Hennie,* he cried inwardly, *DAMN you. You could have been fine! You had to go and... Flak it!*

He averted his eyes, turned his back on the body and hurried through the gate into the complex. His heart ached at the thought of Hennie's blood on his hands, after she had saved him. Of course, she hadn't done it knowing all the facts, but he couldn't help but feel for her.

Still, it would be easier without her, he noted grimly. Particularly in the next step, which was every bit as important as his own escape: the crippling of this doomsday weapon, and thereby the saving of countless Ganzabi lives. He wasn't completely sure how it might be done, but he felt that he had to try.

He skulked down a corridor lit with countless naked bulbs hanging from the ceiling. Finally he found himself in a wide cylindrical room with banks of important-looking machinery. A young man was stooped over part of the exposed machinery, and Hamel was just considering ways he might remove him when the man stood and left the room through the far doorway.

Hamel ran to the door and shut it behind him, drawing the bolt across it. He then turned to the innards of the monster and set to work.

44 - Chenkov

Laronor Gundar

Hennie rose slowly. Any faster and her head might just fall apart, after all.

She gathered the effort to push herself up with her palms and twist around to sit. There was a red mark on the snow where she'd lain. Working out why took a lot longer than she felt it ought to.

Reaching up gingerly to her head, she felt a nauseating curiosity at the wetness meeting her fingers. Inspecting them confirmed her suspicion. How strange. She found herself impressed that she was still alive. Not dead, just leaking red, as the old joke went. *Gosh. Red, everywhere. I need to get out of here*.

She immediately looked about for her rifle, but of course he had taken it. She spotted a stack of metre-long metal marker rods, the kind used for setting up makeshift perimeters by slotting them into holes set along the ground. She scooped one up, finding herself angrier as her most recent memories realigned themselves in her head. Karak—no, Hamel. Everything—it was *his* fault.

She stared at the length of steel in her hand. What if she just let him be? She could simply let him escape, and she could return to Waltov. She pictured returning to Miran and the family, explaining all that had happened. How she'd stolen the ship, given Hamel a free ride, then just... well, let him go.

No. She couldn't face them like that. She had to redeem herself. If she stopped him, they might even forgive her. Perhaps.

She went to stand, but her legs didn't quite get it right the first time and she fell to a knee.

Snowflakes were the only sense of time she felt, as she caught her breath and looked up in determination. She fought back to her feet, leaning on the steel rod for support.

'Hamel...' she muttered bitterly. Her head pounded, but she was beginning to care less and less. All she could think of was wringing that bastard Ganzie's neck.

Venturing inside the Gundar confirmed that it was just as deserted as the dock. She followed a long corridor of hanging lights, realising that if she were seen she'd surely be suspicious. Her head was beginning to clear. With the clarity came anxiety and apprehension. Hamel was a soldier; she was not. But then, she had surprise on her side. He clearly didn't think she'd survived the blow; if he had, he wouldn't have just left her there, to raise the alarm.

She passed rows of doors. Hamel could have been behind any one of them, but she tried a couple, and they didn't seem to go anywhere. Besides, she figured he would head for the airfield, so she crept across the Gundar.

It seemed as though the facility was running on a skeleton crew. Hennie spotted a few guards in the distance, but the station was mostly endless pillars of humming machinery without a soul around. The smell of grease and industrial grime reminded her of transit stations, but in truth there was really nowhere she had been that was quite like this.

Soon the airfield came into sight: a long flat strip of smooth deck plates running alongside the side of the main tower structure. A trio of Brazak soldiers in long beige coats stood beside a parked transport plane warming their hands on a heater. Hennie figured being seen by them would be nearly as bad as being seen by Hamel, so she made sure to keep low.

It was then that she saw him.

He was also attempting to close on the transport plane, hiding behind stacks of luftwood crates and metal boxes. She considered how she could possibly take him down. Hamel still wore his stolen uniform; she was just wearing a pinafore and an old coat. The guards would find her and she'd be left with one heck of a flimsy explanation.

As she agonised over how to stop him, a klaxon blared. The infantry guarding the airfield whirled around to look at the main tower, then seemed to confer for several moments. No doubt the mysterious circumstances around the Mygos had finally raised an alarm, Hennie thought.

Two of the soldiers stood beside the plane hurried back towards the tower; Hennie shrank back as they passed her hiding spot. That left a lone sentry by the transport plane—a woman of maybe thirty. Hennie took a deep breath. Hamel was bound to make his move now. But could she stop him once he'd revealed himself to be the enemy?

There was no time to think about it, for at that moment Hamel stood quickly and crept forward, rifle in hand. The soldier was looking the other way, scanning the sky curiously, unaware of the death closing in on her.

'Look out!' Hennie yelled.

Both Hamel and the soldier turned to her with matching expressions of surprise, albeit for totally different reasons. Hennie suddenly realised she'd made a terrible mistake.

'You there!' The soldier had raised her rifle in the bat of an eye. 'Identify yourself.'

Hennie raised her hands and dropped the rod with a clatter. 'I'm a Reserve!'

'Reserves aren't authorised access to the Gundar,' the guard replied. Then she spotted Hamel. 'And where in Sky's name did you come from, Private?'

Hamel looked apologetic. 'Me? I've been looking for her,' he said, his fake accent back again. 'Don't let the civvies throw you; she's a Ganzabi spy.'

'Liar!' Hennie shouted back, wincing as the pain in her head intensified.

'Come out of there! Arms up!' the soldier instructed, taking a step forward, her rifle trained on Hennie.

Hennie really didn't like where this was going, but nothing could be done now. If she made a false move, this guard was on the edge of her trigger. So she stepped forward slowly, arms above her head.

When the soldier reached her, she motioned for Hennie to move over to one of the large luftwood crates. Hamel joined the guard, standing a little behind her. Hennie began to try and explain. 'You can't trust him, he's the spy here—'

'Silence,' Hamel barked. The sentry glanced at him uneasily. She clearly wasn't totally convinced by Hamel's claims. Hennie figured she had to press that.

'You must know all the others on this station, right?' she protested. 'And you've never seen him before, have you?'

'Different unit,' Hamel growled, his eyes laying challenge to Hennie.

The soldier narrowed her eyes slightly. 'Which unit are you with, anyway?'

'The fifty-second,' Hamel said.

'There's no—'

Hamel raised and fired in a heartbeat. The soldier wore a look of blank shock, mouth open silently, then collapsed forward clutching her chest.

Hennie stared, starting to hyperventilate, at the slick dark pool of blood growing beneath the guard's crumpled body. 'No!'

Hamel turned the rifle on Hennie. 'Enough. She is only going to die because of you. I would have knocked her out, but you had to interfere. You had to complicate it again! Flak, I thought you were dead!'

Hennie felt her eyes water. 'No... Please, Karak—'

'I said *enough*!' Hamel gritted his teeth. 'If you make another sound, I swear I'll shoot.'

Hennie fought back the whimper of terror that fought to escape her throat. Her eyes stung with tears.

'Now,' Hamel said, turning to the plane. 'Get up on the wing with one of those fuel cans and fill it up. You've cost me time, so you're gonna repay it.'

Hennie kept her hands raised meekly as she walked over to one of the fuel cans. Hamel opened the door of the small plane and leant in, keeping his rifle pointed in her direction.

She thought about running away, but decided she couldn't get far. Besides, she didn't *want* to run away. She wanted to kill him. But it was hopeless. He'd won.

She hung her head, looking down into the front of her pinafore. There she saw the Chenkov pistol that she had confiscated from the kids in Voxton. She'd never fired a percussion pistol, but it couldn't be much harder than the rifle. She could hit him if she was close enough. And of course, if it was loaded...

She peeked to one side. Hamel was starting up the plane and appeared to be mostly ignoring her. And why not? She wasn't much threat to him without a weapon; he was twice her size in muscle.

She closed her eyes. *Only one chance to do this. He could kill me anyway, when he's done with me.*

She took the fuel can in her hand and stepped towards him. Three. Two...

... One.

She pulled the Chenkov pistol from her pinafore and stared down the barrel at Hamel, her eyes ablaze.

Hamel froze. He was far away enough to be unable to snatch the pistol but close enough that she could hardly miss.

'Raise that rifle so much as a hair-width and you're flakking dead,' Hennie said.

'Well, now.' He smiled uncertainly, but didn't move. 'The Chenkov? Y'know, I'd forgotten 'bout that. Too bad it's probably not even loaded.'

She realised her aim was wobbling noticeably. She fought to keep her hand steady, but the gun was heavy and she was nervous.

'You're just a frightened little girl. Put it down before I shoot you. I mean it. Put it down now!'

Hennie's brain decided to comply with his orders, but her finger made a different decision: it pulled the trigger instead.

The pistol kicked back and thundered. Hamel was thrown back, the rifle falling to the tarmac. He looked down at his wound, then back at Hennie in surprise. She didn't know whether she felt vindicated or mortified, but it was anger that took over.

'I am *not* a frightened little girl,' she declared, still pointing the old pistol at him. She felt she should have more to say, but that was all that came to her at that moment.

'You never cease... to surprise me, Hennie,' Hamel said, clutching his wound. He slid from the open cockpit seat to the floor.

Hennie kicked his Bluebell well out of reach. She wanted to go find someone to help the guard, but she felt it would be a mistake to leave Hamel, even wounded as he was.

Fortunately, several of the garrison forces had been drawn to the gunshots and were running across the airfield to them. In less than a minute, they'd surrounded the plane.

'Put the gun down, miss!' one of them instructed.

Hennie tossed the Chenkov away, keeping her eyes on Hamel. The soldiers took her by the arm and picked up the two wounded, leading them both inside. Hennie followed without resistance.

Hennie was led to a small room in the Gundar's central tower, where she was bound to a chair and told she would be questioned by the installation's commanding officer. She didn't bother arguing with the soldiers or even speaking to them; she knew they were acting under orders.

It wasn't long before an intense and elderly woman with faded brown hair entered the room. She eyed Hennie coldly, but before she could speak, a soldier ran in and whispered something in her ear.

'What do you mean, it's no longer tracking?' the woman demanded.

'The calputer storage on deck eight has been wrecked, ma'am,' the young man reported bleakly. 'Guidance system smashed. Repairing it could take weeks.'

'We don't have weeks, Goswyn! The Armada is headed this way; we've got an hour, at best.'

The young man looked to his feet, but it was to Hennie that the woman turned. 'Seems you have some explaining to do, girl.'

'Me?' Hennie exclaimed. 'It was Hamel!'

'Hamel?' The woman frowned. 'Are you telling me the infantryman you shot is the saboteur here, 'cause I find that a little hard to believe.'

'He's not really from the army, he's a Ganzie; he crashed here, like, months ago! Then he stole a uniform.'

The looks that confronted her told her she wasn't necessarily presenting this story necessarily in the most believable way.

'Then what are you doing here?' The officer folded her arms expectantly. She had a haughty, chiselled face with some years to it. It seemed to suit her lean physique.

'I came to stop him. I mean, I brought him here, but I didn't know that he—I...' She sighed and slumped in defeat.

'We will see what he has to say—if he lives. You'd better hope he does.' The woman stared long and hard at Hennie. 'But for now I'm keeping you both tied up. The last thing we need right now is more complications.'

'Commander!' A young woman had appeared in the doorway. 'The Armada... it's here!'

The commander pivoted and strode out. 'Assume battle stations.'

'Yes, ma'am!'

45 - The Battle for Laronor

Laronor

The sky was filled with Ganzabi ships, too many to number, engulfing the sky southward like a swarm of insects.

Lines of cannons awoke, and the air was filled with the percussive thumps of ships' guns. Ganzabi Dragonfly monoplanes met head on with Brazak Foxtail duplanes. The skyfighters weaved in and out of each other's formations, spitting streams of tracers and chasing tails.

A string of independent cannon emplacements on the border of the city, huge coastal guns, fired on the Ganzabi ships, but even scoring several hits they did little to dent the approaching mass of the Armada. Defensive ships, too, leapt at the attacking mass, but they encountered a wall of deadly shells in response and were little more effective than the cannons.

The streets descended into disarray as people fled from the southern rim zones and the terrifying shadows of invaders. But some stood fast, arming themselves with outdated and makeshift weapons, fortifying their homes. Determination was written on many a face: *Sooner die than face the occupation again...*

Inside the Gundar, Hennie watched the flashes and smoke columns from afar through a large round window, the sounds dulled. She and Hamel had been placed in the same room after his gunshot wound was patched up. Hennie wasn't too thrilled with his company, but they'd at least tied his wrists. Having her own bound as well was a fair price to pay.

It had become clear that Hamel was in no state to escape. He sat on the floor, chin almost on his chest, not saying a word. Hennie kept wondering if he was actually dead, but watching him carefully revealed the slight swell and sink of his chest.

The battle beyond the window frustrated her. There had been no sound from the Gundar itself, so it was most likely still disabled. Guilt surged within her like bile at the thought. If it weren't for her, the Gundar would have been shooting Ganzabi ships before they got anywhere near the city. Instead, the Gundar was sitting here like a distracted child while the battle was being lost. And it was all her fault.

A deep rumble shook the tower, snapping her from her thoughts. Had the Gundar finally fired? Even Hamel gazed out of the window with a kind of stunned intrigue.

'By the Gates of Arkaedis! Hennie, that you, m'lovely?'

Hennie turned, eyes wide, to the source of the familiar voice. Stood at the doorway and dressed in infantry fatigues with a Bluebell rifle in his hands was a boy she'd never have expected to be so pleased to see.

'Sput!' she blurted. 'What are you doing here?'

Sput raised an eyebrow. 'I might verily be asking you that very question.' He motioned to the gash on her forehead. 'Looking worse for wear, I must say.'

'Well—it's a long story.' Hennie shifted, almost forgetting the rope that bound her hands to her chair. 'But what about you?'

'Me? I'm stationed here, m'lovely.' He regarded her a moment. 'I heard we took a pair of spies, but—they can't mean you, can they?'

Hennie felt hugely better that someone else could vouch for her. '*He* is a spy. But they think *I* am too!'

Sput looked livid. 'Preposterous!'

'Glad you think so. What the hadnar is all that noise, anyway?'

Sput glanced down the corridor. 'Enemy transports. There's Ganzies landing on the lower decks. No time to chat I'm afraid, m'lovely.'

'Wait! Get me out of here!' Hennie tried to stand, but was stopped by her binds.

Sput's face showed a flash of dilemma. 'I could get into a lot of trouble for that, m'pearl.'

'Please!'

Sput's shoulders drooped. 'Ohh... you know I can't disappoint a lady. And while you may be aware and reckoning on this little vice o' mine, I still cannot find it in myself to refuse—'

'Then hurry up!'

Sput moved swiftly to untie her, his hands working the rope quicker and surer than she'd have imagined for so skittish a boy. As he did, she watched Hamel, who simply stared out the window at the distant battle.

'We need to get you out of harm's way, Hennie m'lovely.'

'I came here on a ship. I need to get back to it.' Hennie stood and rubbed her wrists, then took one last look at Hamel. He didn't meet her eye—whether through shame or defiance, she couldn't tell.

Sput gestured for her to follow. 'The dock is this way. Follow along and keep apace, Hennie m'darling.'

'Thanks Sput.'

She took one last glance over her shoulder as they left Hamel behind. She wondered what would become of him. Shooting him had made her realise that his suffering wasn't going to make her feel any better. Perhaps it was for the best that they simply part ways.

She followed Sput down a curving stairway that led into the depths of the installation. The sounds of gunfire, yells and screams grew closer. Then they emerged onto a long exterior walkway, and Hennie felt her heart thump as she got a look at the attacking waves of Ganzabi soldiers for the first time.

'Down!' Sput shouted, pulling Hennie to a stoop just as bullets impacted above them. Hennie cried out and put her hands to her ears despite all the firearms acclimatisation with Jerra. When the bullets were out to get her, they just seemed so much louder.

Sput kept them both below the level of the parapet, slinking along, moving closer to the dock level.

'This is no good, pet,' Sput reported grimly, taking glances over the top. 'The whole dock is swarming with Ganzies.'

'What're we gonna do?' Hennie asked, trying to avert her eyes from the corpse of a fallen Brazak soldier on the walkway.

'We shall have to devise a new plan, m'lovely.' Sput's eyes betrayed worry, but he was making every effort to appear confident.

An explosion plumed up from the lower deck, and they both flinched. Hennie raised her hands around her head protectively.

'What the—'

'Shelling!' Sput said, pulling her along back the way they'd come. 'This is too dangerous, pet, we've got to get back up the tower.'

They ran through the rooms and corridors of the installation, the sounds of the firefight some levels below creeping after them. The cracks of rifles and rings of blades were accompanied by screams and battle cries. As they passed a window, Hennie caught sight of an open-top troop transport tumbling down in flames, the Ganzabi aboard it being flung out into the mercy of the endless sky. Apparently they had been bold—or foolhardy—enough to try and attack the complex at a higher tier, where most of the defences were still intact.

As they emerged onto another defensive walkway strewn with fallen defenders, she stopped.

Sput tugged her arm urgently. 'What is it? Come on, Hennie m'lovely, we can't stay here.'

'Where can we go? We're trapped.' Hennie grimaced. She swiped up a Bluebell from the side of a dead Brazak soldier.

'You can't seriously—'

'Just try and stop me,' Hennie said, anger rising. 'I've been running for too long now.' She loaded the rifle and hinged it closed again with brimming frustration. 'Sooner or later, there will be nowhere left to run. I'm not going to let them go any further. Not anymore.'

Sput looked taken aback, but nodded.

Hennie found herself hoping her practice was going to be enough. She'd never been in a battle before. Everyone here was going to be better than her. No, that was negative, she thought. Had to stay positive. She had the fighting spirit; Jerra had said so.

This was it. She could do this.

They hurried across the gantries towards the central tower, which housed the Gundar control station. The Ganzabi force was attempting to cross an open gap to reach it. Hennie knelt behind the short wall running along the walkway. On the other side of it, along a metallic bridge, was a desperate hand-to-hand scuffle. The enemy were on the outer section of the installation, attempting to push their way down the bridge and reach the elevator.

On the next defensive bridge down from Hennie and Sput, a Brazak officer stood amidst a group of soldiers. 'Fire on my mark. Aim behind the main line, not the struggle!' the line sergeant called to his men. 'Line, aim! Fire!'

A cluster of rifles errupted.

'Fire between their shots, m'lovely,' Sput said, placing his rifle on the edge of the parapet and taking aim.

Hennie followed his lead, finding a target some way down the sight. They were a little farther than the practice targets on the range had been, but Jerra had taught her to aim her shot a little up to compensate. How much, she had to guess.

She pulled the trigger, the rifle made an almighty crack, and she froze, still staring at her target. The mass of marines was moving along the far walkway towards the bridge, and she had no idea if she had hit anything or not.

Sput pulled her back 'Get back down!' A moment later a bullet rebounded off the wall behind them, and Hennie cried out.

'Careful, m'lovely. They know where we are now.'

She nodded and took another cartridge from her front pocket. She slid it into the breech of the rifle and locked it closed with the lever below the stock. If she just hit one of them, it would be something better than cowering in a hole.

She took aim and fired another round into the approaching masses. To her disbelief, one of the soldiers collapsed to the deck, clutching his belly. She ducked back quickly to reload. Perhaps someone else had hit the man, but he *had* collapsed the precise moment she fired. She hoped it was her.

Then she stopped. How could shooting Karak have felt so awful, yet the prospect of hitting this nameless Ganzie was positively thrilling? She shook the thought away. Now wasn't for thinking—but for fighting. They had to fight.

Two other soldiers took up position with her and Sput. Hennie felt it odd that neither of them gave the soldier in a pinafore a second look, but perhaps having Sput alongside her made her less conspicuous.

She locked another round into the Bluebell and raised it to fire. A shot whizzed by her ear, and she faltered. Realisation dawned on her: the marines on the far side of the gap were making an active effort to take shots at the two of them on the high platform.

'Watch yourselves, comrades! They're firing this way,' Sput called.

Gathering courage, Hennie rested the rifle on top of the parapet, fired it, and ducked quickly. She flung back the lever, sending the expended cartridge flying out of the breech as she fumbled for another round in the front of her pinafore.

With a deafening boom, the station beneath them shook. A glow of flame and thick smoke marked where a cannon shell had impacted the Gundar tower some way behind them.

'What are they trying to do, capture the Gundar or blow the flakking thing up?' she heard an indignant soldier yell.

She raised the rifle again and again, taking more shots, but the marines continued to advance. She confirmed another kill for sure, as she got used to the particulars of the rifle.

Then suddenly, to her horror, Sput flew backwards with a cry and a splash of crimson.

'Sput!' she screamed.

He lay on his back, letting off a stream of curses that were more elaborate and profane than anything Hennie had ever heard.

She rushed over, trying to see where he'd been hit. He was still moving, so that was good, she figured. Blood oozed from his arm onto the bronzed plates of the walkway.

'Easy, Sput!' she said, trying not to panic. 'Oh, Sky and Moons...'

One of the two newly arrived soldiers turned to the other. 'Karsky,' he said, 'we've got one down.'

The young man responding to the name shouldered his rifle and fumbled with the pack on his chest, extracting various first aid tools. He tore the sleeve from Sput's wounded arm and had just started to treat the wound when the other soldier tapped Hennie on the soldier.

'Look, I've no idea what you're doing here, but you can shoot, so don't stop,' he said. A serious frown pressed his heavy eyebrows together.

'Right,' she said. She looked back to Sput a moment. 'You still with us, Sput?'

'Still... kicking.' He winced, but forced a smile.

'Stay that way,' she instructed, then turned back to the battle.

46 -   Fall of the Gundar

Ganzabi Battleship Grace of Gnost

The *Grace of Gnost* was teeming with activity as the Ganzabi fleet geared up for battle. Officers strode purposefully, barking orders, while the lowly airmen, bottom rung of the Ganzabi naval ladder, scurried around attempting to enact those orders.

A rhythmic beat of marine footsteps passed by Marc and Leo's hiding place. Marc craned his head to watch as they passed.

The pair of them had found refuge in a pile of discarded cargo in one of the hangar bays. The bay was an expansive, cavernous space that was apparently used for storing whatever fit through its doors. There were containers of ammunition, food and spare parts, huge cylindrical water tanks, trunks of firearms and even a volatile-looking cannister labelled 'petroleum'.

And of course, there were also a number of fighters strewn about; this was what had drawn Marc. Unfortunately, the fleet seemed to be gearing up for battle, and the hangar was filled with Ganzabi personnel intending to use those fighters.

'Aw, this is frustratingly close,' Marc whispered, watching a Ganzabi with a clipboard wander around the plane he'd been eyeing up. 'That Dragonfly is gonna be so mine.'

'Easy, big guy,' Leo hissed. 'They 'int gonna just let you fly it out of here.'

'No,' Marc agreed. Then his face lit up with an idea.

Leo looked worried. 'Why do I feel like you're about to do something mental?'

Marc merely grinned.

A short while later, the last of the Ganzabi pilots was preparing to launch his Dragonfly fighter from the hangar. He was tall, with short black hair showing streaks of grey, and a weathered face. As he got ready to climb into the cockpit, he felt a tap on the shoulder.

'Hey there, wanna see a neat trick?' Marc said with a friendly smile and a somewhat convincing Ganzabi accent.

The pilot gave him a stony glare. 'What the—hey, are you one of them punks from maintenance? I've had just about enough of your pranks. This is a flakking battle, airman!'

'Watch this! I can make a plane come to life.'

'That's the stupidest thing I ever—'

At that moment, the Dragonfly shuddered into life, its propeller building momentum until it was a circular blur.

'Hey! Get out of...' The pilot frowned at what appeared to be an empty cockpit. 'What the blazes is going on here?'

'I told you!' Marc raised his hands with a showman's flair. 'Mind control, ain't it?'

'Propwash! Cut this out right now.'

The plane began to roll forward down the runway. The Ganzabi pilot had to dash aside to avoid being hit by the wing, but Marc deftly rolled under it and climbed up into the cockpit as the plane trundled onward.

As he was about to sit, Leo appeared from the cockpit's depths.

'Nice work, kid!' Marc said.

Leo flashed a grin, but his expression instantly switched to alarm and he pointed over Marc's shoulder, where, Marc saw, the pilot had taken up pursuit of the plane.

Marc leapt into his seat, displacing Leo into the compartment behind, then yanked the throttle fully open. The craft lurched forward.

Marc wrestled to keep the plane pointed in a straight line as it accelerated out of the hangar and down the portside runway. Approaching rapidly, was the edge of the strip—a sheer drop into open sky. The main bulk of the ship was to their right, and to the left was an unbounded edge with only sky beyond.

The Ganzabi pilot's hands suddenly appeared at the left side of the cockpit, and he hauled himself up, one foot on the wing. Marc swung at him, but the pilot grabbed hold of his wrist with a grip that was firm with desperation as much as determination. The plane swerved as the Ganzabi tried to pull Marc from the cockpit.

Leo lunged forward and bit down on the pilot's hand, who gave a yell of pain and tumbled out of sight. The sudden loss of weight on Marc's left caused him to fall to the right—and the imbalance on his feet made the plane swing sharply in that direction as well, towards a wall of steel.

'Left, left!' Leo cried.

'I know!'

Marc hammered the rudder back the opposite way, but it was far more responsive than he'd expected and the plane jolted to the left, lifting the wing with the severity of the move. The plane went right over the side of the airstrip and plummeted into the sky.

The force of the rushing air slammed the canopy shut, and Marc realised the screaming he heard was just as much his as Leo's. The craft's nose was pointing into the depths of the Understorm some kilometres below. But as their airspeed rose, Marc was able to pull up and gain something resembling a controlled flight.

After a few moments of uncertainty, he caught his breath and stole a look back at Leo, who looked numb.

'We did it, mate!' Marc said triumphantly.

'Not yet!' Leo pointed.

Marc followed the direction of Leo's finger to see Brazak fighters heading towards them. He groaned inwardly. Smart kid. If they were flying around in a Ganzabi monoplane, they were going to have to deal with Brazak skyfighters.

'Hold on to something, dude!' Marc called back.

Hennie reckoned she was firing maybe a shot every thirty seconds—not as fast as the others, but she was fending them off. They all were.

The Ganzabi marines were a hardy lot though. They didn't go down easy, and they stayed hidden, coming forward only in surges with determined covering fire from those behind them. It was only a matter of time before they would overwhelm the few remaining Brazakkers around the central column. Hennie's handful of ammunition had quickly vanished, too.

'Sput, you got any more rounds?' she called over the sporadic gunfire.

Sput now lay in a feverish daze, trying to keep himself conscious and focused. He fished a handful of shells from a pocket on his belt and handed them to her. She took them eagerly, emptying all but one into her pinafore, then loading the remainder into her Bluebell as he watched.

'You show 'em, Hennie m'lovely,' he said groggily. 'You're a trooper. A blazing fire, a hurricane through their ranks, girl.'

She turned to face the parapet and couldn't help but smile. All armies should have a Sput, she thought to herself, locking the lever back into place with a little extra gusto. *Look out, Ganzabar! Hennie Litvyak's here, and it's payback time.*

With gritted teeth, she popped out over the parapet and fired a shot into the marines piling forward. There were several ricochets as bullets answered, scraping the top of the wall just an instant after Hennie had dived back behind it. The fire from the enemy was getting more intense. She'd begun to move slightly back and forth along the parapet, so as not to continually appear in the same place. Around her, at least a dozen Brazakkers lay dead where they'd fallen.

A loud rumble from one end of the walkway announced that the Ganzies had broken through and were pushing up to their level.

Sput turned to her. 'Quick, Hennie, the Ganzies are coming. Time to fall back.'

'You're in no state to run!' Hennie protested.

'I'll stay here, m'lovely. You go while you still can.'

'No!'

Sput lay a hand on her forearm like a father might. 'Hennie. I'll be fine, m'lovely.'

Her expression fell. She doubted that was true, but there seemed little sense in them both dying here. 'Surrender when they come, Sput. Promise me.'

'I'm no hero, Hennie. Believe me, I flakkin' will.' Sput's cheerful grin was distorted by pain into an ironic smirk.

'Arispas'ba,' she said, then backpedalled to the main building with the other retreating defenders.

As she withdrew towards the central column of the Gundar, one of the soldiers with her—a man who'd been alongside for enough of the battle to take her seriously—suddenly cried, 'Girl, look out!'

She ducked just as several shots rebounded off the wall beside her. She and the soldier darted into a doorway that led across an internal bridge to the core of the tower, where the entrance to the stairway was being fiercely contested.

'Byrant, take your girlfriend to the top level while we hold them off!' a man called from another walkway. Hennie grimaced at the remark, but she was contented that at least this Byrant didn't seem to think of her as superfluous.

'Ganzies, north entrance!' Byrant shouted.

The two bolted up the stairs as shots echoed behind them. Hennie made to go back, but Byrant insisted they continue.

'We need to form a defensive wall at the upper tier,' he said. 'They're breaking through above these floors, so we'll be surrounded if we don't move soon.'

She gave no argument, and they took up pace again. When they reached the top, heaving for breath, there was already a firefight going on across the upper tier walkway.

'Bastard Ganzies are everywhere!' Byrant cursed, letting off a crack of his rifle.

Hennie knelt beside him and took aim herself, landing a shot to a marine's shoulder that knocked him back, tripping down several stairs.

'Nice shot!' Byrant yelled, taking cover behind a pillar as he slipped another cartridge into his rifle.

Hennie hid behind another pillar opposite and took out a round to reload her Bluebell. Her fingers fumbled on the casing, and the bullet slipped, falling through the grating they stood on.

'Shyut!' she cursed, delving into the front of her pinafore. 'That was my last one!'

'Take mine.'

Byrant offered her another round from his belt, but as he leant forward to throw it, a bullet hit his waist and sent him spinning to the floor.

Hennie screamed and pulled away. Byrant was alive, but he was face down and barely moving. And he was fully in the line of fire of the approaching Ganzabi.

Somewhere nearby another cry was cut short, and Hennie knew that the only other Brazakker still resisting the advance had just perished.

She was alone.

She did her best to stay concealed behind the pillar, trying to think of what to do. Then she saw a marine approach the groaning body of Byrant next to her. To her horror, he raised his bayonet.

She leapt at him without thinking.

The attack of a seventeen-year-old girl in a pinafore had likely not been expected by the Ganzabi marine, who spun with confusion to face his shrieking assailant. His eyes went wide as his bayonet disappeared into Hennie's shoulder.

She froze, her face drooping in dazed shock. She'd felt an almost supernatural force stopping her at the shoulder. It was succeeded an instant later by pain—immense pain, gathering exponentially until it was almost matched by panic. Her left shoulder seemed to be screaming. She looked down to it and realised it was now a part of the long, silver bayonet at the end of the Ganzabi's rifle. She saw her blood pouring out of the wound and down the blade.

The pain alone she might have borne; but when combined with the panic, the dread of mortal danger and the terrifying unknown sensations, the pain was unbearable. She submitted to it and cried out in anguish, too scared to move.

The marine faltered, unsure what to do. Two other marines appeared behind him.

'Pull it out, you idiot,' one said, finally breaking the endless agonising moment.

The man pulled the bayonet from her with a sickening jolt, and she dropped to her knees and fell to one side. Her head felt light, but she fought to stay conscious. The pain made her eyes water.

Around her, marines rushed over the battered defenses and dead defenders of the last level of the installation.

The Gundar belonged to Ganzabar now.

47 - Takeback

Laronor

In the highest frozen wisps of cloud above Laronor, the sweeping organic engine pods of the Proctor's yacht left a pair of white trails, condensed vapour crystals tracing its flight path. The setting sun shifted the sky's hues into oranges and reds here above the main cloud level. But the city, as well as the battle embroiling it, was somewhere below a heavy canopy of cumulonimbus.

'I think we're coming up on Laronor,' Elzie said.

Kiy nodded, his gaze outside the downward-facing window. 'I guess I owe you thanks, after all. You got me home. Just like you said.'

'No, Kiy,' she said, not able to look at him. '*I* owe *you*. An apology, in fact.'

'You too?' Kiy didn't seem to take her seriously.

She stepped up beside him. 'The mixup with the Domestic Ministry—it was because of me. I leaked the story that there was a cloudgazer on the *Akron*.'

Kiy knew he should be annoyed, but all that felt like it had happened in another life. 'Why?'

Elzie sighed. 'It wasn't supposed to happen the way it did. If it hadn't been for the whole Beyer Fields ambush, Mestphura would have been able to quietly end your services and that'd be that. But then we ended up going back to Nubylon, Domestic got involved, and the whole thing went to Hadnar.'

Kiy nodded to himself. 'Huh. Well, I guess I should be thankful that you tried to get me off the ship.'

Elzie's face creased. 'You're not bothered that I sold you out?'

Kiy shrugged. 'I imagine it infuriated Mestphura more than it would ever perturb me.'

Elzie gave him a smile. 'Well, you're right there. He was every kind of furious. I don't think I'll be going back to the *Akron* again.'

'Well, you didn't mean anything against him.'

'Stop defending me!' she said, though her face still retained amusement. 'Did anybody ever tell you you're far too agreeable?'

Kiy turned as though he hadn't heard a word until now. 'No, actually. Just you.'

A smile grew slowly on her face.

The Proctor entered the room behind them. 'We've arrived,' he said, hands clasped behind his back. 'Laronor is below us.'

'What's the situation?' Kiy scanned the sky beneath them in the hopes of catching a glimpse of something other than cloud.

'Worse than I expeculated. Longpulse transmissions confirm Ganzabar have captured the Gundar already.' The Proctor stroked his chin. 'I hadn't estimated their attack to be so soon. I believe they're already turning the barrel to the west.'

'To fire at Nubylon?' Elzie asked.

'Possibly. But—we detect no sign of the *Postremo* yet.'

'I thought it was invisible,' Kiy said.

'Well, yes,' the Proctor replied, 'but if it was doing the calculations, it would have to transmit. We've not picked up any such signals. So there may still be time to stop this... multipocalypse.'

'How?' Elzie asked, her arms folded as she scowled at the sky below. 'This yacht doesn't have anywhere near the firepower we need. What we need is... we need the *Akron*.' She kicked her heel. 'Ugh, dammit!'

The Proctor rubbed his chin. 'It is unclear if even the *Akron* would be enough to stop the whole Ganzabi Armada at once. I've requested help from an old friend with the interest of the Brazakkers at heart. It wasn't hard convincing her to come back.'

Kiy frowned. An old friend of the Proctor's that'd help Brazak West?

'However, even destroying the fleet may not stop the Gundar in time,' the Proctor added somberly.

'If we can't destroy them, perhaps we can get past them —deactivate it somehow?' Kiy offered.

Elzie snapped her fingers. 'The Foxtail could make it through. The one docked to the underside.'

The Proctor nodded. 'But you can't get an infantry battalion on a Foxtail.'

Elzie gave Kiy a wry smile. 'We don't need to. We've got something better.'

Kiy realised what she was suggesting. 'Are you out of your calputer-calibrated mind?'

'What, you aren't up to it?' Elzie had that playful look again. 'We both know a cloudgazer in the right place is worth a hundred soldiers.'

Kiy stared once more at the cloud below. 'Are you suggesting I squeeze into the back of a Foxtail, then you fly it right up and land on the Gundar? 'Cause there's no way the Ganzies will—'

'No, no,' Elzie said. 'We don't land.'

'We don't—' Kiy stopped and stared. 'So I ride on the back of the plane...'

'Yes.'

'... you fly us close enough...'

'Yep.'

'... then I jump onto the Gundar...'

'With the sling,' she added.

'Of course. And then I stop the Gundar firing... somehow?'

'Something like that.'

Kiy raised an eyebrow at the Proctor, who shrugged and replied, 'It is, without a doubt, a plan, Cloudgazer Tanthar.'

'Well,' Kiy said, 'this may not even be the craziest thing I've ever done.'

48 - Return of the Red Star

Laronor Gundar

In the room below the control centre of the Gundar, Hennie considered her position. She was slumped against a bulkhead with a bandaged shoulder and her wrists bound by rope to a wall bracing post. The Ganzabi bayonet was no longer in her flesh—one of the Ganzabi medics had tended to her—but the pain it had left behind was worse somehow. Just the thought of it made her feel like vomiting.

She leant her head back and tried to fight the ache that pulsed outward from her back and neck.

Around her, the last Brazakker defenders lay incapacitated or dead, and Ganzabi soldiers hurried about them as though they weren't even there. She'd seen no sign of Sput and could only hope he was alright. She doubted he'd have been killed if he'd surrendered, but if that was the case, she had to wonder why he wasn't here. She wanted to ask someone, but she knew they'd never speak to her.

Her attention was suddenly drawn to a tall man in a cloak and fine uniform as he made a grand entrance. He stopped to brush the snow from his shoulders with a look of disdain.

One of the marines saluted. 'Admiral Moller. We have secured the facility.'

'Excellent.'

'Unfortunately, sir, there appears to be a problem with the gun's tracking system. Likely explains why they weren't firing on our approach.'

Moller's brow creased. 'I want it fixed as soon as possible. Get the cannon turned to aim north-west. The central power station is our first target. Tracking or not, we'll fire.'

'Sir... won't that inflict high civilian casualties?' the marine asked tentatively. 'I thought we were to capture the Gundars.'

'It could sink the whole miserable city for all I care,' Moller growled. 'It must be done. Or do you have a problem with eliminating the enemy, marine?'

The marine cleared his throat. 'Sir. No, sir.'

Hennie ground her teeth together, wishing there was something she could do.

'And who is this?' Moller asked irritably. Hennie looked up, fearing that the man was speaking of her, but it was Hamel who now stood before them—and prouder than last she saw him. Evidently this turn of events had revived him.

'One of us, sir,' the marine explained to Moller. 'Says he disabled the installation before we arrived.'

'Oh, is that so?' Moller said. Hamel looked up at the taller and more senior officer, who regarded him with a careful gaze. 'State your name and rank, soldier.'

'Flight Sergeant Hamel Jerome, sir. Seven-fifty-six squadron.' He stood to attention, but it was a slouch compared to the marine beside him.

'A pilot? Well, I suppose we have you to thank for the Gundar not being able to shoot down any of my ships,' he said pleasantly. But then his mood turned sour. 'But I have plenty of ships, if you hadn't noticed. I could afford to lose a few. Time is far more precious, and your *meddling* has left this facility inoperable and has delayed the entire operation. In light of the previous point, I shall not have you expelled from service. You are merely demoted to airman and stripped of your honours, effective immediately.'

'But... sir!'

'Don't test my patience, Airman Jerome. You had no orders to do what you have done, and your actions have jeopardised a lot more than this battle. Next time you might try sticking to protocols. You are dismissed.'

Hamel glared in protest, and it looked as if a thousand curses fought to pass his lips, but he held his tongue and lowered his gaze.

The admiral turned and stepped through a doorway to the firing control room. Hamel stood still until Moller was gone, then he turned, and his eyes met Hennie's. There was a moment of recognition before he looked away.

Some distance from the Gundar, the heavy cruiser *Sentinel* edged forward. Her captain, Gregor Nesterov, held the rank of voenkom and as such was the most senior officer left amongst the ramshackle Brazak defenders. His ship was trying to lend support to another of the larger and more senior defenders, the destroyer *Steadfast*.

'Come about!' he yelled. 'Give them everything we've got!'

The *Sentinel* had begun to turn to duel with a Ganzabi ship when they noticed the hulking form of a battleship approaching. Its cannons were the size of houses, and it was bristling with guns in every possible direction. As it closed, it fired. And the shells shook the world. The bridge of the *Sentinel* was tossed by the onslaught.

'It's the *Grace of Gnost*! Evasive! Evasive, dammit!' Nesterov shouted.

The Brazakker cruiser swung back to port and slid below the larger, slower Ganzabi ship. As it passed beneath it, it fired into the belly of the beast using the cannons running along its top edge. The shots found their mark, but it was like blowing breaths at the sky for all the difference it seemed to make. And when the Ganzabi ship's lower cannons struck back angrily, smoke rose from fires on the Brazakker craft.

As the *Sentinel* climbed up and away, another group of enemy ships ahead of it closed in. There must have been eight to ten ships, all readying their cannons to concentrate their fire on the leading Brazakker ship.

'All hands... brace yourselves!' Nesterov yelled.

Then something broke out of the cloud just off to port. A flotilla of swift ships raced forward, headed for the Ganzabi group. There were not more than five or six of the dark slender shapes, but the ship at their lead was unmistakable.

It was entirely black, its size and lithe profile suggesting a destroyer, but it moved like something smaller, faster. And at its crest was the large flapping standard that even Brazakker schoolchildren knew: a black field with a red five-pointed star at the centre.

The *Rhiannon*.

'Natalya Ataryk,' Nesterov said in disbelief.

Ataryk's ships immediately attracted the attention and shells of the Ganzabi fleet, but they were by now almost on top of their targets. A long vessel trailing Ataryk's ship emitted a volley of anti-ship missiles before accelerating ferociously and passing beneath the Ganzabi cruisers. The missiles caused utter chaos in the Ganzabi line, smashing through decks and causing command towers to topple.

The *Rhiannon* changed direction sharply and launched a savage attack at the rear of one of the Ganzabi cruisers. Firing something that looked like massive nails from its forward cannons, it dived past the volley launched in return and swooped up between another two craft. The Ganzabi efforts to attack it largely resulted in them hitting each other.

Nesterov realised he had stopped to watch the deft work of the old veteran and her flotilla. Regaining his composure, he ordered the *Sentinel* to support them with a bit of firepower. The feeling of hopelessness that had crept up on him just moments before had now dissolved, replaced by a bright sense of hope that only Ataryk's red star could bring.

49 - Cloudgazer

Laronor

The pristine white and gold Foxtail duplane punched out of an overcast ceiling of stratus cloud and swooped over the rooftops of northern Laronor.

Elzie glanced back at Kiy. He gave a thumbs-up with one hand, his other firmly attached to the rear of the skyfighter by the clamp of the sling. The slipstream was furiously wrestling with his coat. Elzie nudged the throttle higher, and the Foxtail sped on into the chaos of battle.

A group of Ganzabi Dragonflies swooped in to attack, and Elzie seemed to want to give them something to chase. One of the enemy fighters came from the side, its guns flashing a stream of tracers across the Foxtail's nose. With a wrench of the control column, Elzie sent the plane into a series of tight turns, attempting to throw the enemy off her. Kiy gripped the small handhold with his non-sling arm and held on as tightly as he could. He felt as though he weighed a hundred times his usual weight as the craft spiralled, each jerk and feint coming close to tearing his arm at the elbow.

The plane changed roll and swung to the right, narrowly skimming a Ganzabi frigate that slid along at a much grander pace. Kiy's hand finally came loose, but the sling held fast, and after slamming hard against the fuselage, he managed to grab the handle again. He caught sight of an explosion against the huge ship they had narrowly missed; their pursuer had evidently not flown as deftly as Elzie.

Their plane swooped to the right and the left through the raging battle, past flak and explosions. All around them, cannons fired, ships spewed smoke, and flames leapt up from impacts. The Foxtail skirted underneath a huge Ganzabi cruiser dotted in fires. Exploding shells punctured the clouds, black smoke mingled with a flurry of snow, and streams of bullets criss-crossed the view.

Then Elzie climbed and banked the Foxtail towards the Gundar's massive barrel, which was turning ponderously. To Kiy's alarm, it appeared to actually be turning past west, northwards, to bear on the city of Laronor itself.

One of the Ganzabi planes swung in behind them, perhaps seeing the cloudgazer and sensing something grand, but more than likely just looking for another target. Its shots sprayed over the Foxtail's canopy. Kiy swore. Unless that Ganzie was a useless shot, they wouldn't last more than a few seconds.

Kiy abruptly felt the terrific heat of an explosion and craned his neck to see the remains of their pursuer drifting down in flames. Almost immediately, another Dragonfly came up behind them from below. This one was so close, Kiy was able to see inside the cockpit. He could have sworn he saw Leo give a wave, and then the plane rolled away without firing a shot.

Was that really Leo? He wasn't sure if he was imagining things, but perhaps it really was. The thought filled him with hope.

Soon they neared the edge of the Gundar's fortification. It was a ridiculously huge thing; the barrel alone must have been over a hundred metres long. The Foxtail swooped just below it, and Elzie carefully slowed the craft to the absolute minimum before it would stall, curving inwards so that they passed just below the barrel. Kiy waited for his moment, then fired his sling.

The line traced for what felt like minutes, missing the steel cylinder of the cannon. Kiy cursed, snapping the cable back as Elzie swung around and repeated the careful manoeuvre again. It was pushing both of them to their limit; landing a sure hit on the smooth surface of the barrel was no mean feat, and to top it off, the barrel, too, was moving.

Kiy steadied himself, trying to relax while still clinging with one hand to the handle on the back of the cockpit—at this point, that hand was the only thing keeping him alive.

The barrel passed overhead, and again he fired.

With a thunk, the clamp scored a sure hit on the bottom of the barrel. Kiy let go of the plane, and the cable went taut, swinging him up and around.

He landed on top of the barrel. It was not a dignified landing; he scrambled to find hold on the shiny surface. But he got to his feet in time to see Elzie dive and accelerate away.

It was up to him now.

Retracting the sling, he began to run down the length of the huge weapon, gusts of wind tugging him to either side as though trying to knock him off. When he reached the wall of the tower from which the barrel extended, he spotted two Ganzabi marines staring down at him in disbelief from a walkway above. They were so stunned that someone had come at them down the barrel of the cannon, they hadn't even drawn their rifles yet.

Kiy fired the sling and flew up into the air. Too late, the men fired their rifles, but now Kiy was coming right at them, far too quick, and their shots were hopelessly off the mark.

Kiy landed on one of the gantries, right on top of a dumbstruck marine. Flicking the sling's cable out to one side, he hit another marine, knocking him to the floor. Without pausing, he had taken off once again.

He continued to fight his way up through the gantries, swinging over heads, pulling rifles from hands and flinging his clamp into the skulls of others. The Ganzabi tried to stop him, but he had the element of surprise, and for the most part they simply didn't know what to do. *Who even was this guy?*

Then, below them, with a decisive metallic thud, the Gundar barrel stopped turning.

50 - Cataclysm

Laronor Gundar

Hennie could hear the commotion somewhere below the control deck. One of the officers picked up a phone to communicate with the admiral in the room above.

'Sir, we've got a problem on the upper tier. Some sort of elite infantry attack. Our forces report at least a dozen enemy men.' Indistinct yells sounded from the other end of the line. 'Yes! Yes, sir, of course.'

He put down the phone and turned to his inferior. 'Send a call to base level—get some more men up here!'

'Leave the men where they are,' a voice intervened.

Hennie looked around to see Hamel stood with a rifle trained on both men, a cigarette in his mouth. His posture was slouched, his injured arm slack.

'What is the meaning of—'

'Shut up a sec,' Hamel said. He kept the rifle on them, then walked over to Hennie.

'What are you doing?' she said.

'I've had it with these assholes. They said it was all about stopping this weapon, but they just want to use it themselves. Well, enough's enough. My service record is flakked anyway.' He fished a knife from his pocket and slipped it through Hennie's binds easily, keeping his attention on the two officers.

He offered her the knife without looking. 'Go on, get out of here.'

'Give me one good reason why I shouldn't stab you,' Hennie said venomously, looking at his combat knife then up at him.

'I don't think that's who you are, Hennie. You could be just a sweet girl if the world didn't hate us all so damn much.' He allowed himself a quick glance at her. 'Also, I'm stopping these two from killing you, you crazy dame. Now, you gonna split or what?'

The Ganzabi officer made a sudden grab for the phone. Hamel fired, and the officer's neck exploded. He dropped to the floor, the phone dangling by the wire. At the same time, his subordinate pulled a pistol and fired, blowing a hole in Hamel's chest. The wound made Hamel stumble, but he drew up his sidearm with his weaker hand and took a skewed shot that somehow hit the other Ganzabi in the head. The man spun violently, a spray of red across the wall behind him, before falling motionless.

Hamel's legs gave out and he collapsed onto his back.

Hennie hurried over. 'Oh, Sky and Moons,' she said with weary concern. 'Karak, can you hear me?' She knelt down and rested his head on her lap.

He looked at her with confusion. 'Sure...' he said after a pause.

'Karak...' Hennie muttered, lifting the man's head forward gently. 'Can I call you Karak?'

'I think... perhaps...' the wounded pilot said with a faint smile, 'you ought to remember me that way.'

'Wait, you're not dying! I already shot you, and that didn't work, so—'

'Hennie...' he said chidingly, but with a smile. 'Look. I think...' He paused. 'I think... I'd like to go home now. It's over.'

'We can do that. We can do that,' she said.

'I can see it now,' he said warmly. 'The little red rooftops. The cloud farms. Pontuck's beautiful in the fall. You know...?'

Hennie didn't know what to do but nod.

'Hennie.' He grasped at her suddenly. 'Hennie! Do you still hate me?'

She smiled sadly. 'No, of course not, Karak.'

'Oh,' he said softly. 'That's good.'

She waited on his next word, then saw that his eyes had ceased to focus.

Hennie lowered his head to the cold steel floor, then closed his eyelids. So far from home; so uncared for. His passing had to be marked by something, even if it was only a moment's peace from her. It was all she could give him.

There was a light tap of leather on metal as Kiy's boots landed smoothly on the top walkway of the control tower. But when he stepped inside, he found the control room itself apparently deserted, even though its workings clicked and whirred with activity.

'So I presume you're the source of this mayhem?' said a gruff voice.

He spun to face a tall man, dressed in the uniform of a Ganzabi admiral, emerging from the doorway on the far side of the room. Kiy brought his pistol to bear on him in one smooth motion.

He then saw the man's face, and his mind took him back eleven years. Julene screaming as she was carried off. The soldiers beating him into submission. And all the while, the white-haired man in that blue uniform...

'Moller,' Kiy said.

The admiral looked down at him with a frown of disdain. 'It appears my reputation precedes me. Unfortunately, I cannot say the same for a scrapgull like you.'

'Oh, we have met,' Kiy said, his rage barely contained. 'Eleven years ago. Nantez.'

Moller seemed uninterested. 'I don't recall. It was a long time ago.'

'Of course you don't,' Kiy spat. 'You didn't give a flakking damn.'

'Did you come here to lecture me, boy?' Moller growled. 'I'm sure you beat a lot of good men in getting this far, but do not mistake me as vulnerable. I can have you killed in a moment.'

Kiy eyed the room uneasily. He suddenly realised that the room was far from deserted; within every nook, every shadow, he now spotted the beady eyes of soldiers and the shiny black of rifle muzzles aimed directly at him. There were too many for him to have any chance of dodging them.

He kept his aim firmly on the admiral. 'They can't stop me from pulling this trigger,' Kiy said defiantly.

'Oh?' Moller smiled. 'And what will that achieve? The best case scenario for you is, I will be dead, and an instant later so too will you. And these men will see through my instructions.'

Kiy ground his teeth together. Indeed, killing Moller wouldn't change anything. And what good could Kiy do dead?

'Place the pistol on the ground in front of you,' Moller said. 'Let us talk like men, for before long you may be one.'

Kiy ignored the insult, but placed the pistol on the floor.

'You probably don't even realise the evil this contraption is capable of, do you?' Moller said. 'But Brazak West will soon give in. Now that we can strike your capital.'

'But that's not possible,' Kiy replied. 'Well, not unless you have a Gold Age battleship to do your calculations.'

'What are you talking about?' Moller's expression sharpened so much it could draw blood. 'A Gold Age battlesh—wait, how could you possibly—'

Kiy gave him a sideways look that gave way to a slight, knowing smile. Now he understood. 'Only... you didn't know that, did you?'

One of the Ganzabi men looked at Moller like a child needing guidance, but the admiral's expression was equal parts rage and panic as Kiy continued, '*That's* why she tricked you into coming here. You didn't realise the Gundar's limitations. But she figured a fanatic like you would ensure it fell right into her lap—'

'Enough!' Moller roared. 'Spare me your lies and propaganda.' He looked around at his soldiers. 'Don't you see? He's caught like a gutter rat and is trying to confuse you. Forget his words. Glory Is A Straight And Narrow Path.'

The soldiers immediately repeated the phrase back to him and became visibly more focused.

'It's clear to me,' Moller continued, 'the only way for you to pay for this affront is by feeling its results yourselves. How poetic that Laronor's destruction should come from the very instrument constructed to defend it.'

Kiy saw with horror that the barrel's direction was aligned with the inner city.

'Moller... that's genocide!'

'What is genocide, boy?' Moller's bottom lip protruded in thought. 'Death of countless millions? War can kill a million soldiers, yet not be genocide.'

'Those aren't soldiers, they're *families*. Children—'

'Does that really make any difference?' Moller said. 'Why should a soldier's life mean less than a child's?'

Kiy shook his head, searching for the words. 'A child has not signed their life away for their country...'

'You are wrong,' Moller said in an instructive tone. '*All* should be prepared to die for their country. That is the Ganzabi Way.'

Moller stepped up to the control panel. There was a deep clank as he slid a lever forward.

'Stop!' Kiy said, his voice faltering.

The admiral's features darkened. 'Do not cry for them. They shall have a place in Arkaedis, if indeed they are righteous.'

Moller fired the Gundar.

With a sky-shattering noise, the barrel of the cannon was flung backwards. Through the windows, Kiy could see the skyline of Laronor light up. He cried out, but the sound was lost in a roaring blast that drowned out everything. The sky was blinding. The pulse of the Gundar's shot passed through half the city almost instantly, but the fallout of white brilliance came a flicker afterward, and everything was in slow motion.

Tiny fragments spun, lost in mid-air, glittering points of light floating upwards as the brightness swallowed everything. Towers toppled, crashing down through walkways and houses. Roof tiles were ripped free, glass panes torn from their windows. Islands were broken apart, cracking and shrieking. The iron bracing beams were pulled apart with them, protruding from stone slabs like ribs.

Kiy watched helplessly as fire engulfed the city's heart. The Gundar had cleaved through lines of buildings, and they were falling away, disintegrating, tearing, weeping. Steel blew its rivets, pipes burst in protest, and the pieces and remains drifted down towards the endless stormy grave below.

And then a wave of debris and destruction sped from the cataclysm towards them. The windows trembled as a blast of air rolled over, then shook when a wave of junk and debris struck the tower. Perhaps it was the exceptionally close range or a quirk of chance, but as the hail of wreckage struck the control room, a steel beam smashed right through the main window. Chaos unfolded; two of the guards were tossed aside like discarded dolls, and the main targeting console was uprooted and thrown into a third soldier.

Kiy saw his chance. His body moving automatically, he fired the sling out and whipped the clamp viciously into one of the soldiers.

The other men quickly turned their attention to him, but Kiy was already on the war path and moving too fast for them. He fired the sling's clamp out again as he dived to avoid gunfire. One man's neck snapped around, likely killing him from the full force of the sling's maximum acceleration, but Kiy was too angry to care or to stop. Moller had to pay. They *all* had to pay.

He ensnared another man and yanked him backward, sending him tumbling down a stairwell.

That left only one soldier besides Moller, but he was a hulking giant of a man. He launched himself at Kiy, who dodged just in time, reeling the sling back in with a flick of the wrist.

The guard threw a punch. Kiy managed to deflect most of it, but wished he had done so with his sling instead of his shoulder. He expected the next punch though, and this time he blocked it with the sling's bulky metallic form. The man gave a yell of pain and stumbled back.

Kiy saw his rotary pistol still on the floor. He snatched it up and pointed it at the guard. Moller remained at the control panel, looking suddenly pale.

'Step away from the console,' Kiy demanded. When Moller didn't move, Kiy struck out with the sling like a whip, causing a bleeding gash to appear on Moller's lip.

'... Kiy?'

The sound of Hennie's voice seemed like it was coming from a dream. It threw him for a moment, and he lowered the pistol, only marginally, as he glanced at the stairwell, incredulous to see Hennie stood there, clutching her shoulder. A million questions formed on his tongue.

Then Hennie shrieked in warning, and Kiy had barely turned back to his adversary when the man's full weight knocked him over. He lay on his back, dazed, then two great hands like bear paws lifted him up and threw him into a set of instruments that broke from the impact.

Glass fragments cut his skin, and his body ached. But his adversary wasn't done. Kiy was hauled back onto his feet, and his arms were pinned behind his back.

Beaten, Kiy blinked, focusing on the figure ahead of him. Moller stared back at him with disdain, dabbing his bloodied lip with a hankerchief.

'Miserable rat!' he spat. 'Make sure he sees this. I want him to watch every shot, until this city is nothing but a rockstorm!'

He stepped to the firing switch again. Hennie screamed, running forward to stop him, but Moller threw her backwards easily with a shove, his hand pressed to her face. When she fell, her head cracked against the floor, and she remained motionless.

Then Moller threw the switch again.

This time, however, a red light blinked on the panel, and above it appeared a large block of text:

—COOLING PERIOD INCOMPLETE—

Moller was thrown into a rage. He slammed his fist down on the bronze control levers. 'Just fire, you useless contraption!'

Looking quickly about the base of the unit, he uncovered the manual override lever.

The big man looked at Moller with concern. 'Sir, shouldn't we—'

'Silence, Carver!' Moller barked.

He threw the lever down, and there was a deafening crack. But no bright flash lit up the sky this time. Instead, the entire tower shook violently. Moller stumbled sideways, and the big guard, Carver, stumbled back, releasing Kiy, who fell forward to his knees.

Kiy was still scrambling to his feet when behind him, the deck underneath Carver was flung upwards—and just like that, it was as if the big man had never existed. Only a brightly glowing fissure in the floor remained where he had once stood.

Moller cried out fearfully. The deck was crumbling and falling away in clumps. The whole installation rumbled indignantly, as though gearing up to punish its occupants. With a cascade of concrete, a portion of the outer wall fell away. Pieces of machinery and masonry were coming down all around them.

Kiy made his way to Hennie and shook her shoulder. 'Hennie?'

She stirred. 'Kiy? What's going on here?' He could barely hear her above the noise.

Before he could answer, Moller shouted in surprise and fear. The floor had apparently crumbled underneath him, and he was now clinging to the deck, his legs dangling into an abyss below.

'Tanthar!' he cried.

Kiy glared. 'So you do remember.'

Moller scowled, his anger nearly overcoming his fear— but only nearly. 'I can tell you what happened to your sister, if you pull me up.'

Kiy stepped cautiously closer and looked down. Beneath Moller's dangling feet was a drop of some twenty metres to the hungry flames of the breech-loading bay.

'Tell me first,' Kiy countered.

Moller resisted, struggling to pull himself up.

'Where did they take her?' Kiy said angrily. 'Tell me and I'll save you!'

Moller growled. 'Don't try to trick me, boy.'

Kiy stood back, looking down in disgust. 'So be it. Go to your precious afterlife.'

The portion of the deck that Moller clung to began to tip, coming loose. As Kiy stepped back onto the safer part with Hennie, Moller yelled, 'No—wait! It was Carricksgate! They took her to Ca—'

The slab snapped and Moller fell from view. Kiy lunged to grab him with the sling, but the admiral had vanished into the inferno below.

'Shyut.' Kiy lay on his front, his arm dangling over the edge. He drew a deep breath and pushed himself back onto his feet.

'Kiy...' Hennie said. 'We've gotta get outta here.'

'Right.'

With his arm under her healthy shoulder, he carefully led the way outside to the walkway by which he'd first entered. They were met with a wide view of the snow-flurried battlefield, which had taken a clear and dramatic turn. Ganzabar's forces were evidently in full retreat, with the Brazakkers hounding them.

'Look!' Hennie cried.

Kiy followed her finger to the shape of a tiny, odd-looking craft, a very small airship, backing away from the Gundar as explosions ruptured the dock.

'Hang on tight!' Kiy said.

Hennie locked her hands around his shoulder as he raised his sling arm. It was a small target to hit, but there was no other choice. The tower was being ripped apart beneath their feet.

'Wait!' Hennie cried. 'Wait, I'm not ready—I don't know if I can do this.'

'Just trust me.'

She blinked at the snowy view, then buried her face in his shoulder. 'Okay,' she said. 'Go!'

They dived from the walkway into the sky. As they fell, Kiy fired the sling's clamp. It seemed to travel forever.

51 - Triumph

Laronor

Ganzabar's Armada was in complete disarray. Most ships had begun a hasty retreat upon receiving news of the Gundar's destruction, and the Brazakker ships had responded by pressing them harder.

Countess Katrinn de Saufon surveyed the field with dismay, one side of her upper lip tensing. The arrival of the *Postremo* had evidently come too late, but they remained concealed by the optical camouflage system.

'Ma'am, the Brazakker ships are technically outmatched, but our forces are routing. We could intervene to support,' Talot said, licking his lips nervously. He never liked giving the countess bold suggestions; there was always the chance she might flippantly enact them.

She stared at the Armada and then dismissed them with a shrug. 'No, I think there's little use in us lingering here. The Gundar's gone. There ain't nothin' more we can do here.' She allowed herself a small, smug smile. 'Take us outta here, Mr Mofkan.'

'Miss, the grand fleet!' Mofkan protested. 'We can't just abandon them.'

'Can't we?' the countess said, with wide, innocent eyes.

'No, Miss Saufon,' the officer replied, more sternly. 'We have a duty to assist our comrades.'

The countess stepped up to him slowly, the swagger of her hips communicating her aggression despite a sweet expression. 'You also have a duty to follow my commands, though. Don't you?' She stopped so close she almost spoke to his collar.

'With all due respect, miss, you aren't even—'

With a gargled choke, Mofkan flinched. A black line shot from his back into the ceiling, which it struck with a loud clash of metal. He looked down in disbelief at the cable which had just passed through him.

'It's "Countess", sweetie.' Then, with a sharp pull, the countess retracted the cable into the device on her wrist, and Mofkan keeled over onto the ground, falling still.

She looked around the bridge with wild, accusative eyes. 'You all saw him assault me, didn't you?'

Talot stared in fear at the device on her arm—the device that, up until this point, had been concealed by a half-cloak. *Is that a sling?* He dared not ask. 'Yes, m—Countess.'

She smiled, raising her chin. 'Now. As I was saying... get us out of here.'

Smoke poured from the crashed monoplane, rising into a pillar that loomed over Voxton Park. The plane had left an ugly furrow in the turf behind it that dug all the way to the floatrock beneath, yet it had mostly held together—a single, buckled wad of wreckage.

Marc kicked the canopy again and it came away, releasing the smoke from the cockpit, but he wasted no time in diving out onto the dirt. Leo followed a moment later, and the pair of them lay on the disturbed earth in fits of coughing. Then, as their coughing subsided, Marc looked over and cracked a triumphant smile.

'We did it, mate.'

Leo just smiled and nodded, still catching his breath.

Then the two of them looked up—and froze at the sight of all the rifle barrels being aimed at them.

The individuals holding those rifles weren't uniformed soldiers, but rather a varied and disorganised rabble. Still, no one was smiling.

'Whoa, now, we're not Ganzies,' Marc said diplomatically.

'Save it!' said a burly man at the front. 'That's a Ganzie plane, that makes yer Ganzies!'

'I'm not a flakkin' Ganzie!' Leo protested, coughing again. 'I'm a Brazakker! My name's Leo Litvyak.'

The armed rabble hesitated, and then a girl's voice piped up from the back of the group.

'Did you say Litvyak?'

The girl pushed her way forward. She was about Olya's age, with blond hair and blue eyes, and was wearing elaborate yellow lace. Leo thought she was as beautiful as the fairest painting.

A smile of recognition crept across her face as she looked at Leo. 'You have a sister called Hennie?'

Leo was baffled and awestruck, but managed to nod.

The girl nodded. 'I see the resemblance. I'm Jerra Lightlock.' Jerra extended a hand to help Leo up. He tried not to stare at her. 'And these are the Laronor Reserves,' she added.

The rest of the Brazakkers lowered their weapons, and Marc got to his feet. 'Well, nice to meet you guys when you 'int pointing guns at me. Don't you have a battle to be fighting?'

Jerra slung her rifle onto her shoulder. 'The battle looks to be over. Ganzabi forces are retreating south.'

'I guess they must be about done with destroying everything,' the burly man said, motioning towards the orange glow at the city's core.

'Come,' Jerra said to Leo. 'There's someone I'd like you to meet.'

They walked from the crash site towards Waltov.

Beyond the sky, the Gundar smouldered.

Miran, Hennie, Kiy and Sput sat in the spacious garden of the Rathbones' manor, drinking tea and Pure, courtesy of Mrs Lightlock. They'd returned the Mygos to its builder, and he had taken it pretty well, Hennie thought. The idea of having to face him again had filled her with dread, but after hearing the full story he had been remarkably magnanimous. In a way, that had made her feel even worse.

Or maybe it was just that Kiy's news of Leo was not what she had hoped for.

'I'll resume my search immediately,' Kiy was saying. 'I would have waited until I'd found him before coming to find you, but when I heard about the attack I couldn't wait.'

She smiled sadly. 'I understand. So glad you got him off the *Municipal* when you did. If it weren't for you he'd be gone for sure. At least now... there's still hope.'

Kiy nodded. 'There is, yes—'

'Holy Hadnar's Belly!'

The exclamation made Hennie sit up straight, her mouth hanging open. That voice. She would know that voice anywhere. She turned.

Leo was striding towards them from the house, with a pleased-looking Jerra alongside him and Marc in tow, towering over both.

'Am I dreaming?' Hennie said.

Leo was laughing. He didn't break step, just threw his arms around his big sister as they collided. They rocked for a few moments.

Kiy's look of surprise turned to a bewildered smile as he looked to Marc, who was watching the reunited siblings with satisfaction. 'I take it,' Kiy said, 'that if I was to ask where you'd been, it'd be a long story?'

Marc chuckled. 'I'll say, mate! I'd better pull up a chair.'

The group recounted their ordeals and adventures for some hours. But at a quarter to six, with the loud whoosh of a turbine, a sleek white craft landed on the lawn in front of the house, and all of them—joined by Mr Rathbone and Mrs Lightlock—went out front to see who it was. Many of the neighbours had also gathered around the landing site, intrigued.

Kiy recognised the ship, but it was Marc who exclaimed, 'Is that an Azrunite yacht?'

Kiy nodded. 'The Proctor's.'

'Get outta town!' Marc laughed. 'The Proctor is *here*?'

Kiy didn't need to convince him, because at that moment a ramp extended from one of the hatches and the Proctor himself descended it. Elzie followed, and they made their way to where Kiy and the others stood.

'To what occasion do we owe the honour of Azrunite company?' Rathbone said.

The Proctor smiled at that. 'Oh, just a friendly visit. You know. Popping by, as the saying goes.'

Elzie seemed a little embarrassed. 'We're here to pick up our friend.' She looked at Marc.

'Hey, Zi!' Marc said, then frowned. 'How'd you know where to find me?'

She looked unsure, but the Proctor was smoothly confident. 'A little birdie told me. Well, a sling.' He gave Kiy a meaningful look. 'You'll take care of her, won't you?'

Kiy blinked. 'Wh—I mean... yeah, of course.'

'The old folks, they keep in touch,' he said, to nobody in particular. Then, apparently satisfied, he boarded the craft again.

Elzie and Kiy exchanged a look of respect. 'You did good back there, Cloudgazer,' Elzie said.

'I could have done better,' Kiy replied.

She shrugged. 'You can always do better.'

Marc laughed. 'Yeah, she always says that.'

Elzie turned to go. 'You may wish to know that the *Akron* appears to be in the clear. The Domestic Ministry's case fell apart after they, ah, lost their evidence.' She smirked. 'And the Proctor has smoothed things over with Mestphura. I hear he's accepting postings for ambitious acrobatic mercenaries...'

Kiy laughed, but shook his head. 'If it's all the same, I think I'll pass. I'm not keen to get myself caught up in the First Nation's business any time soon.'

Elzie's smile faded like evening light. 'I understand. Perhaps our paths will cross again, all the same.'

'Maybe so.'

She gave him a lingering look, then a nod. 'See you 'round, Cloudgazer.'

52 - Departure

Laronor
November 18th 9329

The deep, brilliant blue of the clear sky enshrined a half-decayed tower of scrap metal, ripped bulkheads and melted floors. A stack of tangled iron and concrete rubble was all that now crowned the Gundar. The structure was motionless, silent. It was pitted with black, gaping cavities like weathered holes in an ancient tree. A flock of skinny kerrons drifted past, just a smattering of tiny white flapping shapes dwarfed by the mighty wreck.

Kiy stood beside Hennie, admiring the view of the wreck from the passenger liner *Arlandale*. The sight was peaceful but sad, Kiy thought—though he wasn't sure what it was about it that saddened him. As pitiful as it was for a patriotic Brazakker, he'd never thought himself a patriot. But it now occurred to him just how much the Gundar's meaning varied depending on who was perceiving it. This behemoth had been a symbol of pride and safety to some, but to others that same creation was a monstrous superweapon of destruction and evil.

In the Battle of Laronor, the people of the city had seen both sides of the Gundar. The damage wrought on the central districts was devastating. Hundreds of homes, stores, factories—and nearly fifty thousand souls—had gone to the Understorm. It would be a long time before the people of the city would recover from that. He knew someday they would, but certainly they'd never forget.

Ganzabi forces had been quickly routed after destruction of the Gundar, though Kiy suspected there was more to it than that. Word was that the Armada was regrouping in the south somewhere. The tide might have swung in Brazak West's favour—for now—but the conflict felt far from over. After all, the Gundar was now useless, Laronor had been crippled, the *Postremo* was still at large and, despite being on the defensive, Ganzabar's Armada was still in Brazak West. The more Kiy thought about it, the less there seemed to be to celebrate. The Second Nezzu War, they were calling it. And it was only getting started.

But he had to remind himself what they'd accomplished. Leo had made it back from the maw of the Ganzabi navy, and Hennie had survived the hottest zone of the Battle of Laronor by some miracle. And he himself had only narrowly escaped being locked up in Azrune for the rest of his days.

And there was other good news, too. A few days after the battle, Kiy and Hennie had been at Rathbone Manor when Edwark had thrust an envelope into Hennie's hands with a grin. She looked at him in wonder, but he simply made a gesture that she should open it. Her face lit like a sunrise when she saw the hand in which it was written.

'It's from Mum'ma!' she said ecstatically, looking at the faces of her friends before reading it aloud.

> *My Dear Hennie,*
>
> *You would not believe my relief, honey, at hearing you and Leo are alive and well in Laronor. I should have known you could make it; I saw you with Kiy as we left. Your host Mr Rathbone was able to find me through his contacts at the War Office. He has also kindly arranged for your passage on a ship so you can come join us in Risley! Please thank him for me. I will be counting down the days!*
>
> *Take care my love,*
>
> *Mum'ma*
> *& the Girls*
>
> (to which the scrawl of '& NAKI' had been added in crayon)

Hennie's eyes were wet when she finished the letter. She looked up at Rathbone and smiled, but could only manage a muted, 'Thank you.'

Kiy had offered to accompany her and Leo on the trip, as had Jerra. So the following day, the four of them said their farewells to Rathbone, Mrs Lightlock and Miran at the docks.

Now they stood on the ship that was taking them west, sliding across the sky towards a new horizon.

Beside Kiy, Hennie shifted her left shoulder absently. A bandage encased her chest from mid-rib to collarbone, half covered by a strapless blue dress that fought with the wind, and another gauze pad was bandaged to her forehead. Her expression was distant and heavy with memory. She'd only told him a little of what had happened since leaving Brudor, but her demeanour and mannerisms seemed different—more like her mother, he thought.

Just behind them, Jerra and Leo sat on a wooden bench, quietly watching the clouds pass by. Leo had been infatuated with Jerra since they'd met, and it seemed the interest was mutual.

'A skyfighter pilot,' Hennie said, after some minutes' pause.

'Really?' Kiy replied. He'd asked her what she wanted to do as a job, but hadn't expected that. Although she'd always adored skyfighters, he'd thought it was a passive interest. 'You want to avenge Feo? Follow your aunt's footsteps?'

'Not because of that,' she answered, pensive. 'I want to fly. And these are dangerous skies we live in now. I feel an urge... to make them safe.'

'Have you told your mother?'

Hennie looked down with a coy grin. 'I'm working on that one.'

'Well, don't know about you, sis,' Leo declared, 'but I think I've had enough of war and adventure. Think I might settle down, y'know?'

'What? You're barely even fourteen!'

'Marry a fine woman, maybe become a baker—'

'You? A baker? Yeah, right; I've tried your scones!' Hennie laughed.

Jerra looked to Leo with undisguised idolatry. 'Well, I would rather like to try some of this baking of yours.'

'That so?' Leo looked ready to take the challenge there and then. 'It's a deal! I bake a flakking mean pie, Hennie can shut up. Come on, let's go find the kitchens.'

Jerra followed him away eagerly, with an expression that suggested she didn't much care where they might actually be going.

Hennie watched them go with an almost parental look of satisfaction, then returned her gaze to Kiy, who seemed preoccupied.

'Kiy?'

'Hmm?'

'Back on the Gundar, you mentioned...' She paused, her brow furrowing. 'Julene?'

Silence lingered a while, as though Kiy wasn't even going to reply at all. 'She was my little sister,' he said. Then he corrected himself: '*Is* my little sister. Taken over ten years ago, at Nantez. And she's probably still out there today, somewhere in Ganzabar, maybe completely unaware of who she is. She'd be seventeen by now.'

Hennie absorbed the information quietly. 'Why don't you look for her?' she asked. 'You found Leo.'

Kiy nodded thoughtfully. 'I always wanted to. I didn't have any leads.'

Hennie considered this for a moment. 'But not anymore.'

He nodded. Something in his eyes said the rest.

She looked away, squinting in the brilliant sun. 'I see. How long will you be gone?'

'I don't know. But if I find her, I'll come home. Perhaps we both will. I suppose that depends.'

Hennie smiled. 'I'd like to meet her.'

His face took on a wistful expression. 'As would I.'

'When will you go?'

Kiy glanced over the side to see a cargo ship chugging along just below and ahead of them. It looked like they might just pass over the stern. 'Probably sooner than later.'

'Kiy... Are you about to do what I think you're about to do?' Hennie cocked her head to one side.

'Maybe.' He swung his legs over the railing and looked at her over his shoulder.

Hennie sighed and hugged herself. 'You are a strange one, Kiy Tanthar. Promise me you'll take care of yourself.'

'I'll try. Tell the family I'll miss them.'

Leo and Jerra returned just in time to see him leap from the rail and disappear. Jerra stared in disbelief. 'What? How... how did—why did he...'

'He's a cloudgazer,' Hennie explained, turning to her with a warm smile. 'And he's not very good at saying goodbye.'

Acknowledgements

I would like to thank all those that, over the many years, have helped to bring this book into the light of day. Thanks to the excellent David Gatewood for his thorough and patient editing. To all my supportive first/second/fiftieth draft readers; to those who offered their critique, feedback and ideas. Thanks in particular to Connor Barr, David Pearson, Richard Britt and Jonathan Coy. Additional special thanks to my father, for the motivation I needed to get the paperback version into print.

And of course, thanks to my wife Lucy—without whose endless support and encouragement this book might still be just a pile of made-up words in a drawer.

About the Author

Alexander Webb recently congealed from supernova remnants and is still trying to come to terms with the lifestyle change. He lives in the United Kingdom with his wife Lucy and is some kind of games-designer / writer / artist hybrid; or just really indecisive.

Captivated by airships and flight almost his whole life, he's been writing about Azimuth since around 2003. *Cloudgazer* is his first novel and, incidentally, was first drafted as his 2009 entry to National Novel Writing Month; which really puts procrastination into perspective.

He enjoys playing piano, gaming (both board and video) and hopes to renew his pilot license someday.

You can find him at:

www.novodantis.com (Blog)

novodantis@gmail.com (Email)

@novodantis (Twitter)

...and mostly anywhere else he can make use of a monopoly over a fictional word.

Glossary of Azimuth

The world of Azimuth probably has a few unfamiliar terms. Some of the more relevant ones are listed below, but you can also get much more in-depth info at the Crystal Archives wiki! Although its primary purpose is an author reference, it's open for all to see at the following URL.

Crystal Archives Wiki:
  http://www.novodantis.com/crystal_archives/wiki/

Akron: the ancient flagship of Azrune. The Akron is a Wingstar-class battleship and said to be some 700 years old.

Antimass: a tank of liquid in which there are spinning rods, which cause an inversion of gravitational force on the tank. This can be amplified, as a product of the tanks mass times the rotation speed; producing more lift.

Aquitano (*ah-kwi-TAH-no*): an ethnic group, mostly found in Ganzabar and the USK. They are recognised by tan skin and almond-shaped eyes.

Autocab: a condensing of **Auto**-altitude **Cab**riolet. These are common vehicles carrying a floatrock ballast, which holds them at a certain altitude. A propeller engine is then used to move people and goods around at that level.

Azbuka (AZ-bu-ka): the most widespread, commonly spoken language in the world.

Azimuth: the world in which Cloudgazer is set. It appears to be a gas giant, having no tangible surface. It has 4 seasons: first winter, first summer, second winter and second summer. How humans ended up living there is thus far a mystery.

Azrune: also known as the First Nation, is the rump state of what was once a global government; dating back to the Gold Age.

Brazak West (b*rah-ZAK West*): a rebellious remnant from the nation of Great Brazak, which was conquered by Ganzabar. Brazak West gained its independence from Ganzabar over ten years ago, in 9317.

Cabletram: a carriage suspended from a cable track with its own propulsion. The track has three cables: two safety lines clipped to either end station and a main track line that the wheels drive along.

Calputer: a portmanteau of Calculation-Computer. Calputer is the name used in Azimuth for Gold Age devices that are vastly more complex than the simple thermionic-valve arithmetic machines of the New Age. Capable of complex behaviour, some Gold Age devices are said to be able to think for themselves.

Chenkov: the common name for Chenkov Armaments' outdated but rugged pistol.

Cloudgazers: a type of mercenary that uses a powerful Gold Age tool called a sling. As the sling is no longer made, their use is spread among all kinds of scavengers. Cloudgazers are generally distrusted, but in some places—such as Azrune—they are banned altogether.

The Collapse: a short period, some 500 years ago, in which the world is said to have rebelled against political unity and ripped itself apart.

Duplane (DU-playn): a powerful skyfighter configuration that uses two propeller engines.

Flak: A highly versatile curse word.

Floatpack: a backpack containing a quick-setting compound similar to floatrock. On pulling the cord, the compound rapidly crystallises, halting vertical movement. For this reason, they are used as a safety device in the event of sinkings and other dangers.

Floatrock: this substance is what the cities of Azimuth are built on. Starting in liquid form, it crystallises to a quartz-like material that resists vertical movement, like an anchor to both rising and falling.

Ganzabar (*GAN-za-bar*): the large superpower to the south. The Ganzabi people are proud and lively; their nation expansive and boisterous.

Gold Age: a peaceful era, hundreds of years ago, when the world was largely united as "The Azrune". It ended with The Collapse.

Gundar: a portmanteau of Gun-Radar. This huge fortress has a massive cannon, used to hit targets at distance with the assistance of radar.

Laronor (*LA-ro-nor*): also known as the City of Winter. Laronor is one of the biggest cities in northern Brazak West and the site of one of its new Gundars. It also gives its name to the svalic subgroup from that area: the Laro.

Lystrata (lih-STRAH-ta): western neighbour of Ganzabar. Often in conflict with them, most recently with the Merchant Wars. Many Ganzabi personnel have real combat experience from fighting the Lystratans.

Maroni *(ma-RO-nee):* a human splinter-species. They are thin, palid and often exceptionally intelligent; but only live for around 10-15 years.

Meedish: an ethnic group of humans. Very dark skinned and dark haired, they are found mostly in southern nations.

Megaprop: massive engines with windmill-like propeller blades, used in airship propulsion.

New Age: the modern era; marked by a less electronic, more mechanical technology. Cloudgazer is set in 9329, the height of the New Age.

Nubylon (*NU-beh-lon*): capital of Azrune. Said to be the oldest city in the world.

Poltiax class: a civilian freighter airship commonly used in Ganzabar. It is named after the Poltiax, a species of bird.

Rhiannon: the Valyan goddess of night; also the name of the airship of famed revolutionary Natalya Ataryk.

Sentinels: a state security force in Azrune, using a grappling tool similar to the sling, called a 'hook'.

Shyut: a curse word; generally an exclamation.

Sky-Hop: the name of a common cloudgazer technique to transfer to a ship using the sling.

Sling: an ancient, highly advanced grappling tool. Slings vary, but all fire a small magnetic clamp attached to a strong cable, which can be reeled at will. Its users are potent enough that they are known by a special name: 'cloudgazers'.

Svalic (SVA-lik): a northern ethnicity often identified by fair hair and pale skin.

Transpulse: a form of communication, used to send messages with high resilience using neutrinos. However, the bandwidth is severely limited, so all messages are in the form of short lines of text.

Understorm: the lowest cloud level, an ever-raging hurricane of turbulence that would be the doom of even a Gold Age airship. It isn't known if anything is below the Understorm and few who venture there survive to tell of it.

Voenkom: a high-ranking Brazak officer, below an Admiral.

Printed in Great Britain
by Amazon